Trained as an actress, Barbara Nadel used to work in mental health services. Born in the East End of London, she now writes full time and has been a visitor to Turkey for over twenty years. She received the Crime Writers' Association Silver Dagger for her novel *Deadly Web* and the Swedish Flintax Prize for historical crime fiction for her first Francis Hancock novel *Last Rights*.

By Barbara Nadel

BARBARA NADEL

BRIDE PRICE

HEADLINE

First published in Great Britain in 2022 by
HEADLINE PUBLISHING GROUP

First published in paperback in 2022 by
HEADLINE PUBLISHING GROUP

1

Cataloguing in Publication Data is available from the British Library

ISBN 978 1 4722 7354 3

Typeset in Times New Roman by Palimpsest Book Production Ltd,
Falkirk, Stirlingshire

Printed and bound in Great Britain by Clays Ltd, Elcograf S.p.A.

Headline's policy is to use papers that are natural, renewable and recyclable
products and made from wood grown in well-managed forests and other
controlled sources. The logging and manufacturing processes are expected to
conform to the environmental regulations of the country of origin.

HEADLINE PUBLISHING GROUP
An Hachette UK Company
Carmelite House
50 Victoria Embankment
London EC4Y 0DZ

www.headline.co.uk
www.hachette.co.uk

To my husband

Acknowledgements

Enormous thanks go to Professor Joann Fletcher, Honorary Research Fellow at the University of York, Department of Archaeology. A world expert in ancient Egyptian funerary archaeology, she very gladly gave her time to explain to me the ins and outs of mummification. Not only was this fascinating but also invaluable for the completion of this book. Any errors around mummification that may appear in this book are mine and mine alone.

Cast List

Çetin İkmen – retired İstanbul detective
Çiçek İkmen – İkmen's eldest daughter
Kemal İkmen – İkmen's youngest son
Bülent İkmen – İkmen's fourth son
Hülya İkmen – İkmen's second daughter
Berekiah Cohen – Hülya's husband
Hülüsi – Kemal's partner
Defne Yalçın – Hülüsi's mother
Samsun Bajraktar – İkmen's Albanian cousin, a transsexual
Inspector Mehmet Süleyman – İstanbul police detective
Murad Süleyman – Mehmet's brother
Nur Süleyman – Mehmet's mother
Beyazıt Süleyman – Mehmet's uncle
Edibe Süleyman – Murad's daughter
Patrick Süleyman – Mehmet's son, by Zelfa Halman
Gonca Şekeroğlu – Mehmet's fiancée
Asana Şekeroğlu – Gonca's eldest daughter
Rambo Şekeroğlu – Gonca's youngest son
Rambo Şekeroğlu Senior – Gonca's brother
Erdem Şekeroğlu – Gonca's eldest son
Didim and Sema – Gonca's sisters
Hürrem Solak and Buket Teyze – Gonca's friends
Dr Arto Sarkissian – police pathologist
Selahattin Ozer – police commissioner
Sergeant Ömer Mungun – Mehmet's deputy

Peri Mungun – Ömer's sister
Inspector Kerim Gürsel – İstanbul detective
Sinem Gürsel – Kerim's wife
Melda Gürsel – Kerim's daughter
Madam Edith – Elderly drag queen, Sinem's carer
Sergeant Eylul Yavaş – Kerim's sergeant
Inspector Haluk Keleş – police art fraud expert
Technical Officer Doğan Tuğrul
**Constables Kerem Akar, Mustafa Gölcük, Tan, Alp and
  Tuncer**
Drs Yaşova and Özil – forensic scientists
Dr Aylın Akyıldız – archaeologist
Professor Bilal Gezmiş – historian
Officer Pervin Deniz – night watch officer
Officer Yıldırım Yaman – Pervin's lover
Fındık Elvan – Gölcük's mistress
Fahrettin Müftüoğlu – jeweller, deceased
Canan Müftüoğlu – his wife
Muharrem Aktepe – Canan's father
Osman Aslan – Canan's lover
Lazar Alfandarı – Berekiah Cohen's employer, a jeweller
Atyom Mafyan – jeweller
Sema Kılıç – jeweller
Rahul Mengüç – haberdasher
Neziye Mengüç – Rahul's daughter
Huriye Can – seamstress
Şaziye Can – Huriye's daughter
Hızır and Ziya Can – Şaziye's brothers
Munir Can – Huriye's brother-in-law
Şevket Sesler – Romany godfather
Burhan Sezai – Romany musician
Nilüfer, Meryem and Barcın Hanıms – Fahrettin's
  neighbours

Alev Hanım – another neighbour
İbrahim Atılla – male neighbour
Rasım Tandoğan – gangster
Güven – Rasım's son
Şişman Hanım – bath attendant
Juan-Maria Montoya – Catholic Bishop of İstanbul
Müge Topbaş – landlady
Şeymus Düzgün – Kurd
Soğut Hanım – prostitute
Vahan Bey – caretaker
Ramazan Albayrak – lawyer
Nilüfer Deniz – old actress

Pronunciation Guide

There are 29 letters in the Turkish alphabet:

A, a – usually short as in 'hah!'

B, b – as pronounced in English

C, c – not like the 'c' in 'cat' but like the 'j' in 'jar', or 'Taj'

Ç, ç – 'ch' as in 'chunk'

D, d – as pronounced in English

E, e – always short as in 'venerable'

F, f – as pronounced in English

G, g – always hard as in 'slug'

Ğ, ğ – 'yumuşak ge' is used to lengthen the vowel that it
follows. It is not usually voiced. As in the name
'Farsakoğlu', pronounced 'Far-sak-orlu'

H, h – as pronounced in English, never silent

I, ı – without a dot, the sound of the 'a' in 'probable'

İ i – with a dot, as the 'i' in 'thin'

J, j – as the French pronounce the 'j' in 'bonjour'

K, k – as pronounced in English, never silent

L, l – as pronounced in English

M, m – as pronounced in English

N, n – as pronounced in English

O, o – always short as in 'hot'

Ö, ö – like the 'ur' sound in 'further'

P, p – as pronounced in English

R, r – as pronounced in English

S, s – as pronounced in English

Ş, ş – like the 'sh' in 'ship'

T, t – as pronounced in English

U, u – always medium length, as in 'push'

Ü, ü – as the French pronounce the 'u' in 'tu'

V, v – as pronounced in English but sometimes with a slight 'w' sound

Y, y – as pronounced in English

Z, z – as pronounced in English

It waited. Halfway down a pile of other, less fabulous pieces. It stuck out slightly, but just in case there was any confusion, there was a label, with a name. All morning it didn't move.

Lunchtime came, with köfte and pide and boza, because it was getting cold now as autumn drew into winter. In the afternoon, the women arrived with the children they had collected from school. Girls mainly, entranced by gold and silver thread, by lace and velvet and bows. The boys played outside in puddles with half-deflated footballs. Drug deals went down on the opposite corner organised by men who changed every day.

It was almost evening when it went. The cavernous streets outside were darkening and within seconds it had gone in a flurry of gold bracelets, untamed hair and laughter.

The front door of the shop closed after it as night proper began to fall.

Chapter 1

He'd heard her come in and go straight up to the bedroom. A lot of things like that happened now. A sister or three would turn up and sew for an afternoon, an aunt from Romania he hadn't even known existed appeared carrying an amphora, and of course her children came and went as they pleased.

Ever since he had moved into his fiancée's big, noisy house in İstanbul's Balat quarter, Mehmet Süleyman had become largely irrelevant. Except in the bedroom. Gonca Şekeroğlu, his older gypsy lover, was a demanding woman, which he appreciated, but now that they were getting married, everything except her body had slipped from his grasp.

He'd made himself a den in the basement of the old Greek house in a room that had been used as a wine cellar by the original owners. In more recent times it had been turned into a larder. Now, with the addition of a small window, it was his office, cool in the summer, warm in the winter, a place to escape to – or not.

He'd seen Gonca's youngest boy, twenty-year-old Rambo, creep by to look at him. Roma people didn't really understand the need he had to be alone from time to time. As a police inspector in one of the most populous cities in the world, Mehmet Süleyman was surrounded by people and their noise, their aggression and their misery every day of his life. Sometimes, when he got home, he didn't want that. This damp late-October evening was a case in point.

He looked at his watch and was surprised to see that it was already 8 p.m. Nobody in İstanbul ate early, even in the winter, but if someone was going to cook, someone should make a start. He stood and made his way up to the kitchen. At some point Asana, one of Gonca's daughters, had arrived from her apartment in nearby Fener. Sitting at the kitchen table, she looked up briefly from a stack of very official-looking papers and said, 'Good evening, Mehmet Bey.'

'Asana.' He sat down and lit a cigarette. 'Looks important.'

Asana was a property lawyer. Beautiful, like her mother, she was as sharp as a sword and had what Süleyman considered to be a measure of disdain for her soon-to-be stepfather.

She said, 'Mum's TAPU documents. Just making sure the title to the house remains with her.'

He'd learned over many years dealing with Gonca's family that it was as well to be straight with them.

'So I can't get my hands on it,' he said.

'That's right.'

He nodded. 'You're a good daughter,' he said, 'but you've no appreciation of just how much I love your mother.'

'She's twelve years older than you are,' Asana said. 'My father used to beat her, then the man she was with after he died robbed her. She's got a bad track record, Mehmet Bey.'

She left to go into the garden. Mehmet Süleyman decided to go and see his fiancée, who had been upstairs for a very long time.

When he opened their bedroom door, he saw that she had her back to him. Her floor-length black and grey hair hung down, swaying gently against her heels. She stood at the end of the bed they shared. When he approached her, she didn't even turn her head.

'Gonca? Are you all right?'

4

Still she didn't move, and so he walked up and put a hand on her shoulder. She gasped. Then he saw what she was looking at on the bed.

Alarmed, he said, 'Are you hurt?'

'No.'

'So . . .'

She seemed incapable of tearing her eyes away from what lay there. It wasn't surprising.

Because she was neither a young bride nor one who hadn't been married before, Gonca Şekeroğlu didn't possess a chest full of linen she had personally prepared for her wedding day. But because this was to be the first time she'd been legally married to a man she loved, she had wanted to have beautiful bed linen for their wedding night. This she had ordered from a shop run by a Roma man in Tarlabaşı, where lots of her people lived. The rich families always did this, and compared to most Roma, she was rich. What lay before them now was the white lace bedcover trimmed with silver thread she had paid to have specially made.

Except that the centre of the cover was red, soaked in blood.

She turned to him. 'Who would do this to us?' she asked.

The blood was fresh, he could smell it.

'Who hates us this much?'

He put his arms around her. 'Sweetheart, this must be a mistake . . .'

Gonca wasn't a woman who cried easily, but her eyes were wet. He kissed her.

'Baby, this is a curse,' she said. 'This is a message – our marriage will end in blood.'

'No it won't.'

'You don't understand.'

'This is a mistake,' he repeated. 'This isn't meant for you.'

'It is!' She threw her arms in the air. He struggled to hold her. 'You and a "dirty gypsy" – I know what people say! All the people you work with, all the women who want you, your mother!'

He led her across the bedroom to the chaise longue below the window that looked out over the garden and made her sit down.

'Darling, none of those people would do this,' he said. 'Even if that's true!'

'Oh, so my people would?'

'No. As I say, this is a mistake. Where did you get it?'

'From Rahul Bey in Tarlabaşı. I've known him all my life! He makes the most beautiful bed linen. All the big families go to him. He wouldn't let something like this happen! Mehmet, what do we do?'

He took his phone out of his pocket. 'Let me make a call.'

Friendship wasn't something Dr Arto Sarkissian had ever taken lightly. And although the police pathologist didn't know Inspector Süleyman well, he was the oldest and dearest friend of Süleyman's mentor, Çetin İkmen.

Three years retired from the police, Inspector İkmen was still a highly respected investigator, who had, over the decades, built up a large cache of owed favours amongst the people of İstanbul. This included Arto Sarkissian, who, while resenting the fact that he had to drive all the way from his home in the Bosphorus village of Bebek to Balat in the Old City, at night, nevertheless did it, for İkmen's sake.

The doctor had never been to the old Greek house opposite the Church of St Mary of the Mongols where Gonca Şekeroğlu lived. Long before she had taken Süleyman as her lover, Gonca had been – and still was – one of the nation's most sought-after artists. And although her stock had dropped somewhat in recent years, her tactile, Roma-inspired collages could still fetch thousands of lira.

As he eased his tired, overweight body out of his car, the doctor looked up at the eighteenth-century house and found it

6

beautiful. It had been restored to its former glory in a very sympathetic way. Although the clearly renewed plasterwork was pink, which was entirely in keeping with all the other brightly coloured houses in Balat, the metal grilles at the wonderfully crafted wooden-framed windows were clearly original and consequently shabby. But that all made sense, and when the Armenian got inside, there were lots of other delights for his eyes.

Süleyman let him into a small marble entrance hall and shook his hand.

'Doctor, thank you so much for coming,' he said. 'I know it was an imposition.'

'Not at all,' Arto said, knowing he didn't mean that and that Süleyman would know it too. But Turkish politeness and care had to be observed.

Süleyman led him up a fine wooden spiral staircase. On the second floor, a young boy looked out of one of the rooms, stared at him and then closed the door behind him.

Süleyman explained. 'Gonca's youngest son, Rambo. He's not a bad boy, but he likes to pretend he's hard, so if he gives you an odd look, ignore it.'

'I will.'

Lots of what Arto imagined were Gonca's artworks lined the walls of the staircase, canvases studded with boncuks, horse tails and stylised Hands of Fatima. The superstitious nature of the Roma was almost a cliché, but it did have a very strong basis in fact. And when he saw Gonca's strained face, this bore that contention out.

'Oh, Dr Bey!' She ran over to him and kissed his hand.

'Hanım . . .'

'It's so good of you to come, especially in the middle of the night!'

Süleyman put his arms around her and said, 'Sit down, Gonca. Let Arto Bey do his job.'

The Armenian knew Gonca to be a woman who didn't take well to being told what to do by anyone, but she sat down meekly on a chaise longue underneath a bay window. Süleyman gestured to a large gilded bed. On it was an ornate white and silver cover, heavily stained in the middle with what looked like blood.

Süleyman said, 'It came in a zip-up plastic bag, which gave off what I recognised as the smell of blood.'

The doctor peered down at the stain and sniffed.

'Faintly metallic,' he said.

From across the room, he heard Gonca say, 'Someone is cursing us. Someone jealous.'

The two men looked at each other. They both knew that Süleyman had taken many lovers in his fifty years of life, and that there were women who were jealous of Gonca. But would any of them do this?

'I know that bloodstains can be deceptive,' Süleyman said to the doctor. 'Is this a lot of blood, or . . .'

'It's less than it looks,' Arto said. 'I wonder if it's animal.'

'What kind of animal?' Gonca asked. Then, darkly, 'Not a dog!'

Dogs are considered unclean by some Muslims, and so Arto was accustomed to prejudice against them. But then Süleyman whispered, 'The Roma deem both dogs and cats unclean.'

'I see.'

'So . . .'

'So I will photograph this *in situ*,' the doctor said as he took out his phone. 'And then I will take it away.'

'Thank God!'

He looked over at her. 'To test, Gonca Hanım,' he said. 'To find out what kind of blood it is, put your mind at rest.'

'Thank you, Doctor,' she said. 'I don't frighten easily, but this . . .' She lit a cigarette and then turned to look out of the window.

As he took the photographs, Arto said, 'Do you know where Gonca Hanım got this?'

'Yes,' Süleyman replied.

'You know that if it's human blood, you will have to follow it up?'

As the pathologist began to remove the cover from the bed, Süleyman drew close to him.

'That's my main concern,' he whispered. 'That someone has been attacked, tortured, killed . . .'

'I'll have some results for you by mid-morning,' the doctor said. 'I'll email you.'

'Thank you.'

Once the bedcover had left the house, and after a lot of rakı had been drunk, Süleyman finally managed to get Gonca to go to bed at midnight. However, when he woke up at three, she had gone. She'd not been comfortable sleeping in her bed after the cover had been placed upon it. But where was she?

He got up and wrapped a bathrobe around his body. There were five other bedrooms in this house, and only one other occupant. He didn't know why he looked out of the window into the garden before he left the bedroom, but when he did, he saw her immediately. Curled up in a pile of blankets, rugs and cushions, she was sleeping underneath the olive tree.

When he opened the back door into the garden, the cold autumnal air hit him hard. There could easily be a frost by the morning. He put his shoes on and walked over to the tree. He squatted down.

'What are you doing?'

She put a hand up to his face. 'Oh baby, I'm sorry,' she said. 'I couldn't sleep in that bed, not after that *thing* . . .'

'It's gone now,' he said. 'Dr Sarkissian took it. The bed's fine.'

'No, it's not! It's dirty!' she said. 'I can't go back in there!'

9

He shook his head. 'It's freezing out here.'

She pulled her covers aside and he joined her on what seemed to be a mattress of garden furniture cushions. 'This is crazy.'

'I won't sleep in that bed! I won't!'

He put a hand on her shoulder. 'Our bed,' he corrected. 'It's our bed, Gonca, and I for one like it very much.'

'I did too, but not now.'

'Oh for God's sake! Sweetheart, our bed is not cursed. Quite the reverse,' he said. 'That's a good bed, a fortunate bed, it's a bed we've made love to each other in many, many times . . .'

'It'll have to go!' She was actually trembling. Obviously with the cold, but also with fear. 'I'll need to clean everything. The bed will have to go, and the bedding.'

Inwardly, Süleyman groaned. Today was his only day off this week. He had hoped to spend it picking up the wedding rings he'd had made in the Grand Bazaar. Now it seemed they would have to look for a new bed too. But Gonca was adamant. Frightened and determined, she was not to be denied, and he knew it. He kissed one of her shoulders and she leaned back against him.

There was a pause, then she said, 'You go back inside. I can feel you're cold.'

'So warm me up.'

She wasn't in the mood for levity. 'Just go.'

But he didn't. He loved her too much to leave her. He lowered himself down, pulling her with him. 'I'm not going anywhere. I don't like sleeping without you. We've not gone to bed outside since the summer. It will be fine.'

'There's always a rational explanation,' Çetin İkmen said to his wife. 'Of course, that isn't always the actual truth, but . . .'

He often sat on the balcony outside his apartment. It had one of the best views in the city. Just off the main Divan Yolu

10

thoroughfare, the İkmen place looked out over Sultanahmet Square, the Blue Mosque, Ayasofya and, if you turned your head to the right a bit, the Hippodrome. Because he had retired from the police force three years before, and because his wife was dead, he could come out on the balcony and be with her whenever he liked. Three o'clock in the morning meant nothing to ghosts.

'One can say that gypsies like Gonca are naturally superstitious and simply reason it away like that,' he continued. 'But that's too glib. She's an intelligent woman; she felt something coming out of that bed covering. Not that Arto said that, and of course he didn't feel a thing except to say that it was "creepy".'

Arto Sarkissian had called İkmen once he'd taken the bloodied cover to the lab. Shocked by how badly the experience appeared to have affected Gonca, he had called İkmen both as his friend and as his 'go-to' person when it came to affairs of a supernatural nature.

'Mehmet, poor boy, will be at a loss with all this, of course.' İkmen lit a cigarette. 'A man's body was found in an apartment in Vefa last night – cyanide poisoning – that's his case. Could be suicide, given the state of a lot of people's finances these days, but who knows? What I'm saying is that Mehmet has a lot to think about without this. His work, his wedding next week, money . . . He doesn't need crazy superstitious stuff in his life.'

His wife, Fatma, looked at him. She was very bright, almost tangible this night.

'And yes I know I always get involved in things like this, but I care. Anyway, she will expect me to at the very least talk to her about it. I mean, she can't talk to Mehmet, can she? Not really. Not about this. The poor man's out of his depth. Don't get me wrong, Fatma, I think those two were made for each other, but even in the best marriages there are always differences. You and I, we're all difference, always were.'

He poured himself a large brandy and leaned back in his chair.

'They're going to the Grand Bazaar tomorrow. Berekiah has made their wedding rings and they're going to pick them up. Really expensive, apparently, but I'm not complaining. Our son-in-law is a craftsman, and he and Hülya need the money, even if Mehmet can't really afford it. Which he can't. Gonca's sisters are making the dress, which will be a huge production and also costly. Arto told me the bloodied bedcover cost her over a thousand lira. Still had the price on. Mehmet's paying for everything. And this of course is just the civil wedding. When they have the Roma ceremony, it will be even more elaborate.'

He shook his head. He'd been to a few Roma weddings over the years. They were often held, as Gonca and Mehmet's was destined to be, during the spring festival of Hıdırellez, and hundreds of people came from all over the country and beyond, transported in big shiny cars, all firing off rounds of ammunition into the night, fed to bursting on a wedding cake that could be seen from space. İkmen secretly loved these almost Hollywood-esque productions.

He drank. 'So I'll probably go along to the bazaar and see the happy couple tomorrow,' he said. 'I have an interest.'

If a ghost could be said to have a wry expression on its face, that was what İkmen saw when he looked at Fatma.

12

Chapter 2

Boza had always appalled Inspector Kerim Gürsel. His favourite winter beverage was sahlep, a sweet, warm milky drink made from orchid root and sprinkled with cinnamon. Boza – although those who enjoyed it said that once inside the body it was warming – was served cold with a topping of leblebi, toasted chickpeas, and was too sour for his taste. It was said that it had been one of the mainstays of the Ottoman army when it conquered half of Europe in the sixteenth century. Full of vitamins and minerals, it was certainly nutritious, and when one was in the İstanbul district of Vefa, known as the home of boza, one just had to get some. Or not.

As they walked away from the famous Vefa Bozacısı, Kerim looked at his colleague, Sergeant Ömer Mungun, in amazement. He was lapping the stuff up.

'People say that's the best boza in the city, and I think they're right,' Ömer said. 'It'll set me up for the day.'

Kerim lit a cigarette. Just as Ömer wasn't his sergeant, this case, which concerned the death of a man called Fahrettin Müftüoğlu, wasn't strictly speaking his either. Like Ömer Mungun, it belonged to his colleague, Inspector Mehmet Süleyman. But the inspector had booked this day off months ago in order to go and collect the rings for his upcoming wedding to Gonca Şekeroğlu. And although Müftüoğlu's death could be murder, the number of suicide-by-cyanide cases in the city in recent months had spiked. For those at or near the bottom of society, the economy was no longer delivering. Profits were

13

falling and prices rising – a lot of people were in debt. The police were in the process of discovering whether Müftüoğlu was one of their number. What they did know was that in life, he had worked in an industry – the jewellery trade – that routinely used cyanide. The evening before last, a neighbour in the downstairs apartment had heard a huge crashing sound from above, and when the front door had been kicked in, Müftüoğlu had been found apparently collapsed in his hallway.

They walked to Kayserili Ahmet Paşa Caddesi, where the man had lived. Scene-of-crime officers in white overalls were in attendance, and the whole sagging wooden apartment building was cordoned off by tape. Kerim introduced himself to the team, who had already met Ömer Mungun, and said, 'So – quick overview . . .'

An older man called Sergeant Ertan said, 'It's a big job, Inspector. Bigger than we first thought.'

'In what way?'

Ertan looked at one of his colleagues, then said, 'Where the body was found . . .'

'The hallway, yes, I know . . .'

'That wasn't in any way typical of that apartment. We didn't really get the measure of it yesterday when Inspector Süleyman was here, what with the pathologist, and closing down the scene because of the noxious substance . . .'

'Sergeant, get to the point,' Kerim said.

'The man was a hoarder, sir,' he said. 'Every room, floor to ceiling, stacked with every sort of thing you can imagine and probably some you can't. We need multiple skips and we need more officers.'

Not much sleep had been managed under the olive tree in Gonca Şekeroğlu's garden. She'd been upset and so they'd talked for hours, then they'd made love. Just as Mehmet Süleyman had been about to fall asleep, the dawn azan had rippled across the city. For two hours after that, he'd lain beside Gonca staring up into the lightening sky. Then he'd gone inside to make tea and get his phone. Gonca was awake when he returned to the garden. He offered her his tea, but she refused it.

'I'll go and get mine later,' she said. She pulled the covers on their makeshift bed aside and said, 'Get in. It's cold.'

He got in beside her and they put their arms around each other.

'I'm sorry about last night, Mehmet,' Gonca said.

'Sorry? It was great!' He kissed her neck.

'Not the sex!' she laughed. 'The hysteria.'

'Oh.'

'What you have to understand is that I can't just brush this away.'

'Which is why Dr Sarkissian came and took the bedcover to be analysed,' he said. 'I'm taking it seriously too.'

'I'm sure,' she said. 'As a crime, or possibly . . .'

She looked down.

He said, 'I know you feel as if this is a message from someone who means us ill will.'

'A curse.'

'A curse if you must, but . . .'

'I know I made it sound as if I was blaming your people, but I'm not,' she said. 'A lot of *my* people disapprove of our marriage. In the past, even touching a gaco was thought to pollute us.'

'Yes, I think I knew that,' he said.

He'd heard what some of the gypsies were calling him. The main insult and the one that disturbed him the most was 'the bewitched bridegroom'. That he was 'henpecked' just made him angry.

'It's not enough for some people that our marriage will be childless,' she said. 'And it's true, you could marry a younger woman and have more sons.'

'I'm happy with the son I have,' he said.

'And when I am eighty and you are still in your sixties . . .'

'We've been through this,' he said. 'It doesn't matter.'

'It might.'

He knew that. It might. But he wanted to be happy *now*. She made him happy, he loved her, and he was endlessly fascinated by her.

Or bewitched . . .

Kerim's deputy, Eylul Yavaş, was already at the scene. As the inspector picked his way towards her, he said, 'Any idea what this room was used for?'

'Same as all the others, sir. Storing junk.'

As far as anyone could tell, Fahrettin Müftüoğlu's apartment, on the first floor of a dilapidated wooden Ottoman building, had five rooms. Everything sloped at an angle, which made for a slightly queasy feeling amongst those attempting to move around. There were also signs that the floorboards were broken in places, which, given the amount of things piled up on them, was hardly surprising. And there was a smell, like no other. Everyone had their own ideas about it.

Kerim Gürsel said it was like old fur, while Eylul Yavaş said it had some characteristics in common with leaf mould. Ömer Mungun claimed it reminded him of saints' relics he had seen in the many Syrian Orthodox monasteries in and around his home city of Mardin. There were only two rooms that could actually be entered. One was the bathroom, which featured an ancient, filthy shower above a tub that appeared to be full of some sort of viscous scum, a squat toilet and a rancid sink.

Kerim asked Ömer, 'How old was Mr Müftüoğlu?'

'Thirty-nine.'

He pulled a face. 'This place looks to me like the home of a middle-aged or elderly eccentric. Thirty-nine? Are you sure?'

'What it says on his kimlik.'

'Oh, well . . .'

'He worked in the Grand Bazaar,' Eylul Yavaş said as she

16

opened the door into the second just-about-accessible room. 'Although as you can see, he also did some work here.'

A scruffy workbench covered in soldering irons connected to gas canisters, and what looked like cutting tools, stood in front of a vast heap of clothes.

'A tub containing sodium cyanide was taken away by forensics yesterday,' Eylul continued. 'Under Inspector Süleyman's authority.'

'Well thank God we managed to find that, at least!' Kerim said. 'Apart from the fact that this place is a fucking nightmare, anything else?'

'The neighbours say that Müftüoğlu was always very smart,' Eylul said.

'That from the local teyzes?'

'Of course,' she smiled. 'I've an appointment for tea with a group of them in ten minutes – including the one who called in the night watch when she heard that loud crash from this apartment.'

'When Müftüoğlu collapsed,' Kerim said. 'Excellent.'

Teyzes, or 'aunties', referred to the local housewives, who knew everyone in a particular neighbourhood and their business. Every street in the city had at least one teyze, whom Çetin İkmen had once scathingly dubbed 'women who should have been brain surgeons but who settled for stupid men instead'. A lot of teyzes were clever women with not enough to do.

'Sir, this thing about getting a skip,' Ömer said. 'I know that makes some sense . . .'

'Oh, it's all right, Sergeant,' Kerim said. 'I'm on that. There's no way any of this stuff will be thrown away until it has been properly sorted.'

'The boss'd have a breakdown,' Ömer said.

Kerim smiled. Although he'd been drafted in to assist, this was still Süleyman's case. He remained, and probably always would, the boss to whom his sergeant referred.

17

Looking around, Kerim said, 'I suggest we clear this room first. It's not quite so full up as the rest of the place, and will hopefully be cleaner than that bathroom. There's some space to begin sorting through that wall of clothes behind the bench. Then if we can bag them up and move them out, we can start shifting things from other rooms into here.'

'Where will we store it all, sir?' Eylul asked.

Kerim shook his head. 'I have no idea. I'm not sure our evidence storage provision can cope with this.'

'The effect I was going for, which was Mehmet Bey's idea, was of a sprinkling of stars. Some large, some small, some barely visible.'

Berekiah Cohen, the jeweller, was a tall, thin man on the verge of middle age. He wore bifocals, which together with the fact that his right arm was stiff and almost useless made him look like an exotic insect.

But Gonca Şekeroğlu wasn't looking at the jeweller. Her eyes were fixed on what he had made for her. Although neither the thickest nor the most expensive wedding ring she had ever seen, it was the most beautiful – and clever. A ten-carat white-gold band, slim and tall on the finger, was studded with diamonds so small they were little more than dust, together with larger stones, giving the whole piece, in the correct light, the look of a shimmering sky filled with stars.

'Even the smallest stones have been individually set,' Berekiah continued. 'So hopefully you shouldn't need to worry about losing them. I tried always to keep in mind your work, Gonca Hanım. You need to be able to work with your wedding ring on.'

Gonca looked up at her fiancé. 'This was your idea?'

He smiled. She flung her arms around his neck and began to cry. Mehmet Süleyman mouthed his apologies to Berekiah, who just shook his head. He'd seen this sort of display many times before, albeit not quite so excessive.

When she finally disengaged herself from Süleyman's neck, Gonca said, 'That is the most beautiful ring I've ever seen in my life! How did you get the idea for it?'

'What? Because I'm a rather dull police officer with little imagination?'

'No!'

He laughed. 'One night back in the summer, I was out in the garden when I looked up and saw this . . .' He took his phone out of his pocket and showed her the photographs he had taken of the night sky back in August. 'It was one of the most beautiful things I had ever seen, and so of course I wanted something like it to be replicated on my darling Gonca's wedding ring. The genius in this production is not me, but Berekiah. To enact what was simply a vision with such skill and artistry is a miracle.'

The younger man blushed. 'As you know, Mehmet Bey,' he said, 'I enjoy a challenge. Now, Gonca Hanım, I'd like you to make sure for me that the ring fits. We still have time to make adjustments.'

'It's perfect!' she said.

'Doesn't pinch anywhere? You can move it easily without it falling off?'

'Yes! Yes!' Then she said, 'What about your ring, Mehmet?'

The jeweller handed a similar, if larger, ring over to Süleyman, who slipped it on his finger. He turned it around a few times.

'Fits perfectly.'

Berekiah supervised, frowning as he too manipulated the ring.

Gonca, watching, said, 'You have diamonds too.'

'Yes, but fewer. If I'm cuffing someone, I don't want small pieces of diamond to get embedded in their flesh.'

'That shouldn't happen.'

'No, because you are a clever man, Berekiah.'

19

'Just working to the brief,' the jeweller said. 'You told me that once you're married, you never want to take it off. So that's what we're aiming for.'

Süleyman glanced at Gonca. 'Anyway, I didn't want to out-glitter you, did I?'

'No. The bride must always be the centre of attention,' another voice said. Çetin İkmen had quietly entered his son-in-law's cramped workshop.

'Do you remember when Fuat Bey died, Nilüfer Hanım?' the old lady asked the fat middle-aged woman in whose apartment they had met.

'Not exactly,' she replied. 'Fifteen years ago, maybe?'

'Oh no, more like twenty,' an uncovered woman in a nylon tabard said. 'The mother died ten years ago.'

The old woman, Meryem Hanım, touched Eylul Yavaş's arm. 'The mother,' she said, 'was a strange one.'

'In what way?'

'Egyptian,' she said.

Eylul was waiting for more information, but she didn't get it. 'Egyptian' was clearly strange enough to need no further explanation.

But then Nilüfer Hanım added, 'Never learned to speak Turkish. They all spoke French to each other, her, Fuat Bey and Fahrettin. Not that I ever heard them myself. Faruk Bey told Doğan Bey, who told me when he came home from the coffee house.'

'When was this?' Eylul asked.

Nilüfer Hanım laughed. 'Oh, years ago!' She leaned in closer to the policewoman. 'Fahrettin was a jeweller, like his father was. Worked for Armenians in the Grand Bazaar, both of them. People say that Fahrettin was better than his father. An artist.'

'We know he was a jeweller.'

'Oh.'

Eylul said, 'We're trying to find out about his life outside work.'

'Not sure he did much,' said Barcın, the nylon-tabard woman. It had been this woman who had called the nightwatchman when she heard an enormous crashing sound coming from Müftüoğlu's apartment upstairs. 'He never married, as far as I know.'

'Brothers and sisters?'

'Didn't have any,' she continued. 'I think old Fuat Bey and whoever the wife was . . .'

'Isis.'

'Yes, Isis.' She frowned. 'Funny name. Anyway, they were quite old when they had Fahrettin. He was fat when he was little.'

'Oh yes,' old Meryem said. 'Fat and lazy. Sitting at his bedroom window watching the other boys play football in the street.'

'Did the other boys make fun of him?' Eylul asked.

The women looked at each other, then Meryem said, 'No.'

'Seems a bit strange,' Eylul said. 'Children who are fat or wear glasses or are different in any way . . .'

'He used to do their homework for them,' Barcın said. 'My little brother Ali is only a year older than Fahrettin. Used to do his. Went to the Lycée, see.'

'What? Galatasaray?'

That was where Inspector Süleyman had gone. It was the most famous boys' school in the country.

'Yes. Had ideas, did Fuat Bey,' Barcın said. 'When he used to go off to the bazaar in the mornings, he'd be dressed up like a lawyer or a doctor or something.'

'Fahrettin carried that on,' Meryem said. 'Always very smart. What did he die of, dear?'

'We don't know yet,' Eylul said.

'Oh. Was he murdered?'

'Again, I can't—'

21

'Don't take this wrongly, I mean him no harm,' the old woman said, 'but he did attract the Eye round here.'

If he had attracted jealousy attributed to the Evil Eye, then why and from whom? As far as Eylul could see, Fahrettin Müftüoğlu hadn't had much of value. And even though he was a craftsman, he couldn't have made a lot of money, otherwise why was he still in that squalid old apartment that his parents had lived in?

'The Eye?' she said. 'Why?'

The women looked at each other, and then Meryem said, 'Haven't you found all his money yet, then?'

Lazar Alfandarı had run his jewellery shop and atelier in the Grand Bazaar ever since he had taken over the business when his father had died in 1975. His father, Moris, had in turn inherited from *his* father in an unbroken line from the beginning of the nineteenth century. The name of the shop, Melek – or Angel – was an oblique reference to the fact that the Alfandarı family were and always had been practitioners of Kabbalah. Lazar's second in command, Berekiah Cohen, said that you could pick those influences up in pieces that Lazar Bey made for his family.

Walking out of the atelier and into the shop, Gonca Şekeroğlu greeted the old man, who sat behind his counter in a vast velvet chair and kissed his hand. She showed him her wedding ring.

'Oh, Lazar Bey,' she said, 'you clearly trained Berekiah Bey in the dark arts. This is almost beyond my understanding!'

The old man laughed and made room for her on the chair beside him, and the two of them cooed over the ring and talked about magic as they smoked Lazar Bey's brightly coloured cocktail cigarettes.

Above the shop, in the atelier, İkmen and Süleyman sat on old chairs on the inner corridor just below the roof of the bazaar. Around them, groups of soot-blackened silversmiths drank tea, laughed and spoke Armenian.

Both men lit cigarettes, and then İkmen said, 'I don't think I've ever seen Gonca look so happy.'

Süleyman smiled.

'Thank you,' İkmen continued, 'for letting my son-in-law make your rings.'

'My pleasure.'

'It must've cost you a lot of money.'

'Mmm.'

İkmen knew that his friend was always in debt. He also knew that he considered it coarse to talk about money. İkmen, however, was compelled.

'I've heard about the house on Büyükada,' he said.

There was a silence. The house to which he was referring was a nineteenth-century villa that had been built by one of Mehmet's illustrious Ottoman ancestors and was still owned by the Süleyman family. Mehmet himself owned a fifth of this house, together with his brother, an uncle and two cousins – or rather, that was how it had been. Now, İkmen had heard, he was attempting to buy his relatives out.

'Balat is very hot in July and August,' Süleyman said. 'We would all benefit from a summer house. And of course Patrick loves the place.'

Patrick was Mehmet's teenage son by his second wife, Zelfa Halman. At present, he lived with his mother in Dublin. But apparently when he'd visited his father earlier in the year, he had fallen in love with this house.

'It's a lot of money,' İkmen said. 'I mean, a cheap one would cost you a million dollars.'

'I already own one fifth of the property,' Süleyman said.

'What does Gonca think of the idea?'

'She thinks it will be nice for us all to have somewhere to go in the summer,' he said. 'And I want Patrick to have something from my side of the family eventually.'

23

İkmen could understand that. It was why he himself kept hold of his vast apartment in Sultanahmet, for his children. But it was still a lot of money for Mehmet to find. Of course, he was borrowing . . .

He changed the subject. 'Are you back in Vefa tomorrow?'

'You've heard about that?'

'Of course. Don't know any details . . .'

Süleyman smiled. İkmen was, he knew, someone upon whom he could safely unload.

'Connection to this place, actually,' he said.

'Melek?'

'No, another jeweller in the bazaar. An Armenian-owned business.'

'Going to tell me who?' İkmen asked. 'You know I know most people, and I have particular friends amongst the Armenians.'

He was referring to pathologist Arto Sarkissian, his oldest friend, but Süleyman knew that there were others too. In fact, it was difficult to find a group of people in the city İkmen didn't have a connection to.

'It's called GülGül,' he said.

İkmen's face lit up. 'Owned by Garbis Bey's cousin, Atyom,' he said. 'You know Garbis Bey? Custodian at the Üç Horan church in Beyoğlu?'

'Of course.'

'Well, Atyom Bey is a jeweller, and his shop is called GülGül.' He pointed across the empty space to the opposite balcony. 'His atelier is there.'

'Yes, I know, I was there yesterday.'

'Atyom Bey is very charming,' İkmen continued. 'But never play poker with him. He's an absolute devil with cards and will take the skin off your back. I know.'

Süleyman leaned forward in his chair. 'Çetin,' he said, 'I think Atyom Bey's employee's death was probably suicide.'

'Oh.'

'Suicide?'

They both looked up and saw Berekiah Cohen standing over them with a tray full of tea glasses.

Back from her meeting with the teyzes, Eylul Yavaş was telling her boss about the conversation she'd just had.

'Sir, I hadn't noticed that this apartment didn't have any electricity until the ladies told me,' she said. 'These lights are gas lamps. The women said that Fahrettin, as a youth, used to sit beside the one nearest the window in that room opposite and count his money of an evening.'

Kerim pointed at the door. 'That room?' he said. 'You can't get in that room without a bulldozer!'

'I'm just telling you what they told me. And this was years ago. They said his doing that attracted the Eye . . .'

'God! Superstitious rubbish!'

'I think, sir,' Eylul said, 'that people round here were afraid of Fahrettin Müftüoğlu. He was an odd, distant man, but clever. He used to do homework for other boys in the neighbourhood when he was at school. Charged them for it. He went to Galatasaray Lycée.'

'And yet his parents had no electricity,' Kerim said.

Ömer Mungun, who had been helping a team of scene-of-crime officers catalogue and bag up some very rancid clothes, said, 'Not to speak out of turn, Kerim Bey, but this set-up sounds a bit like an old Ottoman family we both know of . . .'

He meant the Süleymans. But Kerim didn't want to get into personal details about a colleague in such a public setting, so he said, 'Yes, Sergeant Mungun. Thank you for that. How are you getting on?'

'There's some quality clothes here, sir. All rotten, though. Almost as if he bought them and then just flung them in a corner.'

Kerim's phone rang; it was the pathologist.

'Dr Sarkissian,' he said.

Süleyman had attended the post-mortem on the body of Fahrettin Müftüoğlu, which seemed to point to either suicide or death by misadventure. There had been, however, some test results outstanding when he went on leave.

'As you know, Inspector,' the doctor began, 'it was my contention at the PM that Mr Müftüoğlu in all probability took his own life. The seemingly deliberate ingestion of potassium cyanide, together with no sign of defence wounds, leads me to believe this is probably not murder. An accident or misadventure, however, is something else. Given the—'

'Fuck!'

The word had come from the mouth of a scene-of-crime officer. It had been so loud that the doctor had heard it on the other end of the phone.

'What's happening, Inspector?' he asked.

Gürsel turned and saw that the officer was holding up something familiar.

While Süleyman took what seemed to be a very serious phone call, Gonca appeared and sat down next to İkmen on the balcony outside the atelier.

'I'm glad you're here, Çetin Bey. I wanted to talk to you.'

'I thought you might.'

She lit a cigarette. 'Yesterday,' she said, 'I went to Tarlabaşı to pick up my wedding bedcover.'

'I know,' he said. 'Blood.'

'Really?'

He smiled. 'Arto Sarkissian told me,' he said. 'A man of science and scepticism, like your beloved, but he knows me and he knows you and he thought I ought to know.'

'Bless him!'

26

'Indeed.'

'Çetin Bey, a lot of people don't want this marriage to go ahead,' she said. 'Some members of my family, other Roma. Then there's his people: police, his mother, jealous women . . .'

'And then again, it could be completely unconnected to you,' İkmen said.

'That cover was ordered by me,' she said. 'It had my name on it! Why that one, İkmen? Why?'

'Have you spoken to Rahul Bey?' İkmen asked. 'I'm assuming you bought it from his shop.'

'Yes,' she said. 'No, I've not spoken to him.'

'Then you must.'

'Mehmet and I need to go and buy a new bed now,' she said. 'Otherwise we'll have to sleep in the garden again.'

The look on his face made her slightly angry.

'That cursed thing was on my bed, İkmen,' she said. 'What would you have me do?'

'If there was no blood on the bed itself and Arto had taken the offending article away, I would have got in and gone to sleep.'

'That's what Mehmet did. I tried,' she added, 'but once he was asleep, I went out into the garden. I laid a few cushions down under the olive tree. I've hundreds of blankets. It was fine. But then Mehmet got up in the early hours and came down. I didn't want him to. I tried to make him go back, but he wouldn't. So you see, the new bed is really for him. I could sleep in the garden again, provided it doesn't rain . . .'

İkmen laughed.

'What?'

'The way you put the onus on him,' he said. 'It amuses me. I also find the idea of him sleeping on the ground hilarious.'

'Oh, he can be quite adventurous!' she said with a sparkle in her eye that matched that emanating from her wedding ring.

27

'So I gather,' İkmen said. 'Now, Gonca, about this bedcover. I know that Rahul Bey and his daughter make their own pieces, but I also know that he contracts some of his work out.'

'I wanted him to make it,' Gonca said. 'I assume—'

'Don't assume. Ask him.'

'Well, I could, but it's a bit delicate, so I don't want to just phone.'

'Go and see him.'

'But we have to buy a bed!' she said.

'So let me do it!'

'No!'

'I know Rahul Bey, and although I'm not Roma, he'll talk to me.'

She thought about it for a few moments. 'All right.'

'You do want to know the truth, don't you, Gonca? Even if the truth is rather more prosaic than your fantasy.'

Süleyman finished his call and walked back to them, frowning.

'Problems?' İkmen asked.

He shook his head. 'Possibly. But that's for tomorrow.' He put a hand out to Gonca. 'Come along, we've more shopping to do.'

She stood.

'Oh, and the ring, if you please,' he said. She still had it on her finger.

Gonca pouted. 'Oh, please let me keep it, Mehmet Bey!'

He clicked his fingers. 'No,' he said. 'You're not Mrs Süleyman yet. When we're married, I will insist you wear it all the time, but not until then.'

Reluctantly she returned it to him, then they bade İkmen farewell and went on their way. Alone, the one-time inspector was left to wonder what Süleyman had meant about 'possible' problems with his latest case.

28

Chapter 3

It wasn't easy to make out where the eyes had once been. The mouth too was indistinct. It was the nose that gave it away – long and curving, like the blade of a scimitar.

The officer who had found the head, deep, deep inside the wall of clothes at the back of Fahrettin Müftüoğlu's work room, was now outside the building, sitting down and drinking some water. The two other scene-of-crime officers were in the hallway. This left sergeants Yavaş and Mungun and a seriously intrigued Inspector Gürsel.

In order to describe what had been found to Süleyman on the phone, Kerim had put the head down on the floor and viewed it from the front whilst lying on the floorboards. He remained there, staring, while his colleagues sat on the jeweller's stools behind his workbench.

Eventually Ömer Mungun said, 'It looks like some kind of wood.'

'I can't guarantee it isn't,' Kerim said. 'Until the doctor gets here, we won't know. Perhaps not even then . . .'

'The SOC team had quite a visceral response to it,' Eylul put in.

'All their parents probably come from Nowhere Anatolia,' Kerim responded. 'I expect they grew up with stories about how you can be cured of diseases by being shown to the moon.' Then, realising that one of their number was not an İstanbullu, he added, 'Sorry, Ömer Bey.'

29

Ömer smiled. 'That's a Black Sea custom, Kerim Bey,' he said. 'We don't do that in the Tur Abdin.'

The Tur Abdin – or Slaves of God – region of the country was in the far south-east, where the local customs and beliefs were more in line with Mesopotamian myths.

'If it is a human head, it's beyond desiccated,' Eylul said. 'Be interesting to see if there's any more.'

'Can't touch it until the doctor gets here.'

'No.'

They fell into uneasy silence again.

'I'll tell you what, if anything, all this head business is about once I've seen it,' Arto Sarkissian said into his phone. 'I'm sitting in the car outside the building, just about to go in, actually.'

'So . . .'

'Inspector Süleyman, I've got the test results on your blood-soaked bed covering,' he said. 'Human, common blood type – A – but interestingly, I am told, menstrual blood.'

'Really?'

'Really. I baulk at asking the question, but do you have any idea what blood means to the Roma? I am aware there are certain taboos.'

Süleyman sighed. 'I don't know a lot,' he said. 'And Gonca is atypical, of course. But blood and other bodily fluids are considered unclean. Clothes from the upper body, which is clean, have to be separated from those at the bottom, which is dirty, when washed. Men's and women's clothes mustn't be washed together. Menstrual blood is viewed with horror; all sorts of cleanliness rituals pertain to that.'

'Well, that is a common taboo,' the doctor said. 'Is Gonca Hanım with you, Inspector?'

'Depends how one interprets the word "with",' Süleyman said. 'She is in a furniture shop looking at a bed she has informed me

30

is called "Versailles". She is currently agreeing a price with a young salesman who keeps looking at me nervously through the window. My function in all this is to appear with my wallet at the right moment.'

The doctor laughed. 'I will see you tomorrow, Inspector,' he said. 'I wish you good fortune with the shopping. Oh, and let me know whether you would like me to do any further tests on the bedcover.'

'I will.'

'And what you'd like me to do with it ultimately.'

'Of course.'

Süleyman cut the connection. The doctor knew that Kerim Gürsel was anxious for him to look at this mysterious head he'd found, but he stayed where he was. There was something oddly disturbing about the idea that the blood on that bed covering was menstrual blood. How had it got there? Whom had it belonged to, and did it mean anything? In a way, it was comforting, inasmuch as this was not blood from a wound that had killed someone. But on the other hand, even he, a modern agnostic Armenian, had to admit that he was what Americans would call 'grossed out' by the idea of period blood.

If anything summed up the nature of the İstanbul district of Tarlabaşı, it was washing. No matter what time of year, day and night, the lines of amazingly snow-white vests and multicoloured towels that were strung in their thousands across every narrow street gave the place a feeling of vibrancy, even if there were no people around. Which wasn't often.

As Çetin İkmen wandered smokily into İstanbul's most contentious quarter, he saw a lot of people, many of whom he knew. Before he'd walked a hundred metres, he'd tipped his head towards two distillers of moonshine rakı, smiled at a trans prostitute and watched a drug deal go down between two Syrian lads.

Famed for its 'artistic' population, Tarlabaşı was also home to thousands of Roma – some indigenous, others like Gonca's family, who had moved into Tarlabaşı when Sulukule quarter had been redeveloped back in 2008. Parts of Tarlabaşı were being redeveloped now, although it was difficult to see those buildings when he was in the thick of the quarter, where the roads were barely two-people wide and the air smelt of drains.

Eventually he came to a tall, terraced building leaning precariously onto its left-hand neighbour, and stopped. Like most of the old buildings in Tarlabaşı, Rahul Mengüç's shop was in what had once been a Greek house. The entrance, which was four large stone steps up from the filth of the street, was via an ornate wooden door, which at this time of day was open for customers. The old man was serving two mismatched women – one covered as the strictest dictates of Islam required and the other dressed for belly-dancing. The belly-dancer, a Roma girl by the look and sound of her, was instructing her entirely obscured friend in the art of buying linen for her wedding night.

İkmen, who took himself back outside until the women had finished their business, heard the belly-dancer say, 'You get the best you can afford. Then you tell him you made it all yourself, with your own hands.'

İkmen smiled. Clearly the covered girl hadn't paid enough attention to her trousseau chest when she was a child. Maybe she was a Roma girl who had opted to marry a conservative Muslim man. The possibilities were endless.

When, finally, the two women left, without apparently buying anything, İkmen went inside. Rahul Bey, a thin, walnut-patinaed Roma in his eighties, was putting a bolt of cloth back on the shelf behind his counter. His daughter, Neziye, limped towards İkmen, took his hand and kissed it.

'Çetin Bey.'

'Neziye Hanım.' He smiled.

Neziye, who was in her early sixties, was that rare thing in Roma society, an old maid. Tall and thin like her father, she was a gentle-faced woman, unsmiling and yet always pleasant. It was said that men had rejected her because she had one leg longer than the other.

'Ah, Çetin Bey!' the old man called out. 'How are you? Come and take rakı with me. Neziye! Get the rakı and some water.'

The doctor shook his head. He went to say something, and then stopped.

Kerim Gürsel spoke. 'Well?'

Arto Sarkissian pursed his lips, then said, 'It appears, from what I can see, that this mask, this resinous . . . whatever it is . . . thing, is built around a human skull.'

'Really?'

He turned it over in his hands and pointed to an area at the bottom surrounding a hole. 'This is where the spinal cord enters the skull, through this trapezoid structure here, the occipital bone. Were this a mannequin, there would be no need to do this. The head and body could be all of a piece. Unless it were a doll of some sort, in which case some articulation might be required . . . I won't know for certain what this is until I can scan it.'

'You'll take it away.'

'Yes,' he said. 'I can get back to you in a couple of hours. But in the meantime, it might be wise to proceed here with caution.'

Kerim nodded.

'If this is part of a skeleton, there may be more. Any idea how it came to be here?'

'None,' Kerim said.

The doctor carefully wrapped the head in foam and placed it gently into a cool bag. 'As you know, it's my belief that the death of Fahrettin Müftüoğlu was probably suicide – that or misadventure. I can't find any evidence of outside involvement and I really don't think that a professional man like him would have ingested cyanide without knowing what it was and what it does. But he was an odd man, wasn't he?'

'A hoarder,' Kerim said.

The doctor looked around. 'Of the most clinical variety. Jeweller, wasn't he?'

'Yes, sir,' Kerim said. 'Worked for a firm in the Grand Bazaar. GülGül.'

'Oh.' Dr Sarkissian smiled. 'Atyom Bey. Yes, he's distantly related to my wife's cousin Etyen's wife, Jaklin. Very high-end. Mr Müftüoğlu must have been good at his job.'

'Apparently so,' Kerim said. 'A model employee, by all accounts. And yet he seemingly did some work here too.'

'Mmm. Not easy without electricity, I should imagine.'

'No.'

'I wonder whom he made things for in this sort of environment, and why.'

How Gonca got the boys in the shop to both deliver the new bed and take away the old one that afternoon, Süleyman didn't know. He'd seen her make soft, sexy eyes at the young men and was aware that the boys sweated when they spoke to him. Maybe they thought he was her gypsy husband who would rip them apart if he caught them looking at her. But it didn't matter. The bed was now in, and she was making it up, fussing about linen and dancing around the room.

Süleyman sat in the garden in his overcoat and called Kerim Gürsel.

'What's happening, Kerim Bey?' he asked.

'Dr Sarkissian reckons the head is human,' Kerim said. 'We'll carry on here for another few hours and then the scene will be all yours tomorrow. The doctor recommended we search very gingerly in case there are more body parts in evidence.

But this man was a massive hoarder. I mean, every room, to the ceiling.'

'Yes,' Süleyman said. 'He was a good worker, though, according to Mr Mafyan, his employer. But I got the impression that his death was not a surprise. I'd like to go and see Mr Mafyan in the morning again, and speak to some of Mr Müftüoğlu's co-workers.'

'I can be here at the scene.'

'Thank you,' Süleyman said.

'I'll let you know if we have any more dramas.'

He smiled. 'Thank you, Kerim Bey.'

He put his phone down on the table, and it was then that he noticed her for the first time. Gonca had an almost incomprehensible number of siblings. Süleyman realised he probably didn't know half of them. But he did know Didim. Hunched on her haunches underneath the olive tree, she was sewing – and watching him.

Süleyman bowed his head. 'Didim Hanım . . .'

Gonca always told everyone that Didim was decades older than she was, but it wasn't true. She was the second of her father's who-knew-how-many daughters, and was probably only a year or two older. But she had lived even more of a life than Gonca. Famously pregnant twenty-three times, she'd raised her surviving eighteen children with a husband who had been in and out of prison, until he'd eventually given up a life of crime in favour of becoming a bonzai – synthetic cannabinoid – addict. Didim had always survived by selling flowers on the streets – and of course, living off her sister's money. She was also, other Roma had told him, a black witch. Whatever that meant.

She pointed upwards. 'She's up there.'

'I know,' Süleyman said. 'New bed.'

'She did right,' Didim said. 'It was cursed.'

He didn't often challenge Gonca's family's assumptions, but he said, 'No, it wasn't.'

'Was,' she said. 'People mean you and her harm.'

'Yes, well they're entitled to their opinions,' he said.

At that moment, thankfully, Gonca called him.

'Mehmet Bey,' she said, 'come and see our bed!'

'What am I supposed to do with these, eh?' Rahul Bey said as he held his hands up for İkmen to see. He had a point. Twisted out of shape by arthritis, his fingers looked like bunches of dried twigs.

'May it pass quickly,' İkmen said. It was an old formula denoting concern, but they both knew it meant nothing. 'Didn't you say anything to Gonca Hanım?'

'Sometimes it's best to just solve problems and keep your mouth shut,' the old man said. 'I wear gloves most of the time these days; she didn't notice. Neziye's are going the same way, although she can still work with a needle to some extent.'

'So did Neziye Hanım make the bedcover for Gonca Hanım?'

'She created it,' he said. 'But Gonca Hanım wanted a lot of embellishment, and so we had to send it out for decoration. She marries your colleague, I hear.'

'Yes,' İkmen said.

'I wish them much happiness. I can't tell you how sorry I am for what happened with the bedcover. No wonder Gonca Hanım is distressed. She put her wedding bedcover in my hands and I let her down.'

'No.'

'I did. I should have checked the work. But it only came in on the morning before she took it away. I will get Neziye to write a letter to her and, of course, I will refund Mehmet Bey's money. I know he's a gorgo, like you, but she loves him and I think people who wish them ill are wrong. Their hatred will rebound upon them.'

36

Rahul poured more rakı for himself and İkmen. Out in the shop, İkmen heard Neziye speaking in Romani to a customer.

'Rahul Bey,' he said, 'do you think that whoever you contracted the work out to might have a grudge against Gonca Hanım?'

'No! No! The Can family are good people. The mother, Huriye Hanım, is one of the finest seamstresses in the city. Eight boys and one daughter she has, God bless her, and not a word from the husband for over a decade.'

'Oh?'

'A bad Roma,' the old man said. 'There's nothing worse. Gambling, drinking . . . Much like Gonca Hanım's husbands, worthless. At least with Mehmet Bey, we know he has a job. And – I expect you know this, Çetin Bey – he is buying her a house! In the islands! I said when she told me, "You can all spend summers out there now!" and she said they would.'

İkmen tried to imagine Gonca's extended family ranging around Süleyman's ancestral villa on Büyükada, but decided not to dwell on it.

'I said,' the old man continued, '"Mehmet Bey must love you a lot", and she blushed.' He laughed. 'Can you imagine?'

'Rahul Bey,' İkmen said, 'would it be possible for Gonca Hanım to speak to this Can family about the . . .'

'Maybe.' The haberdasher shook his head. 'But not now. Not until I have spoken to Huriye Hanım myself. It is my place,' he added. 'And, well, she has trouble . . .'

'Trouble?'

He leaned in close. 'Money.'

'With eight sons? Are they children?'

'Oh no, no.' He took a swig from his glass and then topped it up with water. 'All but one is like the father, and that one, Hızır, can't do anything.'

'Why not?'

'Spina bifida. Then there's the girl, Şaziye. To be honest, it is

Şaziye I employ to do my intricate work. Tiny nimble fingers. Now she *is* a child – not that she leads a child's life.'

'What do you mean?'

'Supporting her family,' he said. 'Poor girl doesn't just work for me; she gets work all over the city from those in the know.'

'They live in Tarlabaşı?'

'Yes. But let me speak to them, Çetin Bey. They will be mortified that this has happened and I am sure they will wish to make amends.'

'And I am sure that Mehmet Bey will not want his money back, given the circumstances,' İkmen said. 'His wedding is only a week away now, so he and Gonca Hanım have much to do. If you could speak to this family and then get back to me, I would be grateful.'

Arto Sarkissian put his phone back on his bench and reviewed his latest conversation with Kerim Gürsel.

The scan of the object found in the apartment in Vefa had shown that it was very clearly a human skull. But how old was it? Indeed, what was it? It certainly didn't look like anything he'd seen in his laboratory before. He'd have to order a full chemical review of whatever covered the skull, and also, he felt, a radiocarbon dating test too.

Some years ago, the body of a dead Greek, killed in the riots of 1955, had been dug up in the grounds of the Galatasaray Lycée. He'd had that radiocarbon dated, which was how he'd been able to tell the police its approximate age. Now it seemed that yet again he would have to employ the services of his archaeological forensic friends.

When he arrived in the bedroom, Gonca was yelling out of the window.

'Fuck off, Didim! I know what you're doing and it's disgusting!'

Ignoring their altercation, Mehmet Süleyman looked at the new bed, which had a massive gold headboard and was covered with a red and gold quilt.

'It looks . . .' he began.

But she wasn't listening.

'Didim! Fuck off!'

His phone pinged to let him know he had a message. It was from Kerim Gürsel. It said, *Head is definitely human. Will talk tomorrow.*

A strange twist on a suicide, he thought. Had Fahrettin Müftüoğlu been a murderer? And if he had been, what was his victim doing in his home?

While he pondered these things, he was vaguely aware that Gonca had left the window and got into the bed. He put his phone back in his pocket and looked at her.

She said, 'Come here, Şehzade Mehmet. Come and see our lovely new bed.'

He walked across the room and she pulled the quilt to one side. Underneath she was naked. She had clearly undressed very quickly.

'Oh.'

'I thought we might make this bed our own,' she said.

He took his jacket off and placed it on the back of a chair. Her body showed many signs of the twelve times she had given birth, of the beatings her husbands had given her in the past, of the bullet wound that had nearly taken her life, but he loved her all the more for that. With her spooky long hair, her fine skin, hard muscles and big breasts, she was like a goddess from a fairy tale. She had magic.

He took his clothes off and got into bed beside her. She wrapped her legs around his hips and he licked her nipples.

'Oh baby, you love those so much!' she said.

'I do.'

'I wish I'd known you when I was pregnant. They were huge!'

He looked up at her and smiled.

She began to run her fingers up and down his penis.

'I breastfed all my children,' she said. 'It was beautiful.'

She must have been like some sort of sexy earth mother. How could her previous husbands have used her so badly? And why, given the abundance of Gonca on offer to him, was part of his mind still on a desiccated head in some strange apartment in Vefa?

Many years ago, Çetin İkmen had given voice to his own thoughts on such things. He'd wondered why he would leave his beautiful, loving and intelligent family in a heartbeat to go and attend to the death of some old man at the hands of his lazy son. His words came back to Süleyman now:

'It's because anyone who becomes a detective isn't right. The thrill of it intoxicates us every time. It blocks out everything else in our lives. We are only a whisker away from the murderers who obsess us. And of course, we in our turn obsess them too. It's a kind of twisted romance.'

Police guards were posted outside the Müftüoğlu apartment, securing the site overnight. As the three detectives walked away from the building towards their vehicles, Kerim lit a cigarette. Now that he had a three-month-old baby, no one was allowed to smoke in the Gürsel apartment.

'Do you know when the boss is getting here tomorrow, Kerim Bey?' Ömer Mungun asked.

'Not sure,' he said. 'He's going back to the Grand Bazaar to speak to Müftüoğlu's employer again.'

'Why?'

'I think he feels there might be more to discover from that quarter.'

Ömer laughed. 'He's always suspicious.'

40

'Which is why,' Eylul said, 'he's so good at his job.'

Ömer shrugged.

Kerim stopped beside his car and called his colleagues over.

'So tomorrow,' he said, 'I'll be in charge of the scene until Mehmet Bey arrives. I'd like your help supervising scene-of-crime officers. We should get through that wall of clothes by the end of the morning and then I want to move the workbench out and decant items from other rooms into that space.'

'OK.'

'I know it's not a comfortable feeling, not knowing what we might unearth next, but it has to be done.'

'Even though he committed suicide?' Ömer asked.

'We've discovered no family, as yet,' Kerim said. 'And because he owned the property, there's no landlord.' He shrugged. 'And now there's this head. Mr Müftüoğlu seems to have been a mystery. Hopefully we won't find any more human remains. But we have to be sure.'

As they went their separate ways, Kerim still felt uneasy. There were seventeen million people in the city of İstanbul, and so it was logical to assume that many of them lived lonely existences. But the jeweller's place had made his skin crawl.

He picked up his phone and called his wife's carer.

'On my way, Edith,' he said when she picked up.

'Well thank God for that!' the elderly drag queen said. 'I'm dying for a cigarette.'

'Was Sinem not up to looking after Melda at all today?' he asked.

'No, poor thing,' Edith said. 'And the little one just cried and cried. I did all the things you do. Bottle, nappy, wind. Just fractious.'

'She'll be better when her daddy gets home,' Kerim said.

'Well I hope so,' Edith said, and ended the call.

Kerim's wife, Sinem, had suffered from rheumatoid arthritis

since childhood and was prescribed pain-killing drugs that sometimes rendered her unable to function. Madame Edith helped the couple look after their new baby. It was an unusual arrangement. In the past, Sinem had been cared for by a trans woman called Pembe. She had been a friend of Edith's, although the real connection was through Kerim. Until her death earlier in the year, Kerim and Pembe had been lovers.

Driving home to Tarlabaşı, Kerim tried not to think about Pembe. He'd been attracted to men for as long as he could remember, and Pembe, though outwardly a woman, had still retained her male sexual organs and much of her male allure. Sinem had always known. She was Kerim's best friend from childhood and had married him because she was in love with him. Now they had a baby and his life as any sort of gay man was over. And much as he loved Sinem – enough to have made her pregnant – he mourned the passing of his true self.

Life wasn't fair. Not so many years ago, İstanbul had held Gay Pride marches and festivals, and it had seemed as if things for people like Kerim were changing for the better. But the world had taken a different path, a more conservative one, and such parades and marches were even being banned in parts of Europe.

In future, his life would consist of Sinem, their daughter Melda and the job. He was lucky to have so much.

So why did he want to cry all the time?

Chapter 4

All the boys attacked the bread as if they were starving – except for Hızır, who probably was. A tiny, twisted boy in a wheelchair, he just let his siblings do what they were going to do anyway and held back – like his sister.

Şaziye Can, at twelve, was the second youngest of the nine siblings. A thin, light-brown-skinned girl in a torn dress, she looked a lot younger than she was. Like Hızır, who was a year younger, she had bruises up her arms and down her legs from the frequent less-than-gentle attentions of her older brothers. Mother Huriye had given up trying to control her children a long time ago. As soon as her useless husband was out of the picture, her eldest son, Ziya, who was twenty, had taken over from the old man, using fear to get what he wanted from his family.

As the other boys fell on the bread Huriye had put out for them on the breakfast cloth, Ziya moved to push himself to the front. Two of the boys got their heads smashed together, while poor timid Çağatay found himself pushed right out of the way, stuck underneath the broken window. Huriye tried to grab hold of some food for her less aggressive children, but when the boys had all eaten what they could and gone out, she was left with nothing.

As she bent down to pick up the breakfast cloth, she said, 'It's all right, I held some back.'

She took a corn-husk-shaped loaf out of her apron, pulled it in half and gave it to Şaziye and Hızır.

43

'With luck, you've some more work coming in today, Şaziye,' she said.

'From Rahul Bey?' the girl asked.

'Maybe.'

Şaziye looked at her brother, who just carried on eating.

'You did good work on Gonca Hanım's bedcover,' Huriye said. 'Maybe there will be a bit extra for you. You know that Gonca Hanım's fiancé is a prince . . .'

'No, Mama,' the girl said, 'he's a policeman.'

'His family were princes.'

'A long time ago.'

Some people said that Huriye had always been simple; others that all the beatings her husband had given her had damaged her brain. Whatever the cause, she was a bit of a dreamer, and so when she said, 'Uncle Munir will be here later,' she failed completely to see the look that passed between Şaziye and Hızır.

As Mehmet Süleyman began to knot his tie, Gonca hopped out of bed and took over.

'Is this what wives are supposed to do for their husbands?' she said as she finished making the knot and then folded his collar down.

'Only if they want to,' he said.

She took his lower lip between her teeth and kissed him. He drew her close.

When it was over, he said, 'I must go. I've an appointment in the Grand Bazaar.'

'Really?' Gonca threw herself back on the bed. 'Another jeweller's?'

'GülGül,' he said. 'But don't get your hopes up. There may be some more nice things before our wedding, or there may not. Don't forget I'm buying a house.'

'Mmm.' She licked her fingers playfully. 'But you know,

Şehzade Mehmet, my husband, a few more sparkly rocks, especially in GülGül's fabulous settings, would gain you a lot of freedom in my bed.'

He laughed. 'I thought I had that already!'

'Oh, let me tell you,' Gonca said, 'there are still things I can do to you, with you, against your will . . .'

'I'm going,' he said as he picked up his keys, phone and cigarettes. When he got to the bedroom door, he turned. 'Gonca, is GülGül particularly extraordinary or just simply expensive?'

'Both,' she said. 'Expensive and amazing. Their rings move.'

'Move?'

'Articulate,' she said. 'They have little secret chambers.'

'What for?'

'I don't know! Poison?'

He left.

The whole atmosphere of the place acted as a depressant to Çetin İkmen. From the heavy black wooden furniture to the dusty velvet curtains to the massive ornate candelabra. The Süleymans' nineteenth-century wooden villa in Arnavautköy on the northern shore of the Bosphorus was like a preserved corpse – fascinating but corrupted. Back in Ottoman times, it had been one of many small summer houses the family used when their palace in Nişantaşı became too hot. The only other one that remained was the villa on Büyükada that Mehmet Süleyman was in the process of buying.

Nur Süleyman, Mehmet's mother, was well into her eighties. A small, proud figure, once a peasant woman who had caught the eye of Mohammed Süleyman, an ex-prince with no kingdom or status. As his wife, she had become more Ottoman than her husband and had been instrumental in sending her sons to expensive schools, where they had felt poor and disadvantaged in comparison to the sons of the then secular elite. İkmen didn't like her, but he respected her, which was why he was here.

A teenage maid brought them both sahlep and lokum and then left.

As Nur Süleyman picked up her cup and saucer, she said, 'I suppose you're here to try to persuade me to attend Mehmet Efendi's wedding.'

'I am,' İkmen said. 'I know it's not my business . . .'

'You are correct.'

In the light from the one lamp by her shoulder, she looked like a venerable idol. Her dark grey hair scraped back in a bun, her neck and ears glittering with jewels, her hard eyes outlined in thick black kohl.

'I'm doing this for your son,' İkmen continued. 'Because I love him and because I know it will make him unhappy if you don't come.'

'I went to his first two marriages; why do I want to go to a third?'

'Because whatever you may think about Gonca, madam, Mehmet loves her.'

'She has bewitched him!'

'Ah, come now, you don't believe that!' İkmen said, aware that he sort of half believed it himself.

'She's sixty-two! An old woman! What does he want with her? Have you seen my son? He's such a handsome man, and yet he chooses to marry a woman who looks like a falçı in a cheap coffee house!'

'Madam, I am the same age as Gonca Hanım, but I do not consider myself old,' İkmen said. He did when he felt low, but he wasn't telling her that. 'She is a remarkably beautiful woman, one of the most successful artists this country has ever produced.'

'And she's a gypsy.'

'And she is Roma, yes,' he said. 'I know you met my daughter, Çiçek . . .'

'Now she was better for him!' Nur Süleyman said. 'Hardly

46

his equal, but I am led to believe your family is decent, and you are not gypsies. I told him that if he married her, I would not object. In her forties, the girl may even still have been fertile!'

It wasn't comfortable hearing his daughter talked about in terms of her fertility. Her short affair with Mehmet Süleyman had never been the right thing for either of them, and were İkmen not trying to get the old woman to do something for him, he would have given his opinion, and his anger, in full.

'Yes, well that was never to be,' he said. 'Which leaves us with now. Nur Hanım, it is my understanding that a considerable cohort of your family will be attending the wedding, including your son Murad and his daughter Edibe; your late husband's brother Beyazıt Efendi; Mehmet Efendi's son from Ireland—'

'Hah!'

Mention of Patrick Süleyman seemed to unsettle her.

'That is a strange child,' she said. 'I don't understand it.'

İkmen cracked. Patrick was a great kid. He stood up.

'Well, Nur Hanım, it's up to you,' he said. 'I am very happy to escort you to your son's wedding, but I see you are intractable. Not only, I fear, do you not appreciate Mehmet's finer qualities, but you fail to see any in your grandson either – which I find unforgivable.'

'You think what you like, sir,' she said.

Once outside that house, İkmen went straight to his car and sat for a few moments in order to calm his nerves. Mehmet hadn't known that he was going to see his mother, but İkmen had felt he had to try to persuade her. Although Mehmet Süleyman would never say so himself, İkmen knew he would be very hurt if his mother didn't come to his wedding.

Attempting to sort out other people's lives – especially Mehmet's – seemed to be his purpose at the moment. No one had asked him to track down a missing person, find lost family gold or help identify some unknown etiolated body for months. Desperate acts of cruelty gave his life meaning.

But then his phone beeped to indicate he had a text message. It proved interesting.

'Your fiancée is quite right,' Atyom Mafyan said as he held a ring with a prominent blue stone up to the light and then removed a small core from the middle of the sapphire. 'Rings with compartments were often designed to conceal poisons. It's said it was via a poison ring that the famous Italian murderess Lucrezia Borgia killed her enemies. But we, Inspector, we make these rings for the amusement of our customers, not to facilitate murder. These compartments we build are always empty. People can, and do, put tiny gifts for their loved ones inside. Small diamonds or slivers of birthstone, lapis lazuli maybe.'

The jeweller was an affable elderly man. Unlike his cousin Garbis, the custodian of the Üç Horan Armenian church in Beyoğlu, Atyom Mafyan was a man of considerable girth, and possessed the kind of body hair that sprang out from every opening in his clothes – sleeves, shirt collar, even his socks.

'Did Fahrettin Müftüoğlu make things like this?' Süleyman asked.

'Yes, he did. He was very skilled.'

Müftüoğlu's laptop computer, which was owned by his employer, had been sent for analysis by the police technical team. With no electricity, he could not have used it for long periods of time in his apartment, and so, were there anything of concern on the machine, it would probably have been something he had sent or received elsewhere. Possibly at work.

'Atyom Bey,' Süleyman continued, 'you described Fahrettin Bey as a good employee.'

'He was. Most imaginative.'

'And yet . . . forgive me if I am wrong, but I feel he was not a person without, shall we say, controversy.'

The elderly Armenian slumped a little. 'Fahrettin Bey was . . . Well, he wasn't very gregarious,' he said. 'Kept to himself.'

'Was that a problem?'

'No. No. Jewellers are a strange breed, Inspector. People often imagine we are flamboyant because of the rather outré pieces we create, but actually we are a solitary group in general. We work away in our ateliers and workshops creating bespoke pieces for people with more money than we can imagine, making rings and tiaras for princesses both real and celluloid and indulging our own fantasies. We can disappear into our creations.'

'Did Fahrettin Bey disappear?'

'Sometimes. All work that passes through here and bears the name "GülGül" has to have my approval. The atelier has a reputation to uphold. I know you are friendly with Berekiah Bey at the Lazar atelier, so you will realise this. What you may not know is that we, as a community of craftsmen, have a keen interest in each other's work. I can tell you, for instance, that the rings Berekiah Bey created for your upcoming marriage have caused considerable excitement.'

Süleyman smiled.

'They have raised the stakes, as it were, for the rest of us. You may find that for a while, wedding rings are conceived with more of a sparkle effect in mind.' Then the jeweller frowned. 'A long time ago, Fahrettin submitted some very imaginative designs for my approval – which I gave. Or rather, I gave my approval until I discovered the purpose behind his innovations.'

'Which was?'

'Although he always dressed like a lawyer, Fahrettin was an unconventional man in many ways. I remember years ago, before the subject became fashionable, I suppose you'd say, he expressed his views to me about vaccination. I am of a generation that sees vaccination as a sort of miracle, mainly because our parents had known their relatives to die from things like polio and diphtheria.'

49

'I agree,' Süleyman said.

'So I was surprised when Fahrettin, a man younger than myself, expressed his disbelief in it. And it was that which informed a set of jewellery designs he submitted to me in . . .' he thought for a moment, 'just after the great earthquake of 1999, so 2000. Some fabulous designs, some of which I approved. But what I didn't sanction was the use their creator intended for them.'

'Which was?'

'Therapy,' he said. 'I can't say I really understood or understand. Fahrettin came out with lots of terminology about "vibrations" and "healing". I immediately thought about what would happen if a customer bought a piece advertised as possessing the ability to cure cancer and then sued us when that didn't happen. Our customers tend to be wealthy, and by extension litigious. I said no.'

'Can you give me an example of what you mean?' Süleyman asked.

'There were several ideas,' Atyom Bey said. 'One involved semi-precious stones that are supposed to contain healing properties. I wasn't too worried about that. Lots of jewellers, including GülGül, offer birthstones. I just didn't want to move any further in that direction. Other ideas were more problematic. Using the poison ring pattern, he wanted to place substances in his pieces.'

'Substances?'

'Herbs mainly. The one that sticks in my mind is the heart disease pendant, designed to contain digitalis. As I'm sure you know, that is used in the treatment of heart disease but it's also a toxin. It can cause hallucinations, vomiting, even kill.'

Süleyman said, 'So he designed jewellery made to carry these substances, to be used, what – in an emergency?'

'No, Inspector. Digitalis, in the case of that pendant, was sealed into a setting using crystals and pearls, fashioned in the shape of the anatomical heart. It was clever. The digitalis was encased inside rose quartz – you could see it. Acted, as I understand it, as sympathetic magic rather than actual herbalism.'

'So safe . . .'

'What, with digitalis inside? What if it broke? And anyway, some of his other offerings were accessible – hemp, for instance. I told him no, that this was not the nineteenth century and he should really think about getting himself a doctor rather than messing about with this stuff. He accepted what I said. But what he did outside the atelier, I can't say. He worked here alone, as most of us do; he spoke little and worked well to deadlines.'

'Was he suicidal?' Süleyman asked. Searching for his cigarettes to offer the jeweller made him realise, with a jolt, that he had left something behind in Gonca's bedroom.

Atyom Bey took the proffered cigarette. 'I wouldn't say so. I know little about such things, but inasmuch as Fahrettin could be happy, I think he was. There was no woman in his life as far as I am aware. He was somewhat awkward around them. But then I always got the impression that Fahrettin was, well, sexless.'

Huriye put her head in her hands. 'What will become of us?'

Her daughter, holding the linen tablecloth Rahul Bey had given her to work on, said, 'I'll do this as quickly as I can.'

Her mother shook her head. 'We needed all the money from Gonca Hanım's bedcover. How am I supposed to pay the rent now?' She looked at Şaziye and Hızır. 'Are you sure you don't know how it got ruined?'

'No,' Şaziye said.

'You took it straight to Neziye Hanım? You didn't leave it anywhere?'

'No!'

'And you've no idea how it came to be covered in blood?'

'No! How would I know that?' the girl said. 'Maybe Neziye Hanım did it.'

'Neziye Hanım? Are you insane? Why would she damage something so precious, something that would have made her family money? And Gonca Hanım is a witch! Would Neziye Hanım risk her anger? No!'

'Mama . . .'

'Just goes to show that this family is cursed,' Huriye went on. 'I've felt it for years. First you, and now . . . this . . .'

'Me?'

'You know what I mean!' Huriye yelled.

A look passed between Şaziye and her brother.

Huriye began to cry. 'I don't know if I can do this for very much longer! I don't!'

She breathed in again and then told her sister to 'Pull!'

Didim Şekeroğlu was a strong, wiry woman, but even she felt as if she'd reached the end. As she held on tight to the ends of the laces at the back of her sister's corset, she said, 'Gonca, that's it! I'm telling you!'

Gonca gasped as she held onto the front of her wardrobe for support. 'It can't be! I'll breathe in again.'

And she did. Didim pulled tighter.

'I can hear a car outside,' Didim said in response to a squeal of wheels in the street.

'That'll be Rambo,' Gonca said, naming her youngest son. 'Can you do it up now?'

'I think so.'

It was a struggle, but eventually Didim managed to tie the laces into a single and then a double bow. Shakily, Gonca turned around to face her. 'And?'

'Well, you've a tiny waist,' her sister said. 'But your tits are weird.'

'What do you mean, weird?'

'Bigger than normal. Don't know whether they'll fit into your dress even if you've got a tiny waist. Might have to alter it.'

52

Gonca shook her head. 'You've altered it twice already!'

'Well, do you want it to be right or don't you?'

The sisters began to bicker, Gonca fighting for breath as her lungs struggled against the strictures imposed by the corset. Neither of them heard the bedroom door open or saw him until it was too late.

Mehmet Süleyman widened his eyes. 'What . . .'

Didim, seeing a route to escape, took it and ran out of the bedroom. This left Gonca, panting, and a very confused Mehmet.

When she could speak, Gonca said, 'What are you doing here?'

'I forgot something,' he said, picking up his gun and shoulder holster from his bedside table. 'What are you doing?'

She shrugged.

'What is that you're wearing, and why?' he asked.

'Well, it's a corset,' she said. 'Anyone can see that!'

'Yes, but why . . .'

'I'm going to wear it under my wedding dress.'

'Why?'

'Because I . . .' Breathing was difficult, especially when one was angry. 'Look, you know how things are these days with photographs. Everyone photographs everything and at least half of those end up on social media. I don't want to be a big fat old gypsy woman!'

As he put his shoulder holster on, he stared at her.

'What?'

'What? Where do you want me to start?' he said.

'I . . .'

'All right!' He slipped the firearm into its holster. 'Big, yes – you are tall, and that's a good thing. Fat you are not. Shapely and curvaceous you are, which is something I really like. Call me an old-fashioned Ottoman. Old I won't even dignify with a response, and I think that being a gypsy woman is a good thing, don't you?'

She looked down at the floor.

'Take it off,' he said. 'You're not wearing it.'

'Don't tell me what to do.'

'All right. Please take it off.'

She looked confused for a moment, then said, 'I can't. Can you . . .'

She turned her back and let him unlace her. As her flesh began to expand, he said, 'You couldn't breathe! This thing is horrible!'

The corset dropped to the floor. She stood in front of him, her hands covering her breasts, her torso marked with red lines where the corset had pushed her in.

Mehmet shook his head. 'Promise me you won't ever do that again.'

'It gives me a nice waist,' she said.

He put his hand in his jacket pocket and took out a box. 'Promise me, or you don't get this.'

'Oh! What is it?'

'Promise,' he reiterated.

Her eyes were on the box. He knew she could probably read what was on the lid.

'GülGül!'

He held it up. 'Promise!'

Gonca reached out. 'All right, I promise.'

He threw it to her and watched as she grabbed for it, catching it against her naked breasts. She opened the box and smiled.

'Oh, darling!' she said. 'I thought you said no more presents?'

He shrugged and began to leave the room.

In the doorway, he turned. 'I lied.'

'Sir! Inspector Gürsel!'

They'd managed to clear a corridor into what had once been the kitchen. Ömer Mungun, along with scene-of-crime officers, was now clearing a cluttered work surface prior to opening cupboards. However, the young man from Mardin was impetuous and had begun sorting through one low-level cupboard before he had room to remove the items inside. Now it seemed he had been rewarded with something that had looked quite normal but wasn't.

He left the kitchen holding a jar. As he approached Kerim Gürsel at the end of the corridor, the older man said, 'What is that? It stinks!'

'I thought it was tripe,' Ömer said. 'Now I'm not so sure.'

Other officers gagged. Eylul Yavaş said, 'That is like something from a lab.'

'Twenty years ago,' added Kerim.

Ömer gave him the jar. 'It was in a cupboard in the kitchen.'

'Why did you open it?'

'Wanted to see what it was,' he said. 'What is it?'

'No idea,' Kerim replied.

'I think it looks like tripe.'

'Well, then maybe it *is* tripe.' Kerim shook his head. Sometimes when Süleyman wasn't around to control him, Ömer Mungun pursued his own agenda, which, to Kerim, often appeared meaningless. 'What were you going to do with it? Eat it? Close the lid and bag it up?'

A long, slim hand caught Ömer before he could replace the lid of the jar.

'What's that?' Süleyman asked. He'd just arrived back at the scene. 'That smell, if I'm not much mistaken, is formaldehyde. Whatever that is is being preserved.'

He shook Kerim's hand, then said, 'We need to talk, Inspector.'

'Ah . . .'

He turned to Ömer. 'Tell the scene-of-crime officers to go outside for a break.'

Chapter 5

Even pathologists themselves agreed that most of them were odd. Whether, like Arto Sarkissian, they worked for the police or, like Aylin Akyıldız, their field of work was archaeological, they often shared the same, often slightly off-kilter experiences with little or no comment.

'I hoped we were looking at something ancient,' Dr Akyıldız said as she observed what had become known to those involved in the case as the Head of Vefa.

Across the table upon which the head sat between them, Arto said, 'You're sure it's modern?'

'Tragically,' she said. 'I'll be honest, Arto, I've a list that probably stretches to Ankara of missing archaeological pathology from museums and collections all over the Middle East. If I could have linked this to any of those, I would have been a happy woman. But this is modern. However . . .'

'However?'

'However, it's mummified,' she said. 'Like the pharaohs themselves, it is preserved for all time and beyond in this world and that which comes next.'

'Why?'

'I've no idea,' she said. 'An experiment? Perhaps whoever did it wanted to know how to remove someone's brain through their nose with a hook. Basically you have to whisk the brain tissue first, *in situ*.'

Even Arto Sarkissian's strong stomach flipped. This was how

the ancient Egyptians had taken the deceased's brains out prior to mummification.

'And the colour of the thing?' he asked.

'Mummification involved not only drying the body out, using salt called natron, but, once it was dry, applying oils and balms to make it look human again.'

'What sorts of substances?'

'Typically frankincense, myrrh, wood pitch. Gums and resins. Sometimes they'd be poured all over the coffin too. Nothing was left to chance, except of course the fact that human greed was underestimated. Almost every tomb discovered so far in Egypt was ransacked centuries ago. And now, across the region, it's open season, thanks in part to the war in Syria.'

'Because artefacts have gone from that country into private collections?'

'Why just have a Syrian sculpture of Baal when you can also have a Ptolomaic pharaoh mummy?'

Arto shook his head. 'Doesn't help me with this character, however.'

'No,' she said. 'This is modern. But maybe someone wanted to pass it off as ancient. These things can fetch high prices if you know the right people. But why just the head, and why no bandaging?' She rubbed her face.

Arto said, 'By the right people . . .'

'Oh, inevitably online,' she said. 'Not that I can show you how that operates. What I know about the darker side of the World Wide Web is minimal to say the least.'

'Can DNA be extracted from it?'

'To be honest, I don't know,' she said. 'The mummification process is extremely destructive, as you can imagine. I can give it a go, but it will take time.'

*

57

Çetin İkmen didn't know the Can family. In a way this was a good thing, as it might mean they were law-abiding citizens. But then he also knew that a lot of apparently law-abiding citizens were also crooks.

They lived in one of those desperate Tarlabaşı buildings where all the windows had been smashed or shot out years ago and where at least some of the accommodation was used to dump rubbish. He imagined that the people who had to live in such places felt dumped as well.

According to Rahul Bey, the haberdasher, the Can family – Huriye Hanım and her nine children – lived a hand-to-mouth existence supported by the mother and her daughter's handiwork and a little petty robbery courtesy of the sons. On occasion, according to Rahul, they were helped by Huriye's husband's brother, Munir.

He'd seen a large middle-aged man go into the shabby building ten minutes before, and now there was yelling. He couldn't understand what was being said. Why had he never learned Romani? But he'd seen a woman who could be Huriye Hanım in one of the non-existent windows, shouting, and had heard a man's voice reply. Nobody on the street even looked up out of the gutter. This was Tarlabaşı at its most deprived, and it made him angry. Nobody should live like this.

İkmen lit a cigarette and thought about what Rahul Bey had told him. The Cans had denied any knowledge of the blood on the bedcover. The girl who had produced the work said she had folded it up with help from her brother and put it into its bag in pristine condition. She denied meeting anyone else or letting the thing out of her sight until she gave it to Rahul Bey's daughter, Neziye Hanım. According to Neziye, she'd put it on the shelf designated for completed work. Her only error, if it could be called such, was that she hadn't checked the bedcover before she put it away.

Rahul Bey had described the Cans' daughter as a child, but was she so young as to not yet be menstruating? But then if that were the girl's blood, why? The family needed the money, and like most Roma they were probably frightened of Gonca. It didn't make sense. But then any involvement from Neziye didn't make sense either. She was beyond menstruating, and whatever she might or might not feel about Gonca, she was a businesswoman who now, Rahul Bey had told him, was obliged to write her a grovelling letter of apology.

Şaziye Can must have left the parcel somewhere. Something must have happened that meant that somehow it was out of her care. But what?

The man he'd heard speaking to the woman in the window came out of the building fastening his belt. Men, generally older men, who wanted people to know they'd just had sex did that. He was fat, but also muscular. İkmen wouldn't like to meet him in a fight, although he suspected he was the sort of man his younger, fitter colleagues could take down easily. And he fitted the description Rahul Bey had given him. This was probably Munir Can.

When he'd gone, İkmen approached the house and found himself confronted by a group of boys.

Arto Sarkissian was making a habit of visiting the crime scene in Vefa. Süleyman had just started telling his colleagues about his visit to GülGül jewellers when the pathologist arrived. Eylul Yavaş, who had been sitting on the only chair they had found so far, got up and gave it to him.

As he lowered himself down, he said, 'I know that strictly speaking, I should allow you to continue to sit, Eylul Hanım. But my back is terrible these days. Bless you.'

The three men leaning against the wall looked like male models, Arto thought.

Süleyman said, 'I was just telling my colleagues about my visit to GülGül, Doctor.'

'Oh, yes, Atyom Bey. He employed this Fahrettin Müftüoğlu, didn't he?'

'Yes. Like most jewellers Müftüoğlu was a somewhat self-contained artist,' Süleyman continued. 'But he had an angle that was all about therapy.'

'Therapy?'

The inspector explained. When he had finished, he added, 'Which is why I wanted to alert you all to the possibility that we may uncover some more potentially toxic substances in this apartment.'

Ömer held up the jar of 'tripe'.

'And I was nearly too late,' Süleyman said. 'Yes, that's the sort of thing.'

The doctor frowned. 'May I please look at that, Sergeant?'

'Of course.' Ömer handed it over.

Arto adjusted his glasses. 'Ah, oh yes, you're probably wondering why I'm here.'

'It's always a pleasure,' Süleyman began.

'Mmm.' Given the nature of his work, the doctor found that statement rather odd. Then he said, 'The head you discovered . . .'

'Oh?'

They all seemed to lean in on him suddenly.

'Yes,' he said, 'human, definitely. And . . . mummified.'

'Mummified? As in ancient Egypt mummified?' Kerim said.

'Exactly.'

'Fahrettin Müftüoğlu's mother was Egyptian,' Eylul Yavaş said. 'Do you think she brought a mummy with her when she came to Turkey?'

'A pharaoh,' Ömer Mungun suggested.

'Well, no,' Arto said. 'When I say a mummy, I mean a modern mummy.'

60

'What?'

'Yes,' he nodded, 'according to the archaeological pathologist. She assures me it has been well preserved, adhering to the letter of the Egyptian mummification model. Whoever did it even drew the brain out through the nostrils.'

'Really?' Kerim Gürsel shook his head. 'So we've a suicide who was a hoarder and a bit odd about vaccination, and now a mummified human head that is actually modern . . .'

'Yes,' the doctor said. 'Cause of death on the head, I cannot tell as yet. Obviously any further body parts you may find will be most useful in this venture.' He looked at the jar again. 'However, you may have already found some of them.'

Süleyman frowned.

The doctor held the jar up. 'If I'm not much mistaken, Inspector Süleyman, these are human intestines. Although whether it will be possible to extract DNA from them for the purposes of identification is something I will need to take advice on. The Head of Vefa, I am reliably informed, could be difficult and costly to identify.'

It was a work of both deduction and magic. Çetin İkmen deduced that the boys were Roma, and the effect Gonca's name had upon them was pure sorcery.

'She's my friend,' İkmen said. 'I'm going to her wedding next week.'

However, the tallest boy, who was smoking a soggy roll-up and had threatened to beat İkmen to paste, was still sceptical. 'You come to have a go, have you?'

'Have a go? About what?' İkmen said.

'Our women was working for Gonca Hanım, but they got it wrong and now she's angry,' the boy said.

'Oh? No,' İkmen said. 'Far as I know, if Gonca Hanım has a problem with someone, she can take care of it herself.'

'She's a witch,' a small boy said. A slightly larger boy slapped him.

'I want to speak to Huriye Can,' İkmen said. 'I believe she lives here.'

'Who are you?' the biggest boy said.

'Told you, I'm a friend of Gonca Hanım's.'

'So you have come—'

He grabbed the boy by the collar. 'Listen, kid. I want to speak to Huriye Can. I want to help her. You either take me to see her or it all gets a bit ugly.'

The boy, who was called Ziya, began to front up to İkmen, until the latter said, 'Oh, and I should also add that I know Gonca Hanım's fiancé, Inspector Süleyman Efendi, very well too.'

Mention of the police made the boy take one step back, then he said, 'What do you want our mum for?'

Neziye Mengüç had started and stopped her letter to Gonca Hanım when the woman herself appeared in the shop. She could see her standing at the end of the counter while Neziye's father served a man she knew to be one of the local godfather's heavies.

What she should do was go and help her dad. He couldn't just stop serving one of Sesler's men, even if that was in favour of the local witch. As she put her pen down, Neziye curled her lip. She could remember Gonca Şekeroğlu from when they were both children, back in the days when they'd lived in the old quarter of Sulukule. With her big breasts and her sultry eyes, Gonca had always been confident. Her father had got her married off at fifteen, but it hadn't tamed her. With her art and her strange lifestyle, she went her own way. Now that was culminating in marriage to a handsome gorgo twelve years her junior, who, it was said, worshipped her.

Neziye limped out into the shop. 'Good afternoon, Gonca Hanım.'

Gonca smiled. 'Neziye Hanım, good afternoon to you. I wondered whether I might speak to you for a few minutes. In private?'

Of course she wanted to talk about the bedcover. Neziye shrugged and led her through to the small office behind the shop. She saw her father's eyes follow her as she went. She offered Gonca Hanım a seat, which she took, and tea, which she also accepted. Once settled and seated, Gonca said, 'Neziye Hanım, I've come to ask you about the unpleasant incident with the bedcover.'

'We did nothing wrong, Gonca Hanım.'

'I didn't say you did.' She smiled. 'Had I imagined that for a second, I would have been to see you already. But so far I have left the pursuit of this matter in the hands of my fiancé.'

'Papa is working on a replacement, Gonca Hanım.'

'That is very kind. And for your information, I do know that Rahul Bey contracted the work out, and I fully understand. But Şehzade Mehmet Efendi is displeased . . .'

She'd used her fiancé's title in full, to intimidate.

'. . . and anything that upsets me upsets him,' she continued. 'Neziye, you and I both know the significance of the blood, don't we?'

'Yes, hanım. Çetin Bey has been to see my father.'

'I know, I sent him.'

'Mmm.'

'Now, Neziye, what Çetin Bey won't have told you is that the blood on my bedcover was of a particular type. It was dirty.'

Neziye said, 'Oh.'

'Menses blood,' Gonca said. 'So I know it can't be yours.'

Did she say that just to be cruel? Gonca Hanım herself was well past child-bearing age, but she, of course, had a much younger lover to compensate.

'Someone,' Gonca said, 'thinks that my marriage is dirty.

63

Someone wants to curse my love for Şehzade Mehmet Efendi, and when I find out who that is, they will wish they had died at birth.'

An iron silence entered that room, and Neziye found that her hands had become icy cold. Not only was Gonca Hanım a witch, she was also the personal falçı of Şevket Sesler and the lover of a powerful police detective. She could hurt someone.

'And so I should like you to tell me when the bedcover was returned to the shop from the embroiderer, who brought it and also who worked on it.'

'They say they know nothing about it,' Neziye said. 'The girl brought it here a few hours before you came to collect it. I didn't check it, I will be honest. I should have done, but we were so busy . . .'

'It's all right,' Gonca said. 'But Neziye, dear, you know I have to find out who did this, and why. You do understand that, don't you?'

'Yes.'

'So the name of the girl who did the work, if you please,' she said.

'I think Dad told Çetin Bey . . .'

'Well, then you can tell me too, can't you?'

Sergeant Yavaş had learned from the local teyzes that Fahrettin Müftüoğlu's mother had been Egyptian – probably. That was maybe an assumption based upon her name, which had been Isis. It was said she had only spoken Arabic and French, but that didn't necessarily mean she had come from Egypt.

Ömer Mungun had returned to the office he shared with Süleyman at headquarters to try to find out more. He'd been at the scene in Vefa for longer than anyone else and needed a break. If there were more body parts to be found, someone else could do it.

Isis Müftüoğlu must have become a Turkish citizen through

64

her husband, Fuat, who, Ömer had discovered, had been born in 1932 in the apartment in Vefa, which he had occupied all his life. A jeweller; had the equipment found in the apartment actually been his?

Ömer's phone rang. It was the front desk.

'Sergeant, there's a woman here says she needs to speak to Inspector Süleyman,' the officer on duty said.

'He's not here. What's it about?'

'Says she's got some information about that suicide in Vefa.'

'All right. Send her up. What's her name?' Ömer asked.

'Canan Müftüoğlu,' the officer replied.

Ömer put his phone down and waited, intrigued.

She had blood on her skirt and a large bruise was coming up underneath her left eye.

'I saw a man leave here ten minutes ago,' Çetin İkmen said. 'Did he do this to you?'

The woman, who he'd been told was Huriye Can, didn't say anything.

'You know that whatever is going on here, you don't have to put up with that.'

She looked at him as if he were insane. He shrugged. Why should she take his word for anything? He wasn't a police officer any more; he couldn't do anything. And even if he could, that would probably just end in even more abuse for this woman. And it *had* been abuse – both physical and sexual. He could smell sex and reasoned that the man had probably not bothered to use a condom.

The room İkmen found himself in was devoid of furniture. He asked whether he could sit on one of the cushions on the floor, and she said that he could. After a few moments, she sat down too, on the other side of the room, blood dripping down her legs.

He said, 'You are Huriye Hanım. I am Çetin Bey. I come from Rahul Bey.'

She cleared her throat. 'About the bedcover. I told Rahul Bey, we know nothing.'

'No one is accusing you of anything, hanım,' he said. 'We simply need to know how this happened.'

She nodded. 'Gonca Hanım must be so angry!'

'I think she is more concerned than angry,' İkmen said. 'Her wedding is next week. The poor lady is nervous as it is.'

'Mama!'

The yell came from outside. Huriye Hanım excused herself to İkmen and got up to look out of the window.

'What is it?' she called down.

A male voice shouted, 'Witch!'

Inwardly, İkmen groaned. Gonca. That wasn't going to help.

She was probably in her early thirties, so about Ömer's own age. Small and delicate, she had very long, straight dyed blonde hair, and cute dimples in her cheeks when she smiled. Canan Müftüoğlu was pretty rather than beautiful, but then Ömer Mungun had always favoured pretty.

When she walked into his office, he rushed to pull out a chair for her. If this were some long-lost sister of Fahrettin Müftüoğlu, she was clearly from either a different mother or father.

'I am afraid,' he said as he partially cleared his desk of old sweet wrappers and coffee cups, 'that Inspector Süleyman isn't here at the moment. He's at the site of an investigation.'

'In Vefa?' she asked. She was wearing a very short skirt and a figure-hugging coat. She crossed her small but shapely legs.

'Yes.' Ömer sat down. 'I am his sergeant, Ömer Mungun. And you are?'

'I am the wife of Fahrettin Müftüoğlu,' she said.

Ömer was shocked. Everyone they had interviewed had believed Fahrettin Müftüoğlu was single.

The woman smiled. 'I expect that comes as a surprise to you.'

'We thought he'd never married.'

'We kept it quiet,' she said. Then she handed over a marriage certificate, dated 2004.

Ömer turned it over, looking for some way in which it was not genuine. But he knew it was.

'You'll see,' she said, 'that we married in Ölü Deniz. I was twenty.'

He checked the document, tearing his eyes away from her with difficulty. Fahrettin wouldn't have been much older, at twenty-seven.

'We were both on holiday,' she said. 'Me with my father, he with his mother. She didn't like me, but we were in love.'

Ömer was having real difficulty imagining dowdy Fahrettin Müftüoğlu with this exquisite woman. Seemingly reading his mind, she said, 'I understand, of course, that my husband grew old before his time in recent years.'

'So how . . .'

'Well, Isis Hanım was enraged when she knew we had married, and whisked him back to İstanbul with her,' she said. 'I returned home with my father.'

'But you were married . . .'

'Yes,' she said. 'Technically. And we still are, although . . .' She put a hand on the top of his desk. 'Forgive me, Sergeant, this must seem very odd to you . . .'

That was an understatement.

'. . . but I do know that Fahrettin is dead. I knew the moment it happened.'

'How?' he asked.

'Because we had a psychic connection. I felt him leave this world.'

'And, er . . . why didn't you alert someone?' Ömer asked.

'For the same reason you're looking at me as if I'm mad now,' she said. 'I knew the police would not believe me.'

*

It was difficult for İkmen to get his mind around the idea that Şaziye Can was twelve. She looked more like a seven-year-old. He watched Gonca look at the child and could see pity in her eyes.

Sitting on the only chair in the apartment – Huriye Can had rushed to find it for her as soon as Gonca had entered – the artist, characteristically covered in jewellery, looked like a Byzantine empress.

She held her hand out to the girl. 'Come over here, child.'

The girl walked slowly, a hand covering her mouth as if she wanted to silence herself. Gonca watched her carefully, and when she got close, she said, 'Now, Şaziye, I am not angry with you. But I will be angry with you if you don't tell me the truth. Do you know who damaged my bedcover?'

The girl looked at her mother.

Gonca caught the child's chin and held it between her polished fingernails. 'Don't look at her!'

Huriye Hanım said, 'Tell Gonca Hanım the truth, Şaziye! Please!'

İkmen hadn't realised just how much fear Gonca could command from her own people until he saw Huriye's eyes, heard her wavering voice. It made his hair stand up just a little.

The girl said, 'I do not know, Gonca Hanım.'

'Are you sure?' Gonca looked into the girl's eyes.

'Yes, hanım.'

'Because if you lie to me, I will know,' Gonca said. 'And so will Şehzade Mehmet.'

'Me and Hızır,' Şaziye said, 'we put the quilt into the bag and I took it to Rahul Bey's.'

'Hızır is my youngest son,' Huriye said. 'He cannot walk, hanım.'

'Ah.'

Rahul Bey had told İkmen the child had spina bifida.

'Do you want me to get him?' Huriye asked.

'Yes,' said Gonca.

Huriye and Şaziye left the room.

İkmen turned to Gonca. 'And?'

'And what?'

'You're a bit . . . arrogant, brutal . . .'

'I need to know who is trying to ruin my life!' she said. 'And anyway, the girl is lying. I think the mother might be too.'

'Really?'

'Tell me I'm wrong, İkmen.'

'I wouldn't dare!' he said.

'Because you can't,' Gonca replied.

He leaned in close to her. 'I was doing very well without you, you know.'

'Were you?'

And for a moment, he wondered, until he realised that, as usual, Gonca was playing absolutely everyone, including him.

Chapter 6

'What are you doing here, Sergeant?'

Süleyman was staring right at him, in front of everyone in the cordoned-off street, and his voice was low and menacing.

The woman beside Ömer said, 'Oh well, that's my . . .'

The boss's eyes switched to her face and then back to Ömer's. 'Who is this?'

'Oh, this lady is, er . . .'

'Canan Müftüoğlu,' she said.

Süleyman looked at her again. 'A relative?'

'Fahrettin Bey's wife,' she said.

Süleyman paused for a moment. 'Fahrettin Müftüoğlu didn't have a wife.'

'Yes, he did,' she said. 'Me.'

He looked her up and down, his face, to Ömer, completely unreadable.

Ömer said, 'There is a marriage certificate.'

'Is there.'

'I can show—'

'Why did you bring this lady here when I specifically instructed you to remain at headquarters?' Süleyman cut in.

'I am sorry, sir, but . . .'

'That is my fault, Inspector,' the woman said. 'I insisted upon coming here. Sergeant Mungun told me the area was cordoned off, but I thought—'

'You thought what?' Süleyman asked.

'I thought that maybe, sir,' Ömer began, 'seeing as this lady . . .'

Süleyman looked at the woman with actual disgust. 'No civilians, Sergeant Mungun. You know that. Take this woman away, and I will join you later, when we will discuss this matter.' He turned his back and left.

Canan Müftüoğlu said, 'He's stern!'

'I'm afraid he is, hanım,' Ömer said, his face burning with embarrassment. 'I am so sorry.'

'It's not your fault,' she said.

'I know, but . . . He's quite right,' Ömer said. 'I will need to take a statement from you, hanım, and we will proceed from there.'

'Of course,' she said, smiling.

So far, there was a distinct lack of jewellery in Fahrettin Müftüoğlu's chaotic apartment. For someone apparently so besotted by his profession, this was, Kerim Gürsel felt, strange. He clearly did some of his work at home, evidenced by his bench covered with cutting tools, soldering irons and scraps of gold and silver, but there was no product. Maybe, after all, using cumbersome gas bottles to power some of his tools had been too much for him?

His sergeant put some of his thoughts into words. 'What was it with this man and clothes?' she said. 'I mean, I know I'm stereotyping here, sir, but he wasn't that young, nor was he some slim and attractive . . .'

She saw that her superior was laughing.

'Oh, I'm sorry, sir, of course I don't mean that men in their late thirties or forties can't be stylish . . .'

'I know exactly what you meant, Sergeant,' he said. 'And it baffles me too. All these clothes, some of them very fashionable, on a man who, though smart, was hardly groomed, and may even, from the look of that bathroom, have been quite lacking in cleanliness. And no jewellery.'

'Absolutely,' she said. 'And no phone so far.'

'He had to have had one, surely,' Kerim said. 'Everyone has one; even the most ancient teyze who can hardly walk has a phone.'

They finally reached the kitchen. After Ömer Mungun's brief assault on the room, scene-of-crime officers had now cut a swathe through stacks of empty olive oil tins, plastic mixing bowls and heaps of dubious towels that hid several mice nests, to allow Kerim and Eylul to approach the crammed sink and barely attached kitchen cabinets. There was a smell of burnt garlic, rancid fat and mould. Grateful for the white coveralls and plastic gloves they had been given, the officers sifted through surfaces crammed with often unrecognisable things.

In places there was a thick layer of a viscous black material studded with hair and dust that Eylul attempted to sample to put into an evidence bag. As she finally got hold of some, she held it up for Kerim to see.

'Do you think this is mummification fluid?' she said.

'Who knows?'

Kerim opened one of the lower kitchen cabinets and squatted down to look inside.

'Do you think he ever actually cooked, sir?' Eylul asked as she dripped some of the substance into the plastic evidence bag.

'He may have done.' Kerim's voice came from inside the cupboard. 'There are some tins of white beans in here, some okra in a jar . . . biscuits . . . all open, may in part explain the mice . . .'

'How could he live like this?' Eylul asked.

'I don't know,' Kerim said. 'I just keep thinking about how my mother would react to something like this.'

Eylul laughed. 'My mother would just walk out.' Her mother

was a wealthy society woman from Şişli, so they both knew she would have 'people' to deal with such things.

Kerim said, 'My mother would have to tidy and clean. Poor Mama, she'd probably end up dying. I mean, we're just sorting through all this; can you imagine actually having to . . .'

He didn't finish his sentence, which was odd. Eylul imagined he was probably straining to reach the back of the cupboard, and so she didn't say anything. But when she heard him begin to extricate himself and stand up, she looked down, and gasped.

What he had in his hand looked like a sunburst.

The woman and the girl carried the boy into the room. İkmen got up to help, but they waved him away. He sat down again on a floor cushion beside Gonca's chair, which was not comfortable.

Eventually, once the boy was settled, Huriye Can said, 'This is my son, Hızır. He is ten.'

Ten and twisted into such shapes it made İkmen want to weep for him. No living creature should be subjected to the pain he knew this poor boy had to experience. Oddly, though, the child's voice sounded both unforced and cheerful.

'Hello,' he said as he twisted his head away from his shoulder to speak.

Gonca, visibly shaken, said, 'Hello, Hızır.'

İkmen too made his greeting.

'Mum says you want to know how that bedcover Şaziye made got blood on it,' he said. 'But I don't know. Me and Şaziye put it in the plastic bag and then she took it to Rahul Bey's.'

Gonca looked at the girl. 'You didn't stop anywhere on the way?'

'No, Gonca Hanım.' She looked down at her feet, afraid, for many reasons that İkmen could easily discern, of meeting the woman's eyes.

'Are you sure?'

'Yes, Gonca Hanım.'

'We just put it in that bag,' the boy elaborated.

Suddenly angry, Gonca incomprehensibly took her rage out on the boy.

'You know the blood that was on my bedcover was unclean, don't you?' she snapped. 'Menses blood! You know what that is, do you, Hızır?'

The room became silent. Huriye Can was visibly shaking with fear.

The boy said, 'I do, Gonca Hanım. So it can't have been us, because boys don't do that and Şaziye is too young.'

'Is she?' Gonca grabbed hold of Şaziye's arm and pulled up her dress. Nobody tried to stop her, although İkmen felt that he should. Underneath she wore a pair of grey knickers. They were clearly not bloodied. Gonca let the girl's skirt drop and then said to her mother, 'And you?'

Horrified that she might want Huriye to raise her skirts too, İkmen put a hand on her arm. 'I don't think we need any more of that, Gonca Hanım.'

Huriye said, 'Gonca Hanım, I do not have such things any more. I am too old.'

She had to be forty at the most, İkmen reckoned. It was always possible she had been through her menopause, but, he felt, it was more likely that hunger was at the root of her failure to bleed. She was so thin she looked like the pictures one sometimes saw on TV of starving Yemeni children. And now she had been humiliated.

He held his tongue until he left with Gonca a few minutes later. Struggling to keep pace with her as she headed for his car, he said, 'Why did you have to embarrass those people? You saw how they live!'

Ever the grand dame, Gonca stood beside the car waiting to be let in. 'Well,' she said, 'are you going to drive me home?'

Infuriated, but at the same time realistic enough to know that arguing with her did no good, İkmen opened the door of the ancient Mercedes and she got inside. Flinging himself down in the driver's seat, he said, 'It was clear to me that they were terrified of you.'

'So they should be!'

'Really?' he said. 'Do you honestly think they meant you harm, Gonca? Why?'

'I don't know,' she said. 'But they all had guilt stamped upon their faces.' She paused for a moment, then added, 'As well as Neziye Hanım, of course.'

İkmen fired up the engine. 'Neziye Hanım, Rahul Bey's daughter?' he said. 'She's well past child-bearing—'

'Well, maybe she got someone else's blood,' Gonca said.

İkmen laughed.

She turned in her seat to face him. 'You don't understand how serious this is,' she said. 'Someone hates me enough to wish for my marriage to end in blood!'

He lit a cigarette. 'I know exactly why you're worried, but I don't understand why you suspect these people.'

'Opportunity in the case of the Can family. Neziye was always jealous of me back in Sulukule.'

'When dinosaurs roamed the earth,' İkmen said. 'Do you really think she has held a grudge against you for so long?'

'She knows I've never been truly happy with a man until now,' Gonca said. 'Mehmet Bey is the kind of man she knows would never look at her twice!'

'That's as maybe,' İkmen said. 'But you behaved badly with the Can family.'

'Oh, did I?' she said. 'Did you see the mother's skirt? Covered in blood. All lying! All three of them!'

İkmen shook his head. 'I'm not so sure. However, what I do know is that Huriye Can was visited by a man, I think her husband's brother, just before I arrived.'

'And?'

'And I believe I turned up just as he had finished beating and possibly raping her.'

'So why didn't you do anything?' Gonca asked.

'Because I need to find out more. If I just go blundering in on a situation I don't understand, I could put that family at even greater risk.'

'So you're going to find out more about them, are you?'

'Yes.'

'Good.'

Eylul Yavaş turned the thing over in her gloved hands.

'Do you think it's gold, sir?' she asked.

'It looks like it, and Müftüoğlu was a jeweller,' Kerim Gürsel said. 'But what do I know? I don't even know what it is. Do you?'

'No, sir,' she said. 'But I imagine if you tried to wear it, it would be very uncomfortable.'

What she held was a round metal starburst, about a third of a metre in diameter, with a large transparent crystal at its centre. The rays of the sunburst appeared to be made of gold.

Someone knocked on the open kitchen door and they both turned to see Mehmet Süleyman. Frowning, he said, 'What have you got there?'

'No idea,' Kerim said. 'I just found it in this cupboard.'

Süleyman walked over to them and Eylul handed him the object, which he turned over in his hands. Then he said, 'I've a notion I may have seen something similar . . .'

'Really?'

He put the object down and took a photograph of it with his phone. 'I know someone who will know . . .' He sent a message.

'Oh, who?' Eylul asked.

He didn't reply. Instead he said to Kerim, 'Did you find anything else?'

76

'Only out-of-date white beans and a lot of wafer biscuits so far,' Kerim replied. 'But if he made that, whatever it is, then why hide it in a food cupboard?'

Süleyman's phone pinged and he snorted with irritation. 'Why? she says . . .' he murmured, then sent another message. 'Because I need to know . . .'

He turned back to his colleagues.

'Let's see what else we can find. Was that thing wrapped in anything, Kerim Bey?'

'No. Just out in the wild on its own.'

Süleyman opened the cupboard at eye level in front of him, and all three officers frowned.

Again gold, this object stood about two thirds of a metre high and consisted of a seated female figure wearing a gold crown, its robe or gown littered with jewels.

Süleyman's phone pinged. He glanced at the screen. 'Well, my ex-wife is of the opinion that the first object is something called a monstrance. They have them in churches.'

'What are they for?' Kerim asked.

'My understanding is that a monstrance holds the host,' Süleyman said, 'which is basically the wafers the Christians eat when they honour Christ.'

Kerim, whose knowledge of his own religion was scant, said, 'Really?'

Eylul explained. 'It's all connected to Christ's order to his followers to eat bread and drink wine in honour of his body and blood,' she said. 'It's called "transubstantiation", which means, as I understand it, that the bread and the wine actually become Christ's body and blood during the ceremony.'

'Really?' Kerim reiterated.

'Well, not really, no, sir,' she said. 'But that's what they believe. And this . . ..' she pointed to the golden statue in the cupboard, 'looks to me like a saint.'

They all became quiet for a moment, then Kerim said, 'So was Müftüoğlu making these things for churches?'

'Possibly,' Eylul said. 'But then I've a feeling churches get things like this from specific places. I don't know, but I imagine they come from abroad. Rome maybe?'

'And where, if these objects are made from gold, was he getting it?' wondered Süleyman. 'Was he stealing from his employer?'

'So you both came from here in the city, but you didn't meet until you were on holiday in Ölü Deniz?'

'Yes, I know!' she said. 'Mad!'

That two İstanbullus should meet whilst on holiday in Ölü Deniz wasn't either crazy or unusual, but Ömer agreed with Canan Müftüoğlu. She was far too lively to fit the template for a grieving widow, but she was also very pretty.

'Fahrettin and I were staying at the same pansiyon,' she said.

'Alone?'

'No. My father and me and Fahrettin and his mother,' she said. 'When I come to describe it now, how we got together is totally mad too.'

The whole 'mad' motif was beginning to irritate Ömer, but he made sure he didn't show it.

'In what way?' he asked, smiling.

'Well,' she said, 'we took this trip to Efes. It's a long way from Ölü Deniz and so we travelled on one day, then had a full day at the site and travelled back on the third day. You know Efes, Sergeant?'

'Um, no,' he said.

He knew it was a big tourist hot spot. An archaeological site that had been mentioned in the Christian Bible.

'It's Greek,' she said. 'Ancient. The very birthplace of Western art. Ruins and amphitheatres and suchlike. So we went on this

78

bus. Fahrettin and his mother were on the same bus, but we didn't speak until we got to Efes. My father was tired and so I left him to go and explore on my own.'

'Your father allowed you to go off alone?'

'The reason we went to Efes was for me. For my studies. My father wasn't interested.'

'But still, you were very young to be going off alone.'

'I found him at the amphitheatre,' she said.

'You found him? Who?' Ömer asked.

'Fahrettin. He was drawing it. I thought, "Oh, a practising artist!" but of course he wasn't. He did draw well, though; as a jeweller, he needed to sketch his designs. He was ever so gallant.'

'Gallant?'

'Respectful,' she said. 'Boys that age can be so coarse. I'm sure you never were, Sergeant, but so many are. Boys will grab a girl if she doesn't cover, and sometimes even if she does! But not Fahrettin. We talked and talked and we fell in love there and then. When we got back to Ölü Deniz, he asked my father to allow me to marry him. I'd told my father all about him by this time, and so he said yes.'

Unbeknown to anyone except his sister, Peri, Ömer was having his own brush with marriage. His parents had finally found a suitable girl for him back in Mardin. A virgin, apparently pretty, an adherent of the same ancient religion as the Munguns. But she was just eighteen, and Ömer had long ago moved on from wanting to be with a teenager. His most recent lover had been a woman in her forties. Marriage, he knew, was a serious business, often requiring considerable negotiation. How had Canan Müftüoğlu managed to persuade her father to let her marry Fahrettin so quickly? Or had Fahrettin himself done the persuading?

She said, 'Fahrettin's mother was against it, but she couldn't stop him, and so we went to the town hall, and the nikah memuru

79

came to the pansiyon where we were staying at the end of that week. It was so romantic!'

Was this woman really in her thirties? She sounded as if she was still a teenager.

'Fahrettin didn't have a witness, of course, as his mother didn't approve, but the manager of the pansiyon stepped in and it was done! Such a wonderful day! Fahrettin paid for a buffet in the garden for Dad and me. It was lovely!'

But then what had happened next? Ömer wondered. He'd have to ask her. If a marriage wasn't consummated, it wasn't legal. He'd only ever seen Fahrettin Müftüoğlu as a corpse on the verge of middle age. Fat, dirty and poisoned. He must have looked very different at twenty-seven. Canan must have looked amazing. Of course the marriage had been consummated!

She took a photograph out of her handbag and put it on his desk. 'A wedding photo,' she said.

Ömer looked at it, and yes, Canan had been a very pretty young girl. But Fahrettin? Fat and ugly, his face twisted into something resembling a sneer. He must have been unable to believe his luck.

The kitchen had clearly been a storage facility for Fahrettin Müftüoğlu's home-based professional life. Every cupboard contained at least one artefact of a seemingly religious nature. Made from either gold or silver, or maybe even platinum, these boxes, statues, candlesticks, monstrances represented a huge body of work. Then, in a large black plastic bag, Eylul found the angel.

A metre tall, its wings folded across its chest, its face looking down, it was so heavy it took all three of the officers to lift it. Even then it was tough. When they finally put it down in the hall outside the kitchen, they all stood breathing heavily, looking at it in silence, until eventually Kerim said, 'Do you think that's solid gold?'

'I don't know,' Süleyman said. 'But we need help.'

'That is an understatement!'

Süleyman took out his phone and scrolled through his directory.

Kerim Gürsel said, 'Mehmet Bey, there are at least four constables under thirty in the next room!'

'Oh, we'll deal with moving the objects later,' Süleyman said as he put his phone to his ear. 'What we need here is an expert.'

One of the last people to leave the old gypsy quarter of Sulukule had been Burhan Sezai. A disappointed-looking man in his seventies, Burhan had run a coffee house of which Çetin İkmen had once been very fond. The coffee house was long gone, one of the victims of urban redevelopment, and like a lot of Sulukule's Roma, Burhan had moved to Tarlabaşı.

'I'm semi-retired,' he told İkmen as the latter sat down next to him in the tiny tea garden between two garages where he usually holed up. 'I'm not the world's best cümbüş player, but the tourists don't know that.'

Like a lot of Roma men, Burhan now played in a 'gypsy' band, mainly touring the fish restaurants of Kumkapı. His instrument, the cümbüş, was a type of mandolin. When such roaming bands arrived at these restaurants, a lot of the tourists would simply pay them to go away. It was a depressing way to make a living.

İkmen, who had bought Burhan a large glass of tea and given him a well-received packet of cigarettes, said, 'Burhan Bey, I've a problem.'

'What problem? If I can help you, Çetin Bey, I will.'

'Do you know the haberdasher Rahul Bey?'

'Everyone knows Rahul Bey,' Burhan said. 'Rich women in and out all day buying his work. An artist. One of the few of my people who can make a living now. Do you want to talk about that business with Gonca Hanım, Çetin Bey?'

81

'I do,' İkmen said. 'But I'm accusing Rahul Bey of nothing.'

Burhan shook his head. 'I understand that. And I know you are a friend of Gonca Hanım . . .'

'But?'

He looked up. 'But, Çetin Bey, you must know that some people have feelings about the man she is marrying. I've often thought it must be the same on the other side. What do you think about it? You're Mehmet Efendi's friend, you're a gaco.'

İkmen smiled. He had feelings about it, but not as a gaco, or non-gypsy.

'They've been in love for a very long time, Burhan Bey,' he said.

'This we know. But why do they have to marry? Gonca Hanım is a very beautiful woman, but she's no longer young. She won't give him sons.'

'Mehmet Efendi has a son,' İkmen said.

'Only one?' Burhan shook his head again. 'But it's their business.'

'It is,' İkmen said. 'Burhan Bey, these people who have feelings about this marriage . . .'

'I'll name no names.'

'I wouldn't expect you to. But what if I gave you some names? The first one being Neziye Mengüç.'

Burhan looked into İkmen's eyes. 'Ah.'

'Ah?'

'You have been speaking to Gonca Hanım . . .'

İkmen smiled.

'She has no doubt told you there is no love between them,' Burhan said. 'Never has been. Poor Neziye was born with that limp. One leg longer than the other. Her father always knew he'd have her forever. I know you people can be afraid of deformity. We are too, maybe more so. And then there was Gonca Hanım. In those days the Şekeroğlu family lived in the same street as the Mengüç.' He laughed. 'Bunch of rogues! The father a thief, the mother a witch, fifteen children, all clever but wild. Şükrü and Gonca were always the most striking, until the old man took another wife and had the boy Rambo. He's a looker too. Gonca, though, like a movie star and she knew it. Used to make fun of poor Neziye. Of course nobody chided her or tried to protect Neziye back in those days. Kids rose or fell on the streets, there were always fights. Not between those two, you understand. Neziye was always a gentle girl.'

'And Gonca?'

'Ha! No one crossed her,' he said. 'You know when she started doing that art, a lot of people were surprised a Roma woman could do such a thing. But not me. Right from young, it was as if she wanted everything she could squeeze out of life – and a bit more. Husbands, lovers, money, all those children, magic . . . It was said that if Gonca Şekeroğlu spoke, even Hasan Dum listened.'

Now dead, Hasan Dum had been a Roma gang lord famed for his viciousness.

Burhan moved his head closer to İkmen's. 'I've heard it said, although I don't know this myself, that Gonca Şekeroğlu has a rather different relationship with Şevket Sesler.'

Şevket Sesler, a successor to Dum, was an equally terrifying local don.

İkmen frowned. 'What do you mean? What different relation-ship?'

'Oh, nothing improper,' Burhan said. 'She's about forty years too old for him. And anyway, why would she want Sesler when she's got Mehmet Efendi in her bed? Be like going out for kokoreç when you've got fresh fish at home.'

'A lot of people like kokoreç,' İkmen said.

Burhan shook his head. 'You know what I mean. Gonca Hanım is Sesler's personal falçı. Reads his coffee cups, his cards. Goes to his house to do it, they say.'

'Who do?'

'People.' He shrugged.

He was obviously not going to elaborate. İkmen lit a cigarette. Some time ago, there had been a rumour that Gonca had been in debt to Sesler's now-deceased father. By becoming the son's falçı, was she paying back this debt? Burhan probably wouldn't tell him that even if he knew, and so he changed tack.

'Do you know the Can family?' he asked.

'What, Munir Can and his family?'

'I mean his brother's wife, Huriye.'

'Oh, Recep's woman. Yes, I do, poor soul,' Burhan said. 'Just left her, he did. Drunk out of his mind, he wobbled out of Tarlabaşı about five years ago and has never been back. Wouldn't be surprised if he's dead, which is what I think Munir is hoping.'

'Why?' İkmen asked.

Burhan moved closer again.

'Munir Can is not the sort of man to take the dictates of Islam too seriously. He's often drunk like his brother, and he likes a game of cards.'

'Gambling?'

'Poker.' He moved still closer. 'But it suits Munir to have more than one wife. That aspect of Islam is very dear to his heart. So at the moment, he has his first wife, a Roma woman called Fındık, then last year he took a Kurdish girl. Some said she was only fourteen, but I don't know. Don't know her family or anything. Now it's said he lusts after his brother's wife.'

'I see,' İkmen said. Of course this came as no surprise, given how he'd witnessed Munir Can coming out of Huriye's apartment. 'Isn't Huriye Hanım a bit old for a third wife?'

'Oh, Munir's always wanted what Recep had,' Burhan said. 'Old Recep was a handsome man before he ruined himself with drink. Good dancer, could play a violin to make your heart weep. Munir was like their mother, an ugly, fat, lazy lump. Huriye Can

84

for all her poverty is a talented woman with a needle, and if you really look at her, she's a very handsome lady.'

'What does this Munir Can do for a living?'

The old gypsy smiled. 'He works for Şevket Sesler. He brings tourists to one of his gazinos on Turan Caddesi. Kızlar, it's called.'

'I thought the police shut that down,' İkmen said. The Kızlar, or 'Girls', gazino had attracted a lot of complaints from ripped-off tourists in the past.

'They did,' Burhan said. 'But you know how people like Sesler operate, Çetin Bey. And let's be honest, not all of your police colleagues are as honest and upright as you and Mehmet Efendi.'

'You just keep up the flattery, Burhan Bey,' İkmen said.

'Oh, but it's true . . .'

'So Munir,' İkmen said, 'what does he actually do?'

Burhan shrugged. 'The old scam. Hang around on İstiklal until a lone male tourist comes along, hopefully a bit drunk already. Promise him a night out to remember – girls, dancing, booze – then get him to the gazino, set him up with a girl and get him ordering "champagne" at five hundred lira a bottle. Or just rob him and have done with it.'

İkmen knew the scam well. Tried and tested over many years, it tapped into the orientalist fantasies some Western men still held onto about İstanbul's famed 'sexy belly-dancer sirens'.

Chapter 7

Inspector Haluk Keleş, a senior officer only a year older than
Ömer Mungun, was much more than he seemed. On the surface
a foul-mouthed misogynistic slob, he actually had a degree in
history of art, hence his position in the police as head of the art
fraud division. In his everyday dealings with his colleagues,
however, he adopted an aggressive macho man style, laced with
crude jokes and almost constant swearing. Although Keleş was
a lot younger than Süleyman, the latter knew he was also a
graduate of the same school he himself had attended, the exclu-
sive Galatasaray Lycée. It was said that the way he behaved was
his shield against those who believed that a policeman who was
interested in art was, somehow, not a real man.

Unimpressed by both the monstrance and the statue, Haluk
Bey was nevertheless silenced by the winged angel. He walked
around it several times, attempted to lift it without success, and
then touched it very lightly.

Süleyman said, 'I am loath to say that it's made of gold . . .'

'Could be,' Keleş cut in.

'I mean solid gold,' Süleyman elaborated.

'I know what you fucking meant.'

That awful, stinking corridor lapsed into silence again. Kerim
Gürsel, who was tired by this time, just caught himself before
he leaned on one of the greasy walls.

Süleyman, Gürsel and Eylul Yavaş watched as their wiry,
messy-haired colleague examined the item. Süleyman imagined

Keleş' internal dialogue, which he always reckoned was a cleaned-up, more precise version of his speech. Eventually the art man said, 'Can I take a surface sample to kick things off?'

'What do you mean?'

He took a small penknife out of his pocket. 'Tiny scrape from the base. See if at least the outside is gold.'

'OK,' Süleyman agreed.

Keleş crouched down on his haunches like a teenager and scraped a very small amount of material from the base. When he stood up, he said, 'What you gonna do with it? Can't fucking leave it here.'

'No,' Süleyman said. 'We'll remove all valuable objects we've found so far and then I will seal the site until tomorrow.'

Keleş looked around. 'Bit of a shithole,' he said. 'What's the story, Mehmet Bey?'

'An apparent suicide,' Süleyman said.

'So why are you involved?'

'Because it's only apparent. The dead man was a jeweller by trade, also a hoarder, and these artefacts are not the only odd things we've found here.'

'Mummified head,' Keleş said. 'Yeah, heard about that. Also heard it was modern. You said this man was a jeweller . . .'

'With some unusual interests. He worked at home, but mainly at the atelier of GülGül in the Grand Bazaar.'

'I know it,' Keleş said. He shook his head. 'I've never come across a fake mummy. Egyptian artefacts, Syrian icons, statues, but not mummies.'

'Any reason for that?' Kerim asked.

'No fucking money in it. Not unless it's fucking Kleopatra.'

'Really? Why?'

'Famous and fuckable. Find the Queen of the Nile – or create the Queen of the Nile – and people'll pay millions for her.'

'And this?' Süleyman pointed to the angel figure again.

'That?' Keleş said. 'Dunno. I've an itch at the back of my eyes telling me I've seen it before, but I don't know where. I'll have to sleep on it.' He pulled a face. 'Bit shit, isn't it?'

Ömer Mungun knew that what he was doing was wrong, but he couldn't help it. If he wasn't deluding himself, Canan Müftüoğlu had barely looked at the boss when they'd briefly met. He, however, was another matter. She didn't seem to be able to stop looking at him. So once he'd finished taking her statement at about seven that evening, he took her to the Irish pub in Taksim. He knew this would be a quiet night. Midweek evenings in the autumn tended to be.

Not the most romantic place to take a woman, but then Ömer was still very conflicted as to whether he wanted to give Canan that impression. It was also somewhere he knew well. A bit dingy and basic, but he did at least know what the drinks cost.

Canan, like a good Muslim woman, ordered a Diet Coke, while Ömer opted for Guinness. Süleyman had told him that his Irish son made cakes with it, which seemed strange. There were no Irish people here this evening as far as Ömer could tell, just a load of quiet Turks drinking whiskey. But he hadn't come to the pub to get drunk. He'd come to clarify some of the points Canan had made in her statement – or so he told himself.

'We still haven't found your husband's phone,' he said once they were settled with their drinks.

'No? Well, won't the number you took from my phone help you?' she asked.

He'd called it as soon as he'd obtained it, but none of the officers at Müftüoğlu's apartment had heard it ring. Other ways of tracking the phone existed, although he didn't know whether any of those had been employed yet.

'If it's out of charge, it may not,' he said.

'Oh.' She paused for a moment, then said, 'We did talk often, you know. As I've already told you, he was frequently suicidal. I always managed to talk him down. If only he had rung me that night!'

The story she had told about their relationship had been strange. Apparently, after their hasty marriage, once back in İstanbul, Fahrettin's mother had forbidden Canan entry to her home. Her son had been either unable or unwilling to defy his mother, and so the couple had lived apart. However, even when Isis Müftüoğlu had died, that arrangement had persisted, for no reason Ömer could fathom. All Canan would say was that her husband had 'thought it best'. And yet the suicidal phone calls she claimed he had made to her were precisely because they could not be together. Why this pretty woman hadn't sought a divorce and moved on, Ömer could not imagine.

Eventually, although with some difficulty, he had managed to ask her whether the marriage had been consummated, and she had told him that it had. She'd said, 'Our wedding night was lovely.'

Given that her husband had looked not unlike a slug, Ömer had doubted that. But then maybe Canan liked her men that way. And maybe she was as guileless as she appeared. Or was she?

She said, 'My father really liked Fahrettin. He's very upset that he's dead.'

There was little Ömer could say to that, and so he remained silent.

'He was very impressed by Fahrettin's trade,' Canan continued. 'He said I could do myself a lot of good marrying a jeweller. But I was in love with him and so I didn't think like that. And he was in love with me.' She sighed.

'I think I can see that,' Ömer said. 'But when his mother wouldn't let you be together, didn't you ever think about divorcing him, having a more . . . conventional marriage?'

'Oh, but I loved him!' Canan said.

89

'So why didn't you live together once his mother had died?'

'Well, because by that time we were happier apart,' she said. 'I never stopped loving him, which was why I remained always available to him, but we couldn't live together.'

'Why not?'

'You've seen his apartment,' she said. 'Could you live there?'

'She's called St Foy,' Zelfa said. 'Patron saint of pilgrims, prisoners and soldiers.'

It was nice to talk to his ex-wife in a civilised fashion again, even though Mehmet Süleyman knew that Gonca was probably listening. Not that she'd be able to understand anything; she didn't speak English.

'That photograph you sent me has to be a reproduction of Foy's reliquary,' Zelfa continued. 'The original is in France.'

'Why would someone make a copy of such a thing?' Süleyman asked.

'No idea. Maybe to sell online. There's all sorts on there these days, Mehmet. You can buy the arm of John the Baptist if you've a mind, and the foreskin of Christ has to be at least a kilometre wide given the number of pieces out there for sale. It's like a rerun of the fecking Middle Ages.'

He smiled. She'd always been irreverent and funny. It had been one of the things that had attracted him to her. Also, she was right. In recent years, or so it seemed to him, people appeared to be happy to believe almost anything. Even complete fabrications, like the blood libel against the Jews, was spoken about as fact in some quarters.

'The reliquary in France is made from wood covered with gold,' Zelfa said. 'The head, I read earlier, is probably made from a fifth-century Roman helmet. Oh, and there's a genuine – if you're daft – piece of St Foy's skull embedded in the thing.'

'So this is in France?'

'At a place called Conques,' she said. He wrote it down. 'If you look online, there's no report of it having been stolen. That's got to be a copy. Bloody good, though.'

'The man who we think created it was a jeweller,' he said. 'The same place we found the other thing, the starburst . . .'

'The monstrance,' she said.

'Yes.'

'You find anything else?'

The incredibly heavy angel was so extraordinary he hardly dared mention it. All he said was, 'Some candlesticks, boxes. So far, only one other thing of note. I'll send you a photo.'

'OK.' Then she said, 'Patrick's looking forward to next week.'

'I'm glad.'

'Me too. Mind you, all the magic stuff İkmen put in his head has become a bit overwhelming. I'm not sure his new interest plays well at Gonzaga . . .'

'I told him to keep up with his school work, and so did Çetin Bey,' Süleyman said.

'I know. He told me.' He heard her laugh. 'Much as I may have dreamt about him becoming a doctor, I'm more pragmatic now. If he does, he does, if he doesn't . . . it's not the end of the world as long as he's happy.'

Süleyman was surprised how liberal his ex-wife had become, and wondered why.

Knowing he had to be at least a little confused, she said, 'Pat told me he told you I was seeing someone.'

'Yes,' he said. 'It's not my business.'

'Robin,' she said. 'Orthopaedic surgeon. Divorced, originally from Kerry. It was nice to have some male company, though there were no fireworks involved.'

There was a 'but' coming . . .

'But he was a bigot,' she said. 'Anti-immigrant, Ireland for the Irish. We have a growing number of these now. But then

91

where doesn't? That said, I don't have to be with one of them, so I threw him out.'

'I'm sorry.'

'Ah, don't be,' she said. 'Better be on my own than with a man who thinks refugees drowning in the Irish Sea is a good look. Anyway, I have to go. I'd have that statue scanned. If there's a piece of human skull in there, you may have more than a copy on your hands.'

He hadn't yet considered that, but she had a point. There was a long history of precious artefacts being stolen and then replaced with forgeries. Had Fahrettin Müftüoğlu been a forger?

He wished her well and cut the connection. On Sunday, their son would be boarding a plane from Dublin to İstanbul to come to witness his father's marriage. Mehmet suddenly felt nostalgic for the life he'd once had with Zelfa.

But then, there was Gonca.

Bustling into his makeshift office, she said, 'Are you coming to bed?'

'Yes.'

He was closing the lid of his laptop, when she spotted the picture of St Foy. She put her arms around his neck and said, 'So, art.'

'Work,' he said.

She swung herself around and sat on his lap. 'Since when did you know anything about art?'

Living in Tarlabaşı had its benefits and its drawbacks. The greatest benefit was its cheapness, while probably its biggest drawback, for Kerim Gürsel, was the fact that the district was thick with those involved in criminal activities. A concomitant of the poverty in the district, crime in the shape of drug dealing, prostitution and, latterly, the production of moonshine rakı was rife. And then there were the rent boys. He was looking at one now, lurking in the doorway of a long-defunct bakkal. He was beautiful.

Ever since his transsexual lover had died back in the summer, Kerim had existed almost completely without sex. In a way, there hadn't been time, what with the job, caring for his disabled wife and bringing up his new baby. Sinem loved him passionately, and he could and did make love to her – hence little Melda. But he wasn't happy, because he wasn't being true to his nature. He knew he wanted this boy. As he looked at him, he licked his lips, and the boy knew what he wanted. How he longed to be held by those strong arms, kissed by those lips, take that pleasure that only came with making love to a man.

But that was impossible. Not only was he a respected member of a society that had problems with such people, he was also a husband and father, and he loved Sinem and their little girl. He turned away and walked towards his apartment block.

The widow Müftüoğlu, it seemed, had few boundaries. Ömer Mungun, ever the gentleman, drove her back to her home in Gaziosmanpaşa. She lived, she said, with her father, in an apartment in a run-down block in the Sarıgöl Mahallesi. This area, although not the poorest in the city, was full of people who struggled to make their rent and put food on the table. When they got out of Ömer's car, he smelt the very sharp tang of cannabis on the air.

Her apartment block was dirty, festooned with tangled electricity and other, unknowable cables, and when they entered the ground floor, the shabby stairs were lit by just one jaundiced bulb. She led him up to the first floor, where, on the threshold of her apartment, she informed him that her father was out.

What was on offer here was very clear to Ömer. It was also very obvious to him that he was tempted. She was pretty, the apartment was empty; as far as he knew, no one had seen them arrive . . .

But on the other hand, this woman was the wife of someone who may have been involved in criminal activity. To go with her and possibly be influenced by her, if discovered, would cost him his career. And if Süleyman ever found out, he would demand the harshest punishment. This was the kind of action that brought some supposedly open-and-shut cases crashing to the ground.

He said, 'I must be getting home.'

She frowned. 'I said my father is out.'

'Yes, I know you did.'

She smiled then. 'Oh well,' she said. 'Goodnight.'

Ömer walked down that dingy staircase and out into the cannabis-scented night. A group of boys were hanging around his car, possibly trying to break in. He pushed past them, unlocked the vehicle and climbed inside. As he lowered himself down, he glanced up at the apartment block and saw Canan Müftüoğlu and a young man looking out of a window on the first floor. Not old enough to be her father; was he perhaps a brother?

He put the car in gear and began to move slowly through the small group of boys, one of whom spat at the vehicle. Did they know he was with the police? How?

Ömer knew he had to tell Süleyman about all this in the morning, even if the thought of it made him sweat. Canan Müftüoğlu had started her seduction in the Irish pub. He should never have taken her there in the first place, but it had been she who had rubbed her leg against his thigh under the table.

She wouldn't let it go.

'I simply want to know why you've got pictures of art on your laptop,' Gonca said as she lay down beside Mehmet Süleyman and put her arms around him.

'I told you,' he said. 'It's work.'

'Intriguing work.'

'Yes, it is, actually. But I can't talk about it. You know that.'

94

She kissed his neck. 'Work you talk about in English to someone . . .'

He didn't want to answer, nor did he want to distract her with a caress. Her jealousy was sometimes hard to bear.

'So,' she continued, 'it has to be either Çetin İkmen – I know you two like to use it sometimes as a sort of secret code – or Patrick, and then there's your ex-wife, Zelfa . . .'

He tried to out-stare her, but couldn't. He looked away. Of course she'd heard him use Zelfa's name. He said, 'OK, it was Zelfa, what of it?'

'Nothing.'

'So why—'

She put a finger on his lips. 'You should've told me,' she said. 'Hiding away as if you're doing something bad. I understand, you have a child together. I'm not some teenager!'

He wanted to tell her that at times she behaved like one, but he didn't.

'But then again, what does Zelfa know about art?' Gonca continued. 'She's a psychiatrist, isn't she?'

'I consulted her not because she is a psychiatrist but because she is a Christian,' Süleyman said as he rolled on top of her, pinning her to the bed. 'If you'd looked at my computer screen a bit more carefully, you would have seen that the image I was looking at was a religious statue. I wanted to know who it was a statue of, whether it was famous . . .'

She laughed. 'You are so easy to goad, you know, Şehzade Mehmet Efendi!' she said. 'Baby, this is our last night together before you go back to your apartment! I've been waiting about while you looked at that computer and made your calls. I was expecting you to drag me up to the bedroom and take my clothes off with your teeth at the very least!'

Now he laughed. He was going to leave Gonca's house in the morning and take his possessions back to the apartment he rented, but rarely saw these days, in Cihangir. This was to give him some time to make the place ready for his son's arrival. Although he was working right up until the day before the wedding, he hoped to spend his evenings with Patrick.

He kissed her. 'If you thought I'd forgotten about you, you are very much mistaken.'

He ground his naked hips against hers and she smiled. Then she said, 'You do know you're going to have to work really hard tonight, don't you?'

'Oh?'

'Yes.' She began to move rhythmically beneath him. 'Five nights I'm going to have to be without you. I want all of that in advance.'

Sinem had just finished feeding Melda when Kerim got home. Now asleep in her cot, the little girl was what Sinem always described as 'milk intoxicated'. This happened when she drank so much milk and derived so much warmth and comfort from her mother's breasts that she looked drunk.

Melda was a hungry baby, and Sinem's breasts were sore.

'Have you been putting the cream on that the doctor gave you?' her husband enquired as he got them both a glass of tea from the samovar.

'Oh, I can't find that,' Sinem said, leaning against her husband once he had sat down beside her.

'Ring him up and get some more; we can afford it.'

Sinem said nothing. Instead she unbuttoned the front of her dress and looked down at her breasts. 'It's not that kind of sore-ness,' she said. 'I mean, my nipples aren't cracked or anything. It's because I've got too much milk . . .' Realising what she'd just said, she exclaimed, 'Oh Kerim, I'm sorry! You don't want to hear that!'

In spite of the fact both Kerim and Sinem were educated

people, they both came from working class stock where 'women's problems' were not routinely discussed.

But then she realised he was staring at her. He had to be appalled. She went to do up the front of her dress again, but he pulled her hand away.

'Kerim, I . . .'

Sex was sex. He'd managed to resist the charms of that rent boy on the street. Was this arousal he now felt reward for holding back? As soon as he'd seen her holding her breasts, he'd felt himself harden. It did just happen sometimes, but this felt different and she knew it. He could see it in her eyes. There was a tiny sliver of fear . . .

He unzipped his fly, pulled her on top of him and stroked her breasts. Sinem began to gasp. His tongue lapped at her nipples, then he sucked. His wife ran her fingers up and down his penis.

When she'd been alive, Çetin İkmen's wife, Fatma, had made much of the phenomenon she called 'men's talk'. This was often coarse exchanges between men that sometimes, but not always, took place in coffee houses. The principal preserve of macho men known as 'magandas', men's talk covered topics like cars, fighting, what they had done or would do to 'cheap' women, how useless their children were, and football. İkmen's favourite bar, the Mozaik, which was just outside the entrance to his apartment building, was generally free of this sort of talk. It was a place where locals who liked a drink gathered – men and women – and was also popular with tourists. Not in the depths of a Friday night, however.

There were four men at the table nearest the road, two of whom had already almost come to blows about football. One was a Galatasaray supporter, the other staunchly Fenerbahce. İkmen hadn't bothered to listen to what was being first yelled and then, with help from the other two men, uttered in a slightly more civilised way. He didn't do football. Now, as far as he could make out, they were talking about women. Or rather they were complaining about their wives. Basically, it seemed the wives of these uniformly unappealing men no longer 'did it' for them.

'I didn't expect to find you here,' İkmen's cousin Samsun said as she sat down next to him and took her shoes off. 'Have you seen the time?'

'It's near enough two a.m.,' he said. 'I was waiting for you.'

'You could've waited for me at home,' she said as she lit a cigarette. 'But seeing as we're here . . .'

She called the waitress over and ordered two large brandies. One of the quartet of men by the road looked at her. Samsun smiled sweetly and then murmured underneath her breath, 'You couldn't afford me, darling.'

When their drinks arrived, İkmen toasted her, then said, 'So?'

'So? So another night at the Sailor's Bar passes without my getting kicked or punched, so that's a win,' she said.

Samsun Bajraktar, İkmen's transsexual cousin, had worked at the trans and gay bar in Tarlabaşı for years. The Sailor's was not for the faint hearted. Fights broke out all the time, and although the police didn't raid the place often, the possibility was always a worry. A lot of the patrons consisted of girls on the game, most of whom used drugs; ditto their punters. While officially a barmaid, Samsun as a trans woman of a certain age also acted as confidante, adviser and therapist to a lot of the younger girls.

İkmen, knowing she was teasing him, lowered his voice. 'And did any of the Roma girls . . .?'

'Only one,' Samsun said. 'Bardot. Don't know what her real name is.'

He moved closer to her. The macho men viewed him with disgust. 'And? About what we discussed? What I told you?'

'Oh, she knows Şevket Sesler,' Samsun said. 'They all do. One way or another, all the Roma girls pay money to him.'

'So what—'

'I'm getting to that!' She put one cigarette out and lit another. 'I didn't even breathe your name to her, of course,' she said. 'But Bardot's no fool, and she's been around for years, got to be the thick end of fifty now . . .'

'So she knows of our connection?'

'I imagine so. As I say, she's no fool. But anyway,' Samsun went on, 'alcohol changed hands and lips were loosened.'

The four men at the other table left and İkmen breathed a sigh of relief. Samsun was one of the toughest trans women in the city, but she was seventy now, and he, though younger, was no longer thrilled by the prospect of a fight. The men probably wondered what he was doing with someone they would only expect to find in Beyoğlu – probably when they went to one of Samsun's 'sisters' for some hard-core sex. Hypocrites.

'So tell me,' he said.

Samsun took a gulp of brandy. 'Well, I introduced the subject of Sesler with reference to Gonca Hanım.'

'Being his personal falçı . . .'

'Exactly. I said the word was that she was still in debt to him because she'd been indebted to his father. I mean, we all know that, don't we?' she said. 'Even Mehmet Bey knows she borrowed money from old Harun.'

'Yes, Gonca told him.'

'She did,' Samsun said. 'However, what Mehmet Bey probably doesn't know, and what I didn't know until tonight, is that Gonca Hanım has sworn fealty to Sesler. This was Bardot's point, because if that is true, then why? The Şekeroğlus have always stayed out of that life in the past, gone their own way.'

'Because she borrowed money from Harun Sesler, she still owes,' İkmen said.

'Yes, but Şevket Bey, it is said, wrote her debt off.'

'So she reads his cards.'

'And swears fealty, which could put her on a collision course with her husband,' Samsun said. 'And then there's Harun Bey's death and Gonca Hanım's part in it.'

This was something İkmen had put from his mind.

'A lot of the Roma believe that Gonca Hanım encouraged Afife Purcu to kill Harun Sesler,' she said. 'She was seen in Tarlabaşı earlier in the day before the evening he died.'

'So?'

'So, she's a witch, Çetin. We know how people feel about those, don't we?'

İkmen's mother, Samsun's aunt, had been a witch, and they both knew that those who employed such people were both glamoured by their power and filled with superstitious hatred for them.

'Gonca Hanım was decorating the wedding dress Harun Bey had made for his bride, Afife Purcu's daughter, Elmas. Word is there was some sort of dispute over this between Sesler and Gonca. Don't know what. But also Elmas was only fifteen, the same age the Queen of the Gypsies was when she married her first husband. It's said she has feelings about such things,' Samsun said.

'Doesn't mean she killed Harun Sesler.'

'No. But look, Çetin, Afife Purcu is an addict. She didn't care what happened to her children as long as she got her fix. By all accounts, she knew about the marriage – her ex, Hüsnü Purcu, basically sold Elmas to Harun Bey. Not a word from Afife! Then suddenly she kills the man who is betrothed to her fifteen-year-old daughter.'

İkmen frowned. 'Why would Gonca do such a risky thing?'

'You'd have to ask her,' Samsun said. 'Maybe her dispute with Harun Bey was more serious than we think. Gonca's brother

Rambo had allowed Sesler and his people to use his bar the night Harun Bey died. That had never happened before, as far as Bardot knows. She thinks that maybe Harun Bey was punishing Gonca's family as a result of this dispute between them. But the gypsies are abuzz with it, according to Bardot. Gonca Hanım had a hand in Harun Bey's death; Şevket Bey believes this, and instead of killing the powerful witch, he simply brings her to heel.'

'But as you say, swearing fealty to Sesler could put her in dispute with her husband,' İkmen said.

'Şevket Sesler is a lazy bastard, and if he could get some intelligence about the police free of charge from Gonca Hanım . . .'

'She would never betray Mehmet!'

'Maybe she doesn't have a choice,' Samsun said. 'Mehmet Bey is leaving her house soon, isn't he?'

'In the morning.'

'So you'll have to speak to her before they get married.'

'I will.'

İkmen put his head in his hands. He'd told Gonca she was to have no secrets from Mehmet, and yet by his silence, he would be colluding in her doing just that. She had never admitted to having a hand in Harun Sesler's death, but if that was the case, why was she swearing fealty to a man who could threaten her husband?

Chapter 8

'How old were you when you lost your virginity?'

Lovemaking had turned to talking in the early hours of the morning. Mehmet Süleyman smiled. 'Eighteen,' he said.

'I was fifteen,' Gonca said. 'It was my wedding night. He pushed himself inside me. I was scared.'

'You were?'

'Roma girls have a bad reputation with Turks, but we're always pure when we marry, even girls like me. Anyway, I became pregnant, and nine months later I gave birth to Erdem. I was with my pig of a husband for fifteen years, until he saw fit to die. It's why I always say there is to be no young marriage for my children, especially the girls. I learned nothing about love from that man.'

'Then who did you learn from?' Mehmet turned over so that he was facing her.

'Other men,' she said. 'You . . .'

'I learned some new tricks from you all those years ago,' he said. 'You kidnapped me.'

She laughed. 'You loved it.'

'I have never been able to get you out of my head since.'

Gonca kissed him. 'So tell me about how you lost your virginity.'

They were playing what she called the truth game, where participants had to answer questions asked with absolute honesty.

He sighed. 'My father paid for a woman to instruct me in the arts of love.'

'He took you to a brothel?'

'Not exactly. A very nice apartment in Şişli.'

'Oh.'

'I wore my only suit, which my parents had bought when we attended a relative's wedding. My father drove me to the home of this woman, Yıldız Hanım . . .'

'Yıldız! Seriously?' Yıldız meant 'star' in Turkish.

'Seriously.' He kissed her. 'She was dressed in a very modest silver silk dress, underneath which she was entirely naked. My father left me with her one afternoon and returned to pick me up the following morning.'

'Oh God! So you . . .'

'A maid brought us both tea to begin with, and we talked,' he said. 'I was hideously shy. Not only was Yıldız Hanım beautiful, she was also more than twenty years older than me. I must have sounded so nervous and silly. And when she started talking about sex, well, I think my face probably turned purple.'

'So what happened?' Gonca snaked an arm around his shoulders and pulled him close. 'Tell me everything.'

'Do I have to?'

'You do,' she said. 'I love you and so I want to know everything about you.'

He swallowed. 'Of course, the first time was a disaster. She undressed us both, and well, when I saw her, I became shall we say over-eager . . .'

'Poor little boy!' Gonca said. 'But she was kind, this lady, no?'

He smiled. 'She was kind, patient, gentle, and she taught me how to both give and receive pleasure. I am eternally grateful to her.'

'Me too,' Gonca said. 'When I found you, my darling, you were like a diamond in a dust heap. It's why I've never given up on you.'

'I fantasised about Yıldız Hanım for years,' he said. 'But I never saw her again and I never spoke to my father about what happened that night. I know that money changed hands, because I saw him give her a stack of notes. As I was leaving, she told me I was the most beautiful boy she had ever seen.'

'She had good taste.'

'Mmm. Except that she said exactly the same thing to my brother,' Süleyman said.

'What?'

He laughed. 'That he was the most beautiful boy she had ever seen. But ten years before she said it to me. And because my family are . . . my family, we didn't speak of this for decades. Not until my father died and my brother and I shared stories. Murad had realised years before that our father had a mistress. We both agreed that we were happy for him. For all his many faults, my father was a nice man, and Murad and I were pleased that he had found love.'

'Not with your mother?'

'No. Not with her. I don't think that woman is capable of love.' He hugged her tightly. 'Anyway, that may well be the reason I have always desired older ladies. My first love was old enough to be my mother; she taught me everything I knew until I found you.'

'I have corrupted you,' Gonca said. Then her face fell. 'Mehmet, do you think that your mother loves you and your brother?'

'No,' he said. 'Like my father, we are just possessions.'

She pulled his face still closer to hers and smothered it with kisses.

Mummia . . . now there was an odd thing. Using the ground-up bodies of the Egyptian dead as a cure for fracture, initially by the Crusaders. Europeans from the twelfth century onwards were convinced that dead people could cure them of all sorts of ills. In addition, they believed the powder could also be a very effective aphrodisiac. Kerim Gürsel smiled.

It was all based upon some early Islamic research into the properties of bitumen. The Europeans erroneously believed that Egyptian mummies were preserved in this substance instead of what they were really treated with, which was resin. This didn't answer the question about why Fahrettin Müftüoğlu had apparently either created or come into possession of a modern mummy, but it was interesting. Kerim had also watched a clip from a British documentary from 2011 about a team of pathologists who successfully employed ancient Egyptian techniques to mummify the body of a man who had donated his body to science. That had not been for the faint hearted. But then he hadn't been able to sleep, so why not watch something that could be useful in his current investigation, however gut churning. Also it took his mind off what he'd done earlier.

The dawn call to prayer insinuated itself across the city from its thousands of mosques, and though not a religious man, Kerim felt ashamed. It was one thing to desire and indeed have sex with men and transsexuals, but what he had done with Sinem . . . that was something else.

Not that she had tried to stop him; quite the contrary. She was in love with him and had done everything she could to please him, including allowing him to suckle at her breast. She'd always said that feeding Melda made her feel slightly aroused, but with him that had taken on a new dimension that had left him guilty and confused. That he loved Sinem was not in doubt, but this sexual aspect had only taken on such importance since she had become pregnant. He was beginning to wonder who he was.

'Kerim?'

He looked up and saw her standing in the doorway of the living room.

'Is Melda awake?' he asked.

'No. What are you doing?' She came and sat next to him on the sofa.

'Some research, for work,' he said.

'Why?'

'Why not?'

'Couldn't you sleep?' She took his arm and pressed herself against him.

'Not really,' he said. 'But you don't have to be up until Melda wakes. Go back to bed.'

'Will you come too?' she asked.

'Not a lot of point now.' Kerim looked at the lightening sky outside.

'Not even if I want you to?'

He turned to her. 'Sinem,' he said, 'you know I love you very much . . .'

Suddenly she looked scared. With good cause, because she had always known the truth about him. She'd lied about herself for years, telling everyone she was a lesbian. Just to be close to him. Poor Sinem.

'Please don't think I don't enjoy making love to you,' he said. 'But last night was . . . I was uneasy. It made me wonder who I was.'

'What do you mean?' she said.

There was no easy way to say what had to be said. He cleared his throat.

'Sinem, I am a homosexual man. I've never hidden that from—'

'I think you must be bisexual. You must be,' she said.

He took one of her twisted little hands in his and kissed it. 'Sinem,' he said, 'I am not. The only reason I can feel such passion for you is because I love you so much.'

Her eyes filled with tears. 'But Kerim, you wanted me! I could feel it! You drank from my breasts, hungrily, and—'

106

'And it made me feel as if I'd committed a crime,' he said. 'I'd taken what wasn't mine – from our daughter.'

'But I wanted you to!'

He looked down before he spoke again. 'Sinem, every day I am not at work or with you and Melda, I spend my time at Pembe's grave, crying.'

She kissed the side of his face. 'I know I can never take Pembe's place . . .'

'I love you,' he said. 'Just . . .' He shook his head. 'Sinem, I promised you when we had Melda that I would be your husband. I will not break that promise. It's just that sometimes . . .'

She moved round so that she was sitting on his lap. 'I know,' she said, 'that sometimes you will see a man.'

'I will do nothing to put our family at risk.'

She appeared to deflate. 'But are you happy, Kerim? I love you and I want you to be happy.'

His phone rang – again. Whoever wanted to get in touch with him was persistent, like his mother, or desperate, like Gonca. But Mehmet Süleyman wasn't inclined to speak to anyone who was calling him whilst he was in this nightmare. Yeniçeriler Caddesi was nose-to-tail traffic, and of course he was being yelled at by some over-eager supposed alpha male from behind to get a move on. He'd give him five minutes . . .

His morning had started well enough. He'd been tired because he'd had so little sleep, but Gonca had been asleep and so he had been able to pack, shower and have his coffee in peace. Then she woke up. Suddenly panicked because he was leaving, she wanted to read his cards to make sure he was going to be safe. She was so afraid that someone or something was out to ruin their wedding. Knowing he didn't believe in such things, she didn't even tell him what the cards said. But it was probably not good, because she'd loaded his pockets with amulets and religious totems, including a whole string of boncuk beads, to ward off the evil eye.

Unable to stand it any longer, he picked the phone up and shouted into it. 'What? What!'

But it wasn't Gonca, or his mother.

'I know where I've seen that angel of yours before,' Haluk Keleş said.

Gonca opened her front door, still in her bathrobe, and squinted at the shabby figure standing amid the swirling autumn mist. 'İkmen?'

He bowed. 'Not too early for you, I hope, Gonca Hanım?'

'No, no.' She stood to one side to let him in. As he took his shoes off at the door, she said, 'The neighbours already think I'm a whore. What's one more man calling on me before I'm dressed?'

She led him into the kitchen. As she passed, she switched on the automatic coffee machine.

'So what can I do for you, Çetin Bey?'

Stopping to admire the machine, he said, 'How professional.'

She smiled. 'An early wedding gift from Erdem. It's mainly for Mehmet.'

'You must be glad your eldest child approves of your would-be husband.' He sat down.

'Erdem and his family live in the gorgo world,' she said. 'Why wouldn't he?'

'He's still your eldest son,' İkmen said. 'He's looked out for you since he was a child.'

'He is only three years younger than Mehmet,' she said. 'They are friends. What kind of coffee do you want? Cappuccino? Latte?'

'Espresso?'

She turned to the machine. 'I can do that.'

Once furnished with what he declared to be excellent coffee, İkmen said, 'How are the preparations for your wedding proceeding, Gonca?'

'Well,' she said. 'My dress is nearly finished. My daughters are organising my kına gecesi, and Mehmet Bey and my son are liaising with the hotel about the wedding. All I have to do is sit here and wait.' She sighed. 'What do you want, İkmen?'

The niceties of social interaction were not, İkmen felt, as important amongst the Roma. In a way, he admired that about them, even if it did sometimes catch him off guard.

He said, 'I want to talk to you about Şevket Sesler.'

Unlike most of his countrymen, Mehmet Süleyman had a very keen sense of proximity. And so having four people crowded behind him as he sat at his desk was not comfortable. But as Inspector Keleş had told him when he'd called earlier, it was important they all see what he had on his tablet together.

While Keleş smoked, swore and occasionally wiped his nose on his sleeve as he set up his machine, Ömer Mungun annoyingly asked him too many questions about the oversized tablet, which wound Süleyman up. The young man had an avid interest in technology that neither his boss nor Kerim Gürsel shared. Even if Eylul Yavaş appeared to find it fascinating. Was he, Süleyman wondered, turning into that old technophobe Çetin İkmen?

Eventually satisfied, Keleş pressed an icon on the screen and then mercifully moved away from Süleyman. As the officers watched and listened to the clip, Haluk Keleş observed their responses, and when the right moment came and the golden angels on the screen were revealed in their full glory, he froze the action. For a moment, no one did anything, but then they all looked at him.

Eventually Süleyman said, 'Yes?'

'Yes? Is that all you can say?' Keleş said. 'It's the Ark of the Covenant, isn't it!'

'It's a fictional movie,' Süleyman replied.

'Yeah, but the Ark of the Covenant. That was a real thing.'

'Was it? Is it? Inspector Keleş, we deal in facts here. At present, I have a probable suicide of a man who may or may not have been a forger of historical artefacts, plus a mummified head, and what I need from you and your officers, who have some expertise in this area, is information about whether the objects we have found are genuine works of art or copies.'

Kerim Gürsel, Eylul Yavaş and especially Ömer Mungun, who knew Süleyman well, held their collective breath. This was the boss at his most arrogant, effectively putting down an officer of equal standing, in public.

'I have,' he continued, 'consulted an ex-colleague on the subject of the seated female figure. I have been assured by that person that it is a representation of a Christian holy woman called St Foy. The original supposedly resides in a cathedral in France. It is said the head contains a portion of human skull from, it is believed, the saint herself. I should therefore like to have that figure scanned today. If it turns out to be the original, then we have to contact the authorities in France and begin to wonder what sort of theft and forgery operation our suicide was running. If indeed that is what has been happening. In the meantime, I feel my time would be best employed looking for further body parts in Fahrettin Müftüoğlu's apartment rather than watching *Raiders of the Lost Ark*.'

Chapter 9

'I'm more aware of what people say than you are,' Gonca said, 'because I speak Romani and you don't.'

'So are you comfortable with what they say?' İkmen asked.

'No! I had no part in Harun Sesler's death!' she said. 'Elmas Purcu's mother killed him. She didn't want that pig brutalising her daughter!'

'Afife Purcu cares nothing about anything except the location of her next fix,' İkmen said. 'You know it, I know it. You were seen in Tarlabaşı the day before Sesler was stabbed.'

'Not with Afife Purcu I wasn't! Everyone knows I went to see Harun Bey. I wanted him to go easy on my brother! He was threatening to throw Rambo out of his meyhane. I came to an arrangement with him. Ask his goons! I gave him some money and said he could use Rambo's place free of charge for one night.'

'Why?'

'Well, because Rambo is my brother.'

'Why not just give Sesler some money? Why let him loose in your brother's meyhane?'

Infuriated, she lit a cigarette. She didn't offer one to İkmen. 'To save his honour!' she said. 'Sesler's! Everyone knew he'd thrown Rambo out on the street for non-payment of his dues. If Rambo had just gone back in once I'd paid his debt, it would have made him look like a weak man dependent upon his sister. From Sesler's point of view, having a drunken party in Rambo's

111

place made him look like the big, powerful boss who could trash people's lives if he felt like it. I did what I did to save both of them!'

'And yet, had you spoken to Afife Purcu . . .'

'Which I didn't!'

'. . . then because of who you are, you would have known she'd never implicate you.'

'People saw her stab Harun Bey!' Gonca yelled. 'She was seen! The police don't need to gather evidence, they have witnesses!'

'And yet I am told that the rumour persists,' İkmen said.

'How? How do you know?'

'I never reveal my sources.'

'Oh, I will find out!' Gonca said. 'I will.'

'Why have you sworn fealty to Şevket Sesler?'

This struck her dumb.

'Yes, I know about that too,' İkmen said. 'Personal falçı to a man many believe is even more ruthless than his father. Why is that, Gonca? And don't try—'

'I won't deny it,' she said. 'Why would I? You know how it is, İkmen. Nobody gives a shit about us, they never have. And so in a population of outcasts, the most ruthless, the most cruel, they get the job of protecting the rest of us. And why not? Why should we trust you people when you pull down our homes, take our livelihoods away, eh? Of course we turn to our own! Where else is there to turn? I swore fealty to Harun Bey and Hasan Dum before him. I've always known what they are and I've always kept myself and my children out of their way.'

'Until now.'

She lowered her head.

'You've never been anyone's personal falçı, to my knowledge,' İkmen said. 'You've always been a sole operator, a successful artist, a loving mother, a woman in charge of herself.'

'I . . .'

'And now you have Mehmet Bey. A man so in love with you, he will do anything – and I mean anything – to protect you and make you happy.'

'I love him too! With all my soul!'

'I know you do,' İkmen said. 'Which is why I don't want a psychopath like Şevket Sesler involved in your lives.'

Although he knew that Ömer Mungun wanted to speak to him, Süleyman instructed the sergeant to go over to Fahrettin Müftüoğlu's apartment and help with the search. He would meet him there later. In the meantime, he wanted some time alone with Kerim Gürsel.

As Eylul Yavaş and a resentful Haluk Keleş left his office, Süleyman urged his colleague to sit down.

'Do you ever get the feeling that Turks watch too many movies?' he said.

Kerim Gürsel smiled.

'The tragedy is that Inspector Keleş is a very intelligent man who is good at his job. He studied art history at Mimar Sinan University. And yet . . .' He threw his arms in the air in a gesture of helplessness.

Still smiling, Kerim Gürsel said, 'I think he just saw that image and thought . . .'

'What?'

'I don't know. You have to admit that what we saw on the screen was almost identical to what we have in the evidence store.'

'Yes, but it's not one of the angels from the Ark of the Covenant.'

'Isn't it?'

'You sound like my fiancée,' Süleyman said. 'Talking of which, she has asked me to ask you whether Sinem Hanım would like

113

to come to her kına gecesi on Wednesday night. Eight o'clock, apparently.'

'That's very kind,' Kerim said. 'I will ask her. I am happy to take her and sit with Melda for the evening.'

'Which presents me with a problem,' Süleyman said.

'Why?'

'My son is insistent upon some sort of bachelor party. These things are very big in Ireland. Personally I'd rather just have a quiet dinner and prepare myself for my wedding, but . . . So we are to go to the bars of Nevizade Sokak on Wednesday night, and I would be honoured and pleased if you would come, Kerim Bey. Çetin Bey will be with us, as well as Ömer Bey and of course my brother and my son.'

'I'd love to come,' Kerim said. 'But I will have to deliver Sinem to Balat first, if she feels she can go, and I will also have to get someone to sit for Melda.'

'I understand.' Süleyman returned to business again. 'I wanted to ask you what you think Fahrettin Müftüoğlu was doing.'

'Don't give me all that "a woman is the property of her man" rubbish,' Gonca said. 'Fatma Hanım was never your property; you would have left her had she thought like that.'

İkmen moved his head to one side.

'Yes, you would!' Gonca said. 'I am marrying Mehmet, but I will still work. I don't expect him to keep me!'

'I think he expects to,' İkmen said.

And when she thought about it, Gonca knew that what he said was true. Mehmet did expect to keep her. He already gave her everything she wanted, and he was soon to buy that big house on Büyükada, not just for his son, but for her too.

'Any police officer who gets into debt is vulnerable,' İkmen said.

'I wouldn't put him in danger!'

114

'I know. But because he'd do anything for you, all Sesler would have to do is threaten you.'

'And Mehmet would do what?' she demanded.

'He'd do whatever he had to in order to save you,' İkmen said. 'He could even, I fear, part with information he shouldn't. And don't think this is because I believe that Mehmet Bey is a dishonourable man, Gonca. I don't. I just know, as a family man myself, how vulnerable our loved ones can make us. Minimise that risk. If, as you say, you did nothing to encourage Afife Purcu to kill Harun Sesler, then you have nothing to fear from Şevket. If you did . . .' He shook his head.

Gonca said nothing, which İkmen felt spoke volumes. Eventually he said, 'Think about it. Please.'

Scene-of-crime officers had just started on bedroom two of Fahrettin Müftüoğlu's apartment when Süleyman and Kerim Gürsel arrived. It was probably the most tightly packed room in the place.

Looking at Ömer Mungun, Süleyman said, 'Found anything?'

'Not so far, sir,' Ömer said. 'Sir, can I talk to you, please?'

'Of course.'

They went outside, ostensibly so Süleyman could smoke. His head was still full of the information Kerim had given him about the substance known as 'mummia'. That ground-up corpses could be some kind of aphrodisiac was a strange concept. Had Müftüoğlu really ground up a corpse he had mummified in order to create something so ridiculous? And how had that person died?

'Ömer.' He lit a cigarette. A simitçi walked past, his handcart loaded with fresh sesame-seed-sprinkled rolls.

'Sir, I got a statement from Canan Müftüoğlu,' the sergeant said.

'On my desk, yes.' Süleyman nodded. 'I've not had a chance to read it yet. Interesting?'

'Yes, sir. She claims her husband frequently expressed suicidal tendencies.'

'Does she? Did she inform anyone about this?'

'She said he had often made attempts on his own life. Or rather, he told her that was what he was going to do.'

'To gain her attention, do you think?'

'I don't know, sir,' Ömer said. 'To be honest, I can't really fathom their relationship.'

'And his phone is still to be found.'

'Yes, sir. But anyway, after I'd taken her statement, I offered to take Mrs Müftüoğlu home, but we went to the James Joyce in Hüseyinağa Mahallesi instead.'

Süleyman stopped mid drag.

'I can't remember who suggested that – maybe me. I mean, I do go there from time to time . . .'

'You went to a pub with a suspect. For how long?'

The drawn expression on Süleyman's face was making Ömer sweat – not to mention the absolute fury in his eyes. He couldn't think straight.

'Um, I'm not sure . . .'

'Not sure.' Süleyman threw his barely smoked cigarette on the ground and pulled his colleague around to the back of the apartment block by his collar. 'You're not sure!'

Why had Ömer never noticed before how long and bony the inspector's hands were?

'We just had one drink,' he said. 'Sir, she's not a suspect, is she? Müftüoğlu killed himself.'

'We think he did. We are not certain. Did you pay for the drinks?'

'I did, yes. Then I took her back to her father's apartment in Gaziosmanpaşa.'

Süleyman crossed his arms over his chest. 'And what happened then?'

'I . . . well, she lives on the first floor, with her father, and so I took her to her door and . . .'

'Did anyone see you?'

'I don't think so.' Ömer swallowed. 'On the way up the stairs, she told me that her father was out.'

'Out?'

'Yes.' He swallowed again. 'She was very insistent upon it, sir.' There was a silence between them, then he said, 'I think . . . she wanted me to go into the apartment with her.'

'She propositioned you.'

'Not exactly. She just . . . I said no, I had to get home.'

'And what did she say?'

'That she understood, it was OK, and then I left.'

'Did anyone see you leave?'

'Just some boys who crowded around the car for a bit. You know how they are in quarters like that, sir. A lot of youths on the street, many of them unemployed. They didn't speak to me.'

'But they knew you were police.'

'I imagine so, yes,' Ömer said. 'They seem to have an instinct for us, don't they?'

'Do they?'

'I . . . Yes, maybe. But the point is, sir, that when I looked up at the apartment where the lady lives, I saw her looking at me out of the window.'

'Oh, well done, Sergeant!' Süleyman said acidly. 'You have an admirer!'

'Don't know about that. Point is, sir, she wasn't alone. There was a man with her.'

'The father?'

'No, young. Means she wasn't alone, though. She lied to me. I've been wondering why.'

Süleyman lit another cigarette. 'You are wondering why, are you? Well, let's look at that, shall we? Could it be that the lovely lady was setting you up? You know as well as I do that suspects sometimes attempt to influence police officers by the use of monetary and other bribes. Sexual ones are popular. Perhaps she was seeking to gain control over you, maybe using this man as a witness. Criminal charges can die the most awful deaths in circumstances where suspects and officers have been sexually involved. Why did you take her for a drink?'

'She'd lost her husband. I . . .'

'You fancied her,' Süleyman said.

Ömer looked at the ground.

'Didn't you?' Süleyman roared.

Still Ömer said nothing.

Süleyman's phone began to ring, and Ömer Mungun inwardly blessed whoever was on the other end.

The tea garden between the two garages was entirely empty except for the proprietor and Burhan the gypsy. But then it was still early, and it was as cold as death.

After, he hoped, making Gonca Şekeroğlu aware of some of the implications that could follow from her allegiance to Şevket Sesler, İkmen had got in his car and driven over to Tarlabaşı. He didn't use the old Mercedes much these days, but it was too cold to wait for trams or buses. His body was too thin for a hard winter. And anyway, he was anxious and troubled. He'd told Gonca what he'd felt he had to, but would that now make her call off her wedding? But if he could somehow get to the bottom of what had happened to her bedcover, and why, maybe she would feel more secure. It might even give her the confidence to tell Sesler to get out of her life. If that were possible.

'Çetin Bey,' the old gypsy said as he watched İkmen walk towards his table.

'Burhan Bey.'

'Will you allow me to buy you tea this freezing morning?'

Burhan asked. 'I had work last night and so today I can afford to be generous.'

'Thank you.'

İkmen sat down while the proprietor brought them both tea. He enquired after the gypsy's health, they discussed the state of the world for a while, then he said, 'Burhan Bey, I have a problem.'

'Well, if it's anything I can help you with, you know I will,' Burhan said.

'I am still trying to find out who may have ruined Gonca Hanım's bedcover. The poor lady is unnerved and I don't want her or Mehmet Bey to have this shadow over their wedding day. Someone smeared blood on it and I want to know who and why. I can't believe that Rahul Bey or his daughter would do such a thing . . .'

'It would ruin their business.'

'Precisely,' İkmen said. 'The only lead I have is via this Can family. They deny all knowledge of how the blood came to be on the cover, but both Gonca Hanım and myself have visited them and we feel there are things they are not telling us.'

Burhan nodded. 'That is a sad family. Huriye Hanım and her daughter scratch a living through their needlework, but with so many mouths to feed, it's hard. And those boys, the girl's brothers, just run wild. Only the little one, Hızır, doesn't give her trouble, but then he's stuck in a chair.'

'I want to find out more about the brother-in-law,' İkmen said.

'Munir Can? Why?'

'I know he has sex with the mother.'

'So it is said.'

'When I arrived at their building, he was fastening his trousers with a contented look on his face.'

Burhan shook his head. 'Everyone knows,' he said, 'but what can you do? Family business is family business.'

İkmen moved in closer so the proprietor couldn't hear what he was saying. He was taking a risk sharing his thoughts with Burhan, but it was a calculated one.

'When I met Huriye Hanım, I could unfortunately see that she was bleeding,' he said. 'He'd used her . . . roughly.'

The old man tutted and nervously fingered his prayer beads. Gypsies weren't usually religious, but many of them carried rosaries as aids to stress relief.

'You think . . .'

'Assuming Munir visits Huriye Hanım frequently, I fear that may have been her blood on Gonca Hanım's bedcover,' İkmen said. 'I fear she may have used it to . . .' He let his sentence hang. The blood was menstrual blood, and given how that was a taboo in the Roma community, he could only think that maybe poor Huriye had been obliged to clean herself up before her brother-in-law forced himself on her. But she'd told Gonca that she didn't bleed . . .

'I need a way to get to know Munir Can, and quickly. To convince him I'm like him. As a man given to drink, I imagine his lips can loosen after a few glasses of rakı.'

Burhan smiled. 'Sometimes.'

'Problem is, I don't speak Romani.'

'Like most of us, Munir speaks Turkish,' Burhan said. 'English too, I've heard.'

Given that Munir Can's job was to lure foreign tourists into Şevket Sesler's girly bar this would seem to İkmen to be essential.

'Mmm. But I imagine that when he talks of intimate things, he uses his own language. I speak English and German, but I always tell my secrets in Turkish.'

Burhan nodded.

'I know that even if I tortured that woman, which I would not, I'd never find out from Huriye Hanım's lips what happened to

Gonca Hanım's bedcover,' İkmen said. 'And I do believe that Munir Can is connected to this, even if he doesn't know it.'

The gypsy nodded again, and then he said, 'Çetin Bey, are you any good at card games?'

'A customer had just been trying them on,' Atyom Mafyan told Mehmet Süleyman. 'We always clean jewellery after each customer. In addition, each piece is labelled with a price and a code number that relates to the jeweller who created it.' He held up a pair of earrings made from two large blocks of sapphire. 'These were made by Fahrettin Bey.'

Süleyman held them up to the light and shook them slightly. What appeared to be powder moved around in the capsules at the centre of the pieces.

'Your business is famous for these compartments, Atyom Bey.'

'Indeed, Mehmet Bey,' the Armenian said. 'A gimmick if you will, but it has given us a distinct profile for over forty years.'

'You don't think your customer could have tampered with them?'

'Maybe,' he said.

'Can I look at your camera footage?' Süleyman asked.

'Of course.'

The woman in question wore a niqab. She had simply held the earrings up to the sides of her obscured face. She'd gone on to buy nothing.

Süleyman took an evidence bag out of his pocket and placed the earrings inside. 'I'll get these tested,' he said.

The Armenian sighed. 'Thank you. Given how Fahrettin was . . .'

'You did the right thing.' Then a thought occurred to him. 'Atyom Bey, those jet earrings I bought from you . . .'

'Ah, I'll look them up.' The jeweller walked towards his computer.

'Jet and gold,' Süleyman said. 'My fiancée had always wanted something from your atelier, and jet is one of her favourite stones.'

Atyom Bey scrolled through several screens on his system until he came to the right one.

'Ah, here, yes,' he said. 'Jet and gold, called Doorways.'

That was why Süleyman had liked them so much. Little black doorways into another realm.

'They were made by Fahrettin Bey. The jet we use comes from Erzurum, which is not particularly favoured by jewellers, but it's just as good as the more famous product from England. And if one can assist one's fellow citizens . . . I'm sorry, I'm rambling. Turkish gemstones are my passion.'

Süleyman smiled. 'Gonca Hanım was delighted with them,' he said.

'I am so glad.'

When he returned to the crime scene in Vefa, Süleyman gave Ömer Mungun the task of delivering the earrings to the forensic laboratory. For the moment he didn't want to have anything to do with him. How could he have been so stupid? Someone with Ömer's background, a man of the East who belonged to a little-known and understood religious group, should know instinctively the necessity of discretion. But when it came to women, the sergeant had a blind spot, and Süleyman knew that was, at least in part, down to him. Ömer had never recovered from losing a woman he claimed he loved to his superior. Barcın Demirtaş, a fellow police officer, had been a beautiful, feisty woman for whom Ömer had fallen hard. But Süleyman had taken her for his own sexual satisfaction and because he could. He'd hurt the younger man. It hadn't been his finest hour. It had also been the start of a resentment that had only grown inside Ömer over the years.

*

122

'Were I a paranoid man, I might think the police were after me,' Atyom Mafyan said to Çetin İkmen as the two of them took tea in the former's office.

İkmen had been unsurprised at finding that Süleyman had been to GülGül less than half an hour before him, but he could also see why the proprietor might be a little spooked by it. Even retired police officers were viewed with some suspicion.

He smiled. 'Mehmet Bey comes to you in an official capacity,' he said. 'I don't.'

'So to what do I owe the pleasure of your company?' the jeweller asked.

'Poker,' İkmen said.

Atyom Mafyan's face broke into a broad smile. 'Ah.'

'Not that I am offering myself again as a sacrifice to your poker school, Atyom Bey.'

'Nor would I expect you to. A man is either a betting man or he isn't, and you are not, Çetin Bey. I, as you know, am, and it is both my curse and my delight. How can I help you?'

'There is a gypsy called Şevket Sesler . . .'

'The godfather of Tarlabaşı, yes,' the Armenian said. 'I knew his father, an appalling player. The son's no better – or so I have heard.'

'He has a poker school at his club every Tuesday evening,' İkmen said.

The Armenian shook his head. 'Some people never learn.'

'Oh, he doesn't play. One of his henchmen, a thug called Munir Can, plays for him.'

'Never heard of him.'

'He's good,' İkmen said, 'and I need to get to know him.'

'Ah, and you want me to . . .'

'The school is open to any player in the city,' İkmen said. 'Now, Atyom Bey, you and I both know that if I sit down with serious players, I will lose. But I'm not going to be there to win.

123

I'm going to be there to get into conversation with Munir Can and to watch *you* win.'

'You think I can?'

'I'm willing to pay your way, and mine, into this school in order to find out,' İkmen said.

'Mmm.' The Armenian rubbed his chin.

'I know it's short notice, and these things start late . . .'

'What kind of late?'

'Midnight.'

He smiled. 'Nothing worthwhile starts before then, Çetin Bey.'

'But as I recall, Atyom Bey, the one time I attended your school, it was early evening. My wife was still alive, and she would have taken a very dim view of a midnight assignation.'

'As I say, Çetin Bey, the worthwhile schools begin late. And please,' Atyom continued, 'do not be offended by this. You wanted to play, I gave you the opportunity. But really, I didn't want you to lose your life's savings. You are a friend to my cousin Garbis, who was very concerned that I look after you.'

'I still lost,' İkmen said.

'I am not a worker of miracles.'

He laughed. 'So the gypsies' poker school in Tarlabaşı – how about it, Atyom Bey?'

A smile preceded the Armenian's words. 'You know I like a challenge.'

'Good.'

'But don't you know some of the gypsies?' Atyom Bey said. 'Gonca Hanım, certainly.'

'Oh yes,' İkmen said. 'I don't know this Munir Can, though. That said, of course, I cannot be myself, as it were. But I'll take care of that, so give it no more thought.'

124

Chapter 10

Sarıgöl Mahallesi was notorious even within the confines of Gaziosmanpaşa. To the north of the holy district of Eyüp at the northern end of the Golden Horn, Gaziosmanpaşa had been colonised by Turkish immigrants from Thrace and the Balkans since the early 1950s. However, in recent years, the population of the area had more than doubled, and mahallesi, or neighbourhoods, like Sarıgöl, which were generally poor, had become hotbeds of crime.

A lot of the heavy drug-taking that characterised Sarıgöl came about as a result of unemployment. But there were other factors too, like the smart new apartment complexes that were being built nearby. Not for the residents of Sarıgöl, many of whom still lived in the now broken-down and insanitary gecekondu shanties built by their grandparents in the 1950s and 60s, but for the new middle-class pious elite. Streets scented almost permanently with the cannabis such people would abhor kept the 'real' and the 'fake' areas of Sarıgöl apart.

Canan Müftüoğlu's shabby apartment block was most decidedly in 'old' Sarıgöl, and as Ömer Mungun walked those shabby, puddle-scarred streets, he wondered what her backstory was. Were her parents perhaps originally from the Balkans? If so, was this why someone who appeared as educated and articulate as Canan remained in the area? A lot of people liked to live close to their own, especially in working-class districts. Ömer himself knew he felt far more comfortable in Tarlabaşı than anywhere else in the city because of the large number of people there who originated from the far south-east of Turkey. With them he knew he could speak his own first language, Aramaic.

By contrast, he didn't know Sarıgöl well, and he heard a lot of accents on the streets he could barely fathom, as well as some more familiar tones from his own part of the country. This time, after dropping off those earrings from GülGül at the forensic institute, he'd come to Sarıgöl to . . . what? Yes, he had been attracted to Canan Müftüoğlu, and maybe that was wrong, but was it more wrong than falling in love with a gypsy woman whose family were known for their involvement in crime? Gonca Hanım was no angel, but Ömer knew that didn't change what he had done. Yet was this foray into Sarıgöl, of which Süleyman was unaware, a simple trip to try to understand a suspect better, or was he attempting to see the woman again?

More glittering artefacts were coming to light. Usually wrapped in either newspaper or rags, these articles ranged from a simple silver cross right up to something that was probably a golden headdress.

Inspector Haluk Keleş was now on site permanently in Vefa. His spat with Süleyman apparently forgotten, he said, 'I'm having St Foy scanned this afternoon.'

Süleyman nodded.

'That other thing, the monstrance, that's gold and rock crystal.'

'Solid gold?'

'Yeah.' Keleş leaned against one of the greasy apartment walls. 'What the fuck is all this about, Mehmet Bey? Forgery? Theft? Theft and forgery? Man's dead and yet it seems as if he was some sort of channel for these artefacts. Did he make them? Did he collect them? Little fat bastard, by all accounts. Maybe he did this because he couldn't get laid.'

'He was married,' Süleyman said.

Keleş narrowed his eyes. 'You sure?'

'So it seems.'

'Fuck.'

'We have a woman who is waiting to take possession of her husband's property.'

'Well she won't be able to get her hands on these artefacts until I've finished with them,' Keleş said. 'Anyway, why are you all still here if the man committed suicide?'

'Two reasons,' Süleyman said. 'Firstly, the mummified head we discovered. We know it's modern, but we don't know who it was or whether there's any more of the body in this apartment. Secondly, Müftüoğlu's wife says he often made threats against his own life. But did anyone encourage him? And if so, why? Did his wife encourage him? They didn't live together. I have yet to understand the parameters of their relationship . . .'

His phone began to ring. He took it out of his pocket and turned away in order to answer the call. It was the forensic laboratory.

The sirens that suddenly seemed to be screaming across the whole of the city came to Gonca Şekeroğlu's attention gradually. But once she started hearing them, she couldn't stop. Didim, her sister, who was sitting in the middle of the salon, sewing jewels onto Gonca's wedding dress, looked up. 'It sounds as if Mehmet Bey and his fellows are about some big business.'

Gonca had been thinking about what İkmen had told her. She needed to distance herself from Şevket Sesler. But how?

'Maybe,' she said. She'd had many years to get used to the fact that her lover worked in a dangerous profession in a dangerous city. But now that they were about to be married, the sound of sirens affected her more acutely. Was she wise to let herself in for a life of anxiety about the man she loved so much?

She got up from her sofa. 'Would you like tea, Didim?'

'Be nice.'

As she went down to the kitchen, she heard the front door open. A lot of people had keys to her door, including her children, but this wasn't one of those. It was Mehmet Süleyman. Breathless, he ran into the kitchen. 'Those earrings I bought for you from GülGül, where are they?'

'Why? What are you doing here, Mehmet?"

'Just tell me where the damn earrings are!'

He never spoke to her like that; he rarely looked this stressed. She said, 'On my dressing table.'

He ran up the stairs to their bedroom. Gonca followed at a slower pace. When she arrived in the bedroom, she saw him looking for the box. 'On the left,' she said. 'What's this about?'

He found it and slipped it into an evidence bag. Then he leaned down on the glass-topped dressing table to catch his breath. 'I bought the earrings because they were made of jet . . .'

'I love them.'

'What I didn't know until today was that they had been made by the man I have been investigating.'

'The suicide?'

'Yes,' Süleyman said. 'A suicide who was also, we now think, a poisoner.'

Men and women dressed in white hazmat suits, their faces concealed behind visors and respirators, had caused panic in the Grand Bazaar. Just the vision of these figures from a science fiction nightmare caused some people to scream. Once they arrived at their destination, the GülGül atelier, they disappeared inside in silence. They knew what they had to do.

Meanwhile, Kerim Gürsel, who had left the scene in Vefa shortly after Süleyman got the call from the forensic laboratory, was now outside the Nuruosmaniye Gate, together with several hundred disgruntled and frightened shoppers, as well as a shaken Atyom Mafyan and his employees.

128

'I've never heard of ricin,' the Armenian said as Kerim attempted to get the jeweller away from the crowd.

Somebody screamed, 'It's a terror attack!'

Kerim shouted, 'It's not!'

Uniformed officers pushed people aside and removed a man who appeared to be drunk. Kerim led Atyom Bey and his staff into the doorway of a closed shop.

The Armenian put a hand up to his head. 'I think I'm going mad.'

Kerim, relieved to be out of the crowd, holstered his pistol. 'Hardly surprising. In answer to your question, Atyom Bey, I don't know much about ricin myself, except that it's a poison for which there's no antidote and it has been used in terror attacks.'

'Here?'

'Not to my knowledge, but in the USA and in Europe. Do you know whether Fahrettin Müftüoğlu had any connections or sympathies with illegal organisations?'

Before Atyom Mafyan could speak, one of his employees, an enormous man, both tall and fat, said, 'He rarely spoke. How could we know what he was thinking?'

'What about Fahrettin Bey's home?' Atyom asked.

'Inspector Süleyman is in charge of the scene,' Kerim replied.

This wasn't strictly true, as Süleyman's first thought on receiving the news from the forensic institute had been for Gonca Hanım, to whom he had given a pair of Müftüoğlu's earrings. Keleş had been left in charge until his return.

'Public health measures have been put into practice there too,' Kerim continued.

A female jeweller said, 'They will be careful, won't they, the scientists? I just left my bench. I'd been setting a piece of jade.'

'They're used to exercising extreme caution,' Kerim said. 'Nothing will be removed unless it contains ricin – or who knows what else.'

The Armenian shook his head. 'I blame myself, at least in part.'

'Why?'

'Fahrettin's ideas should have alerted me to the possibility that he was strange in some way. His father always had a good reputation in the trade, and both of them were talented.'

Kerim shrugged. 'Creative people . . .'

The woman said, 'I do know that he hated his mother.'

In spite of the fact that all around them people were yelling, gossiping and bumping into each other, Kerim pushed himself forward so that he was standing next to her. Fahrettin Müftüoğlu had, to his knowledge, failed to live with his wife for fear of upsetting his mother.

'Hanım . . .'

'I heard him on the phone one day,' the woman said. 'Years ago now. He didn't know I was there. He said that he hated the old woman and wished she'd just die. I assumed the person on the other end of the call was a woman, because after that he talked about sex. I wanted the ground to open up and swallow me.'

Çetin İkmen had always liked Ataturk airport. Situated at what had once been the village of Yeşilköy on the shores of the Sea of Marmara, it was an old friend. As children, Çetin, his brother Halil and their friends the Sarkissian boys had sometimes gone to what was then called Yeşilköy airport to watch planes take off and land. Back then, in the 1960s, the terminal had been a low-rise concrete lump with outlying wooden huts. But then it had started life as a military airbase.

Now the airport was only used for cargo. The sparkling new İstanbul airport, thirty-five kilometres away, between the northern end of the Bosphorus and the Black Sea, was quite another affair. Clean, bright and some said elegant, it was also really time-consuming to get to. And so because public transport to the airport wasn't great, İkmen had opted to drive. Now snarled up in a traffic jam on the D020, he wondered whether he'd made the right choice. Patrick Süleyman's plane was due to land in just under an hour. Would he make it?

That İkmen would pick the boy up had always been the plan, which was just as well, as Patrick's father was fully occupied. The Grand Bazaar was shut, it was said, because of a security alert, and while that didn't directly concern Süleyman, İkmen had heard a whisper that the GülGül jewellery atelier was involved. And that most certainly did concern him.

Looking around, İkmen noticed that a lot of people were talking on their mobile phones while driving. And while they were all stationary at the moment, he had no doubt that these people would continue their conversations once the traffic was moving again. That or they'd text. Some might even be watching films or YouTube. He didn't approve. He didn't like that some of his younger children were glued to their phones. But that, it seemed, was just modern life.

Haluk Keleş saw Süleyman walk up the street towards him and said, 'All right?'

'I hope so.' Süleyman shook his head. 'I just hope I didn't frighten her too much.'

'You got the earrings?'

'Yes. Who's in charge here?'

The street had been cordoned off. He'd had to show his ID to some child of a constable before he could get back on site. Now that it was the preserve of the scientists, the police were interlopers.

'A Dr Yaşova,' Keleş said. 'He's in there with all the other hazmat suits. Strictly off limits to us.'

Süleyman took the evidence bag containing the earrings out

131

of his pocket. 'I want to hand these over. I don't think they contain anything, but they're jet and so I can't see inside.'

Keleş, like everyone who worked out of headquarters, knew about Gonca. 'She like them, your fiancée?'

'Yes. Very much. Why I want to get them back to her as soon as I can.' Suddenly Süleyman realised someone was missing, 'Where's Sergeant Mungun?'

Keleş shrugged.

Süleyman took out his phone and called him. But Ömer didn't answer.

They could smell him. As soon as he sat down, men moved away. A boy waiter asked him what he'd like to eat, and Ömer ordered tea and cheese pide. He didn't want to go back to Vefa – and Süleyman. He knew that was cowardly and childish; he also knew he was in the wrong. But that didn't change the way he felt. The widow Müftüoğlu had come into his life out of nowhere and offered herself to him, a man who hadn't had sex for months. Did Süleyman even know what that was like? Burying himself inside Gonca Hanım day after day? And anyway, how could Canan Müftüoğlu be a suspect? Her husband had killed himself. His superior was just being spiteful. He'd always been that way. Fahrettin Müftüoğlu had taken his own life; what did it matter what Ömer did with the man's wife?

'Ömer Bey?'

Lost in thought, he hadn't noticed anyone come into the little pide restaurant he'd chosen to go into when he got fed up with people staring at him on the street. Of course they could smell cop, but it also reminded him of his teenage years in Mardin, when every unfamiliar face was scrutinised minutely. Was he or she a terrorist? A government agent? Someone from İstanbul or Izmir who didn't understand the locals and might have money?

He looked up and saw Canan Müftüoğlu. Smartly dressed in a long black coat, she was just as pretty as he remembered. But she wasn't alone. A small man wearing a blue and white checked nylon suit stood behind her. Elderly by the look of him, he had long grey hair and an even longer grey beard, minus moustache. He appeared to be a cross between a 1970s-style taxi driver and a man given to a strict interpretation of Islam. Not the man he'd seen in the window of her apartment the night before. Who was he?

Canan answered his internal musings immediately. She pulled the man forward and said, 'This is my father.'

Ömer said, 'Hello.'

'Dad, this is Sergeant Mungun.'

'Mmm.' The elderly man stood with his hands clasped in front of him and bowed slightly. Not one to shake hands, so probably Ömer had been right about his piety.

The boy waiter brought Ömer his tea and pide and then went to kiss the hand of Canan Müftüoğlu's father but was brushed aside. Ömer's phone rang. He ignored it.

'We're going upstairs,' Canan told him.

In districts like Sarıgöl, women, whether with men or other women, always dined in the family room on the first floor of such establishments.

Ömer smiled. Then Canan said, 'Do you have any news of . . .'

'We will contact you when we know more,' he said.

The men who had scuttled away to the back of the restaurant when he had arrived moved forward now and, he noticed, exchanged small bows with Canan's father. Was he some kind of local dignitary?

'Oh well,' Canan said breezily. 'Must go.'

She took her father's arm and they both went upstairs. As they disappeared from view, Ömer heard the man scolding his daughter. But not in Turkish; in one of the Kurdish languages Ömer knew so well:

'Stupid girl! What were you thinking?'

*

'Çetin Bey!'

Patrick Süleyman, complete with large suitcase on wheels, waved wildly at him. He was wearing a long, dark overcoat, which made him look like his father, and a tweed flat cap, which didn't.

İkmen attempted to run, but then gave up and let the boy scamper over to him. They embraced. İkmen took the suitcase from Patrick's grasp and said, 'How was your flight?'

Patrick rolled his eyes, then nodded his head towards a dishevelled middle-aged man. 'Would've been better if I hadn't been sitting next to him.'

'Why?'

'He got trashed,' he said, then added, 'drunk.'

'Oh.'

'Cracking on about his Russian girlfriend – like I give a shite.' Then he produced İkmen's watch from underneath his cap. 'Please God, don't let me ever become that tragic!'

İkmen was delighted at the boy's skill. 'No. You're going to be Houdini. Your father is sorry he couldn't be here . . .'

'I didn't expect him.'

'. . . but what he is dealing with today is serious.'

'Look, I'm cool with him now,' Patrick said. 'He's who he is.'

'The case he is working on has produced some surprises.'

They began walking towards the arrivals exit.

'Like what?'

'I'm not sure,' İkmen said. 'I will let him tell you. How is your wonderful mother?'

'Oh, she's grand. I think I'm driving her up the wall with the magic.'

İkmen laughed. Then, as the exit doors swished open in front of them, he said, 'I fear my car has become no tidier in your absence, Patrick.'

'Cool.'

*

134

It was difficult to see what Dr Yaşova looked like behind his surgical mask and hazmat hood. Of very upright, almost military bearing, he was, Süleyman felt, probably in his late fifties or sixties.

'This is going to take us some time,' he told Süleyman and Keleş when they asked him how long his team might be in the Müftüoğlu apartment.

'The owner was a hoarder,' Süleyman said.

'Deceased, I gather.'

'Yes. We've been finding historical artefacts, maybe forged, maybe stolen, for days. Fingertip searching in a space so full of stuff is a long job.'

The doctor nodded. 'I'm told you found potassium cyanide.'

'The dead man was a jeweller,' Süleyman said. 'They routinely use cyanide to brighten gold in a process called stripping. Sadly, this jeweller also used it to end his life. Have you found anything yet?'

'No. The ricin found in the jewellery was in the form of a powder, and that apartment is heaving with tins, packets and all sorts of receptacles, unlabelled, containing all sorts of substances. I'm not going to be able to allow your officers back in today.'

'Uniforms will have to be stationed outside.'

'I accept and appreciate that,' the doctor said. 'But for the time being, it's off limits to anyone except myself and my team.'

As yet, nothing had been found at GülGül, so it was beginning to look as if Süleyman could finish for the day. But then Haluk Keleş, who had been reading texts on his phone, said, 'You fluent in French, Mehmet Bey?'

'Reasonably, yes.'

At Galatasaray Lycée, where both men had gone to school, ability in French was highly prized.

'Just got the results from the scan I ordered on that statue you found.'

135

'St Foy?'

'Yeah. Seems the head contains something that could be human bone.' He looked up. 'Means it could be genuine.'

When Ömer Mungun returned to headquarters, he found his superior staring fixedly at his computer screen. Ömer needed to speak to him – what he had witnessed in Sarıgöl had been interesting. But he also knew that if he disturbed the boss while he was concentrating, he could let himself in for another volley of Süleyman's famously short temper. He deserved it, of course, but . . .

'Where have you been?' Süleyman asked, not taking his eyes from the screen.

'Sar—'

'Because if you think you can hide from me, then think again.'

'I know what I did was wrong . . .'

'It was beyond wrong.' Süleyman's fierce gaze met Ömer's eyes, and the younger man looked away.

'Sir, I need to speak to you. I've found something out, about Canan Müftüoğlu.'

Süleyman picked up his landline handset. 'Well, it will have to wait. I need to find the right person to talk to about one of the artefacts we found at Müftüoğlu's apartment, which means I have to speak a foreign language. Get me a coffee.'

Ömer stood up. 'Yes, sir.'

As he left the office with his tail metaphorically between his legs, he heard Süleyman begin to speak in French.

'So as far as you know, there's no more poison?'

Dr Özil, a slim scientist of indeterminate age, was red in the face from wearing a mask and hazmat hood. She was clearly enjoying the relatively fresh air outside the Grand Bazaar. She looked at Atyom Mafyan with some disdain and then addressed her answer to Kerim Gürsel.

'We don't think so,' she said. 'Only present in those earrings.' She looked back at the jeweller. 'Were they made on site?'

'I don't know,' he said. 'Fahrettin Bey did some of his work at home.'

'So he could have brought them in?'

'I imagine so.'

The scientist was blunt to the point of rudeness, Kerim thought. He wondered whether she was one of those Turks who hated Armenians, or whether Atyom Bey had particularly got under her skin.

He said, 'Dr Özil, have you heard anything from your colleagues in Vefa?'

'That's a much bigger job than this,' she said. 'They won't be finished today, maybe not even tomorrow.'

'So are *you* finished now, Doctor?' he asked.

The scientist began to walk back towards the bazaar. 'I'll let you know when I am,' she said over her shoulder.

When she had gone, Atyom Mafyan looked at his employees. 'There's no point any of you waiting around. Go home. I'll ring you when I know whether we'll be opening up tomorrow.'

They all thanked him and left.

Alone with Kerim Gürsel, the Armenian said, 'If I'd known that Fahrettin was dabbling with such dangerous substances, I would have informed the police. This has all backfired on my business in ways I could never have imagined, Inspector Gürsel.'

Kerim, who knew that a lot of people would actively avoid the GülGül atelier, at least for a short time, sympathised.

'It's not good,' he said. 'And to be honest with you. Atyom Bey, we still have a long way to go with the investigation. All I can say is that it is best for all of us that we know everything about Fahrettin Bey now rather than in the future.'

'Mmm.'

He put a hand on the Armenian's shoulder. 'The work of your atelier is highly regarded, Atyom Bey. I know for a fact that my colleague Inspector Süleyman's fiancée is very keen to get her earrings back.'

Chapter 11

It was dark by the time Mehmet Süleyman finally got through to the right person. Ömer Mungun, although able to understand very little of what was being said, remained in the office, while they were both joined by Haluk Keleş.

When Süleyman came off the phone, he said, 'That was Inspecteur Rafael Weiss from the Brigade de Répression du Banditisme. They're the department covering the detection of art fraud.'

'I know that,' Keleş said. 'I told you.'

'You did, but Sergeant Mungun didn't know,' Süleyman replied.

'And so?'

'And so it would appear that St Foy is still in her abbey in Conques,' he said.

Haluk Keleş, who was annoyed with himself for not having sufficient French to speak to colleagues in France, took his frustration out on Süleyman.

'We know that!' he said. 'The whole world would know if the fucking thing had been stolen!'

Ömer Mungun braced for what could be a clash of egos. But Süleyman remained calm.

'Yes,' he said. 'If you will let me finish, Haluk Bey . . .' There was a tense silence, and then he continued. 'As far as the French are concerned, no attempt has been made to steal the statue in recent years. Inspecteur Weiss would not discuss with me the security arrangements around the artefact, but my understanding is that it is protected. They think that the most likely scenario with our statue is that it is a copy.'

'They don't know that.'

'Hear me out.'

Ömer cringed.

'That said, in light of the fact that our statue appears to have a piece of bone inside, they are going to scan their St Foy. With that in mind at this stage, they do not want to make the matter public. They will get back to us as soon as they can. In the meantime, this goes no further.'

Keleş shrugged. 'I get it. Conques is on the pilgrimage route to Santiago de Compostela. I looked it up. Pilgrims from all over the world stop there to honour St Foy. It's a religious tourist attraction.'

Süleyman smiled. He hadn't known where Haluk Keleş stood on religion but had always assumed it was not something he paid much heed. This seemed to confirm that view.

When Keleş left his office, Süleyman turned to Ömer Mungun.

'So,' he said, 'what were you doing over in Sarıgöl?'

As soon as Patrick Süleyman had arrived at the İkmen apartment, he had been whisked away by Çetin's youngest son, Kemal, to go and meet up with his boyfriend in Karaköy. İkmen had let his son take his car, mainly because Kemal's boyfriend, Hulusi, had broken his leg the previous month and was finding the combination of a plaster and public transport too much to bear.

It seemed that the security alert in the Grand Bazaar had indeed centred around Atyom Mafyan's atelier, GülGül. Something, so Kerim Gürsel had told him, to do with a substance called ricin. İkmen had some knowledge about that. A poison with no antidote, it was rare, and he could only remember reading about one case, which had happened in Saudi Arabia. A man had ingested it in some sort of herbal preparation. How had the substance turned up, if it had, in Atyom's atelier? Maybe İkmen could ask him when they met for that poker school they were going to in Tarlabaşı.

İkmen had always questioned almost everything he chose to do. This poker school was a case in point. Was he going to be able to get into conversation with this Munir Can at such an event? Wouldn't the gypsy be too occupied with his game? And anyway, would he talk about women when he was at poker? Besides, he clearly wasn't the one who had immersed Gonca's bedcover in menstrual blood. So what did İkmen hope to achieve?

Huriye Can, Munir's unfortunate sister-in-law, was obviously a very unhappy woman. She was poor, her children were either sick or unruly and her brother-in-law was using her for sex, probably against her will. An intervention was needed, but was he the man to do it? Messing around in the lives of ethnic minorities one didn't truly understand could be hazardous. With Munir unmasked as a sexual predator, maybe things would become worse for Huriye. Maybe Munir paid her for sex. However, the fact remained that Gonca's bridal bedcover had been damaged either while it had been with the Can family or in transit to the haberdasher's shop, and İkmen knew that she wouldn't be happy until she knew why.

He just hoped that Atyom Mafyan didn't lose any money to the gypsies' school. He always had been a fearsome player; the gypsies had to know of him. Which could mean they'd double down to win against him. But then Atyom Bey had been quick to take up İkmen's challenge, and so either he hadn't played for a long while, or he was just keen to get on and take the money of people he didn't know.

'Sir, I'm sorry . . .'

Süleyman held up a hand. 'Whatever has happened, we need to put that to one side,' he said. 'As long as you've not slept with the woman.'

141

'No, sir! I swear!'

'Well then, what of your walk through Sarıgöl?'

Ömer cleared his throat. 'As you know, sir, it's a rough place. A lot of drugs, unemployment. I stopped at a little pideci because I was hungry, and as expected, a number of men chose to leave at that moment. I swear they can smell us.'

'Yes.'

'So then in walks Canan Müftüoğlu with an elderly man. Thin, cheap clothes, beard. Some of the men in the pideci went to kiss his hand, but he wasn't keen and I felt it was because I was there. Anyway, Canan introduced me as the officer working on her husband's case, and then they went upstairs to the family room. As they left, I heard the father tell her off for introducing us. He was aggressive and he spoke in Zaza.'

'The Kurdish dialect.'

'Yes. I can understand most of them. He said, "Stupid girl! What were you thinking?"'

'Mmm. And your interpretation of this incident is?'

'I got the feeling the father was some sort of made man,' Ömer said.

'A godfather?'

'Yes. But not one I'm aware of.'

'Do you know his name?'

'All I managed to pick up, from another conversation in Zaza I overheard from two men behind me, was the name "Muharrem Bey".'

Süleyman nodded. 'Check the address the woman took you to.'

'That was my next move, yes. And I've got an informant, a Zaza speaker . . .'

'Good.' He nodded. 'This entire situation is . . . . disquieting.'

'With a mummified head amongst our pieces of evidence, that's probably an understatement, sir,' Ömer said.

'No, well yes, but I also mean . . .' Süleyman shook his head. 'We have what would seem to be a suicide, open and shut, and yet so much emanating from the death of Fahrettin Müftüoğlu appears to be leading us down pathways that are almost exclusively criminal. I find myself not so much wondering why he killed himself as trying to interpret what he might have been saying about his life through his death.'

'His life was complicated,' Ömer said.

'Maybe more complicated than he could handle,' Süleyman replied. 'Maybe therein lies the reason he committed suicide.'

Attempting to click the two padlocks in place at the top and bottom of the door into his shop was proving difficult for Rahul Mengüç. Neziye had left hours before to prepare their dinner, leaving her father to struggle with cold metal and arthritic fingers. As he swore and cursed his own ineptitude, he heard a man's voice behind him.

'Can I help?'

A wheezy, harsh use of the Romani words. Rahul turned around and saw that greasy thug Munir Can behind him.

Pulling himself up to his full height, he said, 'No.'

But Munir didn't move. He watched the haberdasher struggle until in the end he pushed him out of the way and clicked the padlocks home.

With some reluctance, Rahul said, 'Thank you.'

Munir smiled, revealing more teeth than Rahul had thought he possessed. It was said that he had sex with poor Huriye Hanım. Whether that was true or not, Rahul Bey didn't know, and he almost didn't want to. The poor woman was at the edge of the community as it was; she didn't need any more people shunning her and her children. In part that was why Rahul employed her and her daughter. Nobody needed money more than the Widow Can.

As if reading his mind, Munir spoke. 'You still employ my sister-in-law, Huriye?'

'I do. She is an excellent seamstress – and her daughter.'

His face clouded. 'That girl should be married,' he said.

'She's a child!'

'Not for much longer. Anyway, our Zeytin was married at twelve.'

'Back in the old days, things were different,' Rahul replied.

'Shame.'

'I think not!'

'Kid's always around in that apartment with her mother,' Munir continued.

Rahul put his keys in his pocket. He'd never had much to do with Munir Can before, or indeed with Şevket Sesler or any of his men. He liked it that way. He'd have to be careful what he said next. Being invisible was a full-time job.

'I'm sure you wouldn't want your niece hanging around the streets, Munir Bey,' he said.

'Course not!'

'Well . . .'

Munir drew close to the haberdasher, who could now smell his rancid, beer-tainted breath. 'If you didn't give them so much money, Huriye would have to sell that girl,' he said. 'She'd have no choice.'

So it was Rahul's fault this thug couldn't be alone with Huriye whenever he wanted, was it? How did he explain that there was no way he was going to stop employing the Can women without risking the ire of Şevket Sesler?

He said, 'Şaziye also helps Huriye Hanım look after young Hızır. I doubt she can manage without her.'

'Well, one day she'll have to,' Munir said as he drew still closer to the haberdasher's ear. 'One day soon, someone'll make her an offer she can't refuse before Şaziye gets too old.

You know all about that, don't you, Rahul Bey? With Neziye Hanım.'

'My daughter . . .'

'You need to stop paying them so the kid can move on,' Munir said. Then, with a curl of his lip, he was off.

Rahul Bey, alone outside his shop, wondered how this was going to play out. If he didn't stop using the Can women, would that put him in Şevket Sesler's eyeline? Or would he simply have to be more furtive in his future dealings with Huriye and her daughter?

Everyone had gone, except Didim. Gonca's older sister had all but taken up residence in her house since she'd started working on her wedding dress. The two women had always had a difficult relationship. Like Gonca, Didim had been married young to a man who had turned out to be a waste of space. The difference was that her husband, Tarik, was still with her. When they left Sulukule, Didim, Tarik and their children had holed up in the same derelict house in Tarlabaşı where they still lived. And although her children had now gone, Didim still sold flowers and cleaned for a living, while Tarik had graduated from booze to the local drug of choice, bonzai, a fearful combination of cannabinoid, kitchen herbs and spices, and oven cleaner. Consequently, there was no joy in her life. And although deep down she loved her, she took out all her bitterness on Gonca.

They sat in Gonca's salon, a small living room at the back of the house, next to her studio. While Didim sewed, Gonca considered her cursed bedcover and wondered whether Çetin Bey had made any progress in finding out who had defiled it. If he had, he would have called. She looked at her phone, which sat silently on the coffee table. But then maybe she had missed a call.

She had just picked up the phone when Didim said, 'Have you got pills for Mehmet Bey?'

It was such a non sequitur, Gonca said, 'Pills?'

'You know,' her sister said, 'pills all the men take now.'

'What are you talking about?'

'Pills as make men, you know, want you . . .'

Gonca felt her face flush.

'My man doesn't need Viagra!' she said.

'Maybe not now, but in the future. I mean, he's not a young man, and you're—'

'Oh, and because I am so old, he'll need Viagra when he goes off me!'

'No . . .'

'That's what you meant!' Gonca said. 'Twisted little whore! I know you listen at my bedroom door when Mehmet Bey and I are in bed! You're jealous!'

'Of a copper? Hah!'

'You should know how much pleasure we take from each other! You do know that! And you *are* jealous!' She picked up her tea glass and threw it at Didim. Fortunately it was empty, but it hit her in the eye.

'Ow!'

'Get out of my sight, you bitch!' Gonca yelled. 'Go back to your impotent bonzai-addict husband!'

Didim rubbed her eye. 'But Gonca, it's cold and dark . . .'

Even as a child, Didim had been a timorous little thing.

'I don't fucking care! Get out of my house and don't come back!'

'But it's—'

'So then . . .' Gonca looked at her sister with disgust. But underneath that, she was also worried. Although younger than Didim, she had always had to look after her, mainly because the list of things that frightened her was so long. 'Get to your room! Just go, not another word, and don't even think about speaking to me again until tomorrow!'

Didim picked up Gonca's dress, her needle, thread and the piece of sea silk she had been using, and slowly left the room. Since she'd been staying at the house, she'd used the bedroom that had been Asana's. However, unused to sleeping in a bed, she chose to lay her bedroll on the floor at the bottom of Gonca's eldest daughter's old bed.

Alone, Gonca put her hand up to her head and sighed. There was enough opposition to her marriage without her own family turning on her too. And that was aside from the doubts that plagued her in the small hours of the morning. And yet her lover had bewitched her just as surely as she had put him under her spell.

She heard the front door open and then close, but paid it no heed until she saw Mehmet Süleyman standing in front of her.

The scientists left. They took all their equipment, their boxes of samples and some larger, bulky items wrapped tightly in plastic hazmat bags. They left behind the uniformed police whose job it was to secure Fahrettin Müftüoğlu's ancient apartment block overnight. All his neighbours had been moved out during the afternoon, and so it was just the cops and the building, a dim street lamp and silence.

The men – on this occasion they were all men – stood around, occasionally looked at their phones, smoked, drank water. A few of them drank boza. Two of them, Constables Akar and Gölcük, spoke quietly to each other.

'What do you think about all this?' Mustafa Gölcük said to his younger colleague.

'What do you mean?' Kerem Akar was a dark man in his early twenties. He came originally from a Black Sea village and was assumed by many of his more streetwise İstanbul colleagues to be both unworldly and superstitious. Kerem knew that was how they felt and was wary of them, especially Gölcük.

'I mean,' Mustafa said, 'all the weird stuff coming out of that apartment.' He moved closer to his colleague. 'And he killed himself.'

'Maybe he wasn't right in the head,' Kerem said.

'And maybe he was mucking around with things he didn't understand.'

'Like what?'

'I've been in there,' Mustafa continued. 'Like a church it is. Angels and saints, statues. Müftüoğlu the jeweller was a Muslim, so they say. But what kind of Muslim makes such things, eh? What kind of Muslim takes his own life?'

'I don't . . .'

'I'm telling you, this place is haunted,' Mustafa said. 'Djinn and witches and the damned souls of apostates.'

Did he really believe what he was saying, or was he just coming out with this stuff to wind Kerem up? If it was the latter, the joke was wearing a bit thin. In fact, Kerem's father was an ex-professional soldier and a passionate follower of Ataturk who railed against every type of superstition. He and his uncovered wife all but owned their village. But Kerem had to be careful how he responded to Mustafa, who was popular amongst his colleagues.

He said, 'I'm sure Inspector Süleyman wouldn't put us in harm's way.'

'Süleyman? Ha!' Mustafa's voice dripped contempt. 'What does he know? Fancies himself an Ottoman! I don't believe it. Look at him. Drinks, swears, smokes, and women . . .' He rolled his eyes. 'He's been through every woman he's ever worked with. That won't stop just because he's marrying that old gypsy witch. I've seen him looking at Sergeant Yavaş, a covered lady. Dirty bastard!'

Not for the first time, Kerem noticed that the irony of Mustafa both smoking and swearing while he bad mouthed Süleyman was completely lost on the man.

'It's his soul,' he said. Unlike his parents, Kerem wasn't an atheist. He was, like his grandfather, a good Muslim. But also like his grandfather, he didn't feel that being religious gave him the right to criticise others. Mustafa could do what he liked, but sniping at Inspector Süleyman for his weaknesses wasn't right. Anyway, Kerem liked the boss. He was successful, educated and handsome, and he could be kind if you got on the right side of him. But most of all he was an honourable man who did his job because he cared.

Mustafa, shuffling from foot the foot, changed the subject.

'I need a piss,' he said.

And then he walked to the end of the alleyway and was gone.

She'd given him tea and made him lie down on the sofa. Now Gonca, sitting on the floor beside her lover, laid her head on his stomach.

'You work too hard, baby,' she said.

He'd come to make sure she was all right after he'd run in to take her jet earrings away earlier.

'I've yet to pick Patrick up from Çetin Bey's apartment,' he said. He stroked her hair.

'You could have phoned to ask me if I was OK,' Gonca said. 'You didn't need to come here.'

'I wanted to.' He moved over onto his side and kissed her. 'Any excuse to see you, touch you.'

Gonca felt her body tingle. They almost always made love when they were together. She hoped that would continue after their marriage. It hadn't for any of her sisters. All their men had either lost interest in sex or gone elsewhere. Didim was as bitter as she was because she'd not had a man for decades. Viagra! Gonca's man was aroused just lying next to her with his clothes on!

She said, 'I love you so much.'

He sat up. 'If I don't go now, I never will.'

'I know.' She stood up, helping him to his feet.

They stood, their arms around each other, kissing again. He broke away first.

'Sweetheart, if I could stay, you know I would.'

'I know.' She smiled.

'When we're married, I won't have to go.'

'When we're married, I won't let you,' she said.

Mustafa had gone somewhere. Either that or he had some really serious prostate trouble. Never mind about Süleyman, there were stories about Mustafa Gölcük and women. Kerem wasn't in the habit of listening to gossip, but he'd picked up some nuggets by osmosis. It was said Mustafa visited a woman in nearby Zeyrek. He was married with two kids. But then that was his own business, unless it impacted on those he worked with.

Kerem looked up at the building in front of him, in darkness, its entrances covered with tape. Typical of Mustafa to leave him effectively alone after filling his head with unsettling images. He might not be superstitious, but he was only human, and although he knew his brother officers were on the opposite side of the building, he felt exposed.

An hour passed. Reporting a colleague, for any reason, was not encouraged. And yet what if Mustafa had come to harm? Maybe he'd been attacked. Perhaps some local had taken against him pissing up the side of his house. But then again, if he was with his woman in Zeyrek, he'd lose his mind if Kerem ratted him out. His colleagues would never speak to him again.

At least Kerem could walk to the end of the alleyway and see whether he could see him. And so he did. Except that he never made it to the end of the alleyway, because someone stuck a knife into his ribs and killed him.

Chapter 12

'Will you be all right, Patrick?'

The boy had only just woken up when Mehmet Süleyman had burst into his bedroom to tell him that he had to go out. Ten minutes later, he was back again. This time Patrick was slightly more awake.

'I told you,' he said. 'Kemal and Hulusi are coming to pick me up at ten. Go!'

Mehmet Süleyman kissed his son on his head and left. It was only when he looked at the clock in the car that he had any notion of time. Four fifty-five – no wonder Patrick had looked so sleep sodden. He put the vehicle into drive and headed in the direction of the Ataturk Bridge and then Vefa. A young constable called Kerem Akar had been stabbed to death while guarding Fahrettin Müftüoğlu's building. In addition, according to Kerim Gürsel, who was already at the scene, Müftüoğlu's apartment had been broken into.

What had Akar's brother officers been doing? What, if anything, had been taken from the apartment, and why? There was still, as far as he knew, no news from the forensic laboratory about the toxicity or otherwise of the apartment. And just because ricin had not been found at the GülGül atelier, that didn't mean the same applied to Müftüoğlu's home. When he got to Vefa, could he even go into the building? He had to hope that Gürsel had some news, or, at the very least, some advice.

*

Rahul Mengüç threaded his way through the dark streets of Tarlabaşı towards his haberdashery shop. He didn't usually leave his house at such an early hour, but he hadn't been able to sleep and so what was the point of trying? Neziye too had been up for most of the night, working on the replacement bedcover for Gonca Hanım. It would still have to go to the Can women for embellishment; she would take it over when she got up. In the meantime, Rahul would busy himself in the shop. There were always too many things to be done. Maybe he could have some time alone to organise his order book.

Tarlabaşı could be a dangerous place in the small hours of the morning. He'd already had to dodge a couple of men he knew to be bonzai addicts ranging about in search of their next fix. But in his experience it wasn't as dangerous as some of the more lurid press reports made out. Ever since first Harun and now Şevket Sesler had taken over the running of so many Roma businesses, most folk had to be on their toes about making their next payment rather than roaming about at night looking for even more trouble. Rahul paid his dues, unlike some. Rambo Şekeroğlu had defaulted, but then he had his sister to bail him out. That whole situation puzzled Rahul. Some said that Gonca Hanım had cursed Harun Sesler, others that she had encouraged the woman who had killed him to take his life. Others still wouldn't hear a word against her.

To Rahul, Gonca had mainly been a good customer. She always paid her account on time and she spent big. But she was also a witch and so she wasn't a person to tangle with. Timid by nature, Rahul had always avoided confrontation where he could, which was why the whole situation with Munir Can had kept him awake.

His customers liked the work that Huriye and her daughter Şaziye did for him. And yet Munir Can, one of Şevket Sesler's most trusted men, wanted him to stop using them, and he didn't want to get into any sort of trouble with him. What to do?

He rounded the corner and saw his shop standing dark and shuttered but not unattended. Munir and Sesler were sitting on the steps leading up to the front door. Rahul flung himself back into the alleyway behind him before they saw him. But he listened to their voices. Talking about 'her' and how what she needed was a real man inside her.

He closed his eyes. Poor Huriye Can, whatever had she done to deserve this?

Süleyman looked up at the building. One of the doors on the ground floor that had been taped up now wasn't, and it stood open.

The tall man beside Kerim Gürsel was almost unrecognisable without his hazmat gear. Süleyman said, 'Is it safe to go inside?'

Dr Yaşova, who with his team had been working through the night on samples taken from the Vefa apartment, said, 'So far we've found no traces of ricin in any of the samples. Doesn't mean it isn't present. As you know, Inspector, that apartment is a large and disorganised site. There is still much work to do.'

'Yes, Doctor, it's also somewhere valuable artefacts reside,' Süleyman said. 'Artefacts left *in situ* when ricin was discovered.'

The larger items – the St Foy statue, the winged angel – had already been removed prior to the alert, but the place was still dotted with pieces of jewellery and some smaller precious articles. Süleyman hoped they had all been photographed either by the scientific team or prior to the toxin alert.

'Do you intend to go in?' the doctor asked.

'On the assumption that whoever killed Constable Akar may also have broken into the property, I have little choice.'

'Inspector Süleyman!'

He turned. Out of the tent erected over the body came a large man in white coveralls.

'Dr Sarkissian.' He walked over to the Armenian.

'Stabbed,' the doctor said. 'Between the ribs, left side. Deep, made quite a mess. I've a notion why that might be, but won't know until I examine the poor boy.'

'Theories?'

'One, but I don't want to pre-empt the post-mortem.' He looked at his watch. 'Can I call it for ten?'

'Fine. Although I can't guarantee to attend in person. Depends what happens here.'

'Ah, your deadly toxin situation,' the doctor said. 'Your jeweller was an interesting fellow, wasn't he?'

'Rather too interesting,' Süleyman said. 'Thank you, Doctor.'

He returned to Kerim Gürsel and Dr Yaşova. Looking at his colleague, he said, 'I believe you knew Constable Akar rather better than I did, Kerim Bey.'

'I did,' Gürsel said. 'Black Sea boy. Some of his colleagues were less than kind about his rural roots.'

'Most of them come from Nowhere Anatolia too,' Süleyman said.

Kerim shrugged. 'You know how they are. Ten minutes in the city and they're all İstanbullus. Akar was a bright kid. Military family, parents live in a village in Trabzon province. I'll make contact with the nearest jandarma, get someone to go out to them in person.'

'Good.'

Dr Yaşova cut in. 'If you do need to enter the building, Inspector Süleyman, I will have to insist you wear full hazmat protection and that I accompany you.'

Süleyman nodded.

'I have everything we need in my car.'

'Good. If you get ready then, Doctor, I will follow shortly. I just need to speak to my colleague first.'

The doctor left to return to his car.

When they were alone, Süleyman said to Kerim Gürsel, 'Who discovered the body?'

'His partner, Constable Mustafa Gölcük. The story is he went off to take a piss, five minutes at the most, came back and found Akar dead. Yelled for help, which meant the other officers ran to his assistance, then called it in.'

'Mmm.'

Süleyman eyed a man in his forties he assumed was Gölcük being comforted by brother officers across the road. The inspector had heard of him. Word was he was inclined to laziness.

Articulating what Süleyman had been thinking, Kerim added, 'None of them claims to have seen anyone in the vicinity. But then they also claim they didn't notice that the crime-scene tape was missing and a door was open.'

A knock on İkmen's bedroom door brought him out of a dream where he was cleaning endless rows of toilets. He thanked a god he didn't believe in for not making that his reality and said, 'Who is it?'

'Çiçek.'

His eldest daughter had come home to live with her father after her mother had died in 2016. Together with İkmen's trans-sexual cousin Samsun, she was one of three permanent members of the household.

'What is it?' İkmen asked as he lit a cigarette.

'If you want my hairdressing skills, you'd better get up,' Çiçek said. 'I've got to leave for work in half an hour.'

And then he remembered. It was Tuesday. At midnight, together with Atyom Mafyan, he had to go to Şevket Sesler's poker school in Tarlabaşı. But he couldn't go as Çetin İkmen, because everyone knew who that was. Çetin Oz, however, was another matter, and Çetin Oz wasn't a man with a moustache. Shuffling on an old dressing gown over his pyjamas, İkmen staggered out of his bedroom and into the kitchen, where Çiçek had set up her barber's equipment.

As he sat down, his daughter said, 'Do you really think no one will recognise you just because you have no moustache?'

'I've not been clean shaven since I courted your mother,' İkmen said. 'Only your Uncle Halıl, Arto Sarkissian and possibly Samsun can remember me without it. I'm making the supreme sacrifice for Gonca Hanım's peace of mind.'

Çiçek began snipping at the ends of his moustache.

'Is it just the moustache, or . . .'

'Your brother Bülent has loaned me one of his ridiculously tight suits. I will look like a living pencil.'

Çiçek laughed. Bülent looked almost exactly like their father, but thirty years younger. He too was skinny, if slightly taller than İkmen. She tested the electric clippers. Now that the ends had been trimmed, she began to take her father's famous moustache away.

Later, after Çiçek had gone and İkmen found himself staring at an unrecognisable face in his shaving mirror, Samsun came into the kitchen to make tea. 'It doesn't suit you, you know. Puts years on you. And you look like Dad.'

Looking like his long-dead Uncle Ahmet wasn't exactly an insult, but it wasn't a compliment either. İkmen wondered how long his moustache would take to grow back.

The scene-of-crime officers who had followed Süleyman and Dr Yaşova into Fahrettin Müftüoğlu's apartment were accustomed to wearing coveralls, visors and respirators. Süleyman was not. Hearing his own laboured breathing wasn't pleasant and, despite the cold weather, he was hot.

As they had entered the building, the doctor had pointed out some bloody footprints on the floor. Upstairs, the door to the apartment had been hanging off its hinges. And none of the officers had heard anything? Something was wrong here, and it wasn't just the fact that the place had very obviously been turned over. There had still been much to investigate in Müftüoğlu's apartment when Süleyman had last seen it, but it hadn't been this disorganised.

When he eventually emerged from the scene, he spoke to Kerim Gürsel.

'We're going to need to interview all our men separately,' he said.

Kerim tipped his head towards the building. 'Much damage?'

'Enough. If none of the men heard it, they must be either deaf or dead.' He drew nearer to his colleague. 'I'd like to interview Constable Gölcük myself. I've a feeling he may have been selective with the truth. Also, Kerim Bey, I know my own reputation. They're more frightened of me than they are of you.'

Kerim laughed. 'I don't know how to take that!'

'Take it as a compliment. I'll go back to headquarters and take Gölcük with me. Then I'll send you some fresh blood to replace the others.'

'İkmen!' She sounded bright – and it was only 9 a.m. What was going on?

'Gonca Hanım,' he said. 'Still the middle of the night for you, isn't it?'

'I'm in marriage mode,' she said. 'So much to do and not enough time.'

'What do you want me for?' he asked. Because he was going to have a late night, he had hoped he might be able to catch some more sleep after Çiçek had left for work.

'I've had a call from Rahul Bey,' she said.

'The haberdasher.'

'The same. Apparently my replacement bedcover should be ready by tomorrow evening.'

157

'That's good.' But why had she needed to phone and tell him?

'He also told me that when he went to his shop this morning, he found two men sitting on the steps. One was Şevket Sesler and the other was Munir Can, Huriye Can's brother-in-law. They were drinking Efes and talking, loudly.'

'Annoying, probably, but so what?' İkmen said.

'Çetin Bey, I know you are still active on my behalf, regarding my original bedcover, and I know that Munir Can is a person of interest for you . . .'

'Yes.'

'Well, according to Rahul Bey, Sesler most certainly knows that his thug is having sex with Huriye Hanım. It seems Can now wants to marry her. Sesler approves.'

'Does he,' İkmen said. 'But Munir Can is already married . . .'

'So, I've heard, are several very prominent men in society.'

'He must have won big at poker to be able to support multiple women. He's fucking poor Huriye Hanım anyway. Why does he want to marry her?'

'I've no idea,' Gonca said. 'Just passing on information.'

And then she was gone, her head and her day no doubt filled with wedding dresses, beauty treatments and flowers.

He'd consulted the professor on several occasions over the years. An expert in early Middle Eastern art, Bilal Gezmiş had spent some time with the photographs Haluk Keleş had sent him of the angel figure from the Vefa apartment.

'It looks modern to me,' the professor said. 'As in not ancient.'

Keleş, in his usual position in his office, with his feet up on his desk, phone propped between his head and his shoulder, asked, 'Why?'

'The face,' Gezmiş replied.

'What about it?'

'Don't you think it resembles someone?'

'No. Do you?'

'Yes. The actor Rudolph Valentino.'

'Who?'

'Italian Hollywood silent movie star. You're probably too young to know about such things.'

'Never heard of him.'

'Famous for playing romantic sheikhs. Google him. I tell you the resemblance is striking.'

'I will.'

'Is it solid gold, do you know?' Gezmiş asked.

'I don't know yet. Being tested.'

'Well, let me know when you do,' the academic said.

'Yeah.' And then, continuing the movie-based theme, Keleş said, 'When I first saw it, it reminded me of *Raiders of the Lost Ark*.'

The professor laughed. 'Load of nonsense. Real Ark of the Covenant, if it exists at all, is in Ethiopia, hidden in a church. No one except some priests have ever seen it.'

Haluk Keleş sighed, put the phone down and then said, 'Fuck.'

Looking more closely at the images of the angel, he could actually see what the professor meant about it looking modern. But until an approximate age was attributed to the item, no one knew. The statue of St Foy was another matter. The French still had their statue *in situ* in Conques, and tests were continuing on the İstanbul version. Keleş felt a tingle all over his body. What was this? A case of straightforward forgery, or forgery allied to theft?

The apartment Canan Müftüoğlu had said she lived in was rented out to an Osman Aslan. Details Ömer Mungun had discovered about her marriage recorded her unmarried surname as Aktepe. Logically, her father would be called Muharrem Aktepe, but was that his real name, and who was Osman Aslan?

Ömer had heard about the death of Constable Akar. He hadn't known him, but he did know his partner, Mustafa Gölcük. Middle aged and disappointed, to Ömer he always looked as if he had a bad smell under his nose. It was said the boss had brought him in to ask questions about the incident. Word was that Gölcük had left Akar on his own outside the Vefa apartment the previous night.

The landlord of Osman Aslan's building was a woman called Müge Topbaş. She sounded as if she either smoked sixty cigarettes a day or was as old as time. Or both. Her entire philosophy of landlordism was summed up in her opening gambit: 'As long as they pay their rent and don't burn the place down, I don't care who lives there.'

'Yes, but hanım, do you *know* who lives there?' Ömer asked.

'Sometimes,' she said. 'I don't go there much now.'

Müge Hanım lived far from Sarıgöl, in upscale Suadiye on the Asian side of the Bosphorus.

'Do you have an agent, or . . .'

'My son collects the rent,' she said. 'He's young and can put up with a journey into hell.'

Ömer frowned. 'You don't think much of Sarıgöl, hanım?'

'I was born in that building,' she said. 'Then I found myself a good Turkish husband and moved out. That was a smart move. Then he died and I found myself with three buildings in Kadıköy. So I sold one, and bought the apartment I live in now and that dump in Sarıgöl where I was born. And before you ask, Sergeant, I bought it because I wanted to show all those scumbags back there that I had made something of myself. I am not a nice woman.'

'Madam . . .'

'There's a type of Kurd, Sergeant Mungun – and I know from your name that your family come from the east – that enjoys pinning all their disappointments on the Turks. My parents were like that,' she said. 'But in life you have to make your own

160

fortune. I did. Anyway, what's been happening in my building that I have to talk to you?'

'We just need to know who lives there,' he said. 'The tenant is named as Osman Aslan.'

'Then that's who lives there.'

'You're sure?'

'No. But I can ask my son. As I said, I never go there. I'm seventy. I don't need to talk to a load of bonzai addicts to know that life can be hard.'

Ömer wondered what Müge Topbaş looked like. An elderly Kurdish woman who had married out of one of İstanbul's ghettos. She was either, he reckoned, all sharp Chanel suits and Botox, or she was a heavily covered woman, dispensing her truth like the Oracle of Delphi.

He thanked her and then addressed the subject of Canan Müftüoğlu's father. Had Müge Hanım ever heard the name Muharrem Aktepe?

She laughed. 'You ask me that?' she said. 'Clearly, Sergeant, you and your fellows need to get yourselves out to Sarıgöl more often!'

'Why?'

'Let me ask you a question,' she said. 'Do you speak Zaza?'

'Yes,' he replied.

She laughed. 'Mungun, such a very foreign name around these parts. Well, Sergeant, you take your language skills and go and speak to the Zaza Kurds of Sarıgöl, or in fact anywhere in this city, about Muharrem Aktepe. Go and look at the apartment he owns in Tarabya. Top floor of a huge white yalı. He owns it. Why would he want to go back to Sarıgöl to live in that open sewer?'

'So he did live in your building at one time, hanım?'

'Oh yes,' she said. 'I grew up with him. But he got out, just as I did, and for that, I admire him.'

161

'And for what do you not admire him?'

Müge Hanım sighed. 'Where do you want me to start? On condition, of course, that you heard none of this from me.'

The way Mustafa Gölcük was behaving, he was either being insubordinate (Süleyman knew he didn't like him) or he was terrified.

'I told you, I went to relieve myself,' he said, looking as far away from Süleyman as he could.

The inspector watched him. 'I went to relieve myself, *sir*,' he said.

Gölcük muttered, 'Sir . . .'

'How long did you leave Constable Akar on his own?'

Gölcük shrugged.

'Answer me!' Süleyman said.

'I just did.'

'No you didn't. You shrugged in the same way my teenage son might do if he is feeling particularly moody. You're forty-six . . .'

'I don't know!' Gölcük said. 'Have you asked the others?'

'The others' were the three officers who had been stationed around the far side of the building.

'No, but I'm sure you've spoken to them,' Süleyman said. 'I saw you all huddled together when I arrived.'

'They were helping me.'

'I'm sure they were.'

Gölcük put his head down.

'How long?'

'Ten minutes! At the most.'

Whoever had broken into the Müftüoğlu apartment had taken three items of jewellery and counting. Not valuable in the scheme of what else had been discovered, but including a haul of two-and-a-half-lira gold Meskuk coins traditionally used for investment purposes. None of Gölcük's brother officers had seen or heard anything untoward, or so they said, but if whoever had taken the items had done so in the complete blackness of a sealed apartment, he or she must have had at least some notion of what to look for and where to find it. In addition, Süleyman was fairly sure that Gölcük had taken more than ten minutes away from his duty, even if he had nothing to do with the break-in.

'Where were you?' he said.

'I told you, I was—'

'Relieving yourself, yes,' he said. 'But in what way?'

This got the man's attention. Süleyman didn't routinely listen to gossip, but it was well known that Gölcük had a mistress in nearby Zeyrek. He even knew her name, which was Fındık.

'You have,' he said, 'a lady friend in Zeyrek. A florist.'

Gölcük said nothing.

'And far be it from me to criticise your personal life, but it has come to my attention that you spend a lot of time with this woman.'

There was a long pause. Süleyman imagined he could hear the cogs in Gölcük's brain working their way through his various options, all of which were limited.

Fearing that the silence might become permanent, the inspector said, 'I will search your apartment.'

'For what?'

He pushed the photographs of the missing items that had been recorded before the break-in across his desk.

'These,' he said.

'I've never seen those,' Gölcük said. 'I didn't break into that building!'

'Then tell me what you were doing. Because believe me when I say that if you lie to me, not only will I know, but I will also punish you and your three colleagues. The security of a crime scene aside, a man died last night. Think about how that man's

163

family must be feeling now. Constable Akar was one of us and he was very young. His death—'

'It was his time!'

'Whether that is so or not, he died unlawfully and it is up to us to avenge him,' Süleyman said. 'Now tell me the truth, unless you want to have to tell your wife and children that you no longer have a job.'

Constables Tan, Alp and Tuncer had returned to headquarters – no doubt to be grilled by Süleyman – leaving Kerim Gürsel with a cohort of replacements. Dr Yaşova and his team had resumed their work when Inspector Haluk Keleş arrived.

Without preamble, he said to Kerim, 'I hear we lost a kid last night. *Başınız sağ olsun.*'

Kerim responded to this exhortation to be healthy with the customary '*Amin*'. Then he said, 'Young lad from the Black Sea, twenty-three. I asked the local jandarma to go round to tell the parents in person.' He looked at his watch. 'I imagine they've been by now. To lose a child must be . . .' He shook his head.

Keleş lit a cigarette. 'Know what happened?'

'Not yet. I'm attending his post-mortem in under an hour with Sergeant Yavaş. It seems his partner, Constable Gölcük, left him alone. Went to relieve himself, he says.'

'Long enough for someone to break into the apartment?'

Kerim shrugged. 'Mehmet Bey is questioning Gölcük and the others. Constable Tan, together with a watchman, was the officer who called in Müftüoğlu's suicide originally.'

Neither said anything, although a look passed between them that they both recognised. Süleyman fitted all too easily into the role of brutal interrogator.

Keleş nodded towards the listing wooden apartment building. 'Can we go in yet?'

'No.'

'Why not? What the fuck are the scientists doing?'

'Curse of the hoarder,' Kerim said. 'You know what it's like in there. Dr Yaşova and his team are trying to ensure there's nothing toxic lurking behind a wardrobe stuffed with coats or a floor littered with rat droppings, slivers of gold and a million overflowing ashtrays.'

'I've been speaking to one of my academic contacts,' Keleş said. 'Reckons that angel statue is modern. Reckons it looks like some old movie star.'

Kerim laughed.

'Made me think,' Keleş continued. 'If Müftüoğlu was knocking out copies of famous works of art, then what is the angel based on? I've looked at a lot of golden angels online all over the world in the last few days, but I can't find that one.'

'None with movie star looks then?'

This time Keleş laughed. 'No,' he said. 'But not just that.'

'Then what?'

'If our St Foy turns out to be a very good copy of the original, maybe Müftüoğlu made it to order, or maybe he or someone else planned to steal the original and replace it with ours. But if, as I suspect, the angel is made of solid gold, why make it if it doesn't resemble anything else?'

Kerim said, 'Art?'

'No, no, no. I looked up this old movie star, Valentino, and it does look strikingly like him., But artistically it's not that hot, believe me.'

'Better than I could do,' Kerim said.

Keleş shook his head. 'With respect, Kerim Bey, you're not an artist and neither am I. But I know art. I know what's good, and that isn't. If Müftüoğlu made both those pieces, he was having a bad day when he made the angel. St Foy is fabulous, but Valentino... Well, he's a bit rough, artistically, and I can't figure out why.'

Chapter 13

'It's called the Sarkis Bey Yalı,' Ömer Mungun said. 'It's in Tarabya.'

'I know it,' Süleyman said. 'Not far from the Grand Tarabya Hotel. Built I believe for an Armenian engineer.'

'Yes, sir. But now it's been made into apartments. There are six, plus the penthouse, which is where Muharrem Aktepe and his family live.'

Süleyman steepled his fingers underneath his chin. 'And Aktepe is a Kurd from Sarıgöl.'

'A Zaza Kurd, yes,' Ömer said. 'There are a lot of them in Gaziosmanpaşa district.'

'Mmm.'

'He bought the apartment in 2006,' he continued.

'What does Muharrem Bey do for a living?'

'Well, this is interesting,' Ömer said. 'His mother was a Turk, apparently, and while it's said he identifies as a Kurd, as a young man, in line with her wishes, he became a pehlivan.'

Süleyman raised an eyebrow. 'The ancestor sport. How very noble.'

Pehlivans, or oil wrestlers, had been feted since early Ottoman times. Every year there was a huge competition just outside the city of Edirne called the Kırkpınar Wrestling Tournament. Pehlivans who achieved success in this competition and became başpehlivan, chief wrestler, were treated like national heroes.

'He wasn't successful,' Ömer continued. 'A lot of injuries, although not from sport – Muharrem Aktepe was a street fighter, always in trouble as a youngster. But that didn't stop his involvement with the oil-wrestling world. He entered several young lads, unsuccessfully. Then in 2010, the only boy he had who was beginning to do well got dope tested and failed.'

'So where does his money come from?' Süleyman asked.

'Müge Hanım, fellow Zaza speaker and landlady, says that nobody really knows. He doesn't work, spends a lot of time at his local mosque, does nice things for people. Bought a wheelchair for a disabled girl, et cetera, et cetera . . .'

'And?'

'And, sir, the word is that Muharrem Bey is big into gambling. Started off, it's said, in the oil-wrestling world. He took a few dives for money when he was a pehlivan and got a taste for the cash and the buzz. He's a fixer. If you want to bet on something – doesn't matter what it is – Muharrem Bey will organise that and take his cut.'

'And manipulate the result,' Süleyman said.

'So it would seem.'

Gonca Şekeroğlu didn't really have female friends. She had her sisters and her daughters, and then there were other women, whom in general she didn't trust. Exceptions to this were a very stylish woman called Hürrem Solak, and one of the Beyoğlu falçıs, Buket Teyze.

It was traditional for brides to go to the hamam with all their girlfriends to bathe, gossip and make themselves clean and beautiful for their wedding, but Gonca went with just these two. Her fiancé had hired the Gedik Paşa Hamamı from nine in the morning until four in the afternoon, and it was up to Gonca whom she invited, even if the hamam staff were a little taken aback by such a small party. With instructions from Mehmet Bey that the ladies be treated like sultanas, they were first served tea and breakfast in the marble and ancient wood reception room. Lying on elegant couches, the three of them helped themselves to platefuls of cheese, bread, rose jam, egg and salad, followed by sweet sticky pastries.

Hürrem, who had been Gonca's best friend at school, said, 'Do you remember when we all used to come here as children? Every Friday, all the mothers and the children, all eating, drinking and gossiping.'

'All staring at my mother,' Gonca said.

'You were the only Romas who came here,' Hürrem replied.

'My mother would go where she pleased.'

Hürrem laughed. 'And because we went to the same school, everyone gawped at how you and I talked so easily.'

'My mother was horrified that I'd made friends with a Turk,' Gonca said.

'But we got on, right from the start.'

'And you weren't a bitch like all those Roma girls.'

'And then you met me,' Buket Teyze said.

Gonca put an arm around the older woman's neck. 'Ah,' she said, 'a young, beautiful Turkish wife and mother you were then. I thought you were so glamorous!'

'And you gave us sweets!' Hürrem said. 'With two tiny boys running around your skirts, you gave sweets to little girls you didn't know.'

'You weren't that little,' Buket said. 'And I wasn't much older myself!' She shook her head. 'My Selim, my soul, teaching at the university now! Who would have thought!'

Nobody talked about Buket's younger son, who had ended up in prison.

Gonca reached out to both of her friends and took their hands. 'So here we are, my lovely ladies, and it's my bridal bath!'

'So every tiny speck of body hair must be hunted down and

plucked, Gonca Hanım!' Buket said. 'I will make it my personal mission to ensure your husband finds not one!'

The young constable's post-mortem had been upsetting. Not just because whoever had killed him had made a mess – the wound was ragged, gaping and ugly. It was the boy's youth that had caused both Kerim Gürsel and Eylul Yavaş to shed a tear. The lad's father was on his way, and it was going to be hard to know what to say when he arrived.

When the post-mortem was over, a short conversation with Mehmet Bey revealed that Mustafa Gölcük had lied. When he should have been with his partner, he'd been fucking his girlfriend in Zeyrek. What Süleyman had done or said to make him come clean was something probably only Mehmet Bey and Gölcük would ever know. Now, having spoken to the girlfriend to confirm Gölcük's story, Süleyman had sent the officer home pending an investigation.

Kerim had heard a rumour that someone he had met a few years before was back in İstanbul after a long period of compassionate leave in his home land, and so, together with Eylul, he stopped off in Beyoğlu to see him. He had questions about art and belief, and Juan-Maria Montoya, the Catholic Bishop of İstanbul, was a person he had come to respect. A few years before, he had helped the police solve the murder of a young girl who claimed to experience visions.

The bishop took Kerim and Eylul to his apartment, which was hidden amongst parish offices and public rooms beside the Church of St Antoine on İstiklal Caddesi. He led them into a book-lined room that smelled of cigarettes and coffee and then asked his housekeeper to kindly provide both for his guests, plus cake.

An attractive man in his fifties or sixties, Bishop Montoya came originally from Mexico, via England. When they had first met, he and Kerim had spoken English to each other. Now, however, Montoya was comfortable with Turkish.

Before their refreshments arrived, they all talked of mundane things and the bishop asked after both İkmen and Süleyman. However, once drinks had been served, Montoya said, 'So, Inspector, how can I help you?'

It was refreshing to be with someone who came straight to the point, and so Kerim returned the favour. When he had first met him, Kerim had always addressed this man as Bishop Montoya. In the intervening time, however, he had learned that that was impolite. He said, 'Your Excellency, I'd like if you have the time to ask you about religious statues.'

Montoya smiled. 'You really don't have to call me "your Excellency", you know, Inspector,' he said. '"Bishop" will do.'

'Ah . . .'

'But thank you for taking the time to discover the approved form of address. Now, what do you want to know about statues?'

'Well . . . actually about sacred relics.'

'Ah, so that is different,' the bishop said. 'A relic is something physically connected to a saint, or indeed to the Holy Family. This may be a part of that person's body, it may be some fabric from their clothing, a shoe, a piece of writing . . .'

'We have the relics of our Prophet in the Topkapi Museum,' Eylul said.

'Yes. I have seen them.'

'Bishop,' Kerim said, 'what do you think about authenticity? It seems to me that in your religion, you have a lot of relics. How do you know whether they are genuine?'

The bishop called their attention to the cake his housekeeper had brought. 'Please help yourselves,' he said. 'Katerina Hanım will be disappointed if we don't eat. This cake is, I believe, called revani; you will be familiar with it.'

Semolina cake was one of Kerim's favourites, so he took a piece. 'Thank you.'

The bishop, who also took a slice, said, 'Well, you ask a big and difficult question, Inspector. Many of our relics are so old, we no longer know really what they are. Some have stories connected to them that may help. Some, like the Turin Shroud, the Vatican has given permission to be scientifically tested. In my own country, we have the tilma, the cloak of the Blessed Juan Diego, an Aztec who had visions of the Blessed Virgin in 1531. The Virgin imprinted a picture of herself on the cloak that is venerated as Our Lady of Guadeloupe. It is important for all Mexicans, a symbol around which we can gather. It is like your flag. But is it genuine?' He shrugged. 'I don't know. I don't even know whether that matters. Faith is the important thing. People see the tilma and they are comforted, reassured and uplifted. What is not to like?'

'I agree,' Kerim said. 'But you must know that if you go online, you can find thousands of relics for sale. Most are Christian.'

'And all are almost certainly fake.'

'Yes, but what if someone buys one, maybe with their life's savings . . .'

'*Caveat emptor,*' the bishop said. 'Buyer beware. I cannot countenance such things.'

'But if "official" relics cannot be vouched for . . .'

'The power of prayer over hundreds of years is by way of being their authenticity certificate.'

'Yes, but, Bishop, what if someone made a copy of a well-known relic and then put that in the place of the genuine article?'

Montoya shook his head. 'Why would anyone do such a thing?'

'Rich private collectors will do almost anything to get hold of artworks that interest them,' Kerim said. 'We know that much of what was looted from Syria and Iraq by Daesh has found its way into private hands.'

'That is appalling.'

'So why not create relics to either sell on as the real thing, or steal originals and then replace them with copies?'

'There is nothing to stop such unscrupulous behaviour, no,' the bishop said. 'But if such a collector was truly a person of faith, I believe that he would know. However accurate the execution, however faithful the materials used, I think he would know, because I think I would.'

Kerim nodded. 'Bishop Montoya, may I take up a little more of your time?'

One of the waiters at his favourite bar, the Mozaik, laughed when it finally dawned on him who was sitting at one of his outside tables.

'I've never seen you without your moustache, Çetin Bey,' he said when İkmen ordered a coffee.

He realised that his face was cold, and thought about wrapping a scarf around his mouth, but if he did that, he couldn't smoke. Also, when the time came, if he covered the lower half of his face, people might well recognise him. So he was stuck with it. Moreover, he'd have to go to Süleyman's wedding with a naked face, which did not fill him with confidence.

While he smoked and drank coffee after coffee, he made a phone call. It was all very well Gonca telling him what Rahul Mengüç had experienced in the early hours of the morning, but he wanted to talk to the old man in person.

After passing a few niceties with the haberdasher, İkmen asked, 'I hear you overheard a conversation on your doorstep this morning.'

The old man sighed. 'I assume Gonca Hanım has been in touch with you,' he said. 'Munir Can and friend.' He didn't use Sesler's name, afraid of who might be listening.

'Yes,' İkmen said. 'I thought Munir Bey was married.'

'He is,' Rahul Bey said.

'Officially?'

'Yes. He married Iris Hanım, daughter of Mihai the Ursari.'

'Who?'

'Ursari is what they call bear men in Romania,' Rahul Bey said. 'Mihai's father came here after the Second World War. It's said he only just survived the Porajmos.'

İkmen sighed. Why hadn't he ever taken the time to learn even a few words of Romani?

'The Holocaust,' Rahul Bey interpreted. 'The family settled in Sulukule. Orthodox Christians, not that we cared. Munir married Mihai's youngest daughter years ago. But as I told you before, it was always his brother's wife he wanted. Now it seems he wishes to marry her.'

'Can he?' İkmen asked. 'I mean it will still be illegal, but what about your tradition?'

'Yes. And if Sesler says it will be so, then it will happen. Remember, Ursari are not like us, Çetin Bey. They are foreigners, outsiders. We Roma marry our own. Munir Can's father, Talaat, made him marry Iris because it was said Mihai had a lot of gold.'

'Did he?' İkmen asked.

'No. A miser he was, a rich man he was not. But Iris was beautiful once. Not now, of course. Now she's just like all the other mothers of ten-plus children round here, hollowed out and old. Gonca Hanım excepted.'

İkmen smiled. 'Ah, Gonca Hanım is, well, special,' he said.

'Yesterday I had a conversation with Munir myself,' Rahul Bey said. 'What he said to his friend this morning underlined that. He wants his brother's woman and yet Munir seems to be intent upon removing the daughter, Şaziye, from the family. The girl is twelve, and he kept on about getting her married. I mean, if you ask me, were I to be considering marrying Huriye Hanım, I'd rather get rid of all those raucous boys than the girl. She's a delicate, quiet and really skilful little thing.'

'And you got the impression that Şevket Sesler was all for this plan?'

'Oh, yes,' he said. 'He'll do anything for his men. They were of course his father's men, and so Şevket Bey is to some extent proving himself to them. Loyalty cuts both ways, Çetin Bey.'

'Poor woman.'

'At least with Munir she'll have enough to eat. I wish I could afford to pay her more, but I'm cut to the bone on my margins . . .'

Life wasn't easy for anyone, what with food prices rising all the time.

İkmen changed the subject. 'What do you know about this poker school Şevket Sesler runs, Rahul Bey?'

'Ah, that's a cancer in that family,' Rahul Bey said. 'Poker, gambling. Harun Bey was useless and Şevket Bey is no better. This is where Munir Can has Şevket by the balls.'

'He plays well.'

'He's like a devil. People think that the Tuesday school is just a casual affair because it happens every week and anyone who can raise the stake can take part. I think this is prejudice against the Roma. All over the city there are schools run by Turks, Armenians, Jews. These are seen as serious schools, where men wear suits and speak perfect Turkish. But make no mistake, Çetin Bey, the Tuesday school is serious business, and if you are thinking of participating in it, then I hope you have very deep pockets.'

The woman who sat at the front desk and took hamam entrance fees and bookings was a large female, swathed in a huge variety of scarves, called Şişman Hanım – 'fat lady'. What her real name was, nobody knew, but just before Gonca and her friends finished their leisurely breakfast, she came over and gave the gypsy a parcel.

Gonca looked confused. 'For me?'

'An old lady just brought it for you,' Şişman Hanım said.

'An old lady?'

'I don't know who she was.'

Şişman Hanım walked away. Wrapped in brown paper, the parcel was an almost perfect square.

'So open it then,' Buket Teyze said.

Gonca, one of whose many virtues was not patience, pulled the parcel open. What she found was an ornate wooden box.

Hürrem Hanım, who knew about such things on account of having a passion for antiques, said, 'Oh, that's lovely! Look, there's Ottoman script carved on the lid. Must be old.'

Gonca lifted the lid. There was a green velvet bag inside. She took it out and undid the drawstrings that held it closed, then put her hand inside and drew out a necklace. Suspended from an elegant gold chain were three emeralds, two small ones either side of one in the middle that was tear shaped and very large.

Buket Teyze's eyes widened and she swore, then apologised. 'Emeralds!'

'Must be worth a fortune,' Hürrem said. 'Oh Gonca, is it from Mehmet Bey?'

'I don't know.' Gonca was in shock.

Buket Teyze, seeking answers, looked inside the box and took out a small envelope with Gonca's name written on the front.

'There's a note,' she said.

Gonca took it from her, and, knowing that her friends would be dying to learn what was in it, read it aloud:

Gonca Hanım

It is traditional for the prospective mother-in-law of a bride to give her a gift when she attends the hamam prior to her wedding. This emerald necklace is therefore my gift to you. It belonged to my husband's grandmother, Nemike

Sultan. I thought it would be appropriate for you given the fact that while Nemike was the daughter of a sultan, it is said in the family that her mother was one of your people. I would deem it a kindness if you would wear this necklace when you marry my son.

Nur Hanım

Gonca didn't know what to say, unlike Buket Teyze, who said, 'Well, put it on then!'

The scientific team were leaving as Süleyman and Ömer Mungun arrived.

Bringing them up to speed, Haluk Keleş said, 'Safe now, apparently.'

'Did they find anything?' Süleyman asked.

'No.'

'So we started with potassium cyanide – a substance used routinely by jewellers – and there we remain. Where did the ricin found at the atelier fit in?'

'Who knows?'

Ömer Mungun said, 'Perhaps it came from one of the other people working for Atyom Bey?'

'Those earrings had been made by Fahrettin Müftüoğlu,' Süleyman said.

'We only have Atyom Bey's word for that.'

Both senior officers looked at Sergeant Mungun.

'I'm just speculating,' he said.

'No, you're right to do so,' Süleyman said.

'Did you hear anything back about Gonca Hanım's earrings?' Keleş asked.

'Yes. Clean.' Süleyman sighed. 'Such a small amount of ricin. Why? Were those pieces targeted at someone?' He looked up. 'The pieces that were stolen last night included jewellery . . .'

Keleş took his phone out and they all gathered around to look at his screen.

'Two pairs of earrings,' he said. 'Modern. One solid gold, the other a line of drop rubies. Not worth a life . . .'

'There was a considerable amount of gold, too.'

'Still not worth a life.'

'I agree,' Süleyman said.

'And yet,' Keleş continued, 'if whoever stole those items had broken in a day or two earlier, maybe it could have been.'

'What?'

Keleş smiled and put a hand on Süleyman's shoulder.

'Just me being my fucking flippant self, Mehmet Bey,' he said. 'I don't mean it. The big brains of the science world got back to me today and told me that angel figure is pure gold. No value calculation on that yet, but I'm working on it.'

Süleyman said, 'That's astonishing. But by value, what do you mean?'

'At the moment, the meltdown value,' Keleş said. 'As I told Kerim Bey, I can't find anything that corresponds to the figure so far. I'm wondering whether it's something that exists in private hands. If it's Syrian or Iraqi, maybe the original was stolen to order, but then again, maybe it *is* original. Sadly for me, one of my tame academics who knows about this stuff made a comparison between our angel's face and an old Hollywood movie star called Valentino. Can't get it out of my fucking mind.'

Süleyman said, 'Valentino? My God, wasn't he a silent movie star?'

177

Chapter 14

Bishop Montoya crouched down on his haunches and looked into the statue's fixed gaze. To Kerim Gürsel and Eylul Yavaş, the figure of St Foy was a disturbing presence. They were not alone. The bishop frowned.

'There is a piece of St Foy's skull in the head . . .' he said.

'There's something in there, according to the scan,' Kerim said. 'We are waiting on scans of the supposed original in France for comparison.'

Eylul, who had been considering the statue for some time, said, 'It looks Byzantine to me. The opulence, there's a sort of almost Roman characteristic to it.'

The bishop stood up. 'It was established some years ago that the head of the reliquary had been constructed from a Roman death mask. As for opulence? I agree that the Byzantines were probably the masters of that, but we in the Western Church have played our part too. Conques is on a very famous pilgrimage route to the Spanish shrine of Santiago de Compostela. In the past, those walking this route were expected to make an offering to St Foy as they passed through. They were encouraged to give things that were valuable, including precious stones. This is why she has jewelled clothes. St Foy was a child martyr from the early years of Christianity, and her cult was very popular. It is said that she cured the sick.'

'What? St Foy herself, or . . .'

'Her relic.' He sighed. 'As for whether I think this is genuine or not, I cannot say yes or no. The idea that another identical reliquary exists in France is unsettling. This is because, I think, I find the idea that this fraud is being perpetrated at such a high and skilful level deeply offensive. Whatever one may think about the power of relics, the faithful do believe, and so doing this laughs at their piety.'

'I think it's just done to make money,' Kerim said.

'Oh, I have no doubt, but it also causes collateral damage.'

The bishop picked up the sheet that had been draped over the statue and replaced it. Kerim thought it was as if he couldn't bear to look at it any longer.

Poker was psychological. Çetin İkmen looked at his own face in the bathroom mirror and asked himself why he was so bad at it.

'Well?' he said. 'Why? You've always been a good amateur psychologist. You know about tells and sleight of hand. I'm sure that you will be instantly alive to any supernatural entities the Roma might have employed to help them as soon as you enter the room. But you'll still be absolutely awful and you will lose.'

The stake money, five hundred lira, was not as high as many of the other schools in the city, but it was a lot for poor Roma folk – and for İkmen. To Atyom Mafyan, it was probably nothing. The sort of games he took part in, it was said, involved staking tens of thousands of euros. But then everything was relative. Five hundred lira to a Roma rubbish picker was a fortune. It was also a vehicle through which Şevket Sesler could control his people ever more firmly. Being in debt to him was not a healthy place to be.

And Gonca Şekeroğlu, İkmen recalled, knew all about that. Much as he loved her, he hoped she would do right by her husband-to-be, whom he loved more, and tell him the truth about her involvement in the death of Sesler's father. Whether one

179

believed in curses or not, Gonca had wished Harun Bey ill, and İkmen strongly suspected she had put emotive suggestions into the head of the woman who had killed him. The way, it was said, the Roma spoke about the incident put Gonca at the heart of it.

What İkmen would do if she didn't speak to her fiancé, he didn't know. Besotted as he was, would Mehmet even believe that story? And yet İkmen knew he couldn't leave his friend in ignorance. That would lay him open to manipulation by Sesler. Perhaps that was how the son would exact revenge on his father's proxy killer.

All three women lay on the göbek taşı, the large stone platform used for massage at the centre of the hamam. Scrubbed, depilated, massaged and soaped to within a centimetre of their lives, they sprawled on the warm stone in various states of undress. Hürrem in a bikini over which she wore a pestemel cloth around her waist, Buket Teyze just in a pestemel, her huge breasts reaching down almost to her waist, and Gonca entirely naked save for the emerald necklace given to her by Nur Hanım.

Watching her lazily run the green stones through her fingers, Buket Teyze said, 'Now, Gonca, you must tell us how you met Mehmet Bey.'

'I've told you,' Gonca said. 'We met, it was love at first sight and then we spent too much time trying to deny that.'

'Oh, not the romance!' Buket said. 'The sex! We want to know about the sex, don't we, Hürrem Hanım?'

Hürrem, a dentist and wife of a wealthy middle-class banker, was in two minds. Born and raised on the edge of Sulukule, where her father went to drink away the family's money with his Roma friends most nights of the week, she was a woman who now enjoyed living a life of moneyed gentility. But on the other hand, this was Gonca they were talking about, and Gonca was daring and exciting.

180

'Oh, all right,' she said eventually. 'Come on, Gonca, tell us about the first time.'

Gonca flopped over onto her stomach, continuing to play with her emeralds.

'I don't know when it was, I'm not good at dates.'

'We don't care about dates,' Buket Teyze said. 'Get to the point!'

Gonca smiled. 'I'd been helping Çetin İkmen,' she began.

'The witch's boy.'

'Yes. He had to go somewhere else and so Mehmet Bey took me home in his car.'

'What did you think of him at that time?' Hürrem asked.

Gonca shrugged. 'I thought he was good looking, very polite, really a bit too much of the honourable man, if you know what I mean. I flirted a little, but I knew he was married. I didn't know until I got in that car how unhappy he was.'

'How did you find out?'

'The look on his face,' she said. 'No one who is happy at home looks that sad. And he was talking about duty and all that rubbish. I took one of his hands and laid it against my tits—'

'Gonca!'

'Oh Hürrem, don't be so coy!' Gonca said. 'It was that or go home alone and feel frustrated. I had to know whether he was up for some fun. Anyway, it was he who moved his hand.'

Buket Teyze, all wide eyes, said, 'So what happened then?'

'Then? We arrived at the house, I chucked the kids in the garden and we went up to my bedroom.'

'Oh!'

'We pulled each other's clothes off, he pushed me onto the bed and fucked me. We were both so horny. We fucked all night. I tell you, he was so hot and I was so turned on I'd've let him do anything. As it was, he was as caring about me as he was about himself. I'd never come so hard before. Never!

When I eventually woke up in his arms, I knew I was lost. I loved him.'

'Did you tell him?'

'Don't be silly, Hürrem!' Gonca said. 'No. I pushed him out into the street and told him to go away.' Suddenly she looked sad. 'He was out of my league. It's what our people do.'

Scene-of-crime officers were much more confident about gathering evidence from the Vefa scene now that the scientists had declared the building safe. The problem of Fahrettin Müftüoğlu's hoard remained, although once the alleyway beside the building had been thoroughly examined for evidence pertaining to the death of Constable Akar, removal of material from the site could begin.

Although Constable Mustafa Gölcük had admitted he'd been with his mistress in Zeyrek at the time of Akar's death, Constables Tan, Alp and Tuncer were still adamant they'd neither seen nor heard anything untoward. Not many people, apart from the other residents of Müftüoğlu's building, lived in the area, and as Ömer Mungun walked the streets, he became aware of how many of the buildings were derelict. Climbing up a rickety set of stairs on the side of an old warehouse, he stepped out onto the roof and surveyed the surrounding area. Not only were there a lot of alleyways between the various buildings, but he could also see how easy it would be to get through the skeletons of what had once been commercial properties. Getting to the apartment block and then leaving it, unseen, wasn't hard to imagine.

'Ömer Bey!'

He looked down and saw Süleyman in the alleyway with a woman. Running down the staircase, he'd come up, Ömer walked out of the warehouse and over to his superior.

'This is Alev Hanım,' Süleyman said. 'She lives in the street behind this one.'

Small, her head covered, wearing a pair of flowery şalvar trousers, she wasn't as old as she first appeared, but she was rural, albeit of a particular urban variety. Or did Ömer think that simply because she was holding a live chicken by the feet?

'Hanım . . .'

'I was telling Mehmet Bey about the bad women who walk these streets at night,' she said. 'It's a sin. I've been telling the bekçiler round here about it for years. They do nothing. Disturb my son, they do, these women.'

'In what way?' Ömer asked. 'Do they taunt him, tempt him?'

'Both! They shouldn't be here. They should be punished! But they're not!'

Süleyman said, 'Alev Hanım, were these "bad" women here last night?'

'They're always here,' she said. 'All these derelict places round here. They take men in and do their filthy business on the ground. I wish we'd never come to this wicked city!'

'Where do you come from?' Ömer asked.

'Our village is in the Çukurova,' she said. 'When my husband, God bless him, died, it was at the same time my fingers stopped moving. Our Muktar, a man of wisdom and religion, said I should go to the city to find work. So I did. I'm an ignorant woman, I know nothing.'

Living on the Çukurova plain, Alev Hanım was probably a cotton worker, and although much of the work in the fields was done by machine, some still laboured picking the cotton by hand.

'And your son?' Süleyman asked.

'Oh, he cannot work, efendi,' she said. 'That is why an old woman like me has to. Not that I complain. What God gives we must accept. The boy is as an infant, his mind does not move.'

'So how do these women disturb him, hanım?' Ömer asked.

'His mind is of an infant, but his body is of a man,' she said. 'They tempt him. I must watch him all the time to make sure

183

he doesn't sin. I am poor and must work, and having this all night every night is making me sick, efendi.'

Süleyman bowed. 'I will speak to your local watchmen and put a stop to it, hanım,' he said.

She shuffled forwards, took one of his hands in hers and kissed it. 'Bless you, bey efendi,' she said. 'May your life be long.'

When she had gone, Süleyman said, 'Have you seen any nightwatchmen on duty since we arrived on site?'

Nightwatchmen – or bekçiler – were officers who patrolled the streets at night, alongside the regular police. Generally young, they were supposed to act as community officers, but that depended upon who they were. Some were very diligent, others less so.

Ömer said, 'No, sir. Only the first night. The one who found the body with our Constable Tan. He put in a report.'

'Mmm. I wonder how much the bekçiler know about the local streetwalkers. From what Alev Hanım said, it would seem they either know nothing or, maybe, I feel, they could know rather too much. We tend to overlook the watchmen, which may be a mistake. Find out, will you, Ömer. Go and speak to the bekçi who called Constable Tan to break down the door.'

'Yes, sir.'

It wasn't the same now that Fahrettin Bey had gone. Although he hardly ever spoke – and when he did, it was generally odd – the atelier didn't seem right without him. Although that in itself was relative. and not why she had come to speak to her superior.

When Sema Kılıç had left art school back in the 1990s, all she wanted to do was make jewellery. Her father, a migrant from Mardin province, had been a silversmith, specialising in filigree work, and it had been through him that she had come to know Atyom Bey. Being apprenticed to such a prestigious atelier had been an honour, and was, Sema felt, a recognition of her skills.

But that was almost a quarter of a century ago. Now Sema wasn't happy – and it wasn't just because she'd not had a pay rise for almost ten years.

Atyom Bey looked at her from the other side of his great desk at the back of his office and said, 'Sema Hanım, you seem unhappy. How can I help?'

She took a breath.

'Everyone was unnerved about what happened yesterday,' Atyom Bey continued. 'But now we know we are safe, there is no more need to think about it again.'

Sema let go of her breath and then took another. 'It's not about that, Atyom Bey,' she said. 'It's about the materials we are using.'

'What about them?'

'I know, Atyom Bey, that you have an enormous and, I should say, patriotic interest in Anatolian materials . . .'

'I do. It is a policy we have pursued for the last decade and it appears to be popular.'

'Yes, sir,' she said. 'And as much as it is an honour for me to be able to work with materials like Turkish jade, anatolite and colemanite, I feel as if I am not utilising all the skills I have learned, long ago now, with precious gems. Colemanite, for instance, is difficult to cut, as you know, and I am more accustomed, or I was, to cutting diamond.'

'Mmm.' Atyom Bey stirred the tea in his glass.

'I know we still use a considerable amount of sapphire,' she continued nervously.

'We do. Much of our compartmental jewellery is sapphire,' he said. 'Our compartments and our Turkish gemstones are what make us GülGül.'

'Yes, but when I started—'

'When you started working here, the world was a different place,' he said. 'It was a different century!'

'Yes, Atyom Bey.'

'A time when people were not accustomed to having their desires fulfilled instantly via the Internet. People saved for what they wanted. And what they wanted then were products they knew like their own children. Diamonds, emeralds, rubies, gold, gold and more gold. Now people want novelty. They want something no one else has and they want it now. This is why, with the exception of the unfortunate Fahrettin Bey, I allow you all to follow your hearts when you design pieces for GülGül.'

'We're all very grateful . . .'

'But?' He steepled his fingers underneath his chin.

She swallowed. 'I should like to practise some diamond cutting,' she said. 'I should be grateful for the opportunity to employ whatever stones I wish in my pieces.'

'And if that makes our pieces too expensive for our customers?'

'Our work is not cheap, Atyom Bey,' she said. 'I'm not talking about using enormous stones, just some small, exquisitely cut pieces, for variation. I have designs that absolutely cry out for precious stones, particularly emeralds, which were so important back in Ottoman times.'

As soon as she'd said it, Sema felt as if she'd done the wrong thing. Atyom Bey was Armenian; what did he care about the Ottoman Empire?

But then he smiled. 'I will see what I can do,' he said. 'I will look at our current margins and I will give it some thought.'

Sema smiled too. But when she left Atyom Bey's office, she remained uneasy.

It had been Defne Yalçın's mother who had first taken her to the theatre, in 1970. Then aged twelve, Defne had seen the great stage actor Yıldız Kenter play Lady Macbeth. She never forgot it, and, when she grew up, she became an actor too. And while some of her mother's neighbours in what was then the run-down district of Bomonti tutted under their collective

186

breath over Defne's career choice, there was no father around to stop her.

Defne Yalçın, while not living up to the accolades awarded to Yıldız Kenter, achieved her ambition, and even now, in her early sixties, she still managed to get enough work to keep her and her son Hulusi in a small, trendy apartment in Karaköy. Like her mother, Defne had no desire to have a man in control of her life, and so Hulusi's father was forever absent. The apartment housed just Defne herself, her thirty-year-old gay son and, latterly, his boyfriend, Kemal İkmen. Devoted to her son, Defne also loved Kemal and was very happy to guide the son of one of his father's friends, an Irish boy, around the local street-art hot spots.

When Defne, Kemal and Patrick Süleyman arrived at Hoca Tahsin Sokak, she told the teenager, 'This street is what we now call Umbrella Street.'

It wasn't hard to see why. Above the narrow alleyway were dozens of rainbow-coloured umbrellas suspended by netting.

'It is a sort of installation,' Defne continued. 'Very pretty. Many people come here for Instagram pictures, so it is lucky that today the weather is bad. In the summer, there are crowds.'

Patrick said, 'Temple Bar's like that.' Then, seeing that neither Kemal nor Defne knew what he was talking about, he added, 'It's an arty sort of part of Dublin. It's fulla tourists Instagramming the pubs and the street art and that.'

'Well, if you don't mind being a little bit cold, we can sit and have coffee under the umbrellas,' Kemal said. 'There are some good murals here of cartoon characters.'

'Cool.'

They began to walk.

'Are the umbrellas a gay thing?' Patrick asked.

'I don't really know,' Kemal said. 'But we have a big LGBT community here in the city.'

'It's a shame Hulusi couldn't come with us.'

Defne smiled. 'He has so much pain with his leg,' she said. 'I am afraid it is not healing properly. But he is a man and so I cannot get him back to the doctor.'

'My dad would be the same,' Patrick said. 'Mammy says Turkish men are bad about stuff like that.'

'I try not to be,' Kemal said. 'But my dad too is really terrible.'

Patrick's phone rang. He took it out of his pocket and answered. 'Hello?'

'Patrick,' Mehmet Süleyman said. 'Are you having a good time?'

'Yeah. I'm with Kemal and Hulusi's mum, Defne Hanım. We're looking at street art in Karaköy.'

'Good. Patrick, I am sorry, but I will be late tonight. I have spoken to Çetin Bey and he says you can have dinner with him and Çiçek and Auntie Samsun tonight. I will have to pick you up from there, but I don't know what time.'

'It's OK,' Patrick said.

'I am so sorry.'

'I do understand,' Patrick said. 'I do . . . I get you, Dad, I really do.'

He heard his father sigh, and then he signed off with 'You are my beloved son.'

Patrick put his phone back in his pocket.

Kemal said, 'Are you OK?'

'That was my dad. He's busy. I'll have my dinner at Çetin Bey's apartment tonight.'

Patrick looked disappointed, so Kemal put an arm around his shoulders.

'Well,' he said, 'I know Çiçek is cooking tonight, so you will have a nice dinner.'

'Not one of Auntie Samsun's strange ones?'

Kemal ruffled the boy's hair. 'No,' he said. 'This will be edible.'

*

188

Kerim Gürsel was alone in his office when his superior, Commissioner Selahattin Ozer, knocked on his door and entered, shutting the door behind him.

Kerim stood up. 'Sir.'

Ozer motioned for him to sit. A slim man in his sixties, he was almost uniformly grey, from his loosely fitting suit to his cold, almost silver eyes.

'Kerim Bey,' he said as he took a seat in front of Kerim's desk. 'You had a priest looking at this statue you have discovered.'

'A bishop, yes, sir,' Kerim said.

'Why did you do that?'

'I believe his perspective matters. We have the French saying their St Foy is the genuine article; tests on ours are ongoing. Bishop Montoya is of the opinion that a man of faith, like him, could possibly tell a fake from the original.'

'How so?'

Ozer was well known to be a pious Muslim, but how would he view the opinion of a pious Christian? Kerim tried to imagine what Çetin İkmen would say. İkmen wasn't a religious man, but he did have a relationship with the unseen, and Kerim had often witnessed him managing to persuade religious people to agree with some of his observations.

Eventually he said, 'Over hundreds, sometimes thousands of years, objects of veneration somehow soak up the prayers and the intensity that goes with prayer.'

'I don't think so,' Ozer said.

'Sir, with respect,' Kerim said, 'I think that most of us would agree that buildings such as our imperial mosques have a certain atmosphere created by faith. I mean, why is the conversion of the Aya Sofya so important for some people if it has no meaning?' He knew that Ozer was one of those who supported the re-conversion of the Aya Sofya museum back into the mosque it had been in Ottoman times.

Ozer raised his eyebrows. He remained silent, maybe in contemplation, for over a minute before he said, 'And the angel figure?'

This sudden sideways swerve was typical of him. Clearly the subject of Bishop Montoya was closed.

'Inspector Keleş and his team have sought advice and seem to think it is modern, sir.'

'It's also solid gold, I've been told.'

Kerim hadn't known this for sure. He had suspected it, but it still came as a shock. That was a huge amount of gold.

'So what was this man Müftüoğlu?' Ozer asked. 'A forger?'

'If the artefacts we have found in his apartment were indeed made by him, it's possible,' Kerim said. 'He, or someone, copied certain things like St Foy.'

'Mmm.' Ozer nodded his head. Then he got quickly to his feet. 'We have a lot of resources tied up in this investigation,' he said.

'Sir, Müftüoğlu's death is still open to question, and now we have the tragic death of Constable Akar. Items were looted from Müftüoğlu's apartment the night Akar died.'

Ozer was trying to cut down the manpower numbers on the investigation, which Kerim could understand. But if the budget was under pressure, that wasn't his problem.

'Inspector Süleyman is still investigating Müftüoğlu's death, I am assigned to that of Constable Akar, and both of us are reliant upon Inspector Keleş for his knowledge and contacts in the art world,' he said.

Ozer nodded. 'I know.' Then he left, closing the door behind him.

A strange man, Kerim thought. His predecessor, Commissioner Teker, had been popular with her senior officers, and it was hard for Ozer to compete. However, unlike Teker, who was still under investigation for alleged corruption, Ozer had the full force of the ruling establishment behind him. He also had the unquestioning loyalty of most of his officers, and loyalty of a more pragmatic kind from his senior staff. What he didn't always have was their trust. Clearly he wanted to reduce the head count on this investigation. But why? It was by definition complex.

Kerim's phone rang. It was Haluk Keleş. 'Ozer been to see you yet?' he asked without preamble.

'He's just left.' Kerim heard Keleş sigh. 'I don't know what he wanted any more than you did.'

Keleş exhaled again. 'Why would Müftüoğlu make a copy of something no one knows about?'

Here was someone else who just changed what he was talking about in less than a heartbeat.

'Maybe it's not a copy,' Kerim said. 'Or maybe it is a copy of that Ark of the Covenant angel in *Raiders*—'

'No!'

It was Keleş himself who had pointed the similarity out, but Kerim said nothing.

'Why make something that is basically shit out of solid gold?' Keleş continued.

'Well, if it's a copy—'

'If it is, it's shit! Who'd want that?'

'I don't know,' Kerim said. 'Maybe it's a copy of some artefact we don't know about.'

'If I don't know about it then it must be fucking obscure!'

'Or maybe it's an original that has just surfaced. Remember, we don't know what's going on here. Was Müftüoğlu simply copying artefacts to sell on to people who just wanted a copy, or was he doing it to order, to replace existing relics?'

'But if he somehow found something nobody else knew anything about . . .'

'Unless they did,' Kerim said. 'If he found this artefact on the Dark Web, say, why not replicate it? He worked with precious metals; maybe he enjoyed the challenge. I don't know where he got that much gold from. Mehmet Bey and I are working on trying to discover something, anything about him. You've contacts in the darker side of the art world . . .'

'Who've given me nothing so far.' Keleş sighed again. 'Not that I've exhausted those particular sewers. It's just . . . Places and people you don't want to go to, you know?'

Kerim did. Every officer he knew who had been around for some time had such contacts. People, sometimes whole organisations, who made your blood freeze. People who could ruin or even kill you.

'I'm calling Mehmet Bey,' he said.

Chapter 15

Ömer Mungun gave Eylul Yavaş his seat and then dragged an old wooden chair in from the corridor for himself. Süleyman's office was larger than most, but still, accommodating five people comfortably around his desk was a stretch. Haluk Keleş had chosen to stand.

When everyone was seated, or not, and had tea, Süleyman said, 'Since we're all investigating different parts of what is effectively the same story, I thought it best that we come together and share intelligence. I understand that Commissioner Ozer is keen to trim his manpower numbers at the earliest possible opportunity.'

'Bastard.'

They all looked at Haluk Keleş, who shrugged. None of them liked Ozer, but only Keleş would express that publicly.

'So, Fahrettin Müftüoğlu,' Süleyman continued. 'Forger, madman, thief or potential murderer? Or all of the above? What do we know about him, and from whom?'

They covered the indisputable facts quickly – his age, where he had worked and lived – then Kerim Gürsel said, 'One of his colleagues at GülGül, Sema Kılıç, told me he hated his mother.'

'What evidence did she give for that?'

'She'd heard him talking about her on the phone to someone,' Kerim said. 'Then the conversation moved on to some embarrassing sexual innuendo. She assumed he was talking to a woman.'

'His wife, maybe?'

'Don't know. But if he hated his mother so much, why didn't he go and live with the wife?'

'Sir, with respect,' Eylul said, 'some men are dominated by their mothers. On the one hand they love them because they view them as perfect women, while at the same time they hate them for imposing standards the men find stifling. We know that Müftüoğlu defied his mother in order to marry Canan, but the old woman then exacted a terrible revenge.'

'If Müftüoğlu had been a real man, he would have stood up to her,' Haluk Keleş said.

They all stared at him in disbelief. It was Eylul who said what they were all thinking.

'Sir,' she said, 'this is Turkey. I will say no more.'

Keleş shrugged again. It was all very well for him to think that Fahrettin Müftüoğlu should have stood up to his mother, but he also knew full well just how uniformly Turkish mothers were adored – even if they were foreigners. To demean the figure of the mother in any way was almost sacrilege.

Süleyman said, 'Putting aside his antipathy towards his mother, Müftüoğlu's marriage was odd. He met his wife on holiday; they married within two weeks and came back to İstanbul, then separated. They continued to live apart even after his mother's death, and yet Canan Müftüoğlu says the marriage was consummated, claims she loved her physically unappealing husband.'

'Maybe he was good in bed,' Keleş said.

'That's possible. But then this woman has, I think, shown herself to be unreliable.'

Ömer felt his face colour.

Süleyman continued. 'The address she gave to Sergeant Mungun on her statement is of an apartment in Sarıgöl she states is rented by her father. However, further investigation has revealed that her father, a Zaza Kurd called Muharrem

Aktepe, owns and lives in with his daughter a penthouse apartment in Tarabya. The lease on the Sarıgöl apartment is held by a man called Osman Aslan. We need to discover whether he exists, and if he does, who he is. I doubt the name Aktepe will be familiar to any of you, but I am reliably informed that Muharrem was a practitioner of the ancestral sport back in the 1980s. He was no star, however, and when his career finished, he became a trainer of oil wrestlers. This then fell apart because some of his boys were found to have been taking performance-enhancing narcotics.'

Keleş shook his head. 'That's so shit.'

'And now it seems he lives on fresh air,' Süleyman continued. 'Word is that he is a man who organises betting opportunities for anyone interested in or addicted to gambling. But he has no record. He doesn't appear to be on any of our organised crime watch lists, but when Sergeant Mungun encountered him in Sarıgöl, it seems he was treated with deference by a considerable number of people.'

'So he's a godfather?' Eylul asked.

'That's a good question,' Süleyman said. 'Which is not easy to answer.'

As soon as they had left the hamam, just after lunch, Gonca suggested alcohol. Had they wanted to, the three women could have remained there until mid afternoon, but it was clear that Gonca wanted to parade her new jewellery.

They took a taxi to Beyoğlu and she led them to a cocktail bar in the trendy Asmalımescıt Mahalle district. Crammed to the walls during the evening, the place was comfortably lively in the afternoon. However, because Gonca and Buket Teyze needed to smoke, they sat outside underneath an awning and patio heater. When the waiter came to their table, Gonca ordered for all three of them. Once he had gone, she said, 'They make all sorts of cocktails here, but this is my favourite.' It was called Afternoon Delight, and both gin and rose water were involved.

'How did you find this place?' Buket Teyze asked as they helped themselves to olives from a small tray on the table.

Gonca took her coat off and pulled the front of her dress down so that people could see her new baubles.

Buket leaned towards her. 'You don't want to flash your jewels round here, girl. You'll get mugged.'

Gonca laughed. 'I won't,' she said. 'But in answer to your question, Mehmet Bey brought me here in the summer.'

'He raided it or something?'

'Oh Buket!' Hürrem said. 'Mehmet Bey does do other things!'

The old girl sank back in her chair and lit a cigarette.

Their drinks arrived, and after taking a sip from a sparkly straw, Hürrem said, 'That's strong! How much gin is in this thing?'

Gonca laughed. 'A lot. The way I like it.'

Buket drank half of hers down straight and then put her glass on the table.

'So, Gonca,' she said, 'you didn't tell us how Mehmet Bey knows this place.'

Some young men, all dressed very trendily in tight trousers and figure-hugging T-shirts, walked into the bar. Gonca followed them with her eyes.

Buket shook her head. 'They're young enough to be your sons!'

Gonca lit a cigarette. 'A woman can look.'

'Don't let Mehmet Bey see you doing it!'

'Ah, he knows my body belongs exclusively to him. Anyway, much as I love him, it's always good to keep men slightly anxious.'

'Darling, you did that with your previous husbands,' Hürrem said, 'and that ended up in cuts and bruises, as I recall. Mehmet Bey may be a police officer, educated and well connected, but

196

he's still a Turkish man, and I think we all know how a lot of them can be.'

'I know,' Gonca said, 'but he's not here, and so . . . Look, I do as I please. That's me. And anyway, when the man on the street sees my long skirts and my long hair, he's going to think "gypsy" and walk in the opposite direction.'

'And yet you've never been short of lovers,' Buket said.

Gonca slapped her hand playfully. 'Oh Buket Teyze, you listen to gossip!'

'And to your wailing when one or other of your young men has walked out on you over the years.'

'Yes, yes, whatever . . . Anyway,' Gonca said, 'Mehmet Bey brought me here in the summer so that we could be somewhere together where neither of us was known. He found it in a listings magazine. I like it.'

Buket Teyze looked around the little alleyway in front of the bar and found that her eye was caught and captured by one aspect of this place. Leaning towards her friends, who in turn leaned towards her, she said, 'And yet, Gonca Hanım, it would seem that your fame precedes you.'

'What?'

Buket tipped her head towards an overweight man sitting outside another bar.

When he saw Gonca Şekeroğlu looking at him, Şevket Sesler raised his glass to her.

Outlining how Muharrem Aktepe was difficult to categorise in terms of crime, Süleyman said, 'Until we can find out more about him, I am reluctant to acknowledge we know where he really lives. The information came to us via someone who wishes to remain anonymous; however, it has been verified by the belediye. Also, we don't yet know who Müftüoğlu was working for or with. His employer, who of course says he and his staff had no knowledge of Fahrettin's at-home activities, may be implicated. Atyom Bey would have access to gold.'

'Mehmet Bey,' Kerim said, 'Atyom Bey was the one who alerted us to the presence of ricin inside Müftüoğlu's jewellery.'

'Yes. But is he telling us the truth? And don't forget he failed to notice that Fahrettin had taken a canister of potassium cyanide home with him.'

'This is art fraud,' Haluk Keleş interjected. 'Since the beginning of the Syrian war, this country has been a conduit for the stuff, real or fake, on an industrial scale.'

'And yet so far, all the items we have discovered have been originals, or copies of artefacts from this country or Europe. Not Syria.'

'Maybe he was working to order,' Keleş said.

'Maybe.'

Eylul turned her head so that she was looking at Keleş. 'Why would someone want something they can go and see in a museum?'

'Good question,' he said. 'Opportunity and insane levels of wealth, I'd say. The war in Iraq opened the floodgates. Half of the Baghdad museum went missing. Tie that in with a world where billionaires can own whole countries if they feel like it, and you have a disaster waiting to happen. There have always been people who, because they're rich, want to collect original pieces of art; that is a market that is always open. What joy these fuckers get out of sitting on their own in a vault with an original Titian or a "genuine" thigh bone of St George, I don't know. They can't show what they've got to anyone in case they tip us off, and the only reason they've got whatever they have is because of money. Twisted bastards.'

His little speech impressed his colleagues with its passion. Keleş was profane, unkempt and sometimes aggressive after a particularly hard night on the rakı, but he was a cultured man who knew his subject and cared about it.

Süleyman nodded. 'A world in which everything is for sale,' he said. 'What do we think about the jewellery and the gold stolen from the Kayserili Ahmet Paşa Caddesi apartment last night? Are they significant?'

'Only in terms of meltdown value,' Keleş said. 'Two thousand lira at the most.'

'So . . .'

'They were looking for something else. Place was left in even more of a shit state than it was before.'

'Do you think they were looking for the angel?'

Keleş shrugged. 'The meltdown value makes your head spin, but I'm still working on what it is.'

Kerim said, 'What are the possibilities?'

'What, apart from being a very expensive piece of shit art? Until I can identify it, I don't know. If we assume that Müftüoğlu made all these pieces, he was off his game when he made that, in my opinion. Waste of gold.'

'Anyway,' Süleyman said, 'what I propose is that Sergeant Mungun and myself proceed from the known, hopefully, to the unknown. To wit, we obtain a warrant to search the apartment Canan Müftüoğlu gave as her home address on her statement. I want to know more about her family. She may well be the ingénue she purports to be, but I'm not entirely buying it. Why marry someone like Fahrettin Müftüoğlu?'

Eylul said, 'Beauty and the Beast, sir.'

He smiled.

'Think about all the femicides that happen in this country, and others, every week,' she continued. 'Most women I know would choose kindness over looks. Their marriage was strange, but maybe it worked for them.'

The men in the room considered this, then Kerim said, 'But what about the fact that she turns up now to claim his property?'

'It's her right. She was his wife.'

'And yet if she loved him so much, why didn't she get him help?' Ömer Mungun asked. 'According to her, he frequently expressed suicidal thoughts.'

Eylul said, 'Stigma? He's a man who couldn't cope, and that's not done, is it?'

'The patriarchy,' Keleş said.

'Yes, sir. Still putting both men and women into roles that don't always fit.'

Nobody said anything. Because Eylul was a woman of faith, some of her colleagues believed that she was also anti-feminist. Kerim Gürsel, who knew her better than the other men, was aware this wasn't so.

'I'll chase the artefacts,' Keleş said eventually. 'I've tapped into my usual sources; now I need to think laterally and more dangerously.'

'Dangerously?'

'I've never come across this myself,' he said, 'but I've got colleagues abroad who have. *This* being that at the end of some Dark Web food chain is a name that is so well known and powerful it makes you shit yourself.'

Süleyman raised his eyebrows. 'OK. And while I am not persuaded that Müftüoğlu's death was suspicious, Ömer Bey and myself will continue our investigation into him as well as into the human remains found in his apartment.'

'Nothing else has been found so far, sir,' Ömer said.

'I know. But that head belonged to someone, and we need to find out who, and what the circumstances of their death might have been.'

'As for Constable Akar's death,' Kerim said, 'of course the pressure's on to get a result on one of our own. I understand that Ömer Bey is planning to go and see the local watch tonight. It was, after all, one of their number who originally alerted our officers to Müftüoğlu.'

'Yes, sir,' Ömer said.

Kerim looked at Süleyman. 'If I may, however, Mehmet Bey, I'd like to take that on myself. In my opinion, if we all concentrate on our own areas of what is a complicated situation, it may well focus our minds.'

Ömer Mungun, for one, was a little nervous as to how the boss would take what could be seen as a rebuke from Kerim Bey. But he smiled and said, 'As you wish.'

'Thank you.'

Then Ömer remembered that Süleyman had more on his mind than most. He only had one full day left to kick this investigation into shape before he was going on leave to get married. When the other officers had vacated Süleyman's office, he said to his superior, 'Thank you, boss, for not talking about Canan Müftüoğlu and me.'

Süleyman waved his thanks away. 'Even had you not done what you did with that woman, we still could not go to the apartment in Tarabya,' he said. 'We may play that card later, but not now. In the meantime, I would like you to use your knowledge of Zaza to find out how this apparently lucrative gambling operation of Aktepe's works. I meanwhile will apply for a warrant to search the Sarıgöl apartment. Then I will put on my best Ottoman kaftan and go and talk to the good people of Kayserili Ahmet Paşa Caddesi. Follow up on Sergeant Yavaş's teatime conversation with the local teyzes.' He steepled his fingers underneath his chin. 'After that, I feel you and I need to return to the GülGül atelier – unless what we discover in the next few hours takes us somewhere else . . .'

İkmen could hear his daughter talking to that fucking djinn in the kitchen, politely telling it to go away. What it needed were some really offensive insults, but Çiçek, although willing and able to swear, usually chose not to. He was just about to go into the kitchen and tell it to fuck off when his phone rang.

'İkmen.'

'It's Gonca,' a slightly rasping female voice said.

'Ah,' he said, 'did you have a good day at the hamam?'

'I was having a good day until I left the hamam and took my friends to a cocktail bar in Asmalımescıt Mahallesi, and there was Şevket Sesler.'

'Doing what?'

'He raised his glass and toasted me,' she said.

'So? You know him,' İkmen said. 'You read his cards, you're one of his own.'

'It rattled me,' she said. 'Thinking about what you said about how my being involved with him could affect Mehmet Bey. I'm wondering whether it was Sesler who smeared blood on my bedcover. Only he could get away with that. Only he could buy the silence of the Can family, maybe even Rahul Bey!'

'Calm down,' İkmen said. He could both hear and feel her hysteria all the way from Balat. 'Sesler isn't directly involved with the Can family.'

'Calm down! How can I?' she said. 'I've been living in denial! I can't marry Mehmet Bey, not with . . .'

As İkmen had always suspected, Gonca had meddled in the death of Şevket's father, Harun, more than she cared to admit.

'OK,' he said. 'I see it's finally hit you that whatever you did with regard to Harun Sesler—'

'I didn't kill him!'

'No. I know. But you . . . Well, some of the Roma believe you at least had a hand in it.'

'I didn't!'

İkmen sat down and lit a cigarette. 'Gonca,' he said. 'You did something. I'm not asking what . . .'

'I cannot marry Mehmet Bey,' she repeated. 'I can't! I will put him in danger!'

She was becoming hysterical. İkmen yelled into his phone. 'Shut up and calm down!'

Çiçek came running in from the kitchen, but he waved her away.

'Look,' he said, 'serious question: do you still want to marry Mehmet Bey?'

'With all my heart!' Gonca said. He heard her begin to cry.

'Well, he wants to marry you too. So stop sobbing and listen.'

He heard her breathe to calm herself down.

'If you don't marry Mehmet, you will break his heart and your own,' İkmen said. 'This means that one of two things has to happen. As far as I can see, either you tell Mehmet everything . . .'

'Oh.'

'. . . or you give me tonight and tomorrow to see what I can do. When I told you I would find out who damaged your bedcover, I was telling the truth. I've said little since because I want you out of the way. But I am working on it.'

'But to what end?' she wailed.

'To the end, I believe, that will lead me to someone close to Şevket Sesler. Someone whose brutality may, I hope, be used against him.'

'Munir Can?'

'I don't know. And I don't want you jumping to conclusions and running off to do something about it.'

'So it is—'

'Leave it to me!' he bellowed. 'Stay where you are, do nothing, and I will get back to you. One way or another, your wedding will go ahead, even if it kills me!'

It wasn't the Dark Web, but the Deep Web. Haluk Keleş knew that, but he didn't say anything to the child-man sitting next to him in front of an array of computer screens. Technical Officer Doğan Tuğrul, like a lot of IT people, was deeply exercised by incorrect terminology. When Keleş referred to 'bitcoin', Tuğrul corrected him with 'You mean cryptocurrency, of which bitcoin is only one.'

But Keleş let it go. Anyone looking for stolen or forged artworks had to be insane if they thought they could ignore the Deep Web. In the past, Keleş' department had been strictly analogue; they had relied on intelligence from tame forgers – many of them ex-cons – shady art students, the occasional rich collector who'd got in too deep, and Italian and American police forces, who informed them about the current activities of the Cosa Nostra. But in the digital world, there were other players, including more recently developed mafias – mainly Russian and native Turkish – terror organisations, and, it was said, proxies for rogue states and some of the richest people on the planet.

One of the methods used to find buyers for looted artefacts from Syria and Iraq by terror organisations like IS was to scour social media for likely customers. Demonstrating an interest in, for instance, Mesopotamian artefacts could deliver results if it came to the notice of the right people. Keleş' department ran multiple fake social media accounts for just this reason. However, what he was doing now, with the help of Officer Tuğrul, was scanning a list of sites already identified as ones that sometimes sold what they claimed were original artworks. And while Keleş was a competent user of IT, he wasn't savvy enough to pass unnoticed – hence Officer Tuğrul.

Unlike Süleyman, Keleş was not fluent in French, but his English, which was the language used on a vast number of these sites, was excellent. Scanning the screens, he said, 'I've heard that cryptocurrencies are sometimes accepted in shops these days.'

'Oh yes,' Tuğrul said. 'It's becoming mainstream. The world moves ever onwards towards the completely cashless society.'

Keleş thought this sounded like a nightmare, but he didn't say

204

anything. Instead, he thought about freeports and how artworks moved through those too. As analogue as it got. Then he thought about Fahrettin Müftüoğlu.

Except at work, the deceased had been a computer-free zone, and nothing untoward had been found on that system. He had to somehow contact or be contacted by those who employed him to make these artefacts. Both new and old mobsters always had a thirst for gold; in fact, anything gaudy. But there had been a lot of religious stuff, exclusively Christian. And then there was the mummy . . .

Kerim Gürsel had suggested that maybe Müftüoğlu, with his interest in sympathetic medicine, had made the thing in order to grind it up into 'mummia' to sell as an aphrodisiac, but Keleş didn't buy that theory. The guy had been half Egyptian, apparently, but that didn't mean he knew how to mummify. And yet the head had been in his apartment . . .

His mind turned to the angel. Amazingly valuable, hideous and poorly rendered, and also rather sexual now he came to think about it. It was at this point that a name arrived in Haluk Keleş' head, along with the possibility of that awful thing making some sort of sense. He got up out of his chair and left Tuğrul and his machines to their own devices.

He both loved and hated his Ottoman act. The perfuming, the clothes-brushing, the having some little grunt tell the good people of Kayserili Ahmet Paşa Caddesi that Inspector Süleyman was really very special. They deserved better than to be cowed by him. Eylul Yavaş had got as much out of the apartment block's teyzes as it was reasonable to expect. The menfolk, who were few, were now his purview. The very old one, two teenagers, a nondescript middle-aged taxi driver and a man who he had been told was mute. They sat on a row of chairs outside his office. He called the first one in, an Osman Dızdar, a man of ninety who called him 'efendi'. It took only five minutes for Süleyman to decide that the poor man was dementing.

Next up was the mute, who came into the office slightly nervously, shook Süleyman's hand and then said, in a very cultured accent, 'Good afternoon, Inspector.'

He was called İbrahim Atılla, and he had been a school teacher.

'I've lived on the top floor for twelve years,' he said. 'When my wife died, I decided I needed somewhere smaller and cheaper than my old apartment.'

Süleyman explained that some of the other residents had told him that he was mute.

İbrahim Atılla smiled. 'I keep to myself,' he said. 'I've my record collection and my interest in history. After thirty-five years in the classroom, I find I rarely need the sound of human voices these days. You want to know about the jeweller, I gather.'

'Yes.'

'I didn't know him,' he said. 'I picked up that he was strange. I found I had, albeit at a distance, something of a kinship with him. Like me, he had no visitors. Although unlike me, he was not fastidious about hygiene.'

'In what way?'

'Well, he was a hoarder,' Atılla said. 'I know you know this. To be fair, I didn't until you people got involved. But there were smells.'

'From his apartment?'

'Intermittent,' he said.

'No one else has pointed this out,' Süleyman said.

'No? Oh, well I suppose they didn't notice. A lot of them are less than sanitary themselves. I am particularly sensitive to odours. I understood that he worked from home sometimes, and so I assumed that some of the smells were connected with the manufacture of jewellery.'

'What sort of smells?'

206

Atılla frowned. 'Well, some were distinctly chemical in nature. Horrible. Like being in a laboratory. I knocked on his door on several occasions to see whether I could have a discreet word with him, but he never opened it. The farmyard smells I let go.' Seeing a look of confusion on Süleyman's face, he continued, 'Organic odours. Rotting vegetables, faeces. Flies.'

'Flies?'

'More than usual.'

'So why did you let that go?' Süleyman asked. 'If flies were emanating from his apartment, you should have informed the belediye.'

Suddenly İbrahim Atılla became volcanically aggressive. He shot up from his chair, which fell to the ground beside him. Süleyman, genuinely fearing he might be about to get hit, stood up too.

'I want to be left alone!' Atılla yelled. 'Why do you think I don't talk to anyone? I'd knocked at the jeweller's door about the chemical smells. He hadn't answered. Now there was this . . . organic smell. I knew he wouldn't do anything about it! Eventually it went.'

Still standing well back from his desk, Süleyman said, 'When was this? The organic—'

'I don't know!' Atılla threw his arms in the air and then sat down again, deflated. 'Years ago.'

'Years?'

'Yes, years.' He shrugged. 'Long time ago.'

'Over a decade, do you think?'

Süleyman had wondered how this probing would play with the man, after his recent explosion, but he had to ask, because something of possible significance had just occurred to him.

Chapter 16

Haluk Keleş had always thought that Rasım Tandoğan was a cut above other criminals. With his beautifully restored yalı on Büyükada and his vast but tasteful art nouveau apartment in Teşvikiye, the old bastard was as crooked as an olive tree, but at least he knew about art and heritage. He'd been to prison a few times, mainly for art fraud, but everyone knew he'd killed one of his rivals, Ömer Öztekin, back in the 1970s. His first wife had probably been one of his victims too, although no body had ever been found. Rasım had friends in high places. He had also, over the years, availed himself of Inspector Keleş' help and, in turn, assisted the art expert in locating seemingly vanished works of international importance. Especially when they belonged to his rivals.

It was his third wife, a woman known to the popular press only as 'the Body', who had changed things. She'd given Rasım the last of his many children, a twenty-something spoilt brat called Güven, who lived in the apartment below his father's. Cursed with way too much money, Güven was arrogant, selfish and a taste-free zone. He was also famously gay, although not as far as his old man was concerned.

The homoerotic properties of Müftüoğlu's golden angel had only really hit Keleş when he'd had time to think about it. But of course it had abs and nipples and . . . There was a definite feel about it. Add to that the belief, according to Google, some people had that silent movie star Rudolph Valentino had been gay, and Haluk Keleş found himself drawn to the person of Güven Tandoğan.

The old man had been glad to receive his call. He had a new Picasso drawing he wanted to show him.

'Completely legitimate,' he said as he pointed to a framed pencil sketch on the wall above his chair.

Haluk Keleş looked at it. It was clearly a fake, but he said nothing except 'Nice.'

Rasım was losing his touch, or rather, his eye. But Keleş hadn't come to talk to him about that. The old bastard knew who and what he was and so he just went for it.

'I've come about Güven,' he said.

'Güven?' For a moment, Keleş thought Rasım was going to bang on about what a good boy his son was, but that no one would give him a chance, blah, blah. But all he said was 'What's he done?'

'I don't know he's done anything,' Keleş said.

'Really? So why are you here?'

Keleş passed the old man a photograph of the angel. 'I'm looking for whoever ordered this.'

Rasım Tandoğan put his glasses on and peered at it.

'What is it?' he asked.

'Don't know,' Keleş said. 'Seems to be an angel. Wings. What do you make of it?'

'Horrible,' the old man said. 'Where's it from?'

'Found in the home of a jeweller. Suicide. It's solid gold.'

Rasım Tandoğan looked up. 'And you thought of Güven,' he said.

Keleş leaned forward. 'Rasım Bey, I know you know there are rumours about Güven's lifestyle . . .'

'My boy is not a pervert!'

'Whatever.' Keleş had gay friends. He'd been an art student and he took people as they were. 'But even as a proud father, you have to admit that he has no taste.'

209

The old man's eyes moved rapidly around the room, trying to avoid the inspector's.

'He drives a gold Ferrari, he spends every winter wrapped head to foot in fur. His jewellery alone is enough to turn your stomach. Rasım Bey, look at the face of that angel – pure gold, remember – and tell me this isn't Guven's sort of thing.'

Eylul held her phone out to Dr Arto Sarkissian. 'It's Inspector Süleyman,' she said.

The doctor had heard her side of the conversation with Süleyman, which had seemed to consist of details regarding the parents of the dead jeweller Fahrettin Müftüoğlu.

He took the phone from her. 'Inspector?'

'Doctor. Good afternoon,' Süleyman said. 'I'm assuming you still have the body of Fahrettin Müftüoğlu.'

'Yes. With only a woman purporting to be his wife to take possession – I have to say I have been awaiting word from you on that – and still uncertain about cause of death in my own mind—'

'You have him?'

'Yes.'

'Good. Where are we with a DNA profile?'

'I have a partial—'

'Tell me about it,' Süleyman butted in. He was clearly in a hurry, which was causing him to be blunt to the point of rudeness. He often behaved like this, it was said, but that side of him was rarely on display to Arto Sarkissian.

'What do you want to know?' the doctor asked.

'Ethnicity,' Süleyman said.

The doctor found Müftüoğlu's results on his laptop. 'Turkic and Afro-Semitic mainly.'

'Meaning?'

'Turkic elements from his father. The mother was Egyptian

210

and so, typically for that part of the world, she possessed both Arab and African antecedents. Why?'

'Doctor,' Süleyman said, 'I want you to do a DNA familial comparison for me.'

'A comparison with whom?' the doctor asked.

'The mummified head. I accept you said it will be difficult, but that is what I want.' Süleyman cut the connection.

Not wishing to criticise the inspector to one of his inferiors, Arto Sarkissian got back to talking to Eylul Yavaş about the wound that had killed Constable Akar.

'It was made using a flamberge blade,' he told her. 'That is a blade that is serrated on both sides.'

'Like a khanjar,' Eylul said.

A khanjar was a small serrated dagger typically worn by Kurds, mainly for ceremonial purposes.

'Exactly so,' the doctor said.

She smiled, the small woman in the brown uniform, and Kerim Gürsel felt a wave of relief pass through him. That some of the bekçiler, the nightwatchmen, were women had slipped his mind. And unlike some of the men he had already spoken to, like Officer Ergin, who had been responsible for finding Fahrettin Müftüoğlu's body, Officer Pervin Deniz was friendly.

She offered him her hand. 'You wanted to see me, sir,' she said as she waited for him to sit, then sat down herself.

'Yes,' Kerim said. 'I understand you are responsible for patrolling Kayserili Ahmet Paşa Caddesi and its environs.'

'I am, sir,' she said. 'Although I was on leave the night Fahrettin Bey died.'

'Yes, I know,' Kerim said. 'I have spoken to Officer Ergin, who covered for you. He, of course, was instrumental in finding the body. Did you know Fahrettin Bey?'

'Not really, sir,' she said. 'I only met him once, which was when I went to introduce myself to everyone on my patch, early last year. He was a man of few words.'

'What did you talk about?'

'As I say, I introduced myself. He told me he worked in the Grand Bazaar, that he lived alone, and that was that. I learned from the other residents that he was a jeweller. They said he brought work home. Once or twice I knocked on his door to make sure he had adequate insurance, but he never answered. I even tried leaving a note in his pigeonhole, but he failed to respond.'

The squad room of a small inner-city police station was a tense and somewhat scruffy place to be. Kerim had spent the first few years of his career at Sirkeci station – a nondescript blue and white building behind the railway station. With hindsight, he wondered how he had survived amongst all that in-your-face machismo. This place was no different, and he wondered how Officer Deniz coped.

'Did the other residents of the building talk about Fahrettin Bey much?' he asked.

'No,' she said. 'There are a lot of elderly people in that building and they don't tend to be out and about late. There are a few working girls round there who use some of the derelict buildings to do business.'

'Do you know any of them?'

'All of them. There aren't many, and they're all past their prime, if you know what I mean. They're poor, what can you say?'

'Have you ever arrested any of them?' Kerim asked.

Pervin Deniz flushed a little. 'No, sir,' she said. 'I've had no cause to do so.'

'You were, I understand, on duty last night when Constable Akar lost his life,' Kerim said.

'I was, sir, but . . .'

'But what?'

'I wasn't in the vicinity of the Kayserili Ahmet Paşa Caddesi. I was at the junction with Vefa Caddesi. That is also my patch, and . . . Sir, the place was crawling with police officers.'

'There were five,' Kerim said.

She looked down.

Kerim had been aware that one of the younger bekçiler had been watching them – or rather, watching Officer Deniz. He had a thick neck like a bull and was clenching his fists.

Kerim changed the subject. 'Returning to Fahrettin Bey, he was at his employment in the Kapalı Çarşı in the daytime and so he wouldn't have had visitors then. But what about at night?'

Pervin Deniz looked a little confused at first, then she said, 'I don't think he ever had any actual visitors, sir. The other residents of his building were shocked to discover he was a hoarder. There was a man I once saw who came to deliver things.'

'At night?'

She shrugged. 'Fahrettin Bey did private work at home,' she said.

'I know, but at night . . . Do you know who this man was?' Kerim asked.

'No,' she said. 'But I do remember ID'ing him. It was last year, in one of my old notebooks; if you wait, I can go and get it for you.'

Nilüfer Hanım, Fahrettin Müftüoğlu upstairs neighbour, was still making sure no one had stolen anything in her absence when Süleyman arrived. As soon as ricin had been discovered in the jeweller's place of work, the tenants of his building had been temporarily evacuated too. She let him in. Doğan, her husband, was out at the coffee house, but that didn't bother Nilüfer, who appeared not to worry too much about what her neighbours might think.

As she led him into her kitchen, she said, 'I looked ricin up on the Internet. Nearly lost my mind when I saw there was no cure. Whoever broke into Fahrettin Bey's old place must have been insane.'

'Is this apartment intact?' Süleyman asked.

'What I was doing when you arrived,' she said. 'Looking.' She ran a distracted hand through her greying hair. 'Anyway, Inspector, what do you want?'

She didn't offer him tea, as most women would have done, and that was so rare it was refreshing. She did ask him to sit down, however, and then sat opposite.

'We have a lot of information about Fuat Müftüoğlu, as the original purchaser of the Müftüoğlu apartment, but not about his wife,' he began. 'We know for instance that Fuat died in 2004, whereupon ownership of the property passed to his son. I know that Fahrettin's mother was called Isis and I understand from the colleague who came to talk to you and the other ladies that she was Egyptian . . .'

'Never spoke to us,' Nilüfer Hanım broke in. 'Couldn't speak Turkish. The three of them, her, Fuat and Fahrettin, spoke in French to each other.'

'Did you see her around?'

'Not much. She'd walk about in the corridors sometimes. I think just before she died she was a bit demented. Fahrettin used to lock her in when he went to work, and if she did get out, he'd quickly take her home.'

'I believe she died about ten years ago,' Süleyman said. 'Do you remember anything about that?'

She frowned. 'I heard about it from someone, but can't remember who.'

'No, I mean do you recall whether she died at home or in hospital? Her funeral taking place?'

She thought for a moment and then said, 'No. Of course, he

didn't talk much, Fahrettin Bey. What with him and that mute above him . . .' She frowned again. 'It was one of those things that we all just came to sort of know.'

'The death of Isis Hanım?'

'Yes,' she said.

'Nilüfer Hanım, did you ever notice any unpleasant smells coming from Fahrettin Bey's apartment?'

'Oh yes,' she said. 'All the time.'

'Did you ever say anything to him about it?'

'No.' She shook her head. 'People don't interfere round here. We're mostly middle aged or older. Just want a quiet life. He worked from home, so it was probably something to do with that.'

Walking back into Fahrettin Müftüoğlu's apartment once he had finished at Nilüfer Hanım's place, Süleyman asked the exhausted scene-of-crime team whether they had managed to distinguish any one room as a possible for the Müftüoğlu parents' bedroom. Only one bed had been found in what seemed to have been Fahrettin's bedroom. However, there was a wardrobe in another room that contained some women's clothes.

It was getting dark outside now, and he was tired, but he knew that if necessary he would work – his team as well as himself – into the night. He was getting married in less than forty-eight hours, and while he knew that this situation might still be unresolved when he returned from leave, he wanted to get as much done as he could.

In the space of the next half-hour, his phone rang three times, after which he headed off to headquarters. On the way, he called İkmen to ask whether Patrick could stay over in Sultanahmet that night.

One of the reasons Haluk Keleş' English was so good was because he had spent his university holidays with his mother's brother

215

and his family in New York. One of the words he had picked up, and particularly liked, was 'kitsch'. Of German origin, Americans used it a lot when referring to artworks or interior design that was deemed to be in poor taste, gaudy and/or sentimental.

Güven Tandoğan's apartment was a tribute to kitsch of the most elaborate and, some would say, offensive kind. There weren't that many statues amongst the hectares of zebra-print carpet, pink light fittings and real bear and tiger skins, but those that were exclusively celebrated the male form. Generally priapic, these supermen were rendered in metal of various types, including – so Güven told him – silver.

And while Keleş could see that the young man's father was clearly appalled by his son's lack of taste, he was probably also reacting to so much homoeroticism.

Rasım Tandoğan said, 'You've always been interested in the human body, haven't you, my soul?'

Güven, who was very tall, very slim and entirely self-centred, said, 'No, not really.'

'You have!' his father persisted. 'You always got top marks in biology at school.'

'Because I copied Ali Demirer,' Güven said. 'You know that!'

Clearly this exchange between moody man-child and ageing father in denial would go on forever unless Keleş took charge. He handed the photograph of the golden angel to Güven and said, 'Recognise it?'

'No.' But he was clearly entranced, his eyes fixed to the image. 'What is it?'

'What do you think it is, Güven?'

'A lovely golden winged man,' he said.

'Bit of the Rudolph Valentino about him, do you think?'

'Well, now you come to mention it . . .' He pursed his lips. 'And how did you come to know it as the divine Rudolph, Inspector Bey? Something you're not telling us...'

216

'It's pure gold,' Keleş said.

'Really?'

'Really.'

'Oh! I want!'

Keleş took the photograph away from him. 'Can't have,' he said. 'Although when I saw it, I thought of you. Ever come across a jeweller called Fahrettin Müftüoğlu?'

'Did he make this?' Güven asked.

'He did, and now he's dead,' Keleş said. 'The two things may be unconnected, but we can't rule it out. At the moment, the department owns this figure.'

'Well, I will buy it from you in a heartbeat!'

'Not for sale. But if you come across anything like it, I want to know.' He looked at Rasım briefly and then turned back to Güven. 'I know the crowd you run around with like this kind of stuff. That figure was a commission for someone, and I can't think of any better candidates for that than you and your crew.'

'Really?' Güven raised an eyebrow.

'So if this kind of stuff comes to market . . .'

'I will buy it,' Güven said. 'Why I should tell you, however . . .'

Keleş saw the old man cringe. Rasım Tandoğan, unlike his son, did not underestimate Haluk Bey. But then there were things that Haluk knew about each of them that the other didn't know.

He leaned in and whispered in the younger man's ear. 'You tell me, or your dad goes to prison,' he said. 'And if that happens, his bank accounts will be frozen.'

The fact that Güven's face went white told Keleş that he had fully understood the need to comply with his request.

While İkmen could see that Patrick was perfectly happy to spend the night with his family, he could tell the boy really wanted to be with his father. İkmen himself was ambivalent – on the one hand, he was happy that Mehmet was attempting

217

to clear his desk before his wedding, but on the other, he felt for the boy. In the morning, the kid was due to visit his grandmother, Nur Süleyman, in Arnavautköy. Luckily, his uncle, Murad, would be there too. A more easy-going version of Mehmet, he would make sure that his mother, whom Patrick called 'Scary Granny', was not openly hostile to the boy. As far as İkmen knew, Nur Süleyman was still refusing to attend Mehmet and Gonca's wedding.

He looked at his watch. He was due to meet Atyom Mafyan at eleven o'clock in Taksim. They would talk on the way to the Kızlar bar in Tarlabaşı, and their appointment with Şevket Sesler and his poker school. Atyom Bey lived a long way out of town, so İkmen imagined he would have to give himself over an hour to get there.

Out on the balcony with Fatma, he watched as his daughter Çiçek, son Kemal and Patrick brought steaming serving bowls from the kitchen to the dining table while Samsun snored loudly in her chair opposite the TV. Çiçek had spent hours preparing köfte, vegetables and rice and even making her own pide. İkmen was aware that while cooking for the family made her happy, it wasn't enough. Back in the day, she had been a flight attendant married to a pilot, but first her marriage broke down, and then, in the wake of the 2016 attempted coup, she lost her job. Dismissed on the paper-thin evidence of having the same app on her phone as certain enemies of the state, she now had to settle for a job in a Cihangir coffee shop. And she was single.

For a while, it had seemed as if a permanent relationship with Mehmet Süleyman was going to happen, but Çiçek had tired of his infidelities and now he was marrying his long-time mistress. Çiçek was going to the wedding because she bore her ex no ill-will, but she had declined an invitation from Gonca to go to her henna night. Watching the gypsy and her female relatives and friends paint their hands and feet while talking about the bride-groom was not for her.

Patrick opened the door to the balcony. 'Dinner's ready, Çetin Bey.'

İkmen smiled. 'Thank you, Patrick. I'll be in soon.'

The boy went away. İkmen looked at his wife. 'I have to go now, my darling. Dinner and then a poker game await. I know you wouldn't approve, but it's all in a good cause.'

Mehmet Süleyman made a personal phone call as he walked down the long corridor towards his office. To his son, as usual, to apologise.

'Information is coming in very rapidly now,' he said. 'If I can coordinate this, then perhaps I can leave things in an orderly fashion for Ömer Bey and Kerim Bey.'

Patrick sounded moody, although he made a heroic attempt at not saying anything inflammatory. His mother had always said that his father had a 'saviour complex' – doing everything he could to minimise adverse effects on others.

'It's OK,' he said. 'But you'd better do the stag, Dad.'

'I will,' Süleyman said with as much fake enthusiasm as he could muster. Patrick was so keen for all the men to go out and get drunk the night before his wedding. He changed the subject. 'What are you doing this evening with Çetin Bey and his family?' İkmen usually organised something for the boy, even if it was just sitting about outside the Mozaik talking.

'Oh, he's taking me to a poker game,' Patrick said.

'A poker game?' Süleyman stopped walking.

'Yeah, in Tarlabaşı.'

A different voice came on the line, speaking Turkish: İkmen's. 'I made the mistake of telling him I would be out tonight with Atyom Mafyan, playing poker. I didn't tell him he could come.'

'You're hopeless at poker,' Süleyman said. 'Tell Patrick he

isn't going. I forbid it. Why are you going, and who are you and Atyom Bey playing?' He'd lost track of what İkmen had been up to in the last twenty-four hours.

'Şevket Sesler . . .'

'Şevket Sesler!' he yelled. 'Is this something to do with Gonca's bedcover?'

'No,' İkmen said. 'I am simply accompanying Atyom Bey.'

'Sesler will know you, at least by sight.'

'No, he won't.'

'He will.'

'He won't. I've changed my appearance.'

Süleyman saw Ömer Mungun come out of his office. He wanted to speak to him.

'Why?'

'Why? Because he won't want even ex-police at his school.'

'No, he won't,' Süleyman said. 'What are you up to?'

'I told you, I'm accompanying an old friend.'

'Who by your own admission is a poker expert. Why does he need you? Is Atyom Bey in financial difficulty?'

'Not as far as I know,' İkmen said.

Süleyman was juggling too many balls and he knew it.

'I know you probably think I'm being a silly old bastard,' İkmen said, 'but you have to trust me on this, Mehmet. This is something I've got to do.'

It *was* something to do with Gonca, Süleyman could feel it.

İkmen seemed to read his thoughts. 'Gonca has nothing to do with this. She doesn't know where I'm going tonight.'

Süleyman sighed. 'So when are you due to be . . . where?'

'Midnight.'

'Oh, how apt!'

'No serious game starts before midnight,' İkmen said. 'This one is at Sesler's club, the Kızlar.'

Süleyman knew it. A girly rip-off bar. But what else could he

220

do but trust İkmen? He wasn't stupid, and in spite of increasing age, he wasn't dementing. 'Well, take your phone. Call me if anything happens, and I do mean anything you don't like. The Roma go tooled up to these things. Do not aggravate them.'

'I won't.'

'Oh, and how, may I ask, have you changed your appearance, Çetin?'

İkmen told him, and Süleyman found that he truly did not know whether to laugh or cry. Would he even recognise his friend when they met again?

Chapter 17

'I had to buy something,' Ömer Mungun said to Süleyman when he walked into his office, which stank of French fries. 'Şeymus Bey works in a Patso burger place.'

He knew that Süleyman had noticed him chewing as soon as he'd arrived. Patso burgers – bread stuffed with French fries and smothered in cheese, ketchup and mayonnaise – were extremely popular snacks, particularly with young people in İstanbul. The little Patso restaurant near headquarters was also the workplace of one of Ömer's informants, Şeymus Düzgün, an elderly Zaza Kurd who came originally from the town of Midyat in Ömer's home province of Mardin.

Süleyman probably wanted to say that Ömer hadn't needed to bring the thing back to his office, but he didn't.

Ömer said, 'He doesn't know Muharrem Aktepe, but he knows of him.'

'So why did you go and see him?' Süleyman asked.

'Because he's got a gambling habit,' Ömer said. 'Whole reason he's here in the city is because he had to leave Midyat before his creditors got hold of him. If there are two flies on a piece of baklava, he'll bet on which one will take off first. He's properly addicted.'

'So he knows of Aktepe . . .'

'Everyone does,' Ömer said. 'Bit of a Zaza legend, him having been a pehlivan, all those bouts he's opened books on over the years . . . But according to Şeymus, he stopped all that a long time ago. Apparently one or more of the gangs put a stop to it. He was always a lone operator, and you know how the godfathers hate those.'

İstanbul's criminal gang bosses only tolerated competition from people like themselves. Unless, of course, they wanted to participate in all-out war. But individuals seeking to snatch a bit of fake cigarette, moonshine booze or gambling action were generally doomed.

'So where does his money come from?' Süleyman asked.

Ömer shrugged. 'Apparently he's very generous to any Zaza speaker in trouble. Explains why those people I saw in Sarıgöl treated him like a made man. He's got one bank account, with Is Bank. Nothing spectacular in that.'

'So he keeps his money under the bed,' Süleyman said.

'A lot of people still do.'

A knock at the door brought their conversation to a close.

It had been a bad day for pain, so Sinem Gürsel had been obliged to take a lot of medication and go to bed, leaving baby Melda in the care of Madam Edith. She hadn't noticed when what had passed for sunlight that day faded into night. It was past 6 p.m. when Edith finally brought her a glass of tea.

Sitting on Sinem's bed with the sleeping baby in her arms, the elderly drag queen said, 'I would've thought Kerim Bey would have been home by now.'

Sinem looked at her phone, but there were no messages from her husband.

'He's working on the death of that policeman over in Vefa,' she said. 'One of their own. I expect he's obliged to work himself into the ground to get a result.'

'An unforgiving organisation, the police,' Edith said.

But Sinem knew it was more than that. Kerim was avoiding her. Although at first she had been happy that her husband seemed

223

to want sex with her now, she was also aware that it disturbed him. He had told her he didn't feel like himself any more, and indeed, the sex they did have included an urgency to the point of violence on Kerim's part. Was she just a substitute for what he'd had with his male lovers? She knew he had loved Pembe, but Pembe had still had masculine sex organs, and although on the surface Kerim had always related to her as a woman, Sinem suspected that what they had done in bed was different. Over the years, she'd tried not to think about it. She'd even bought ear plugs when Pembe had lived with them so she couldn't hear their moans of passion and words of love.

'Anyway, it doesn't matter,' Edith said. 'I'll stay here until he gets home. I'm not working tonight.'

Edith sang Edith Piaf songs – hence her name – in LGBT bars and clubs across the city, as well as helping Sinem look after Melda. But she was nearly seventy now, and so her appearances no longer took place seven nights a week. And she loved the couple and the little one. She was just sad she could do so little to help Sinem with the pain of rheumatoid arthritis she had to endure. Nobody could.

Sinem put her hand out. 'Bless you, darling.'

'So did you manage to get it from her or not?' Süleyman asked Kerim Gürsel.

'Yes.' He placed a small black notebook on Süleyman's desk. 'But only after I insisted. Officer Deniz told me she had written the name of the man she had ID'd down in one of her old notebooks, and left to go and find it. But she came back empty handed.'

'Saying what?'

'Saying that she couldn't find it. What she didn't know was that I'd noticed one of her male colleagues watching her interaction with me earlier. I may not be the most sensitive individual, but I know when a man thinks another man is hitting on his woman. He followed her out when she left to get the notebook.'

'What did you do when she said she couldn't find it?'

'I told her to look again. I said I'd come with her. Then miraculously, she found it, apparently with the help of the same male colleague. She drew my attention to a benign-looking entry featuring a man called Nacı Sak, who was delivering a package to an unspecified person in that building. So I began to go through her notes until I found this.'

He opened the book and showed it to the other men.

'The name of the person she ID'd is not so much crossed out as obliterated. However, his kimlik number remains, and although there has been an attempt to obliterate that too, I suspect it was done in rather more haste, so I played around with it for a while. And while I can't say for certain that the name I came up with is correct, it does match that of someone we know.'

'Which is?'

'Atyom Mafyan.'

'The jeweller?' Ömer asked.

'The same. Officer Deniz ID'd this man on the eighteenth of October last year, which is prior to the date she pointed out to me. Now because I can't be certain the number is correct, that might just be a coincidence. Also, Atyom Bey was Müftüoğlu's employer, so he may well have had a legitimate reason for delivering something to him.'

'Does Atyom Bey's ID number appear anywhere else?' Süleyman asked.

'I've not managed to look at every entry yet, but I don't think so,' Kerim said. 'Officer Deniz told me she doesn't ID everyone she sees. Sometimes she just speaks to them. But what was running through my head was the amount of gold involved in that angel statue. Müftüoğlu had to have got it from somewhere – unless he stole it.'

225

'Did Officer Deniz make a note of what Atyom Bey was delivering?' Ömer asked.

'No.'

'And what about this watchman you said went with her to get the notebook?' Ömer asked.

'Officer Yıldırım Yaman,' Kerim said. 'Thirty-five, married, three children, built like a bull.'

'You said that you suspected Officer Deniz is in a relationship with him,' Süleyman said.

'I'd put money on it being abusive in some way. She was on duty the night Akar died. She told me her patch was crawling with our officers, and that she was away from the scene at the crossroads with Vefa Caddesi when Akar was attacked. I got the distinct impression she was not where she should have been.'

'Could have been with this Yaman,' Ömer said.

'Very possibly. But my main concern is this scrubbed-out name,' Kerim said. 'Why? If the visitor was Atyom Bey, why obliterate his name? He was Müftüoğlu's employer, he knew where he lived; why should he not be delivering something to his home?'

'Well, I've a warrant to search the Aktepe apartment in Sarıgöl tomorrow morning,' Süleyman said.

'Good.'

'I've also had a message from the lab confirming that our St Foy statue has been fashioned from materials that are as much as five hundred years old. It does contain a fragment from a human skull. But it was put together recently, using modern techniques and equipment.'

'So the real one's in France . . .'

'Ours is the forgery, yes.' Süleyman nodded. 'But it's really good quality, and I'm told it would take a high level of skill and knowledge for anyone to be able to tell the difference. If Fahrettin Müftüoğlu did make it, he was more than just a jeweller. We know he worked from home as well as in the Kapalı Çarşı. We know he was an innovator.'

'GülGül, his employer, is innovative,' Kerim said.

'Not enough for him,' Süleyman replied. 'But in light of your evidence, Kerim Bey, maybe his employer was on board with some of his ideas. Fahrettin wanted to use jewellery as sympathetic magic. Atyom Bey wouldn't allow it, so he says, and so Müftüoğlu did . . . well, seemingly something else from home. Maybe something in which his employer colluded.'

'So he occupied himself making forgeries,' Kerim said. 'He had a mummified head in his possession. Was that a forgery, and whose head is it?'

Süleyman nodded. 'In spite of the fact that DNA analysis of the head may well be impossible, and will be expensive, I have ordered it to be carried out. While I can find evidence for the death of Müftüoğlu's father's, I cannot track down that of his mother.'

'You think it might be her, sir?'

'Possibly, Ömer. Allegedly Müftüoğlu didn't like the old woman.'

'Or maybe he treated her body the way she would have wanted,' Kerim said.

'Because she was Egyptian?' Süleyman smiled. 'I don't think they do that any more, Kerim Bey.'

Ömer Mungun said, 'Müftüoğlu was strange, though, sir.'

'This is true.' Süleyman paused. 'Haluk Bey thinks he might have a lead on the angel via the son of an old art fraud gangster he knows. He believes the angel has homoerotic overtones, something that appeals to this man's son.'

Kerim Gürsel frowned. 'How do we move forward?' he asked. 'I'll be honest, I've never worked on an investigation as, well, fragmented as this before. I've three unread messages from Sergeant Yavaş on my phone.'

'Where has she been?' Süleyman asked.

'At Dr Sarkissian's laboratory.'

'Dr Sarkissian, yes,' Süleyman said. 'I need to get back to him.'

While Kerim read his messages, Süleyman called the doctor and told him that he'd arranged to have some items of women's clothing thought to belong to Isis Müftüoğlu delivered to the forensic institute. Hopefully they would yield some hairs. Then he asked the doctor to send the jar of viscera they had found in the Vefa apartment for DNA testing along with the head.

So that his colleagues could hear, Süleyman put his phone on speaker to listen to the doctor's reply.

'As I've told you, Inspector, I'm not sure that either the intestines or the head will yield anything that can be genetically tested. My colleague Dr Akyıldız, the archaeological pathologist, was very dubious about the mummified head in that respect, but we will do our best.'

When the call had finished, they all sat in silence for a moment, then Kerim Gürsel said, 'So what do we do about Atyom Bey?'

People were talking about Huriye Can's screaming. Where had those boys of hers been when she was begging the man for mercy? Everyone, including Rahul Mengüç the haberdasher, knew about it. Fortunately, when he had gone to the Cans' place earlier to see how they were getting on with Gonca's bedcover, it had been before Munir had allegedly made his visit.

People speculated over the reason for their argument, but only in tiny whispering groups or in the privacy of their own heads. Munir Can was Şevket Sesler's man, so no one dared so much as mention his name. The Turks and the Kurds and the immigrants probably didn't know what had been going on, because none of them could speak Romani. But everyone knew a thug when they saw one, and Munir wasn't the sort of man to take questions, especially not from a gaco.

It was Neziye who had picked up on what was being said. At first, Rahul Bey had refused to give it credence, but as the afternoon had worn on into night, he started to realise that he'd been in denial about it for a long time. So monstrous was it that he'd simply turned his mind away. And yet Neziye had been adamant, her source impeccable.

'Papa, I would not have believed it had it not come from Zambak Hanım,' she'd said. Then a thought had occurred to her and she'd put a hand up to her mouth.

'What is it?' her father had asked.

And then Neziye had said, 'Gonca Hanım's bedcover!'

From that point on, Rahul Bey knew what he had to do, even though it made him feel sick to his stomach. While he was not telling the police, he was telling a gaco, and that was usually something to be avoided.

Connections to ethnic Kurds like the Aktepe family were beginning to build. The latest being Dr Sarkissian's thesis that Constable Akar had been killed with a short knife, possibly a khanjar, associated with Kurds, which possessed a blade that waved sensuously on both sides.

Süleyman and Ömer Mungun briefed the team due to accompany them on the following morning's search of the Aktepes' apartment in Sarıgöl, while Kerim Gürsel prepared to go back to the crime scene in Vefa. The examination of Fahrettin Müftüoğlu's apartment and its vast contents was nearly at an end. Despite the fact that it was now secured by a new team of officers, Kerim felt anxious in case whoever had killed Akar came back to search the apartment again. It was unlikely, but in truth it was also an excuse on two counts.

Night-watch officers Deniz and Yaman were both on duty, and he wanted to see if they interacted. He was also, he knew, anxious for Deniz's safety. Had Yaman made her clumsily change the name and the kimlik number in her notebook? And if they were romantically involved, was he hurting her?

However, before he could go to Vefa, he knew he had to make a couple of calls. The first one was to his wife. Edith would probably still be with her, but he owed them both the courtesy of telling them what he was doing. With attacks on trans girls and drag queens escalating across the country in recent months, not even Tarlabaşı was immune, and so normally when he returned to his apartment, he would drive Edith home.

When Sinem answered, he told her he was on an observation. 'Tell Edith she can stay over,' he said. 'But if she wants to go home, pay for a taxi.'

Sinem agreed. Then she lowered her voice. 'Kerim, you're not staying out because of what we did, you know, in bed . . .'

He felt his heart skip a beat. 'No, of course not.'

'Because—'

'I have to go,' he said. 'Kiss Melda goodnight from Daddy.'

He ended the call and put his head in his hands. He hated lying to her. But there was still something else he had to do before he could leave for Vefa, and that was to call Atyom Mafyan – because that was what he and Süleyman had agreed.

There had been a time when the Golden Horn district of Zeyrek had drifted almost entirely from the consciousness of the average İstanbullu. Even its greatest treasure, the vast Zeyrek mosque, once the Byzantine monastery of the Pantokrator, had remained deserted and semi-derelict until comparatively recently. Now under restoration, it and Zeyrek as a whole had joined other parts of the city on the tourist trail, and many new shops and restaurants had opened, taking advantage of the district's quaint Ottoman charm.

Unable to get an answer when he called Mustafa Gölcük's mistress, Fındık Elvan, on her phone, Mehmet Süleyman drove to Zeyrek and visited her florist's shop on İtfaiye Caddesi. Unlike much of the quarter, this part of Zeyrek, opposite the ancient Aqueduct of Valens, was characterised not by old wooden houses but by low-rise apartment blocks and shops. One of these was where Fındık Hanım had her shop, which was called Lale. And in spite of the lateness of the hour, it was still open – no doubt to catch the husbands returning home from work.

Süleyman had never seen Fındık Hanım, so he assumed that she was the willowy, smiling young woman who stood by to serve him. But that young lady, it turned out, was her daughter. Fındık herself was a middle-aged lady, albeit one who eschewed the more traditional clothes of a youngish widow in favour of denim.

When Süleyman told her who he was, she reluctantly agreed to speak to him at the back of the shop. But she didn't offer him a chair.

'I've told you I was with Mustafa,' she said. 'Not going to deny it.'

Mustafa Gölcük wasn't an attractive man either physically or in terms of his personality, but there was no accounting for people's preferences.

'I'm not asking you to, hanım,' Süleyman said. 'I simply want to confirm with you Constable Gölcük's times of arrival and departure.'

'I told you.'

He placed in front of her a written record of the conversation he'd had with Gölcük, who had finally admitted to being with this woman for just over an hour. She glanced at it.

'Seems right,' she said. 'Course, I don't remember exactly . . .'

'Was Constable Gölcük's visit planned?' Süleyman asked.

'He comes over when he can,' she said.

'Did you realise he was supposed to be on duty?'

'No, why should I?'

231

'He must have arrived here in his uniform.'

'He always does,' she said. 'I like it. Know what I mean?'

He did. There were people who were turned on by a uniform. He wasn't one of them, but seemingly Fındık Hanım was. He wondered whether they played out weird fantasies, and decided that it was best for his mind if he thought they didn't.

'So Constable Gölcük was with you for approximately an hour?'

'I told you he was,' she said.

Her confrontational manner was beginning to irritate him. 'You do know, Fındık Hanım, that Constable Gölcük's visit to you resulted in his colleague being murdered, and theft from a crime scene.'

For a moment she looked as if she might be about to shrug these facts off, but then she said, 'I never wanted those things to happen, and neither did Mustafa.'

'I'm sure you didn't.'

'But you must understand that me and him, we don't choose to be together. Us meeting just sort of happened. We fell in love.'

'Constable Gölcük is married,' Süleyman said as his own infidelities briefly came back to haunt him.

She sighed. 'He's not happy.'

Süleyman didn't want to get into this with her. But he also felt she had a right to know what her lover had said about her, which basically boiled down to the fact that he had been feeling horny that night, and because she had been near at hand, he'd gone to see her for a fuck. He'd even described her as 'a bit of fun'. Süleyman didn't pull any punches. If Gölcük had left his post in order to allow someone to get into Müftüoğlu's apartment, and either by accident or design had caused his partner's death, he wanted to know about it. But Fındık Hanım held her tongue. Eventually Süleyman said, 'If you are covering for him in any way, you should own up to that now. Because if we do discover that he was involved in theft, contamination of a crime scene and murder, we will come for you.'

Still she said nothing. Silent time passed until he said, 'Well then, I will leave it with you, hanım.'

But as he turned to go, he heard a gasp or a sob come from her. Then she said, 'I don't care what he's said to you. Mustafa's going to marry me. When his boy goes into the army in two years' time, he'll divorce that old bitch.'

Marlboro, Çetin İkmen's half feral, un-neutered cat, rarely gave anyone apart from İkmen the time of day. But he seemed, strangely, to have taken to Patrick Süleyman. Having slithered into his son Bülent's shiny grey suit, İkmen came into the living room to find the boy, with the cat on his lap, watching BBC World on the TV.

Unaccustomed to wearing trousers that were quite so snug, he first shook his legs and then sat down, gently and gingerly, just in case he put strain on the seams. The boy glanced up.

'God,' he said. 'You look as if you're in your twenties!'

'Apart from my face, my hands and my general deportment, yes,' İkmen said. 'I could not agree more.'

'But you don't look like you,' Patrick continued.

'Which is the point . . .'

İkmen's phone rang. He looked to see who was calling and, having seen that it was Rahul Bey, left Patrick to go out on the balcony.

'Rahul Bey, what can I do for you?'

He heard the old man draw in a shaky breath. 'Oh Çetin Bey, what can I say?'

'What's the matter?' İkmen lit a cigarette. Bülent had warned him not to make any burn holes in his suit, but he was desperate.

'It was my daughter, Neziye, who heard them . . .'

İkmen sat down. 'Heard who?' he said. 'Start from the beginning, Rahul Bey.'

Again the old man took a deep breath. 'Neziye had just gone

to collect Gonca Hanım's bedcover from the Can family when it started. About five, it was. She took the cover from Huriye Can, inspected it, paid the lady and left. But as she walked away – I should say he didn't see her – Munir Can arrived. Drunk.'

'And . . .'

'There was an altercation. Neziye, in common with the whole street, heard Munir slap Huriye around. As you know, people don't get involved. But they were screaming, and what they said could be heard all over the mahalle. It is, Çetin Bey, to my shame, something I have heard rumours about. But it's not my family and I didn't want to believe it. I know that's wrong, but . . .'

'Didn't want to believe what?' İkmen asked. 'You told me yourself that Munir and Huriye Can have been, well, he's been . . .'

'It's not Huriye Hanım that Munir Can wants,' the old man said.

And then it clicked into place. İkmen said, 'The child.'

'Şaziye, yes. His own niece.'

The dress was finally finished. Didim and one of Gonca's other sisters, Sema, helped her try it on. Getting into it alone wasn't an option, as it was far too heavy. Like the Ottoman wedding gowns on which it had been based, it was made from rich silks and velvets and included little squares of golden sea silk from the giant byssus mussel – the most expensive cloth on earth.

Even without the tiara that would be woven into her hair and the purple satin shoes that would be on her feet when she was married, Gonca looked magnificent. But she looked at herself in the mirror with a critical eye.

'Do you think,' she said, 'that the waist could go in just a little bit?'

'No!' Didim said. 'Mehmet Bey said no corset, remember?'

'I could just wear a little one . . .'

'No!'

Gonca sighed. 'When he sees me, I want him to have difficulty controlling himself.'

'Oh, that'll happen!' Sema snapped. 'I've never known a man so besotted.'

Gonca smiled. 'You think it indecent, don't you?'

'I don't know how you do it. But then how would I?'

Even amongst her own family, Gonca was feared. Like their mother, she knew how to bewitch people. Although that didn't work with everyone, and her mind turned back to Şevket Sesler. Oh, the Roma godfather believed in her, but he didn't fear her. Quite the reverse. He could see inside her mind and she knew it. She'd known it that first time he had visited her after his father's death. Şevket Bey knew she had been meddling; it was the whole reason he had her on a leash, at his beck and call with her cards day or night. He was keeping his enemy close and showing that to the world. In common with everyone who had pointed the finger at her when Harun Sesler died, she was waiting for him to strike.

Chapter 18

Mehmet Süleyman knew he should go home. He needed to sleep, especially if he was going out on what his son called his 'stag' the following night. But his mind wouldn't let him rest. Kerim Gürsel had called Atyom Mafyan about his nocturnal visit to Fahrettin Müftüoğlu's apartment the previous October. The jeweller hadn't been able to recall the occasion, but had said, quite reasonably, that as Müftüoğlu's employer, he had to know where he lived and had a perfect right to visit him. This was true. What he didn't apparently recall was delivering anything to him. And yet the bekçi had explicitly stated that the man who had given her Mafyan's ID number – or an approximation thereof – had been making a delivery. Maybe it really hadn't been Mafyan. But then who had Officer Deniz, and maybe her paramour, been trying to protect?

In the world of art fraud, there were some big players; this was a known fact. Various Russian mafias had been early adopters on behalf of interested oligarchs, and maybe even those further up the food chain. They had, after all, been in war-torn Syria for over a decade. But European artefacts were rare. If required, they had to be stolen from peaceful countries, where they were usually heavily guarded. Faithful replacement of items on billionaires' lists, or maybe even those of hostile governments, made sense. But Süleyman had never heard of such a thing. Even Haluk Keleş, from whom this notion had originated, was not actively pursuing such a line of inquiry. As far as Süleyman knew, he was still looking into the activities of some local, fairly low-level art enthusiasts amongst the city's known crime families. This other operation, if it even existed, was at a much higher level.

He walked over to the chart, an identical copy of the one they shared in the operations room, to look again at the connections between the various actors involved with or around Fahrettin Müftüoğlu. What a strange man he had been. Educated, artistic, romantic – according to his wife – clearly secretive, possessed of unusual beliefs about the properties of sometimes dangerous substances . . .

A knock on his door broke his concentration and he called out, 'Come.'

Lurking apparently aimlessly around Taksim Square at night was not, Çetin İkmen knew, a good look. Even, as he was, contemplating the Republic Memorial – that artwork designed to commemorate the Turkish War of Independence – didn't absolve him from scrutiny. Boys in a uniform he himself had once worn approached him to 'move on', which he did.

Where was Atyom Mafyan? He'd called him multiple times on his mobile but had failed to make contact. It was now 11.30 p.m. And while time could be rather an elastic concept in the golden city on the Bosphorus, İkmen was beginning to feel distinctly nervous. Had Atyom Bey forgotten their appointment? He couldn't believe that. The Armenian was, if not addicted, then very fond of poker. Was he maybe stuck in traffic? That was possible, but surely he'd answer his phone if that were the case. It might be illegal, but everyone did it. Something was wrong.

But then something was already wrong that had nothing to do with Atyom Mafyan. İkmen had come to Taksim Square not to go as planned to Şevket Sesler's poker school, but to tell the

Armenian that the trip was off. He'd tried to contact him when he'd still been at home, to no avail. Now it seemed he couldn't find him at their meeting place either. He knew he'd have to leave soon to return home, where he could, without interruption, consider his options.

With one last glance over his shoulder, he finally left Taksim at 11.45.

Was it just because he'd been an art student that Haluk Keleş was so good at recognising images and so apparently poor when it came to recall of names, dates and addresses?

'I know her,' he said to Mehmet Süleyman, pointing at a photograph on his case chart.

'Canan Müftüoğlu?' Süleyman said.

'Don't remember her name.'

'We've been talking about her for days!' Süleyman said. 'She's our suicide's wife.'

'She's not someone I know well,' Keleş said.

He had already demonstrated that he watched probably way too many movies.

Süleyman said, 'Maybe she reminds you of someone on Netflix.'

Keleş shot him a glare. 'Fuck off, Mehmet Bey.' He sat down. 'No, she's an acquaintance.'

'Someone you were attracted to?'

Keleş glanced at the photograph again. 'Not my type. It will come to me.'

'It would be useful to know,' Süleyman said. 'I've a warrant to search her father's alleged apartment in Sarıgöl tomorrow. Maybe seeing her in person might jog your memory.'

He honestly hadn't thought he'd hear from her again. In common with everyone he came across during the course of an investigation, Ömer Mungun had given Canan Müftüoğlu his card, but he had not expected her to call him – not after their awkward parting in front of the apartment in Sarıgöl.

She said, 'I need to see you.'

He'd been in bed when she'd called. Unbeknown to her, he was due to be with Süleyman and his search team in Sarıgöl at 6 a.m. the following morning.

'What do you want, Canan Hanım?' he asked.

'I'm afraid,' she said.

'Afraid of what?'

The line went silent.

'Canan Hanım?'

He could hear his sister moving around the apartment, singing to herself. For the first time in years, she was in a relationship and she was happy.

'I can't tell you over the phone, Ömer Bey,' Canan Müftüoğlu said. 'Can you come over?'

'To Sarıgöl?'

'No,' she said. 'I'm in a bar. Kapielli5 on Sıraselviler Caddesi.'

He knew it. It wasn't far from Süleyman's apartment.

'Please!' she said. 'I'm frightened.'

'Frightened of what?' He had to be so careful. He'd already slipped up with this woman once. He said, 'I will have to tell Inspector Süleyman.'

'I need you to come now!' she said. She sounded terrified, but what could he do? She was possibly involved in art fraud, and maybe even murder.

'What are you doing in a bar?' he asked. He couldn't hear any sort of noise in the background at her end.

Canan Müftüoğlu burst into tears.

He needed at least a few hours' sleep and so Mehmet Süleyman had decided to go back to his apartment – until he realised he'd never sleep there. He'd just stare at the ceiling until it was time to get up. So instead he drove to Balat. As soon as he arrived, Gonca shooed her many sisters out of her bedroom. They had all looked at him with cold, disapproving eyes. He wasn't supposed to be with her until they were married. But he didn't care. Now they were making love, he felt right with the world, almost like a man who didn't have the weight of a complex investigation on his shoulders.

He ran his hands down Gonca's torso and then held her hips tight. As she moved up and down on top of him, she breathed heavily and arched her back.

At that moment, his phone rang. One of his hands shot out to take the call, but Gonca grabbed it and placed it between her breasts.

'Baby, not now!'

In reality, he couldn't have stopped if he'd wanted to. And so he didn't, and neither did Gonca. It was only after they'd both achieved satisfaction and she was lying in his arms in a sex-drunk haze that he picked up his phone and played the voicemail that Çetin İkmen had left for him. All it said was 'Call me.'

He looked down at Gonca. 'It's Çetin Bey. I'll have to phone back. Sorry.'

She stroked his chest. 'Darling, I'm just so happy you didn't stop.'

He pressed callback and heard İkmen pick up immediately. He hoped nothing was wrong with Patrick. He also hoped that İkmen didn't need rescuing from Şevket Sesler's poker school.

'Mehmet . . .'

'I'm sorry, Çetin, I was asleep.'

'Atyom Bey failed to meet me for this poker school in Tarlabaşı,' İkmen said. 'I've tried to call him, but he doesn't pick up. I've a bad feeling about this.'

'In what way?'

İkmen sounded irritable. 'You know how I do and don't know these things!' he said.

Süleyman did, and he had always taken it seriously.

'I don't know where he lives, except that it's out of town,' İkmen continued. 'And I am loath to contact Garbis Bey, even though I know he will be up, because I don't want to alarm him. You must have—'

'I will access his address and go over,' Süleyman said. 'Just need to put some clothes on. Shall I come and collect you?'

'Yes. Thank you, dear boy,' İkmen said. 'You know I wouldn't do this to you if Atyom Bey wasn't already peripherally involved in your investigation. Oh, and apologise to Gonca for me, would you, please?'

On his home turf, in Tarlabaşı, working women just walked the streets. Wearing a variety of revealing outfits, they plied their trade in flesh both locally and further into the depths of the city. In a place like Vefa, prostitution was more hidden. Furtive and shamefaced, it often came with a scarf on its head, a long coat on its back and a desperation born of acute poverty sometimes combined with a home life that involved great cruelty.

Seemingly rising from the earth once the sun had set, these women – wives of outwardly respectable men who drank in secret, mothers of boys addicted to bonzai, sisters to gigolos – plied their trade in dark streets where men came to pour themselves into women who at least looked clean. And they were cheap, Kerim Gürsel thought as he watched them, these women who looked like your wife but who did things she would not even dream about. They were hardly the bold sirens local matron Alev Hanım had described to Süleyman and Ömer Mungun.

One of the women hung about in the doorway of what had once been a house opposite Fahrettin Müftüoğlu's apartment building. Now a shattered wooden ruin, the place could easily have been somewhere colonised by desperate Syrian refugees. Instead it was used by the woman, who gave her name as Soğut, as a place where she could bring men to have sex for money. She of course thought that Kerim was one of their number, and was naturally cautious when he told her he was a police officer. She was also initially afraid.

'Oh, Inspector Bey!' she said. 'What must you think of me? Please, please, please don't arrest me! I'll do anything . . .'

However, when he talked about the bekçiler, the woman's mood shifted, just slightly.

'I know the lady,' she said. 'She's nice.'

In appearance, this woman was about as far away from the popular image of a prostitute as one could get. Over fifty, head scarfed, she told Kerim that she had been pushed onto the streets by her husband, who was unemployed, and by the need to provide for her disabled daughter. She continued, 'Sometimes the watch lady gives me money to go home.'

'Officer Deniz?'

'If that's her name yes,' she said.

'Do you know why she gives you money?' Kerim asked.

She said she didn't. But she was lying.

A man put his head around the open front door and, seeing Kerim with the woman, quickly left without a word.

'I know you don't want to get Officer Deniz into trouble . . .' Kerim began.

But she persisted. 'Why would I? Such a kind young woman. She has a good heart.'

Pervin Deniz had told Kerim that she spoke to the local prostitutes, that she tried to help them . . .

'Are you saying she's done something wrong?' Soğut asked.

'No.'

'So why'd you want to know about her?'

He sighed. 'Hanım, I will be honest with you, I am concerned about her.'

'Oh.'

'As you may know, one of our officers was murdered on this street—'

'I heard,' she cut in, 'I saw nothing.'

'But you were here?' Kerim asked.

She looked at the floor. 'No, Inspector Bey, I wasn't.'

'So where were you?'

'I was at home.'

'You chose not to work that night?'

'No,' she said. He could almost see the internal struggle she was having.

He said, 'Tell me, hanım. You will not be in trouble. Did Officer Deniz ask you to go away that night?'

She began to cry.

'Hanım . . .'

'Ah, she's such a lovely young woman! She would never have done anything to hurt that policeman!'

In spite of questioning people who lived in the area when Akar was killed, Kerim was fairly certain he hadn't seen any testimonies from local working women – which wasn't surprising. In places like Vefa, in the conservative district of Fatih, such activities were deeply shameful and furtive. Even finding out that these women existed had been an accident.

He took her hand and led her to a rotten bench at the back of the old house.

'Hanım,' he said, 'tell me. Officer Deniz will not get into trouble.'

This was not strictly true, but if he was right, he knew he could make a case that she had been manipulated. Whether he was believed or not was another matter.

'They came here to make love,' Soğut Hanım said. 'Officer

Deniz and her boyfriend. The poor things! She told me he is married to a woman he does not love. An alcoholic! I mean, I know men drink in secret, but a woman?' She shook her head. 'So sad.'

Çetin İkmen looked out of the car window at the smooth blackness of the Bosphorus. Having driven through Besiktas, they were on Çırağan Caddesi, passing by the old palace, now a hotel, where Mehmet Süleyman and Gonca Şekeroğlu were due to be married in less than forty-eight hours. It was still a long way to Tarabya, which was situated around a large bay to the north of the posh village of Yeniköy.

Both men were uncharacteristically quiet. İkmen because he was still wearing Bülent's uncomfortable suit and he had a bad feeling about Atyom Mafyan. Süleyman because he had not long ago found out that the Armenian lived in the same apartment building as Canan Müftüoğlu's father. He knew he should have made that connection before, but he hadn't. Was all the razzmatazz around his wedding pulling his attention away from his job? And this was just the gaco wedding! The Roma version, when it happened at Hıdırellez, was set to be way more elaborate and would go on for days.

Eventually Süleyman spoke. 'I should have looked at all and any connections between people,' he said.

'Mehmet, dear boy, that is why you have junior officers,' İkmen said. 'We miss things. I've done it, you've done it . . .'

'It shouldn't happen!'

İkmen sighed. 'I sometimes think you were with Zelfa for too long,' he said. 'All that useless Catholic guilt! Take your hair shirt off and move on!'

'Hair shirt?'

'Monks wear them when they want to distract themselves from thoughts about sex,' İkmen said. 'Whether it works or not, I don't know. But what I do know is that Atyom Bey is not a man to pass up an opportunity to play poker. At least he would have called me, and he hasn't. His phone just rings out.'

It began to rain. The few people still up and about ran for cover. İkmen said, 'So this Canan Müftüoğlu's family you were telling me about . . .'

'The father, Muharrem Aktepe, was a pehlivan back in the 1980s,' Süleyman said. 'Not successful. Then he started training youngsters – mainly in the taking of banned substances, as far as I can tell. Then gambling.'

'Poker?' İkmen asked.

'Not as far as I know. But then suddenly he's got a lot of money and a lot of respect from his fellow Zaza speakers in Sarıgöl.'

'And you think he's part of some art forgery operation?'

'I think it's possible. But I don't think he's the prime mover – far from it.'

'So who do you think might be?' İkmen asked.

Süleyman shook his head, tired beyond his limits. 'I was coming to the conclusion that maybe Atyom Bey, because he was Müftüoğlu's employer, because we know he visited him at home, because maybe he has gambling debts . . . But perhaps not. I just hope that it's not someone exalted and therefore untouchable.'

'Me too,' İkmen said.

They drove on up the coastal road, past Bebek, through Yeniköy and into Tarabya.

Süleyman would have said no and Ömer Mungun knew it. He would have told him to tell Canan Müftüoğlu to call 155 if she was frightened. And anyway, frightened of what?

He called Kerim Gürsel. But that just went to voicemail.

Canan had cried on the phone. He was putting his clothes on

to go out to her. But he still didn't know what was wrong. Was she being followed? Stalked, even? Clearly she was trapped in that bar in some fashion. Did she not trust any of the staff there to keep her safe?

He clipped his watch around his wrist. This had to be some sort of manipulation. At best she had the hots for him, at worst . . . What? Ömer sat down on his bed.

Her husband had been involved in art fraud, maybe even art theft. True, she had never lived with him, but then what was that about? She had to have been married to Fahrettin for some reason. They never lived together, his mother hated her, Müftüoğlu had been, as far as Ömer could make out, ugly, introverted, secretive and greedy. What had there been to fall in love with?

Had the man looked like his boss, would Ömer have thought differently about that? He would certainly have been able to understand it more readily. But then was that just prejudice on his part? What did it mean to say that some people were ugly anyway? That young girl his parents had lined up for him as potential bride material was absolutely beautiful, but he didn't want her. She was an eighteen-year-old virgin who lived with her widowed father, a subsistence farmer, in a mud house down on the Mesopotamian plain. She'd never left the district of the Tur Abdin in her life, and from the one conversation he'd had with her, he'd discovered that her Turkish was poor. The only thing they had in common was their ancient, almost extinct religion.

He tied his shoelaces. He wanted a woman. Not really one like Canan Müftüoğlu. He'd have sex with her; in fact he wanted to do that because he had dreamed about it. But he also knew that at the very least she was complicated. No, what he wanted he couldn't have. Like Gonca Hanım's daughter, Asana, the lawyer. Remote and arrogant and effortlessly sexy. He would be prepared to bet she was as wild as her mother, and that was awe inspiring. He'd seen the bites and scratches on Süleyman's neck and arms. Ömer shuddered. He'd have to go out to Canan, he couldn't just leave her!

Then his phone rang.

The kapıcı of the Sarkis Bey Apartments was an elderly Armenian. He told Çetin İkmen, who had set out to charm him immediately, that Atyom Bey had come home from his business in the Grand Bazaar at 7.30 and had not been out since.

'The last Armenian in the Sarkis Bey Apartments,' the old man said, shaking his head. He pulled a face. 'Got Kurds in the penthouse, God save us! Don't hear a word of Turkish up there now!'

Süleyman resisted the urge to ask about these people he knew as the Aktepe family and let İkmen do the talking. This was about Atyom Mafyan.

'I know Atyom Bey's cousin,' İkmen continued. 'Garbis Bey . . .'

'At the Üç Horan?' the old man said.

'Yes.'

'Ah. He's a good man. Poor but good, God bless him . . .'

İkmen looked at Süleyman's face, which was showing signs of impatience.

'So,' he said, 'I've been trying to call Atyom Bey for the last three hours, but he doesn't pick up.'

The old man, whose name was Vahan Bey, said, 'He's asleep – maybe.'

'Mmm. Through his phone ringing?' İkmen said. 'I don't think so. I mean, you may well be right, Vahan Bey, but . . . Look, we are worried that he might be sick. Sick, living alone, you know . . .'

'I will call him on his landline,' the old man said, and dialled a number into his ancient Bakelite telephone.

But no one answered. Vahan Bey said, 'Well he's definitely

not gone out – not unless he's grown wings.' He took a key down from the board behind his desk. 'Let us look. I will knock on his door, and if he doesn't answer, I will open it.'

He found her talking to a young girl outside the local bakkal. The girl was crying and Officer Deniz had a hand on her shoulder. What was wrong with the kid, Kerim couldn't tell, but as he moved closer, he could see that she was toothless. Had she had her teeth knocked out by some jealous lover? Then she saw him and, with a quick squeeze of Deniz's hand, she ran away.

Pervin Deniz turned to see what had spooked her young friend. 'Inspector Gürsel? What are you doing here?'

'I want to talk to you,' he said.

'What about?'

Kerim could see Officer Yıldırım Yaman at the bottom of the street, waiting for her. When he saw Kerim, he moved away.

'About your boyfriend. And before you try to deny it, know that I am fully aware of your affair with Officer Yaman.'

'Oh God!'

He took her arm and they began to walk.

'But that doesn't interest me,' Kerim said. 'Well, not immediately. What I want to talk to you about is an Armenian jeweller called Atyom Mafyan.'

She didn't have a clue who he meant, so Kerim explained what he had found in her notebook. Then he showed her.

When she saw the entry, Pervin Deniz said, 'Oh, I don't remember that. More recently there was a man delivering to the building . . .'

'Is that your handwriting?' Kerim asked.

'Yes. But . . .'

'But what?'

She shook her head. 'Oh, nothing. It's . . .' She turned, looking around, as if searching for someone, and Kerim knew.

'Was he with you when you ID'd Atyom Mafyan?' he asked.

'He?' She looked away.

'Yıldırım Yaman,' Kerim said.

'I don't know. I told you I don't know this Atyom whoever. I showed you the entry for the other man who came to the building.'

'You showed me on instruction from Yaman,' Kerim said. 'So I would be distracted. I don't suppose you thought I'd take your notebook.'

She looked at the ground.

Kerim said, 'I thought not.' He took her arm again. 'I want you to tell me about it.'

She nodded. 'Oh, but my duty!'

'I think you'll find that Officer Yaman is at the bottom of the street,' Kerim said. 'And I've told your commander you're with me.'

'So where are we going?' she asked.

'Headquarters.'

'I'm going to lose my job, aren't I?' she said as he led her towards his car. 'Bekçiler are supposed to be models of morality.'

'Are they?' Kerim could remember the days of the old bekçi, when they were simply unarmed community officers who knew everyone and were usually called 'uncle' by local people. Nice, helpful men generally, usually quite old. Not like this new, armed young cohort of, it was said, deeply pious officers.

As if to underline this last point, Officer Deniz said, 'I have sinned.'

Unable to contain himself, Kerim said, 'Who hasn't?'

Chapter 19

The door into Atyom Mafyan's apartment was a sturdy-looking thing. Mehmet Süleyman was in no doubt he could have kicked it in, had he been required to do so, but he was also glad the kapıcı had the key.

Once the old man had opened the door, Süleyman and İkmen pushed in front of him – just in case. And they were right to do so. Hanging from a rope attached to a light fitting in the entrance hall, a chair kicked over on the floor underneath, was the lifeless body of Atyom Mafyan. İkmen went back out onto the landing to tell the kapıcı to keep back and inform him that they would be calling the police.

Not wishing to contaminate the scene, Süleyman satisfied himself that the Armenian was dead and then made a call on his phone. Hopefully Kerim Bey would still be awake. As far as Süleyman knew, he was the last member of the police to contact Mafyan, trying to discover whether the jeweller had visited Fahrettin Müftüoğlu at home on the date indicated in the bekçi's notebook.

When Kerim finally picked up, he said, 'What is it, Mehmet Bey? I'm driving.'

'Call me when you can,' Süleyman said and rang off.

He looked up at the hanging body. Why had Mafyan killed himself? *If* he'd killed himself . . .

Canan Müftüoğlu wasn't in the Kapielli5 bar. Of course she wasn't! And now Ömer Mungun was less than popular with staff and patrons after turning up waving his badge and getting female members of the bar staff to check the ladies' toilets.

Who could Canan, daughter of someone who might well be a Kurdish godfather, possibly be afraid of? Unless of course she fancied Ömer, which was unlikely. Maybe she had been trying to set him up. Her last call to him had been frantic. But now she wasn't picking up, and Ömer Mungun felt foolish.

He'd parked his car on Defterdar Yokuşu, which was a continuation of Sıraselviler Caddesi, and walked down the hill. He would have merely glanced at the front of the La Cave wine merchants had he not seen a bundle in the doorway. Although he knew that a lot of Syrian and other refugees still basically lived on the streets, he also knew he had a duty to move them on. He walked over and nudged the bundle with his foot.

'Come on!' he said. 'You can't sleep here.'

Quite why that was such a bad thing, except for the rough sleeper himself, Ömer didn't know. It wasn't even that Sıraselviler Caddesi was an easy place to sleep. The local bars pumped out dance music almost all night long. Quite how Süleyman put up with it, Ömer didn't know. But then he was moving soon, so maybe he just tolerated it until he could go.

'Come on!' Ömer bent down to shake whoever was hiding in the depths of a very large fur coat. A manicured hand fell out onto the pavement.

'I fell in love,' she said. 'I didn't mean to. You have to believe me when I say that I'd always been good until I met Yıldırım Bey. I am divorced, I have a daughter and my parents are old, my mother is disabled. I had settled myself to the idea of being single forever. I am not young . . .'

She was to Kerim Gürsel, but he knew what she meant. Unless they were educated and privileged, Turkish women generally married before the age of thirty.

251

'Yıldırım is a good man,' she continued. 'Pious and loyal. He loves our country, he's passionate about it.'

Conflating piety and nationalism with being a generally good person was something that was heard often. And while that was true of some people, it was simplistic and just sometimes plain wrong in the case of others. Kerim suspected that in the case of Yıldırım Yaman, it was the latter.

'You know he's married?' he said.

'His parents made him marry her,' she said. 'And she's an alcoholic. He's so unhappy.'

Kerim could see that Officer Yaman was good looking in a certain way, if one liked the moody, borderline-thug type of man. But then from the sound of it, this had been the man who had reacquainted Officer Deniz with sex, and that was always a very powerful hook. However, this little affair was not what interested Kerim. He wanted to know about the manipulation that he suspected underpinned it, and how, if at all, that related to the late Fahrettin Müftüoğlu.

He was tired and would have really liked to put his feet up on his desk, but he didn't. In order to get at the information this woman might be able to give him, she needed to be treated with cold respect. After all, the last thing he needed was for her to report him for inappropriate behaviour. He looked at his phone. He had yet to call Mehmet Süleyman back, but at the moment he didn't feel able to take time away from this line of questioning. That said, he knew he needed to speed things up.

He said, 'Officer Deniz, I want you to tell me the absolute truth.'

'I am! I've told you, to my shame. I am in love and—'

'I need to know what Yaman made you do.'

She misinterpreted his words, thinking he wanted details about their sexual activities, and began to cry.

Realising that he could have put it better, Kerim leaned forward and offered her a tissue.

'Hanım,' he said, 'I don't want or need to know details of your private life. What I do need to know is what, if anything, Officer Yaman encouraged you to do when you were about your duties. I know there was something in your notebook he didn't want me to see. He was less than subtle about that, and I want to know what that something was and why.'

She put a hand up to her mouth as if silencing herself.

When Kerim had married Sinem, he had been thirty and she thirty-two. And while theirs was hardly a conventional marriage, part of the reason it had happened had been because Sinem didn't want to be married off to some old man on account of her age. Officer Deniz, a single parent by her own admission, probably thought Officer Yaman was her last chance, even if he was already married. Kerim had no doubt that one of the ways in which he'd managed to persuade her to have sex with him was by saying that he'd leave his wife for her.

'Did you know Fahrettin Müftüoğlu, Officer Deniz? Did Yıldırım Yaman know him?'

She scrunched her face up as if in pain.

Kerim said, 'Look, tell me the truth and it will go better for you.'

Members of the newly resurrected bekçi were usually patriotic, often religious and deeply conservative, which meant that Officer Deniz was worried not only about her job but also her reputation within either the ruling party or their allies. Kerim could do nothing about what others thought, but he could, using Yaman as the villain of the piece, possibly save her job.

'I can't guarantee anything,' he said. 'But I can give you my word that if, as I suspect, Officer Yaman was using your affection for him to manipulate you, I will request that you be allowed to proceed without charges being taken up against you.'

She seemed a little calmer now, and he had hopes that he might be about to make a breakthrough, when his phone rang.

*

Ömer Mungun had called an ambulance five minutes before. He could hear a siren, still a long way off. In the meantime, he cradled Canan Müftüoğlu's head, occasionally holding her over the gutter while she vomited. So far he couldn't see any wounds, and wondered whether she was simply drunk. But it didn't smell as if that were the case. He could see that she was deathly pale. She tried to talk, but he told her to save her strength.

'Canan, it doesn't matter. Lie still . . .'

She grabbed his collar and pulled her face up towards his.

'Poison!' she said.

Blood was coming out of her mouth now. He raised his head to listen out for the siren and noticed that the sound was a little closer. The gutter was littered with cigarette ends, Ülker chocolate bar wrappers, empty beer bottles, sunflower seed husks. Then he saw a rat.

'Canan . . .'

She pulled his hair. 'I'm dying . . .'

'No, no, you're going to be all right.'

And then she said one word that made him almost drop her and run away. It was something that would haunt his dreams for many nights to come.

Gritting her teeth in order to get enough strength to speak, Canan Müftüoğlu said, 'Ricin!'

'Did you tell Kerim Bey?' İkmen asked Süleyman.

'Not in detail, but yes,' Süleyman said. 'He told me he'll get back to me as soon as he's finished with a female bekçi officer.'

'Oh?'

'She ID'd Atyom Bey outside our suicide's building in Vefa last year,' he said. 'But she tried to cover it up. Kerim thinks she may be in some sort of abusive relationship with another bekçi. He spoke to Atyom Bey after I left him earlier.'

'To say?' İkmen asked.

'To ask him whether he had visited Fahrettin Müftüoğlu's apartment, and why.'

'He was his employer,' İkmen said.

'We think that maybe Atyom Bey had been delivering something to Müftüoğlu,' Süleyman said.

'Like what?'

'I don't know. Gold? Diamonds? Things he didn't want his other employees at GülGül to see?'

'So Atyom Bey is a suspect?' İkmen asked.

'Potentially.'

They were standing in the dead man's lounge overlooking Tarabya Bay, away from the scene-of-crime team, the body and Arto Sarkissian. Both of them had seen corpses of people who had died by hanging before, but for İkmen, this was the first time he had known the victim. And while he was perfectly in possession of himself, he had no desire to be around the body any more than he had to.

'Why would Atyom Bey kill himself?' he asked.

The younger man sighed. 'Çetin,' he said, 'while we had nothing concrete with which to incriminate Atyom Bey, I for one was exploring the notion that he could have been at least facilitating Fahrettin Müftüoğlu.'

'You think?'

'Müftüoğlu, from what we have found out about him, didn't seem to be the sort of man who would have the social skills necessary to make connections with people.'

'He managed to get married,' İkmen said.

Süleyman frowned. 'Oh yes, although there's more to that than meets the eye. In four hours' time, I am due at an apartment apparently rented by his wife and her family – except that it's not. We're in the territory of layer upon layer of facts that prove to be anything but, and that only lead to further subterfuge. Our art fraud team think this is a significant operation. Or rather, it is one part of a significant operation.'

'Haluk Keleş?' İkmen asked.

Süleyman nodded. 'Still young, still swears all the time, still irritating.'

'Still knows what he's doing,' İkmen said. 'A bright kid, that one.'

Arto Sarkissian walked into the room.

'Inspector Süleyman,' he said, 'I'm going to have the body lowered so that I can examine it. Would you please supervise?'

'Of course.'

İkmen stayed in the living room, looking out at the Bosphorus. Atyom Mafyan had been one of the foremost craftsmen in the Grand Bazaar. As far as he knew, the Armenian had always made a good living. His apartment had belonged to his father and so there'd never been any issue about rent. But then until his finances were investigated, they wouldn't know. Had his love of poker finally got him into difficulty? Süleyman was of the opinion that he could have been part of an art fraud operation. İkmen couldn't imagine Atyom Bey becoming part of such a thing unless he was coerced. The Mafyan family had always been pious Christians – not that piety meant too much in the modern age, in İkmen's opinion. Much of it was simply performative. But he had always considered Atyom Bey and his cousin Garbis to be the real thing.

A huge tanker moved silently along the Bosphorus en route to the Sea of Marmara. The city always just got on with its business, which İkmen found comforting. People could be as corrupt, stupid and pathetic as they wished, but İstanbul would always look on with disdain. Tomorrow, though, if he was right, one tiny toxic corner of human activity in the city might come to an end, and in doing so, he hoped, would set the lovely Gonca Hanım free.

*

256

Had the medical team at the Cerrahpaşa Hospital not taken the time to protect themselves in full hazmat equipment, was it possible that Canan Müftüoğlu would still be alive?

As he sat outside the intensive care unit, Ömer Mungun didn't know. She hadn't been dead on arrival. As the team had pushed the trolley on which she had been lying through the doors, she had vomited more blood. Now, just over an hour later, she was dead.

When the ambulance had eventually arrived on Sıraselviler Caddesi, Ömer had told the paramedics that Canan was potentially a ricin-poisoning victim. When he'd insisted upon accompanying her to the hospital, they'd made him wear personal protective equipment. They'd prevented him from holding her hand. Then, before they'd transferred her into the hospital, they'd put her into something that looked like a body bag. Maybe it had been.

Ömer's mind was all over the place. What had just happened, and why? Who had Canan been afraid of, and had she already been poisoned when she called him? And of course, here again was ricin – used by terror organisations and rogue states, and potentially stockpiled illegally by the private armies of oligarchs and drug cartels. It wasn't something İstanbul had seen before. But now here it was being employed twice in one week.

The doctor who had told Ömer that Canan was dead came out of the intensive care unit and took off his mask and visor. Ömer noticed he was standing a long way from him.

'We've sent samples off,' he said. 'But at the moment, in light of what you told us, we are assuming that cause of death was ricin poisoning. This means that the body won't be moved until we know what we are dealing with. Do you know anything about her?'

'She's a suspect in an investigation,' Ömer said.

'Investigation into what?'

'Fraud. If you remember, the Grand Bazaar was shut the other day due to ricin having been found at one of the jewellers' ateliers. That was part of it.'

'We were notified,' the doctor said. 'Then told to stand down.'

'Truth is, sir,' Ömer said, 'we only found a very small amount of ricin embedded in a piece of jewellery. No idea how it got there or whether it had been there for very long.'

'The source?'

'Unknown.'

'Do you know the next of kin?' the doctor asked.

'She has a father,' Ömer said. He took his phone out of his pocket. 'I can give you details.'

The doctor gave Ömer his phone number and the policeman sent him Muharrem Aktepe's details.

Then the doctor said, 'In the meantime, Sergeant, I will have to insist you don't leave the Cerrahpaşa. I will have to inform the city authorities that it seems we may have another public health emergency. My observations of Canan Müftüoğlu's corpse lead me to conjecture that the probable way in which the poison was administered was by injection.'

'Why?'

'Puncture wound at the top of her right arm. However, the most common form for ricin to take is powder. So I would like you to surrender your clothing for analysis and let my team examine you.'

'I could see no powder . . .'

'I'm not asking you, Sergeant,' the doctor said.

'The man you ID'd outside Fahrettin Müftüoğlu's apartment building, Atyom Mafyan . . .'

'On one occasion,' Officer Deniz said.

Kerim waved her comment away. 'As you wish,' he said. 'Well, he's dead.'

258

She said nothing.

He leaned back in his chair and braced his feet against the corner of his desk. 'We think suicide,' he continued.

'Oh.'

'But that is just conjecture at this stage. The terrible thought I have, Pervin Hanım, is that I may well be the last person to have spoken to Atyom Bey. This, as you can imagine, hangs heavily upon me. And do you know what I was talking to him about?'

'Well . . . no. How would I?'

'I was talking about the fact that you had ID'd him outside Müftüoğlu's apartment last year.'

He watched that information sink in. Atyom Mafyan hadn't actually missed a beat when Kerim had asked him whether he had ever visited Fahrettin Müftüoğlu at home. He'd said that he'd been there once or twice. His employee, due to his somewhat basic home circumstances, found it easier to order materials for his private work through GülGül. These sometimes arrived after he had left for the evening, or on his day off, and under such circumstances, Atyom Bey would take these items to him. But he had claimed that this had not happened for years. Then, when Kerim had specifically referenced his alleged encounter with Officer Deniz, Mafyan had refuted it utterly. Kerim had asked him whether he was sure about that. Atyom Bey had said that he was.

Officer Deniz said, 'He was Fahrettin Bey's employer. Why . . .'

'Why are you so nervous, Pervin Hanım?' Kerim asked.

'I'm worried.'

'What about?'

'About Officer Yaman. What we have been doing is wrong . . .'

'I've told you, I don't care about that,' he said. 'What I do care about is you.'

She looked up. There was fear in her expression. 'Sir?'

259

'Yaman manipulated you. I saw it with my own eyes.'

'He loves me . . .'

'And if I can prove to you that he doesn't? Officer Deniz, I am in no way impugning your sincerity. Neither am I saying that Yaman—'

'Two years ago,' she cut in, 'I was given that beat. Yıldırım was my mentor because his patch abutted mine. We became lovers. You've seen him, he's an attractive man. His wife—'

'The short conversation I had with your commander confirmed my suspicions about Officer Yaman's wife,' Kerim said. 'She is not what your lover would have you believe. She's an extremely pious lady who wears a niqab. Just the sort of person, I suspect, you would respect too much to be persuaded to take her husband. What she most certainly is not is an alcoholic.'

'You're lying,' she said in a small, weak voice.

'I'm not,' Kerim said. 'And I think you know that. I think you even know the truth about Yaman's wife. According to your commander, a great many wives of bekçi officers cover. And given the nature of the organisation as it is today, I must say that doesn't surprise me. I would say, if anything, that you, Officer Deniz, are the anomaly here. A divorced woman with a child, living alone . . .'

Her face fell, making her look much older.

'Now . . .' Kerim began.

But she was way ahead of him. 'I don't know how Yıldırım knew Fahrettin Bey. All I do know is that money was involved, and that on the night Fahrettin Bey died, everything began to fall apart. Inspector Gürsel, if I am going to be here any length of time, I will need to call my parents.'

'You don't want legal representation?'

'No. I must speak to my parents,' she said. 'My little girl is with them.'

*

260

In common with a lot of his colleagues who were also over fifty, Dr Arto Sarkissian had a complicated relationship with his mobile phone. Whilst he always carried it, he frequently put it down thoughtlessly and then almost lost his mind looking for it later. It was while he was examining the abrasions to Atyom Mafyan's neck that he heard it ping, signalling that he had a text.

'Oh God!' He looked up. 'Where are you?'

'Your phone?' İkmen asked.

'I've put it down somewhere . . .'

Süleyman saw something flash on the floor and picked it up.

'That's it. Can you see who it's from, please, Inspector?'

Süleyman said, 'Dr Mardin.'

Arto Sarkissian frowned. Belkis Mardin was also a pathologist, and a long-time colleague. But she was off duty as far as he knew. What was she doing texting him in the middle of the night?

'Do you mind telling me what it says?' he asked.

Süleyman read the text out. 'Public health emergency declared at the Cerrahpaşa Hospital and in Beyoğlu, centred on Sıraselviler Caddesi . . .'

That was Süleyman's own street.

İkmen said, 'What sort of emergency?'

Süleyman looked back down at the phone. 'Suspected ricin poisoning.' He shook his head. 'There had to be more, didn't there! Why didn't I think of that? Why . . .'

İkmen touched his arm. Süleyman, while outwardly supremely confident, was, he knew, an expert at self-flagellation on the inside.

'You didn't think of it because you're not infallible,' he said. 'Now . . .'

A scream, visceral and agonised, came from the apartment above and silenced him.

*

'Mum . . .'

Gonca lifted her head off her pillow and squinted.

'Rambo?'

He put her bedroom light on.

'Bastard! What are you doing, boy!' She shielded her eyes with her hand and sat up in bed.

Not only was her youngest son in her bedroom, but at least four of her sisters were peering in at the door.

'What is this?' she said.

Rambo approached the bed with his phone in his hand. Although in his early twenties, in his pyjamas he looked about twelve.

'Mum, there's been one of those poisoning alerts again,' he said.

'What?' She remembered. 'Oh . . .'

'I was thinking, was that why Mehmet Bey left?'

Gonca ran a hand through her hair. 'What?' she repeated. 'No . . . He didn't say . . . What do I know?' But she felt a thud of anxiety deep in her chest. Whenever Mehmet was called away, he rarely told her why. It was something she had become if not inured to, then familiar with. 'So where is this poisoning then?' she asked.

Her sister Mirihmah, a widow in her forties, pushed her way towards the front of the pack.

'The Cerrahpaşa,' she said.

'The hospital?'

'Yes.'

'And on Sıraselviler Caddesi,' Didim added.

That struck home. That was where Mehmet lived. Gonca reached for her phone. But then Mehmet hadn't gone home. He'd gone somewhere else, with İkmen, if she recalled correctly. And anyway, even if he were to be in his apartment, that did not necessarily make him a poisoning victim. And there was something else too.

'Call him,' Didim said. 'Make your mind easy.'

And that thing was that as the wife of a police officer, she couldn't call him all the time. As a woman who had lived an independent life for over twenty years, she couldn't and wouldn't do that either. So what if she shook with fear underneath her bravado? So what if what she was about to say meant nothing? Unlike her siblings at least, she had her pride.

'Mehmet Bey is perfectly capable of looking after himself,' she said. 'If I call him, that will distract him from important business. Now you all go back to your beds and don't disturb me again. No poison has yet been invented that can keep my man from my side.'

She lay down and closed her eyes while her relatives filed out. Rambo, the last to leave, switched the light off again as silently Gonca curled herself into a ball.

Chapter 20

There was no one Kerim would rather have had by his side than Sergeant Eylul Yavaş. She was what his dead lover Pembe had always described as a 'no-bullshit Muslim'. She lived the faith in that she was kind, firm and committed to the notion of love for everyone. She was real. She'd also come as soon as Kerim had called her, all the way from her parents' palatial apartment in Şişli.

Officer Yıldırım Yaman had been brought in to headquarters half an hour before Eylul arrived. Kerim then spent another thirty minutes explaining to the sergeant what had happened with Yaman's lover, Officer Pervin Deniz, and what she had subsequently told him. Pervin herself was writing a statement under supervision. No one was leaving while Kerim still had questions to ask.

As they walked into the interview room, Yaman looked Eylul up and down and sniffed loudly. He didn't approve. His lawyer did not approve either, because he was asleep. Kerim knew him. Called Ramazan Albayrak, he was one of those lawyers people only engaged if no other attorney was available.

It was rumoured that Albayrak ran on two substances – cocaine during the hours of daylight and benzodiazepines at night. A heavy-featured, skinny man in his fifties, he had a trophy wife with accounts at some of the most chic shops in the city, and a son, by a previous marriage, who spent his life in and out of psychiatric institutions. He was a man with substantial expenses.

264

Consequently he would take on any client the system threw at him. Kerim kicked one of the lawyer's shins underneath the table to wake him.

Eylul made sure that the camera recording the interview was switched on, and introductions were made. After that, Kerim said, 'We have brought you here, Officer Yaman, to talk about your relationship to a man called Fahrettin Müftüoğlu of Kayserili Ahmet Paşa Apartments in Vefa.'

Albayrak cleared his throat. 'Inspector Gürsel,' he said, 'my client doesn't know this gentleman.' Shakily he rose to his feet, closely followed by Yaman. 'I think this interview is at an end.'

Kerim said, 'You think I brought you here for my own amusement, Ramazan Bey?'

The lawyer grimaced. 'My client has done nothing wrong and you know it,' he said. 'A bit of . . .' he looked at Eylul, 'woman trouble, as far as I can see.'

He was a dinosaur and they all knew it. Even Yıldırım Yaman looked mildly shocked.

'Not the way I would put it, Ramazan Bey,' Kerim said. 'But I take your point.' He looked at Yaman. 'What about Constable Mustafa Gölcük? He was on duty the night Constable Akar, his partner, was murdered. Gölcük, by his own admission, left Akar alone while he went to visit his mistress in Zeyrek. You too were on duty that night, were you not? I mean, I know that according to Officer Pervin Deniz, our officers were very thick on the ground, which was why you felt free to take her away from her beat to be with you, but you all must have realised, surely, how important it was that the Kayserili Ahmet Paşa Apartments were well protected. We did not, after all, at that stage know whether or not poison was present inside the building.'

The two men still stood, but nobody spoke.

Kerim's phone beeped. He looked at it briefly and then put it back down on the table in front of him.

It was eventually Albayrak who said, 'Your officers are your concern, Inspector Gürsel. My client freely admits he had a fling with this Deniz. But on that particular night, he denies the allegation. Anyway, it's only her word against his. Where's your proof?'

'I have a witness,' Kerim said.

'A witness?'

'Mmm.'

'Who is it?'

'Someone who at the moment wishes to remain anonymous,' Kerim said. He meant the prostitute Soğut, who had agreed, albeit reluctantly, to give a statement. He smiled at Officer Yaman, who retook his seat, quickly followed by his lawyer. 'Now . . .' he said, still with a smile on his face, 'shall we start again?'

Ramazan Albayrak scratched his head. 'I should like a few minutes with my client first, Inspector Gürsel.'

'Of course,' Kerim said as he rose to his feet. 'Take your time.'

The kapıcı was too old to go back downstairs, retrieve the key to the penthouse apartment and then climb the stairs again, so Süleyman, his phone beeping with what sounded like an endless stream of texts, kicked the door in. It took three attempts, but it was still quicker than getting the key.

It took seconds for İkmen to identify the direction of the screaming, which was coming from the front of the building. It was difficult to see how old the man who was apparently praying in front of a huge picture window overlooking the Bosphorus might be, but from his cheap shoes and trousers, İkmen imagined he was no longer young. He was also not praying, but screaming and banging his head on the floor. Süleyman unholstered his gun and trained it on the man while İkmen walked over to him.

'Sir . . .'

'I think he's called Muharrem Bey,' Süleyman said.

İkmen knelt down and put an arm around the man's shoulders. 'Please, Muharrem Bey,' he said. 'You are distressed. Let me know why. My colleague and I are here to help.'

The man kept wailing. Now that he could make out his profile, İkmen could see that he was in fact an elderly man with a brown face, deeply lined. He banged his fists on the floor and said something neither of the officers could understand.

If Süleyman was right and the man was Muharrem Aktepe, his first language was Zaza. And in times of distress, people often reverted to their native tongue. If only Ömer Mungun was here with them!

'Are you all right?' Kerim Gürsel asked Ömer Mungun.

The man on the other end of the phone said, 'I think so. I feel OK. They've taken all my clothes and they're running blood and urine tests. The hospital's closed. No one in, no one out.'

'And Sıraselviler Caddesi?' Kerim said.

'It's where I found her.'

Because the phone was on speaker, Eylül Yavaş could hear their conversation. She said, 'Sergeant, what were you doing on Sıraselviler? You don't live in Cihangir.'

They both heard Ömer sigh.

Kerim knew there were time constraints on their conversation. 'Long story?' he asked.

'You could say that.'

'OK. What you need to know is that the jeweller Atyom Mafyan is dead. Mehmet Bey is at the scene.'

'Dead!'

'Looks like he hanged himself,' Kerim said. 'You should also know that Mafyan lived in an apartment underneath the penthouse belonging to Muharrem Aktepe and his daughter Canan Müftüoğlu.'

'God!'

267

'So as you can see, this opens up all sorts of possibilities, none of which must become assumptions or, even worse, facts. I am currently questioning a watchman who, it seems, could have been with his mistress in the vicinity when Constable Akar was murdered.'

'While I'm stuck here!' Ömer said.

'You're stuck there, Ömer Bey, for a reason,' Kerim said. 'Due to you, Sıraselviler Caddesi has been cordoned off, the Kapielli5 quarantined and public health scientists are all over it. Do you know how the ricin was administered to Canan Müftüoğlu?'

'The doctor thinks it was by injection,' Ömer said. 'He's identified a possible site.'

'I'll pass that on,' Kerim said. 'I expect if she was stabbed when she was in the bar, her assailant is long gone. Uniform are taking details from people there.'

'There could be someone on the street carrying a syringe that's been used to administer ricin,' Ömer said.

'Or maybe they've thrown it down somewhere,' Eylul put in.

'That's more likely,' Kerim said. 'Who would want to get searched by a uniform with one of those on you?'

'Then again,' Eylul said, 'if you do have one of those on you and you use it as a weapon . . .'

Now that Muharrem Aktepe had managed to calm down enough to understand and speak Turkish, Mehmet Süleyman left him alone with İkmen. Although in many ways a gruff individual, Çetin İkmen could very easily access a soft side, to which most people responded positively. It seemed from the little he had been able to ascertain that the old man's daughter, Canan Müftüoğlu, was dead.

Out in the opulent penthouse hallway, Süleyman looked at his phone. He'd suspected all those texts were from Gonca. As their wedding drew nearer, she had become more anxious, especially

268

since the bedcover incident. However, they were not from Gonca but from Kerim Gürsel and Ömer Mungun, who was at the Cerrahpaşa hospital.

A short phone call to Ömer confirmed both his texts and what Muharrem Aktepe had said about his daughter. Canan Müftüoğlu was dead, apparently killed by ricin poisoning. As he'd already heard, the Cerrahpaşa and parts of Beyoğlu were cordoned off to be searched by teams of public health scientists. And so the poison nightmare continued.

Another text arrived on Süleyman's phone. This one was from an unusual source – Haluk Keleş. It said, *I finally realised where I've seen Canan Müftüoğlu before. She was in the year below me at Mimar Sinan University.*

He had to be awake, so Süleyman called him.

'I didn't know her, as in *know* her,' Keleş said when Süleyman asked about Canan. 'She was just some clever girl. You know how young men are, Mehmet Bey. Girls are either religious and untouchable, up for it, or clever-clever feminist types who might be lesbians. She was the latter, and so off my radar. The only reason I remembered her was because for one of those girls, she was cute.'

'You fancied her.'

'I was nineteen, I fancied anything female,' he said. 'But I also knew when I was on to a loser. I wasn't completely fucking stupid.'

Süleyman updated Keleş. He was shocked that Canan was dead and, like Süleyman himself, worried about the reappearance of ricin.

'Where the fuck is it coming from?' he asked.

'I wish I knew. There's no precedent for it in this country. Rightly or wrongly, I associate it with Russia and the US.'

'Yeah. But crime's gone global, as you know,' Keleş said. 'Particularly in the art world. If you've enough money, if you're an oligarch or a tech billionaire, you can have anything you fucking want these days. You want the *Mona Lisa*, she's yours. I'll see you at five.'

'For what it's worth,' Süleyman said, 'I'm less sure we'll find anything in Sarıgöl than I was.'

'Why?'

'Don't want to say at the moment,' Süleyman said. 'Everything is moving very fast.'

'I hear you.'

Süleyman hung up and walked back into the living room, where İkmen was speaking quietly to the old man. He heard Muharrem Aktepe say, 'What do you do with a child like that, Çetin Bey?'

'Kayserili Ahmet Paşa Caddesi isn't my beat,' Officer Yıldırım Yaman said. 'The only way I can be there is if Officer Deniz needs me for some reason. She's new and she's a woman and so sometimes she does.'

'You began a relationship with her,' Kerim said.

'She wanted it.' Yaman shrugged. 'On her own with a kid. Calling me over to help her out, telling me how much she appreciated my help. I knew. My wife's never looked at me like that.'

'So you gave her your performance of "my wife doesn't understand me",' Kerim said.

Yaman hung his head. 'You can't do certain things with your wife.'

Kerim knew what he meant. In a country where wives and mothers could be viewed as semi-divine figures, the idea of such women indulging in oral sex or practices like S&M was abhorrent. Men went to tarts for that sort of thing.

Ramazan Albayrak whispered something to Yaman, who nodded then looked at Kerim. 'I had an affair. I admit it.'

'And what about the night Fahrettin Müftüoğlu was found dead? Where were you that night?'

'On my patch. Officer Deniz had the night off.'

'Replaced by an Officer Ergin,' Kerim said. 'Who, in response to a request from one of Fahrettin Müftüoğlu's neighbours, broke down the door into Müftüoğlu's apartment with the help of our Constable Tan. Inspector Süleyman attended, accompanied by scene-of-crime officers and Police Pathologist Sarkissian.'

'Yeah.'

'All very straightforward,' Kerim continued. 'Except that according to Officer Deniz, from the moment of Müftüoğlu's death, "everything began to fall apart".' He looked up. 'Can you explain what she meant by this, Officer Yaman?'

'No.'

'Because you see, Officer Deniz won't,' Kerim said. 'She will admit to your affair . . .'

'Yes, well . . .'

'She says she was with you in a derelict house opposite the Kayserili Ahmet Paşa Apartments on the night Constable Kerem Akar was stabbed to death. Having sex with you, I believe.'

Albayrak whispered something to his client again.

Yaman said, 'Yes, I was there with her.'

'But neither of you came forward to offer witness statements.'

'No, well . . . As I say, we did wrong, but also we didn't see or hear anything that night. We were a bit . . .'

'What were you doing?' Kerim asked.

'We were . . . We had sex.'

Kerim felt Eylul's eyes on him. The use of cringing embarrassment when quizzing suspects was something he'd watched Süleyman employ in the past. And İkmen.

'What were you doing specifically?' he asked. 'Were you doing it standing up? Was she maybe sucking your cock? Well?'

The room lapsed into a shocked silence. Kerim moved some of his notes on the table and then said, 'Officer Yaman, do you know anything about the weapon that was used to kill Officer Akar?'

'Um.' He was still in shock. 'He was stabbed . . .'

'Yes,' Kerim said. 'Specifically with a khanjar. You know what one of those is, Officer?'

'Ah . . .'

Yet again Albayrak whispered to his client, who then said, 'No.'

'No?'

'No.'

Kerim nodded. 'Strange,' he said. 'I thought you would.'

This time Ramazan Albayrak addressed Kerim.

'Why?' he asked.

'Because the khanjar is a serrated dagger traditionally used by Kurds,' he said. 'And Officer Yaman, you are a Kurd, aren't you?'

'Are you sure I can't go to her?' the old man asked Süleyman.

They were all seated in Muharrem Aktepe's vast sitting room. Except for one standard lamp, the room was dark. In the apartment downstairs, Dr Arto Sarkissian and one of his assistants, along with forensic investigators, attempted to discover whether Atyom Mafyan had killed himself. Mehmet Süleyman was to be married to the love of his life in thirty-six hours, and he'd never felt so bleak.

'I'm sorry, Muharrem Bey,' he said. 'But until the hospital gives permission for us to enter, we cannot go. This poison, ricin, is unbelievably dangerous.'

Crying again, Muharrem Aktepe nodded his head.

When the old man had recovered himself, Süleyman asked, 'Sir, do you know who might have wanted to kill your daughter?'

Aktepe said no, but he looked away when he did it.

Süleyman shared a look with İkmen, which informed the older man that things were about to get rough. Not only was Muharrem

272

Aktepe a man who had just lost his only child, he was also an alleged gambler, a known sports cheat and a local godfather. In addition, there was also the location of his home.

'Sir,' Süleyman began, 'do you know your neighbour downstairs?'

Aktepe looked slightly affronted. 'No.'

'He's called Atyom Mafyan,' Süleyman said. 'He's the reason we're here.'

The old man frowned.

'He's dead,' Süleyman said. 'He was a jeweller by profession, and so we will be searching his apartment for signs of a break-in.'

'The jeweller? Downstairs?' Muharrem Aktepe pointed at the floor.

'Yes,' Süleyman said. 'Sir, what did you mean earlier when you asked Çetin Bey what you might do with a child "like that"? Did you mean your daughter? And like what?'

'I don't know,' Aktepe said. He flung his arms in the air. 'Maybe I meant young . . . Silly and young and . . .'

'Did you know that Atyom Mafyan, your downstairs neighbour, was your son-in-law Fahrettin Müftüoğlu's employer?' Süleyman said.

The old man appeared to think about it for a moment, and then said, 'Yes.'

'And yet when I asked you whether you knew your neighbour, you said no.'

'We were not friends,' he said. 'But why are you asking me about these things? These things are irrelevant! My daughter is dead! Poisoned. Who would do such a thing?'

'I believe,' Süleyman said, 'it may very well be the same person who murdered one of my officers two nights ago.'

They had taken a break, and although Ramazan Albayrak knew he was on very shaky ground speaking to Kerim off the record, they were both in headquarters car park, smoking.

'That Kurdish thing was . . .'

'True.' Kerim finished his sentence for him. 'The khanjar is a Kurdish weapon, your client is a Kurd, and it was a khanjar that killed Constable Akar. What's your problem, Ramazan Bey?'

'You know!' the lawyer said. 'You bring up this Kurdish thing and suddenly my client is guilty of murder!'

'I didn't say your client was guilty of anything except adultery and dereliction of duty,' Kerim said. 'But if he was somewhere other than where he alleges he was on the night my officer died, I need to know that. I just want the truth, Ramazan Bey. You can tell him that.'

Kerim watched as the lawyer stomped back inside the building, and then followed him. Pervin Deniz had told him that at the approximate time when Officer Akar was stabbed, she and Yaman had been having sex in the house opposite Müftüoğlu's apartment building. Her story had been confirmed by the woman who usually plied her trade there. Deniz had said that they had heard nothing untoward outside until Akar's body was discovered. Kerim couldn't help wondering what intricate sexual gymnastics they got up to hour upon hour in a draughty building. However, what really intrigued him was Deniz's comment about how, after Müftüoğlu's suicide, 'everything had fallen apart'. She'd not been able to adequately explain it, but he gathered it had a lot to do with Yaman's attitude towards her. Something had changed at that point. Why? And why did Yaman still appear to be concealing things from him? Deniz, as a woman, stood to lose her job if it was discovered she had been involved in an adulterous affair, but Yaman would almost certainly get away with it. So why was he making such hard work of it?

Kerim went back to his office and printed out the statement written by Officer Ergin of the night watch on the night Fahrettin Müftüoğlu died. Then he sat down and read it. When he had finished, he turned to Eylul Yavaş and said, 'I'd like you to go over to Fener.'

'Inspector Süleyman!'

The voice was Arto Sarkissian's. Süleyman excused himself, leaving İkmen and Muharrem Aktepe alone. He found the doctor on the landing, breathless from climbing the stairs up to the penthouse.

'Doctor.'

Sarkissian put a hand on his chest. 'Stairs are unforgiving at my time of life,' he said. 'I'm ready to move the body. I'm almost completely satisfied that Atyom Bey's death was suicide, but you'll need to come and supervise scene-of-crime.'

'Yes. Do you have any idea about who might be next of kin?'

'Well, he never married, and was childless,' the doctor said. 'I only know of a sister who lives abroad somewhere, and of course his cousin Garbis, who is custodian at the Üç Horan in Beyoğlu. What will happen to his business . . .'

They began to walk downstairs.

The doctor said, 'No sign, so far, of a note. But then of course not everyone does that, contrary to popular opinion. Did you find one at Fahrettin Müftüoğlu's apartment?'

'No. Although there remains a lot of sorting to do there.'

Arto Sarkissian shook his head. 'One is inclined to think that a suicide note would be displayed prominently. Nothing on his computer?'

'No. Did Atyom Bey have a machine at home, do you know?'

'I believe your officers have found one, yes,' he said. 'Although I must say I do personally struggle with the notion of something so personal being written on a computer.'

Süleyman smiled. 'It is the twenty-first century, Doctor. Kids have been known to kill themselves online.'

'Yes . . . But someone of Atyom's vintage? I know that were

275

I to take my own life, I would want those around me to know why. I would also, I like to think, write my last words in this world in my own hand.'

Now that transport had arrived to take the body away, many of the residents of the Sarkis Bey Apartments were awake, some out on the various landings looking up and down the stairwell, wondering what was happening. The old kapıcı, Vahan Bey, was back in his office beside the entrance, his sobs audible from the fourth floor. The last Armenian resident of the Sarkis Bey Apartments was dead, and he was bereft.

İkmen held the old man's hand. In reality, Muharrem Bey was only a few years older than him, but the Kurd was distressed, weighed upon by grief, and he looked frail in the light from the lamp in the corner of his vast living room. Out on the Bosphorus, tankers sounded their horns as the first intimations of another damp and mist-enveloped morning began to gather.

'I am a terrible man,' he told İkmen. 'All my life I have taken the easy route, you know?'

'The easy route?'

'I was born poor. In Sarıgöl. Far, far from the fields my father gave up to come to the city. The only thing I was ever good at was fighting. My mother didn't know what to do with me, so she pushed me to train as a pehlivan. I didn't want to do it. I just wanted to win with as little effort as I could get away with. This was why I was mediocre at best. So I cheated, and when I got found out, I set myself up training other young men to do the same. I opened gambling books on my boys and others. It was all rigged.' He shook his head. 'Left to myself, I would have gambled my life away. But then my wife died, leaving me with a bright five-year-old daughter, and so for a while, I took a regular job. We sank still further into poverty.'

İkmen squeezed his hand. A lot of criminals he had come

across over the years had similar tales. Even when they tried to leave crime behind, the system, or so they felt, was against them.

'And now my daughter, my soul, is dead!' the old man cried. 'Also of my doing!'

İkmen let him cry, then he said, 'Muharrem Bey, you must speak to Mehmet Bey, Inspector Süleyman. You must tell him everything you know. The only way you can truly do the right thing for your daughter now is to be honest about everything.'

Muharrem shook his head. 'I don't know who they are,' he said. 'Truly. My hand on the Holy Koran. If I knew, I would tell you, but I don't. You see, in spite of trying to bring my Canan up to be the pure soul her mother was, the part of her that was me took over, and for once, it made us something other than peasants. I let it happen. She was just a girl and I let her do something I knew in my heart had to be wrong.'

İkmen frowned.

Muharrem Bey continued. 'She married that man. Her "delightful jeweller", she called him. A big fat mummy's boy. I couldn't see what my beautiful daughter saw in him. Then she told me what he had offered her, and my greed took over . . .'

'Where's your . . . the woman?' Ramazan Albayrak asked when Kerim Gürsel walked back into the interview room alone.

'Sergeant Yavaş has other duties,' Kerim replied. He looked at a red-eyed Yıldırım Yaman. 'I'd like to go back to the subject of my officer Constable Mustafa Gölcük. Like you, he deserted his designated duty to go and have sex with his mistress.'

'I don't know him.'

'Large man,' Kerim said. 'Late forties, moustache, full of himself.'

'I told you, I—'

'You don't know him, yes.' Kerim lowered his head for a moment and then raised it again. 'My problem here, however,

277

is that on the night Constable Akar was killed, I am finding that the stars appear to align rather more in favour of that being possible than they should.'

Both men frowned at him.

'What I mean by that is . . .' He paused for a moment. 'What are the odds that Constable Akar, who together with Constable Gölcük was guarding the main entrance into the empty building, should suddenly find himself alone? Alone, inexperienced . . .'

'There were other police round the far side of the building.'

'Yes,' Kerim said. 'Constables Tan, Alp and Tuncer. Do you know them?'

Yaman shook his head. 'No.'

'Tan is the oldest,' Kerim said. 'Thin.'

His phone rang, and he turned away to answer it. It was Eylul, with some very interesting news.

Chapter 21

Someone was dead. He didn't know who, but parts of Beyoğlu were cordoned off, plus the Cerrahpaşa Hospital, and word was that Sergeant Mungun was there, as a patient. And the word ricin was being used freely and with confidence.

As Mustafa Gölcük got out of bed, he heard his wife say, 'Are you all right?'

Scratching himself underneath his vest, he growled, 'Go back to sleep.'

He walked into the family's small, time-stained living room and took his phone out of the pocket of his boxer shorts. Then he sat down.

Being at home 'under investigation' by his employers didn't suit Gölcük. Stuck in his home district of Güngören, a nowhere borough whose only benefit was that it was on the European side of the city, made him restless. Working class and conservative, Güngören was all right if all you wanted to do was drink tea in the local coffee house and pray, but Mustafa Gölcük had always wanted more out of life. That was his problem.

His career, such as it was, had never brought him the kind of wealth he thought he deserved. He'd got married twenty years before to a woman his parents had chosen for him, and had three financially rapacious children who lived almost entirely online. Now it seemed his career could be over, while his marriage had ceased to have any meaning years ago.

He'd been on thin ice for a long time. It was why he'd taken

279

the risk he had. What he hadn't reckoned on was not being paid. There wasn't even anyone he could ask. And then earlier, Fındık had been on the phone.

When were they going to go away together? Did he still love her? Would they have a big wedding one day?

Mustafa didn't give a shit. Fındık was a bit of fun and a good girl to cover your back if you needed an alibi for something. She also, unlike the wife, liked sex. But with the money, he could do better. But then now that the jeweller was dead, nobody knew what was going to happen. He'd killed himself, stupid bastard – or so Süleyman and Gürsel had been told by the pathologist. But had he? Poisoned himself, it was said.

He thought he might go over to Fındık's place and have a fuck. If he took his car, he could be back before breakfast, satisfied and in a better mood. But then suddenly a cheeping noise roused him from his torpor. The doorbell.

'He said he would make her rich,' the old man said. 'And me.'

'How?'

'His employer, the Armenian.'

İkmen repeated, 'How?'

'At first I thought that perhaps the boy had just made a lot of money through his work,' Muharrem Aktepe said. 'And she said she liked him. Said he was interesting, that his outward appearance didn't matter. So I gave my blessing. She was at university at the time, Mimar Sinan. I hadn't wanted her to go, but she was a clever girl and she obtained a scholarship. I worried all the time in case some boy at college got to her, you know?'

He meant he feared a fellow student might take her virginity.

'So if she was married . . .' He shrugged. 'I don't know, I always had the feeling that when they met at Efes, that was not the first time. And later, when she would appear with large amounts of money, I became more convinced of that. It was strange, but I closed my mind to it. What kind of man only wants to sleep with the girl he's married when his mother is out?'

'Is that what happened?'

'At first, yes,' he said.

'And then?'

'Oh, by then, she, Canan, was using him. Because by that time, with the Armenian, she was in charge of the work. She spoke to them, her and the Armenian, alone.'

'Spoke to whom?' İkmen asked. 'And what work?'

'Making wonderful things,' Aktepe said. 'For whom? I don't know. My daughter always protected me. Even when I became intoxicated with the power all that money brought, she never involved me. All I know is that they are rich.' He lifted his arms. 'They bought her all this. In my name. I became for the first time in my life a big man in my community. I became the gambler who always won. Because who in their right mind would challenge a man who paid for the wife of the car mechanic to have cancer treatment, who got the thieving son of a bakkal owner out of police cells?'

'The police . . .'

'The tentacles of money reach everywhere,' he said. 'They sit in the place where my soul once lived.' He cried again.

İkmen said, 'Which is why you must confess everything to Mehmet Bey.'

Kerim Gürsel had got his second wind. When Eylul Yavaş and her officers brought Mustafa Gölcük into headquarters, he left Yıldırım Yaman with his lawyer and entered a second interview room. He knew Gölcük and wasn't surprised to see that he had come in wearing jogging bottoms and a stained vest. He had no doubt that Sergeant Yavaş had given him ample time to dress properly; she was very aware of the importance of things like that, mainly to the morale of the person being questioned. But

Gölcük was a lazy man and the expression on his face as Kerim looked at him could only be described as insubordinate.

As soon as those present had identified themselves for the benefit of the tape, Gölcük said, 'What do you want?'

In a nod to Süleyman, Kerim reminded Gölcük that it would be wise to be polite and address him as 'sir'.

Gölcük mumbled the word grudgingly.

'So, Constable,' Kerim began, 'let me get straight to the point. According to your duty roster, you were on duty in Vefa on the night of the twenty-third of October 2019, the night Fahrettin Müftüoğlu was found dead, by his own hand, at his apartment on Kayserili Ahmet Paşa Caddesi.'

'I was in Vefa, but not on Kayserili Ahmet Paşa,' Gölcük said.

'So you have stated,' Kerim said. 'Constable Tan was on duty that night in that area.'

'Yeah . . . sir. He attended when the bekçi raised the alarm.'

'Yes.'

Kerim took a piece of paper out of his jacket pocket and put it on the table between them. He neither looked at it nor referred to it. 'The bekçi officer on duty that night was Murad Ergin. Not the usual officer assigned to that beat; Ergin was providing cover for an Officer Deniz, who was on leave. In his statement about the events of that night, Officer Ergin named the police officer he engaged to assist him as Officer Ümit Tan.'

'Yeah . . . sir.'

'Tan subsequently provided a statement about his activities that night. And because other officers in the vicinity, including yourself, soon came to the scene to assist, plus the prompt arrival of Inspector Süleyman, pathologist Dr Sarkissian and scene-of-crime officers, the actual moment of discovery of Müftüoğlu's body was somewhat overshadowed.'

Gölcük grunted.

'However, in light of more recent events, including the murder

282

of Constable Akar, Inspector Süleyman and myself have begun to interrogate some of the finer details of that night,' Kerim said. 'Not least because the enormous amount of unaccounted-for precious metals and stones found in Müftüoğlu's possession have raised questions about his working practices. However, there is one detail concerning the officers who found the body that does confuse me.'

'Oh?'

'Mmm. The statement given by Officer Ergin states that he called for police assistance in order to break down the door to Müftüoğlu's apartment, and that he was joined by a Constable Tan. However, when I looked at his statement earlier this evening, I noticed that the ID number Ergin gave for Tan was incorrect.'

'So?'

'So I looked up who that number belonged to, and found that it was you.'

'The bekçi made a mistake,' Gölcük said. 'You know what they're like.'

'What *are* they like?'

'Failed cops, everyone knows that.'

Kerim knew that some of them were, but he also knew that to overlook them, as he and Süleyman had done to a large extent, was an error, especially in this case.

He glanced at Eylul. 'Over to you, Sergeant.'

'Thank you, sir.' She looked at Gölcük. 'Can you please explain to us, Constable Gölcük, why when I met with him after Inspector Gürsel had discovered the "mistake" regarding the ID number, Officer Ergin described Constable Tan as a heavily built man with a moustache?'

There was a moment of silence, then Gölcük said, 'He was mistaken.'

'Again?' Kerim asked.

'So ask Tan! And ask the bekçi! He'll tell you!'

'Will he?' Kerim asked. 'Will he really tell me that he was so distressed by the events of that night that he mistook a thin clean-shaven man for a large one with a moustache? The incorrect number I can maybe accept, but . . .' He crossed his arms over his chest. 'What did you do with Müftüoğlu's phone?'

'Nothing! I wasn't there!'

'Our technical team have managed to track its last hours,' Kerim said. 'It disappeared in Balat, they think in the vicinity of the Golden Horn, four hours after Müftüoğlu's body was found.'

'So someone stole it.'

'Who?'

'I don't know! The bekçi?'

'Why?'

'Maybe he wanted a new phone?'

'To throw into the Golden Horn?'

Mehmet Süleyman had left his scene-of-crime officers to harvest possible evidence from Atyom Mafyan's apartment and was now with İkmen and Muharrem Aktepe in the penthouse. The old man had just told him that his son-in-law's death had come as a shock.

'I told my daughter to keep away,' he said. 'Few people knew she had been his wife. But she said that she wanted his apartment, that it belonged to her by right. At first I was shocked at how greedy she had become and told her not to bother with it. But then of course I realised that she wasn't doing it for herself. Müftüoğlu had been working on his wonderful things when he died. She told me she had made friends with one of your officers . . .'

Süleyman and İkmen exchanged looks.

'I told her to leave it alone,' Aktepe said. 'But then he got to her. He's always been able to do what he wanted with my daughter.

284

I told her it was a mistake when we moved here from the old apartment in Sarıgöl. To let him just take over our tenancy. Of course I didn't know she was sleeping with him at the time . . .'

'Who?' Süleyman asked.

'Osman Aslan,' the old man said. 'Or whatever his real name is. He's one of them.'

'One of what?'

He shrugged. 'I wish I knew. But when he came into her life, everything changed. He controlled everything – my daughter, the Armenian, Fahrettin . . .' Then he looked up and added, 'The police . . .'

'Why didn't you come forward to say you were in the vicinity of the Kayserili Ahmet Paşa Apartments on the night that Constable Akar died?' Kerim asked bekçi Yıldırım Yaman.

He'd left Mustafa Gölcük to ponder on his options and was back with Yaman and his lawyer, Ramazan Albayrak.

'Ask her,' Yaman said.

'Officer Deniz? What about her?'

'You know what women are like, Inspector.'

'Well let's pretend I don't, shall we?' Kerim said. 'Tell me.'

'Well, we were . . .' He put his head down. 'I know it's wrong, but some women are devils. Things the dirty whore can do . . .'

'Oh, so back to blow jobs and S&M, are we?' Kerim said. 'So good, so wickedly unusual to a pious man like you . . .'

'We heard nothing! Ask her!'

'I have.'

No one spoke, then Kerim said, 'She says the noise outside frightened her. She was afraid you were going to get caught. You only left – through the back of the building, according to her – when she insisted. You found chaos outside. Then both of you "admitted" you'd been at the bottom of Kayserili Ahmet Paşa Caddesi, apparently talking . . .'

'I didn't kill him,' Yaman said.

His lawyer, Ramazan Bey said, 'Inspector Gürsel, I should like to speak to my client alone.'

'No.'

'What!'

Kerim leaned across the table and looked into the bekçi's eyes. 'Come on, Yıldırım, you know there's no way out of this. Think about your wife and children and do the right thing. Whatever you were being paid to turn a blind eye can't have been much, can it? I mean, you're nothing and no one. A failed police officer, a mere bekçi.'

'Inspector!' The lawyer stood. But Kerim could see that Yaman was broken. What he had done with Officer Deniz, what he'd probably done on his own account, had finally closed its claws around him, and he was ready to do almost anything to break free.

When he eventually did speak, it was subdued. Like the words of someone who had been holding on to too much for too long.

'She knew the jeweller. I don't know how. She said I could make some money.'

'Who did?'

'Pervin.'

'And what did you have to do to get this money?' Kerim asked.

'Like you said, Inspector, I had to turn a blind eye. But I swear to you I never killed that constable.'

'Do you know who did?'

'No.'

'Did you know in advance that it was going to happen?'

Ramazan Albayrak put a hand over his client's mouth. 'That's enough!' he said. 'Inspector Gürsel, I repeat, I need to spend some time with my client! Now!'

Kerim breathed in slowly and then rose to his feet. As he was leaving the room, however, Yaman called out to him. 'You'll never get those behind this.'

Kerim turned, 'Why not?'

The lawyer attempted to silence him again and then gave up.

'Because she'll never tell you, and nor will anyone else,' Yaman said.

Çetin İkmen took a taxi home from Tarabya. Süleyman had offered to provide transport, but İkmen had refused. Travelling along the Bosphorus driven by a complete stranger gave him a chance to think and to look at his great city and its waterways in peace. Thankfully the driver was a man of no words who didn't, like so many of them, listen to blaring music.

İkmen hadn't known Atyom Mafyan well, but it had still been hard to see him hanging from the ceiling of his hallway. Atyom Bey, Muharrem Aktepe's daughter, her husband – all caught up in what appeared to be art fraud. İkmen found himself shivering. That had always happened and always would. Back in the day, art fraud and theft had been the preserve of criminal gangs in the main. But since the war in Syria, with organisations like IS gleefully selling famous works of art to fund their activities, anyone with the right money could get involved. This had opened the door to super-rich art collectors – oligarchs, tech billionaires, corrupt dictators in control of crumbling, impoverished rogue states. Now it seemed they had moved on to European artefacts. Logical in view of the fact that the third world had been so thoroughly exploited.

And what next? he wondered. A perfectly copied version, using carefully sourced materials from another age, of the *Mona Lisa* hanging in the Louvre? He'd told Süleyman that he feared the reason three people had already been killed or committed suicide around the subject of Müftüoğlu's private work was to make sure that no one talked. Whoever the client was had to be someone who inspired great fear. İkmen was familiar with a few of the city's organised crime fraternity, but he doubted it was one of those. From what he'd gathered about the artefacts in question, they were all of Christian origin. Most of the gangsters he knew were if not ultra-nationalists, then in that camp.

And now Süleyman, Kerim Gürsel and the art guy, Haluk Keleş, were going to break into an apartment in Sarıgöl in search of the truth. İkmen rarely advocated for firepower, but he'd advised his friend to go in tooled up. In a world where the rich could command private armies, anything was possible, and there was of course still the spectre of ricin hanging over the city. If that was indeed connected to an art fraud operation, they were dealing with some serious people.

In a way, he hoped they found nothing in Sarıgöl. He'd recently read a book about Colombian drug cartels and the houses some of them had set up just to torture their opponents, including the police. The trade in cocaine was of course worth billions, but so were many works of art.

Since when, he wondered, had the world been so flagrantly consumed by greed? It was human nature to want to better oneself, but this turbo-powered consumerism was new, and affected everyone. Even those who claimed to be too virtuous to be involved.

Whom were Süleyman and his officers up against? God knew. Had he been a praying man, İkmen would have asked God for the safety of his friend and his officers, but he wasn't, and so what he did when he got home, before he walked upstairs to his apartment, was appeal to his city's generosity. As the first rays of the weak autumn sun began to appear above the Bosphorus, he bent down and kissed the ground. 'Keep them safe,' he murmured.

288

Chapter 22

Since his elevation to inspector, Kerim Gürsel had become more careful and fastidious about his appearance. It seemed as if everyone in Mehmet Süleyman's orbit was smarter and more stylish – especially since İkmen had left the force. Now, however, Kerim looked ghastly. Red eyed and unshaven, his suit showing signs of cigarette ash and his face deathly pale.

As soon as he saw him, Süleyman barked at a young uniform to bring them both tea, and then took Kerim out into the car park so that they could smoke. Once his throat had been lubricated by the tea, Kerim said, 'I've three of them. Bekçis officers Deniz and Yaman and our Mustafa Gölcük. Of course no one's killed anyone. Deniz and Yaman were simply having an affair, although Yaman is blaming Deniz. He told me that she knew the jeweller, that she knows who the people behind the fraud are. She denies it, says she was in love with him and did everything he told her.'

'Tell me about Gölcük,' Süleyman said.

'I think he disposed of Müftüoğlu's mobile phone. I've evidence that points to Gölcük and not Tan being the officer who attended the scene on the night Müftüoğlu died.'

Süleyman lit another cigarette. Then he told Kerim about how Atyom Mafyan's death had brought him into contact with the jeweller's wife, and why.

'The old man, Muharrem Aktepe, said this art fraud organisation had infiltrated the police,' he said.

289

'Somebody should have warned them they hadn't picked our brightest and best,' Kerim replied.

'Oh, I don't know. Paying local officers to look out for your investments isn't an entirely bad idea. Anyway, I've brought Muharrem Aktepe in to make a statement, and for his own protection.'

Kerim frowned. 'Mmm. I too have been given the impression that whoever is behind this isn't playing games.'

'And now we must go to Sarıgöl to Mr Aktepe's former apartment,' Süleyman said. 'The old man confirmed that he passed his tenancy on to an Osman Aslan. Young man, he says. One-time lover of his daughter, and also one of "them". By the way, have you heard anything more from Ömer Bey?'

'No,' Kerim said. 'The hospital's still locked down – and parts of Beyoğlu.'

Süleyman shook his head. Sıraselviler Caddesi was still under restriction, and he was beginning to wonder how he would be able to get back to his apartment if that carried on into the evening. His wedding suit and Patrick's were there. Now, however, he had other concerns.

'Can you be ready in ten minutes?' he asked his colleague. 'Briefing in the squad room.'

Kerim smiled. 'Means leaving three suspects in limbo, but who can possibly refuse an early-morning trip out to Sarıgöl, eh?'

Gürsel had taken her phone away, but he hadn't put her in a cell. Officer Pervin Deniz wondered where Yıldırım Yaman was. Men tended to be harder on other men, so he was likely in a cell. And who else besides? she wondered. Would Yıldırım break? Eventually of course he would, because he would become more and more frightened until he couldn't take it any more. But would he point the finger at her?

Probably. But then where was his proof? It was his word against hers, and she was a poor single mother with aged parents to take care of. Or was she thinking about this too simplistically? Had she actually managed to get the balance right when Gürsel had questioned her? She'd tried to concentrate on the affair as much as she could. And that had been significant, even if ministering to some of Yıldırım's baser urges had not always been pleasant. She'd known that his wife was a veiled woman. She'd made it her business to find that out. But she'd gone along with his 'alcoholic' story because it suited her. And she found it amusing. He probably treated his wife as if she was made of fine china. Not for her rough sex on a dirt floor, messy hand-jobs and a pitiful alpha male begging her to suck his penis.

And yet she was scared. Inside or outside police headquarters, things could happen over which she had no control. And she still had to speak to her parents.

Haluk Keleş was sweating. Pistol unholstered, he stood to the side of the door the uniforms were preparing to smash the battering ram through. He'd told Süleyman that he was perspiring with excitement at the prospect of finding more, possibly genuine, artworks in Sarıgöl. But this was only partly true. He was also sweating because he was afraid. The lover of the man who might be in this apartment, according to Süleyman, was dead, killed by ricin poisoning the previous night. What if all they found here was ricin? What if this Osman Aslan was not alone and had a small army of men with him?

But then again, what if the place was empty?

From the outside, the apartment, on the first floor of the building, looked closed up and shuttered. There was a balcony to the rear underneath which two armed officers had been posted in case this Aslan man decided to take a dive into the street.

After first looking at Kerim Gürsel and Haluk Keleş, Süleyman gave the order to break into the apartment. The door collapsed after a single blow and helmeted uniformed officers, their chests rendered bulky by stab vests, stormed inside, followed by the three senior detectives and Eylul Yavaş.

They still wouldn't let him see his daughter. Was it a punishment? Muharrem Aktepe knew he deserved to be punished. To have allowed the girl to have whatever she wanted had been so misguided. He'd known she'd not been right all along. But raising her alone, working whilst being there for her, had necessitated compromises. Canan had been passed around. From aunt to aunt, his ancient mother, a neighbour he knew was on the game. And everywhere she went, he told whoever was caring for her that she could have and do anything she wanted because her mother was dead. When it had all gone wrong, he hadn't believed those who told him the truth.

When she broke all her cousin Meral's dolls, played dressing-up with his mother's dresses and then attacked them with scissors, there was always an excuse. Cousin Meral didn't like her, she bullied her, her grandmother was lying . . . And then Fahrettin. What man in his right mind would have agreed to that?

Well, a greedy one. A serial failure. A man who knew – and he had known – that something was wrong about that mummy's boy. But when the money began to come in, he'd just sat back and enjoyed it. Even Canan herself had warned him. She'd described those for whom her husband and his employer had worked as 'powerful men', and had couched the way they sometimes paid for commissions late, or occasionally not at all, as 'just business'. And when they had once shown their displeasure with Fahrettin's work via a beating, that had just been business too.

The apartment had a familiar aroma. Unventilated, it reeked of cannabis. And like a lot of apartments in poorly constructed blocks, it was damp. The carpets on the floors stank of it, ditto the cheap furniture. Everything about the place was poor, damaged and worthless – except for two things. The first was familiar, the second was not.

292

While the other officers spread out into the four rooms that made up the dwelling, Haluk Keleş stood in the small hallway, transfixed by a golden angel identical in every way to the one that had been found at the jeweller's home. If he remembered correctly, the first one had been orientated to the right, while this one was to the left. Like bookends.

Who would want gold bookends that looked like a dead silent movie star?

A shout alerted Keleş to the second thing of interest in the apartment. He stopped looking at the angel and followed Süleyman, Kerim Gürsel and Eylul Yavaş into a room containing an unknown man. Scrunched up in one corner of a battered sofa, he was young and unshaven, and he held a syringe in his hands.

One particularly eager constable made as if to try to take it from him, but Süleyman pushed him back. Then he said to the man on the sofa, 'Ricin?'

The man, who was sweating heavily, his lips dry and cracked, murmured, 'Yes.'

Süleyman sat down at the other end of the sofa and offered him a cigarette. Either, Haluk Keleş thought, he's gone completely insane, or he's got balls of steel. Or both.

Süleyman lit up, and then said, 'Osman Bey, isn't it?'

The man didn't respond.

Süleyman took his camel overcoat off and put it on his lap. 'Hot in here.'

'Mmm.'

The man was completely surrounded. He couldn't go anywhere. But he was holding, he said, a syringeful of ricin. It had to be assumed he was telling the truth. Süleyman caught him looking at his torso and said, 'Stab vest. We came prepared – almost. Did you kill Canan Müftüoğlu?'

Çetin İkmen looked in on Patrick before he left the apartment. The boy was still sleeping, curled up with Marlboro the cat.

Thank goodness he and Samsun had held the beast down and covered him in flea powder before the kid arrived.

He'd got over not sleeping hours ago, and so he'd decided to hit the streets early. Gangsters, particularly those involved in running flesh clubs and poker schools, tended not to be early risers. And while he knew that Şevket Sesler and his family had a huge apartment in Nişantaşı, he would have put money on the notion that Sesler was still in the basement of his club in Tarlabaşı. Maybe the poker school was still in full swing.

He climbed into his car and drove over the Golden Horn via the Galata Bridge towards Beyoğlu. The weather was still dull, rendering grey everything the steel-tinged sky touched. In this kind of weather, İstanbul took on a strange, quietly menacing beauty. Maybe it was because so much of the available light was reflected off the three deep, dark waterways that shaped the city – the Bosphorus, the Golden Horn and the Sea of Marmara. He'd seen a picture of Venice once taken during what the Venetians called 'Aqua Alta', when the waters rose to cover the city's streets, its basements and crypts. It had looked like a stage set for a horror film. İstanbul, while more open than Venice, had that same strange feel. He hoped that the sun came out for Süleyman's wedding the following day. If it did, he knew that Gonca, at least, would see it as a blessing.

As he edged his way through the back streets of Beyoğlu and Taksim, he wondered what Gonca's friends and family would think of the very formal wedding Süleyman and Gonca's eldest son Erdem had planned. Of all the Şekeroğlu children, it had only been Erdem, and Gonca's daughter Asana who had embraced the gaco world – he was something in IT, while she was a property lawyer. After a wild youth, Asana had now settled down and told anyone who would listen that she never wanted to marry anyone, while Erdem had married a gaco woman and had two conforming children. Their mother's wedding at the Çırağan

Palace Hotel was going to be very respectable, and İkmen smiled as he thought of what Gonca's late father would have made of it. Without a cast of thousands, boys firing rounds into the air from the bridal cars and moonshine rakı for everyone, the old man would probably have been confused.

He parked his car outside Sesler's shuttered nightclub and went down the set of iron stairs leading from the street to the basement. Rubbish gathered in these voids – beer cans, discarded pieces of kebab, squashed tomatoes, cigarette ends, condom wrappers – and sometimes people too. The man standing in front of the door leading into the basement was the type of Roma heavy those not in the know thought was a movie cliché. Like the Russian hit men who had populated parts of the city in the 1990s, he had a chest that could double as a particularly large barrel, and was dressed in leather from head to toe. His face was heavily scarred, his nose clearly broken in more than one place. When he saw İkmen, he said something to him, but İkmen didn't understand what.

'Sorry, my friend,' he said. 'I only speak Turkish.'

The man snorted. 'What do you want?'

'I want to see Şevket Bey.'

The man took a handkerchief out of his pocket. It was wrapped around a knuckleduster. 'Who are you?'

'My name is Çetin İkmen. I used to be a policeman.'

The man narrowed his eyes. 'You ain't İkmen. İkmen's got a moustache.'

'Yes, well I shaved it off,' İkmen said.

'Why?'

'Long story. Now look, I need to speak to Şevket Bey.'

'What about?'

'About one of his men.'

'Who?'

'I'll tell Şevket Bey only,' İkmen said. 'But if he doesn't speak to me now, one of his thugs is going to bring his organisation into disrepute.'

'Did you kill Canan Müftüoğlu?' Süleyman reiterated.

The man with the syringe shook.

'Because, you see, she died from ricin poisoning. Last night. And as you're sitting here with a syringe you tell me contains ricin . . .'

The man looked everywhere but at Süleyman, and then he began to cry. For a moment his fingers loosened slightly on the syringe, and Kerim Gürsel started to think he might be able to snatch it from him, but then the man pulled himself together. 'You're lying,' he said.

'No,' Süleyman replied. 'I am afraid Canan Müftüoğlu is dead. If you don't believe me, then look at the news online and you'll see that the Cerrahpaşa Hospital and parts of Beyoğlu are still cordoned off due to possible ricin contamination. I can show you on my phone if you wish.'

'No. How did she die? Who killed her?'

'I told you,' Süleyman said. 'She died from ricin poisoning. A very unpleasant death, as I am sure you will know. As to who killed her . . . if not you, then I don't know.' He paused for a moment. 'Atyom Mafyan is dead too.'

The man put the hand not carrying the syringe up to his mouth.

'So you know him?' Süleyman asked. When the man didn't reply, he went on, 'His death is a bit of a mystery, to be honest. And before you ask, we have no suspects in custody in relation to either Canan's death or that of Atyom Bey. Someone, it seems to me, is going around this city calmly dispatching people who have known or had contact with the dead jeweller Müftüoğlu and his pieces of large religious art. I noticed you have one yourself, in your hall. Is that why you try to protect yourself using that syringe? Who do you work for, Osman?'

The man looked as though he were in a trance now.

Süleyman extended his hand towards him. 'Give me the syringe, Osman Bey.'

Şevket Sesler smelt like a distillery and looked like shit.

'You're not İkmen,' he said, rather more softly than he usually spoke.

İkmen sighed. Then he coughed. Even by his standards, Sesler's cigarette-end-encrusted games room stank of smoke. When he could finally speak, he said, 'I shaved it off.'

'Why? You look terrible,' Sesler said.

İkmen shrugged. 'I need to talk to you, in private.'

Various men were either sitting in chairs, staring ahead, paralytically drunk, or lying on the floor snoring. One of them farted.

'While I can see that none of these people here could be said to be truly sentient in any constructive way, I should like to go to maybe your office or preferably some sort of outside space where we can talk,' İkmen said. 'I speak as a man not given to fastidiousness, but some of the odours in here, particularly those of a gastric nature, are challenging even me.'

Sesler looked at the man who had let İkmen in. 'Do you know what he's talking about?'

'No, Şevket Bey.'

İkmen said, 'If you've a balcony or a terrace where we can talk, I would appreciate it.' Then he looked at the henchman and added, 'And some tea, please. It's fucking cold outside, even if it is more wholesome.'

Sesler took him around the back of his club to a small, amazingly attractive garden. There were a few such small oases in Tarlabaşı, but İkmen had not imagined that someone like Şevket Sesler would have one. They both sat down on rickety iron chairs, and tea was brought by a young woman wearing a fur coat and not much else.

Once they were alone, İkmen said, 'I want to speak to you about one of your men.'

'Who?'

He offered Sesler a cigarette, which he accepted, and took one for himself. When the gypsy lit up, he coughed for a good minute. İkmen smiled. 'Heavy night?'

When he'd finished hacking up phlegm, Sesler said, 'Poker.'

'I hear,' İkmen said, 'that the man I've come to speak to you about is a good player.'

The gypsy said nothing, so İkmen continued.

'Munir Can. Great poker face, I'm told.'

'He has a God-given talent,' Sesler said. 'Why not use it?'

'Indeed.'

Sesler drank his tea and then yelled for more. 'So what's Munir Bey done to piss you off, İkmen?'

'What he's done so far is . . . unpleasant. But as far as I know, he hasn't broken the law,' İkmen said. 'What disturbs me is that I believe he is about to.'

'What do you mean?'

More tea arrived, for İkmen as well as Sesler. Once the girl who had brought it had gone, İkmen said, 'Munir Bey is married, I understand.'

'Yes. What of it? Married according to your laws. She's not strictly one of us, but . . .'

'So do you, Şevket Bey,' İkmen said, 'regard Munir Bey as married in the eyes of the Roma community? Do others?'

Sesler shrugged. 'Some do, some don't. When we marry our own, we don't generally get it done by the state. Why would we? They don't care about us, why should we care what they do? Your friend Gonca Hanım only ever had Roma weddings until this latest one.'

'And how do you feel about Gonca Hanım's upcoming marriage?' İkmen asked.

'That's her business,' Sesler said.

298

İkmen sat back in his chair. 'OK,' he said, 'let's return to Munir Can for the moment. We'll come back to Gonca Hanım.'

'Will we?'

'Yes.' He leaned forward across the table. 'Did you know, Şevket Bey, that Munir Bey is planning to take a second wife, a child?'

Osman Aslan, if that was the man's name, said something in a language Süleyman didn't understand. For a moment it silenced the room. Süleyman suspected it was probably one of the Kurdish dialects and wished that he had Ömer Mungun with him. But then something unexpected happened. Eylul Yavaş sat down on the sofa between Süleyman and Osman and answered him.

For a moment Osman just stared at her, and then he spoke again. Süleyman wanted to get her out of harm's way, but Osman was still talking, and Sergeant Yavaş was nodding and shaking her head and even interjecting at times. Whatever language they were speaking, she spoke it well, because the man with the syringe seemed to become more animated.

This went on for some minutes before the sergeant turned to her superior.

'Osman Bey says his life is in danger,' she said. 'There is nothing he can tell us and remain alive.'

Süleyman told the man, 'We will protect you.'

Osman Aslan laughed.

'If you surrender that syringe to us . . .'

Osman, still laughing, said something else. Eylul translated. 'He says that if he tells you, then you will die too.'

'I will take my chances,' Süleyman said.

The man spoke again. 'He says you won't have a chance, sir,' Eylul said.

'And because Munir Bey is already legally married, he will be breaking the law if he takes a second wife,' İkmen said.

Şevket Sesler shrugged. 'I don't know anything about that, but so what? Some of the most prominent men amongst the gaco have second and even third wives in this country.'

'Doesn't make it any less against the law,' İkmen said. 'But to be honest, that wouldn't bother me that much if his intended bride were not twelve.'

Sesler flushed. İkmen knew he knew. Rahul Bey had heard him speaking to Munir Can about it – not that İkmen was about to reveal his source.

'And his niece,' İkmen continued. 'Şaziye Can, I understand, his brother's child.'

'No,' Sesler said. 'Where'd you hear that? You hear that from the mother?'

'No,' İkmen said, with absolute honesty. 'I have met Huriye Hanım, I will confess, while I was trying to find out what had happened to Gonca Hanım's bedcover. But she didn't tell me; nobody did.'

'So . . .'

'I used my eyes and ears.'

'You don't speak our language.'

'No, but it's amazing what you can record on your phone these days.'

Sesler lit another cigarette. 'Gonca Hanım . . .'

'A woman preparing for her wedding? No,' İkmen said. 'But now we come back to her, I know that she works for you from time to time.'

'She is my falçı, yes, what of it?'

'Indeed she is,' İkmen said, 'and nothing more.'

'What do you mean?'

'Gonca Hanım was in debt to your father.'

'I wrote it off.'

'On condition?' İkmen stared at Sesler from underneath menacing grey brows. 'Some ugly rumours circulated after your father's death, didn't they, Şevket Bey? As if a person like Gonca Hanım would or even could have had a hand in it. No, he was killed by a junkie. Almost an act of God these days, death by junkie. They're so unpredictable. And of course he had been set to marry the poor creature's fifteen-year-old daughter . . .'

'A lot of Roma marry at fifteen. It's our tradition!'

'Is it?' İkmen asked. 'Anyway, it's all a bit academic now. What is of concern is your man Can's desire to marry a twelve-year-old, an actual child whichever way you look at it.'

'I didn't know about that,' Sesler said.

'I wouldn't be here if I thought you did,' İkmen lied. 'But as Can's employer, I felt you had a right to know. Also, while I'm not a police officer myself any more, I still have friends on the force, plus a continuing respect for the law. That said, however, so far I have kept Can's projected marriage to myself.'

Sesler leaned across the table and fixed him with a stare. 'For which you want . . .'

'For myself? Nothing,' İkmen said. 'For Huriye and Şaziye Can, I would like Munir Bey to cease his association with them.'

'And if Munir Bey doesn't want to do that?'

'I'm sure you can persuade him, Şevket Bey,' İkmen said. 'And if you can't, then tomorrow morning Munir Bey will wake up in a police cell, and your people will wonder why you ever allowed such a thing. Like Gonca Hanım's alleged involvement in your father's death, it will become one of those urban legends that takes on a life of its own. And talking of Gonca Hanım, or rather of Mehmet Bey, do not try to get at him through her. If anything happens to either of them, I will come looking for you, Şevket Bey, and I will tell the world about the paedophile you protect within your organisation.'

They'd reached the kind of stalemate where it was looking increasingly likely that someone was just going to try to grab the syringe. Kerim Gürsel had called for backup, and now they could hear that the rest of the building was being cleared. Another ricin alert. It was dystopian. What next?

Eventually Süleyman asked Osman Aslan whether he was happy to speak in Turkish from now on, so that Sergeant Yavaş could be out of the way in case he dropped the syringe. He said that was fine, so Eylul got up off the sofa and joined her colleagues.

Süleyman, now himself facing the loaded syringe, said, 'I don't know whether you are a mathematical man, Osman Bey. I am not. One of the reasons I've never been a gambler. However, putting my own situation to one side for a moment – I long ago gave up worrying about what my odds of survival might be in any given scenario – looking at you, I would say that coming with me is your best bet.'

'What do you mean?' Osman's eyes were very wide now.

'I mean that if you kill either me or any of my officers, you will go to prison forever – or someone may shoot you,' Süleyman said. 'I don't think you need me to tell you that you can't escape. If you try, you will die, and if you decide to plunge that syringe into your own body, of course you will die. Leaving with me, after handing over that syringe and letting us know if there is any more ricin in your possession, may eventually result in your death. But the odds are better. Who amongst us, after all, can know what will happen tomorrow? You, me, any of us could be run over in the street, die in the next big earthquake to hit the city, or have a heart attack at any moment. These people of whom you speak—'

'There's a jar in the kitchen, underneath the sink,' Osman Aslan cut in. 'There's a small amount of liquid inside.'

'Ricin?'

'Yes.'

Süleyman said, 'Sergeant Yavaş, could you, just you, go and retrieve that?'

Eylul said, 'Yes, sir.'

Chapter 23

The old woman looked down at him, even though she was in a chair and he was standing up. With her deeply lined sallow complexion, her pitiless black eyes outlined in kohl, Patrick's grandmother Nur was like something from a bad dream. If his Uncle Murad hadn't been with him, just the expression on her face would have made the boy run.

He went to kiss her hand, as his uncle had done, but she pulled it away. Murad Süleyman looked away. 'Mama . . .'

'I didn't say I wanted to see this child,' Nur said. 'Why is he here? Why have you brought him?'

Patrick, who didn't understand a word, felt himself begin to panic, until one of his uncle's arms gripped him firmly around his shoulders.

'I am sorry, Patrick, that your grandmother cannot speak any English,' Murad said. 'If you would like to go into the kitchen, the girl is in there and will make you some tea.'

Patrick knew what his uncle was doing. His grandmother didn't like him, something about which she made no secret. Murad didn't want him to actually witness that, however.

'No. I don't want to do that,' he said. 'I came to give her a message and so I have to do that.' He looked at his uncle. 'You said you'd translate.'

'I will.'

Murad turned to his mother. 'Patrick has something to say to you,' he said.

303

Patrick took a deep breath. 'I'd like you to tell her that I think she should come to my father's wedding. Everybody else is coming and it would be nice if she could be there too.'

Nur Süleyman said, 'Is that boy pleading for me to come to his father's wedding? I won't.'

'Mama . . .'

'Did she understand?' Patrick asked Murad.

'In a way, yes. She knew you might try to persuade her.'

'I am not going to see my beautiful son marry that fortune-teller!'

'She says—'

'I know what a falçı is, Uncle Murad,' Patrick said. 'My dad loves Gonca Hanım and she loves him, that's all.' He left the room.

Alone with his mother, Murad Süleyman said, 'You know if you don't go, Mama, you will regret it.'

'I won't. How can he do it? Marrying that woman in a cheap hotel built on the ashes of one of his ancestors' finest palaces! How can such a thing be dignified!'

'Well maybe then it is best you stay home with your dignity. I hope that keeps you warm at night and provides you with scintillating company.' Murad began to walk away, after Patrick.

'How dare you!' the old woman yelled. 'Murad Bey! You don't speak to me like that!'

He turned. 'But I should have done a long time ago. Maybe if I had . . .'

'You never had the stomach for it!' she said. 'Another failure, like your brother! Though at least he had the decency to be handsome. What are you, eh, Murad Bey?'

'I, Mama, am your ugly child,' he said. 'I've always been aware of that, thanks to you. But know this: I never resented my brother because of that, or our father. The way you always treated

304

us differently because of my brother's good looks is entirely down to you. There, I've finally said it.'

And then he left.

The Can boys, with the exception of Hızır, were long gone. Out into the streets, no doubt, to hustle for things other people took for granted, or simply to annoy their almost universally better-off neighbours. Their poverty, one centimetre from the gutter, was so complete, it even made İkmen, who had no hand in their misery, ashamed.

Huriye Can, wearing a stained threadbare dress that hung from her stick-like body, welcomed İkmen into her broken, meagre home and then apologised for not having any tea to offer him.

He said, 'Think nothing of it, Huriye Can. It's not important.' Then he told her about his conversation with Şevket Sesler. He was aware that the remaining children, Şaziye and Hızır, were in the other room, the one the family used to sleep in, so he lowered his voice.

Eventually Huriye said, 'Munir Bey has wanted Şaziye since she was ten. He has always had a liking for . . . girls. I fought him over it. What mother would not? But he has always been protected by the Seslers, both the son and the father. Soon after Munir began asking for Şaziye, I went to Harun Bey and told him it wasn't right. He agreed. He said that he would speak to Munir and tell him he had to marry the girl. Of course I said no, even though I knew I was probably dicing with death. No one says no to that family.'

A large part of the art of keeping your muscle close was making sure they got what they wanted provided it did you no harm. Şaziye was a piece of meat to be thrown carelessly at a tender age into an act of incest.

'Munir beat me senseless,' Huriye continued. 'I was convinced he was just going to take my daughter away from me. But he didn't. He told me that Harun Bey had made him swear that he would wait until the girl started her menses. In the meantime, he has taken me. It's why even when I can eat, I don't. If I bleed, then maybe I will become pregnant, and not eating means that I don't bleed. He hates my husband so much, he seeks to defile everything that reminds people of him.'

'Do you know where your husband is?' İkmen asked.

'No. And nor do I want to. I just want to be left alone with my children, in peace. I can only give thanks to God that Şaziye has so far not started her menses—'

A small voice from out in the corridor interrupted her.

'That's no longer true, Mum,' Şaziye said.

'Give me the syringe,' Süleyman said.

He knew this was the last time he would say it. There had been enough of the deadly toxin in the jar Eylul Yavaş had taken down to scene-of-crime officers to kill everyone in the mahalle. And yet more was unsecured in Osman Aslan's hand. At his signal, the officer standing behind Aslan would pull his head back with his arm while Süleyman took the syringe – if it didn't puncture his skin first. If Aslan didn't just go for it and attack.

Süleyman held out his hand for a second time. Depending upon what Osman Aslan did, it was possible that more than one person could die – not just him. And why did it have to be him at all? He listened to his heart banging against his ribs, felt his body straighten and rise in concert with the adrenaline that was running around his system. It was terrifying and the best feeling possible all in one package. As İkmen had once said, people like them were addicts just as surely as those who snorted coke or shoved bonzai into their arms. Why it had to be him was because he had to have this feeling, like he had to have the orgasm that only Gonca Şekeroğlu could evoke. But then what of Gonca and their marriage? What of that marriage being aborted because the groom had been poisoned and was bleeding out through his eyes, screaming in agony in some isolation ward surrounded by people wearing hazmat suits and breathing through ventilators?

It didn't have to be him and he knew it. But it was too late for that now. He'd put himself in harm's way and there was no going back. Now there was no more time. Osman Aslan knew what his only way out looked like, because Süleyman had told him. He also had to know that he would go to prison for most of the rest of his life, provided the unnamed people behind this art fraud let him live to see his trial; that their long reach didn't extend into prison cells. It all depended upon who they were. Organised criminals? Political grandees, foreign or domestic? Terrorist organisations? None of those options would give Aslan even a shred of hope, or Süleyman a chance of apprehending any but the lowliest operative. The best he could hope for was to clear the city of the present danger posed by ricin.

Slowly Aslan extended his arm. A barrage of clicking sounds signalled the release of multiple safety catches. Süleyman reached his hand slowly towards the syringe. He looked Osman Aslan in the eyes.

When the transfer of the syringe from one hand to another happened, it was almost an anticlimax. Süleyman held it above his head, his vision swimming as his body adjusted to the release of tension.

The next time he looked at Osman Aslan, he was on the floor, with an officer kneeling on his back cuffing his wrists.

She was so tiny, it seemed almost obscene to listen to her talking about such grown-up things.

'It started the day I was finishing Gonca Hanım's bedcover,' Şaziye said. 'It came really quickly and I was embarrassed because Hızır was with me. I was also frightened, because Uncle Munir had just gone and I thought he might come back. You were in here, Mum, and I didn't know what to do. He'd hurt you again and you were crying and there was nothing to soak up all the blood. Then I heard footsteps on the stairs and I really thought that he was coming back. I used the bedcover to mop it up. I knew I would be found out eventually, and that Gonca Hanım might even curse me. But then I am cursed anyway – because of him.'

'Cursed in what way?' İkmen asked.

'Because he wants me for his bride,' she said. 'As soon as my menses begin. I had to hide that from him! Hızır helped me put the bedcover back in its bag so no one would see. I thought I might starve myself like Mum so that it never came again!'

Huriye Can put her arm round her daughter's shoulders and cried into her hair.

İkmen said, 'I know it's silly to ask why you didn't tell anyone, Şaziye, but you know that there are laws about children getting married.'

'My uncle doesn't care!' she said. 'And Şevket Bey lets him do whatever he likes. He knows that my uncle comes here to hurt my mum!'

'Do your brothers know?'

'No,' she said. 'They're always out, except Hızır. He knows, but what can he do?'

İkmen nodded, then took one of Şaziye's thin hands in his. 'You know I told you that we have laws about men marrying children like you? Well, I have just been to see Şevket Bey to tell him that if he allows anyone who works for him to break those laws, he will go to prison. I may be retired now, but my closest friends still work for the police, and they will arrest your uncle if he tries to come here again.'

'Yes, but—'

'Don't worry that he will still come,' İkmen said, 'because he won't. He may shout at you in the street, because he is a crude man who drinks too much. But if he ever touches you, you tell your mum. I will give her my telephone number and my address. If you can't do that, call the police. But I don't think that will happen. I think I have the measure of Şevket Bey.'

'What does that mean?'

He smiled. 'It means I frightened him into telling your uncle to leave you alone. Şevket Bey's business depends upon those he works with being able to trust him not to allow bad things to happen to Roma people in Tarlabaşı.'

'Is Şevket Bey meant to protect us?'

'He says he is,' İkmen said as diplomatically as he could. 'Although to be honest with you, Şaziye, I think you'd do better trusting your mum and nice people like Rahul Bey – and me, if you want to.'

She looked at him with wide, unblinking eyes. 'But what about Gonca Hanım?' she said. 'Will she curse me when she finds out what I did?'

'No,' İkmen said with some confidence. Gonca could be pitiless, but once she heard the truth about her ruined bedcover, she would be relieved to know that it was nothing personal. She would also be furious with Munir Can.

'I will see Gonca Hanım today,' he continued, 'and I will tell her everything. She is one of those people who likes this law preventing children like you from getting married.'

'She has a new bedcover for her wedding now, doesn't she?' Şaziye said.

'She does.'

Huriye Can stopped crying and looked at İkmen.

'I don't know how you did this, Çetin Bey, how you found out these things . . .'

'I started by looking out for a friend,' he said. 'That's all.'

'Well, you have made more friends along the way,' Huriye said. And then she leaned forward and kissed İkmen's hand.

*

309

After having established that the substance Osman Aslan had told them was ricin actually was, they had to question him. This was done with some haste. As far as he knew, Süleyman asked him, was there any more ricin present in the city?

Still traumatised by his arrest, Aslan shakily confirmed that he knew of no other sites where it might be stored. But then by his own admission, he was only a very minor player, while those immediately above him in the food chain – his girlfriend, Canan Müftüoğlu, her husband, Fahrettin, and Atyom Mafyan – were all dead.

Once the threat of mass poisoning began to diminish, Süleyman, Kerim Gürsel, Haluk Keleş and Eylul Yavaş met with Commissioner Ozer to decide how best to proceed. Ömer Mungun, now released by the Cerrahpaşa, joined them.

Süleyman began, addressing his superior. 'Sir,' he said, 'we currently have five suspects in custody: Muharrem Aktepe, father of the deceased ricin victim, Canan Müftüoğlu; the same woman's lover, Osman Aslan; plus police Constable Mustafa Gölcük and officers Deniz and Yaman of the bekçiler.'

'You suspect all these people of involvement in this . . .'

'Art fraud,' Keleş said. 'For what it's worth, it's my belief that the intention was to replace existing works of high art with copies.'

'Copies, I am told, made from the same things – gold and jewels – as the originals.' Selahattin Ozer was not a man interested in art. He didn't know what it was for.

Keleş tried to enlighten him. 'Yeah, but with no provenance,' he said. 'These people want the originals.'

'What for?'

'Well, they're rich,' he continued. 'I mean, like seriously. They want them because these are things they can't buy. So they can sit and stare at them in their private vaults knowing that they've stolen them from the rest of us. That is my interpretation.'

'So who are these rich people?'

'That is what we are trying to ascertain,' Süleyman said. 'Those we have in custody are, we believe, low down in whatever organisation—'

'I thought you believed this was a rich individual?'

'It could be an individual or an organisation,' Süleyman said. 'This could be one of the ways in which organised crime is funded, or terrorism.'

'And you say that some of our officers have been involved?'

'At that very low level, yes. As far as I can deduce, they have been paid to turn a blind eye when necessary. But that may not be all.'

Keleş said, 'So the angel, the second one, where's that gone?'

It was becoming apparent that Haluk Keleş' dislike of Commission Ozer extended to never addressing him as 'sir'. And being curt to the point of rudeness. Ozer, in his turn, chose to ignore this particular question.

'How do you wish to proceed?' he asked.

'We all agree that Osman Aslan and the elderly man Muharrem Aktepe are probably the best sources of information that we have now,' Süleyman said. 'Following on from the death of Aktepe's daughter, her husband, who we think produced the work in question, and the jeweller Atyom Mafyan. The two men I am coming to believe died by their own hand, sir, leading us to feel that when Osman Aslan said that the people who are behind this thing are highly dangerous, he was telling the truth.'

'So do you have any sort of notion, from your own experiences so far, who the people behind this operation might be?' Ozer was very keen to get at, if not names, then what kind of organisation they were dealing with. Perhaps, Süleyman thought, he was concerned in case they turned out to be people at or near the top of society. He then underlined this by saying, 'Could they be foreigners?'

311

'It's possible,' Süleyman said. 'The use of ricin as a weapon has not been seen in this country before. It has been employed by various terror organisations in Europe and the USA. In Great Britain it has been linked to Islamist terror cells.'

'Mmm.'

'Sir, what I propose is that Constable Gölcük and the two bekçi officers remain in custody until we can question them comprehensively.'

'We can't hold them forever, Mehmet Bey.'

'No, but Haluk Bey, Kerim Bey and myself all agree that if we can question Muharrem Aktepe and Osman Aslan first, this may give us more leverage with the other three. While neither of them claims to know much in terms of details about their employers, I am hoping that once the reality of their situation hits home, they may rethink their position. It may also give us more information regarding the involvement of our own officers, both known and unknown.'

'Unknown?'

'Yes, sir,' Süleyman said. 'We have reason to believe that Gölcük, Deniz and Yaman are not the only law enforcement officers involved. Money, after all, as we know, sir, can overturn the most solemn professional commitments.'

Sema Kılıç couldn't stop crying. Atyom Bey had been her first and only employer, and in spite of the fact that she sometimes disagreed with him, she was sorry he was dead. She also had to wonder what would happen to GülGül now that he had gone. He had no children to carry the business on, and so it would be up to his wider family to decide what to do next.

For the moment GülGül was closed, and according to her colleague, Çoskun, the police were back. But why? Both Çoskun and the oldest GülGül employee, Adulkadır Bey, seemed to be of the opinion that Atyom Bey had taken his

312

own life. If that were the case, what were the police doing at the atelier?

Maybe, she thought, it had something to do with the poison that had been found on the premises a few days before. Had Atyom Bey actually been poisoned? Sema felt sad and also unsettled. If he had committed suicide, did it have anything to do with their last discussion?

She had been wanting to use her dormant diamond-cutting skills for a long time, but Atyom Bey hadn't wanted GülGül to go back to using precious gems. He'd been committed to Anatolian semi-precious pieces. The only exception to this had been the continued use of sapphires. He claimed that Anatolian stones made GülGül stand out from its competitors, that they provided a solid, if low-level, revenue stream. But although their pieces were unique, Sema couldn't see that they were ever really busy. For a start, they missed out on the huge diamond ring market that gave businesses like Lazar a constant rate of footfall.

Sema wondered, not for the first time, whether GülGül had been in financial trouble. Maybe that was why Atyom Bey had taken his own life. Just like Fahrettin Bey . . .

'Can I see my daughter?'

Süleyman answered the old man honestly. 'I am not sure, as yet, what the protocols around your daughter's body might be,' he said.

Muharrem Aktepe looked at Ömer Mungun. 'What does that mean?'

'It means that because your daughter was poisoned, we don't know whether you can see her or not,' he said.

'But doesn't she need to be identified?'

'I identified her,' Ömer said.

'You?' And then Aktepe appeared to remember that his daughter had attempted to befriend this man, and said, 'Ah.'

Ömer had told Süleyman how he had gone out in response to Canan Müftüoğlu's call for help the previous evening. Süleyman had told him that would have to be disclosed.

'Muharrem Bey,' Süleyman said, 'let me be frank with you: we have scene-of-crime officers at your apartment now. They have found a computer belonging to your daughter. Any bank accounts you possess, any investments, property, possessions, any money you may have hidden under your bed, will be discovered by us. In addition, our art fraud officers will be examining any possibly valuable artefacts at your address. In looking for those who brought a deadly toxin into this city, we will pursue every lead and every person.'

He let this sink in and watched as the old man lowered his head.

Then he continued, 'Muharrem Bey, you have told us on several occasions now that you don't have any idea about the identity of those with whom your daughter and her partner, Osman Aslan, were working. You have told us about your daughter's husband, Fahrettin Müftüoğlu, who, it seems, produced these copies of famous religious artefacts. You were also aware, you say, of the involvement of the jeweller Atyom Mafyan.'

The old man sighed. 'I know what power you have over me, Inspector,' he said. 'I know I will never see my lovely apartment again. Not that any of that is important. My daughter, my soul, is dead and nothing matters any more. If these people she was working for, those who made me rich, wish to kill me, then so be it. I will not resist. But I do not know who they are. If I did, I would tell you.'

'You know,' Süleyman said, 'that I have to believe you are lying.'

'Yes, efendi.' This time Aktepe bowed. 'That is your job, and if you now desire to beat what I do not possess out of me . . .'

'I don't,' Süleyman said. 'But what I do intend to do is to give

314

you the chance to tell us the story of your daughter's life from the time of your holiday to Ölü Deniz when she met Fahrettin Müftüoğlu until the present time.'

'I told you how she said they first met,' the old man said. 'At Efes.'

'You also told me that you thought they had met before.'

'Yes,' he said. 'The way they were together. They looked comfortable, you know? Talking easily. Canan was so young, and not easy with men – except me. And it was possible, too. With the university, she would go to places where art was exhibited and produced. I know the students visited the Grand Bazaar. But,' he shrugged, 'I don't know whether she ever met Fahrettin.'

Ömer said, 'So this quick romance . . .'

'They wanted each other I now think for different reasons,' Muharrem Aktepe said. 'I could see from his eyes that Fahrettin was completely besotted with her. I am old, gentlemen, and I know full well when a man wants sex. Canan did like him; she treated him like a little pet, I would say. But she wanted him mainly because he was a man of gold and jewels. He gave her so much jewellery in those first years! So much!'

'And then it stopped?'

'My daughter told me that Fahrettin's mother had died,' he said. 'I thought she might move to finally be with him, but it didn't happen. Instead they became business partners, as far as I could see. Canan told me that she was selling Fahrettin's work to foreign buyers. But the amounts of money she was getting were so big! He was talented, but this was . . . unbelievable. And I knew it. But I closed my mind to it. I became more and more able to have things I had wanted for a long time, I became able to help our people in Sarıgöl and become a big man . . . I loved it. And I loved that my daughter told everyone that it was me and not her who had made us rich. For a failure like me, that is compelling!'

He was quiet for a moment, then he said in a more subdued voice, 'When Canan bought our apartment in Tarabya, I knew it was above that of Fahrettin's employer, Atyom Bey. But I didn't know until later that he was involved too. There is a reason people think they can conceal things from me, and that is because I am a silly man. When Canan told me she had found someone to take over our tenancy in Sarıgöl, I just thought it was a friend.'

'You mean Osman Aslan?'

'Yes. But he was her lover. And although my daughter did continue to see her husband – I don't know when or how; I am just telling you what she told me – I think Fahrettin knew about Osman Aslan and I think that is why he killed himself.'

Haluk Keleş tapped one of his colleagues on the shoulder and said, 'Come with me.'

She followed him onto the landing outside the Aktepe apartment, where a table was covered in bagged-up artefacts and a laptop computer. Inside the penthouse, scene-of-crime officers dusted for prints, took hair and clothing samples for DNA analysis and began the long process of looking at Canan Müftüoğlu's files on her computer.

Sergeant Ceyhan Akyol, whose degree subject had been Western European art, had a particular interest in ecclesiastical pieces. Akyol it had been who had identified an extremely early Suriani copy of the Gospels that had turned up on the Dark Web the previous year. And when it came to Christian art, she had passion too. Like her Syrian father, she was a committed Roman Catholic.

Keleş pressed some keys on his laptop and brought up a photograph of a crown.

'This,' he said. 'What do you make of it?'

'It's a crown . . .'

'I know it's a fucking crown! Do you recognise it?'

'No, sir. I mean, it appears to be Christian, because of the cross. Why?'

Keleş pressed a few more keys and brought up a description. 'Says it's the crown put on a statue called Our Lady of Fatima.'

'Oh yes. That's a very revered statue of Our Lady. In Fatima, Portugal.'

'So I gather,' Keleş said. 'I know the stats: 1.2 kilos of gold, 313 pearls, 2,679 precious stones, made in Lisbon in 1942. What I'm struggling with is what it means.'

She shrugged. 'Means? It adorns the statue, sir. Fatima is the site of a miracle in the early twentieth century when some child shepherds saw a vision of the Holy Virgin. It's now a shrine where people go to pray for peace and sometimes to be cured of illnesses.'

'Mmm, so this crown . . .'

'It is placed upon the statue on the thirteenth of each month, which was the date upon which the shepherds first saw the virgin,' Akyol said. 'It's very special.'

'Mmm.'

Keleş put his hand into a hessian sack, also on the table, and pulled out a crown that looked identical to the picture on the screen.

'Found,' he said, 'in Canan Müftüoğlu's wardrobe. I wonder if Mehmet Bey speaks Portuguese as well as French . . .'

Chapter 24

Gonca Şekeroğlu took İkmen's face between her hands and kissed his lips.

'What would I do without you, Çetin Bey?'

'Probably work it out for yourself,' İkmen said. 'If you had time.'

'Well, exactly,' she said. 'But then would I? What with the wedding . . .'

'Well anyway, the mystery is solved. Şaziye Can just grabbed the first thing that came to hand when her menses began and she heard her uncle coming up the stairs. Unfortunately, that was your bedcover . . .'

'Poor little thing!' Then she said, 'Are you sure Munir Can won't go near that family again?'

'Unless he wants to go to prison he won't,' İkmen said. 'But there will be some kickback, Gonca. Rahul Bey will continue to employ Huriye and Şaziye, but I imagine that any more work they might get from Tarlabaşı's Roma may well dry up.'

'Then I will give them work,' Gonca said. 'This house could benefit from some new linen.'

'That's nice,' İkmen said. 'But be careful.'

'Careful?'

'You are still involved with Şevket Sesler, who is duty-bound to protect his man, Munir Can. I did not leave him in a good mood. I told him that if he ever sought to influence Mehmet Bey using you, he'd have me to deal with.'

Gonca's eyes widened. 'With respect, İkmen, what could *you* do?'

'Gonca, dear,' he said, 'a person who cannot be bought is rare. A person who can further hurt you in ways you do not understand is even more unusual.'

'You are your mother's son,' Gonca said. 'You lay a curse . . .'

'Maybe,' İkmen said. 'And maybe not. That is between Şevket Bey and myself. All you have to do is tell me if ever he tries to get at your husband.'

'But you trust Mehmet?'

'With my life. But I fear that the buying of this house on Büyükada will put him at the mercy of those – be it the bank or whoever – to whom he owes money. These are uncertain times . . .'

'These are always uncertain times,' Gonca said. She offered İkmen a cigarette, which he took, and they both lit up. 'İkmen, are you asking me to persuade Mehmet not to buy this house?'

She was too bright for him to be able to get away with a lie. He said, 'Yes. You're the only one who can, with the exception of Patrick.'

'He's really buying the house for him, you know.'

'Yes. But if things stay as they are, Patrick will still inherit one fifth of the property. Mehmet's uncle is too old to make the journey out to the islands now, both his cousins live abroad, and his brother would, I am sure, share occupancy with him in the summer months. He doesn't need to buy it.'

'Yes, but he has said that he will, and you know how stubborn he is.'

'I also know he'd do anything for you,' İkmen said. 'Tell him he need buy you nothing to impress you. Tell him you want just him.'

'I do! I don't care about houses or . . . anything! I love him!'

'Then tell him to leave the house until another time,' İkmen said. 'Anyway, I've a notion that his share in that property may soon increase.'

'How—'

He put a hand up, 'Don't ask,' he said. Then he smiled.

Had Fahrettin Müftüoğlu really believed that his attractive young wife would put up with their strange lifestyle forever? Just because they were also in business together didn't mean that Fahrettin wouldn't be upset if Canan took a lover.

Süleyman looked at his telephone and saw that he had two messages. One from Dr Sarkissian, who said he needed to speak to him, and the other from Haluk Keleş, who also wanted to talk. In the car park outside headquarters, so that he could smoke, he dialled the doctor's number, but it was unavailable. He called Keleş.

'Haluk Bey, I got your message.'

'Another artefact for you,' Keleş said.

'From the Tarabya apartment?'

'Canan Müftüoğlu's bedroom. Reliably informed by a member of my team that it's the crown of Our Lady of Fatima.'

'These artefacts are all Christian,' Süleyman said. His ex-wife had always said that the Christians had the most excessive religious art.

'Except the angel . . .'

'Yes, well we don't know what that is. So . . .'

'This crown is supposed to perform miracles,' Keleş said. 'Like St Foy. It's held in the shrine of Fatima, which is in Portugal, and has not been stolen, as far as I know. You speak Portuguese, Mehmet Bey?'

'No,' he said. 'But we will have to contact the authorities there. I'm sure we can find at least one person in Lisbon who can speak either English or French.'

'I'll book it in,' Keleş said, then cut the connection.

Süleyman, alone, began to think about value.

*

320

Even though it was cold, Kerim Gürsel could smell the accumulated sweat on his own body, soured by the fact that he hadn't slept. Sinem was ill again, according to a text from Madam Edith, and wouldn't be able to attend Gonca Hanım's kına gecesi later on that evening. He wanted to go home to be with her and the baby, but he couldn't. Not only did he have to try and get some information from this man, Osman Aslan, he had also promised to go to Nevizade Sokak with Mehmet Süleyman.

He looked at the man in front of him. 'How did you know Canan Müftüoğlu?'

'We met at university, at Mimar Sinan,' Osman said. 'We're both Zaza, both from Sarıgöl. We sort of bonded.'

'Were you romantically involved with her?'

'Not then,' he said. 'Then she left to get married.'

'What did you think about that?' Kerim asked.

'Couldn't understand it.'

'Why not?'

'She was enjoying the course. And the man she was marrying was weird.'

'You met him at that time?'

'No,' Osman said. 'I met him when Canan met him, when we went to the Grand Bazaar as a group. We visited several jewellery and metalwork ateliers. I saw Canan talking to this strange man making brooches, I think, then a few months later, she married him. Story was that she met him on holiday, but I know they'd spoken before.'

'But you thought nothing of it?'

'Why would I?'

'So how did you come to be her lover?' Kerim asked.

'I lived in the same mahalle,' he said. 'I heard her dad was moving out. Everyone was talking about it because he had got rich.'

'You didn't know how?'

321

'No. But I was working by that time and I wanted an apartment of my own. I asked if I could rent his place and he said yes.'

'So no involvement from Canan?'

'No. But when she heard it was me who was moving into their old place, she visited. It was nice to see her.'

'Did you not,' Kerim asked, 'think it a little strange for a married woman to be visiting you alone, without her husband?'

Osman paused for a moment. 'There had always been an attraction between us, if I'm honest. Nothing happened that first time, just sort of flirting. But the next time . . .'

'You made love?'

He nodded his head. 'I should have known something was wrong then.' He shrugged. 'She was like a bitch on heat. Afterwards she told me that she and her husband didn't do it any more. It went from there.'

'What did?'

'My obsession with her. Everything flowed from that. You know how it is to be a man in this country, Inspector. Or maybe you don't. In families like mine, you're expected to wait until you get married. No one believes that you will, but everybody watches in places like Sarıgöl.'

'Didn't they watch Canan, then?' Kerim asked.

'What, with her father giving out money for medicine to every old teyze with arthritis? People turn a blind eye unless there's something in it for them, and anyway, by that time I was letting Muharrem Bey use my apartment.'

'What for?'

'To store some of the things Fahrettin Müftüoğlu made. Muharrem Bey came often, and from the way he behaved with me, I think he knew what Canan and I were doing.'

'It was all Canan,' the old man said. 'My sins were those of omission. I didn't ask questions. I found out that the Armenian downstairs was Fahrettin's employer, but I never asked Canan why she wanted to live so close to such a person.'

'Why would she not?' Süleyman asked.

'Of course, it all became apparent when I could no longer deny that something wrong was happening. My daughter was always on the phone! She didn't work, and although I used to tell myself that her husband was keeping her, I knew he couldn't possibly be making that much money. I thought that maybe she was blackmailing the Armenian.'

'Why did you think that?'

'Because she spent time with him. She told me it was just business. She said the three of them – Fahrettin, the Armenian and her – were working together. Later she included Osman Aslan. She told me not to worry, said she would take care of everything . . .'

'What happened when Fahrettin Müftüoğlu's mother died?'

'Nothing,' he said. 'My daughter stayed with me.'

'Do you know *how* she died?'

'No. She was old. It was not a surprise.'

'Did you ever go to Fahrettin Müftüoğlu's apartment?' Süleyman asked.

'No. But my daughter told me it was a mess. That he wouldn't clear it up because that was how his mother had lived. Why she wouldn't go and live there.'

'Hardly an ideal son-in-law,' Ömer Mungun said.

'Who can tell,' the old man replied, 'who the heart may choose?'

'Really?' Süleyman leaned back in his chair and crossed his legs. 'Of course, I can only agree with that sentiment, Muharrem Bey, but I also believe that in this case, profit was a driver.'

'In my daughter's case, yes.'

'And in yours.'

Muharrem Aktepe bowed his head. 'Inasmuch as I turned a blind eye.'

'Oh come on!' Süleyman said. 'You knew. I wouldn't be surprised if you'd set the whole thing up. You knew, and you know who is behind what will be, I have to tell you, one of the biggest art fraud cases ever seen in this country.'

'It took Fahrettin Bey a long time to make those things,' Osman Aslan said.

Eylul Yavaş said, 'We know they are copies of famous Christian artefacts. Fahrettin Bey was a Muslim; how did he know to copy these specific items?'

He sighed. 'All I know is that they were being made for one person. I don't know who. I do know that he – Canan always referred to this person as "he" – already had some things from Fahrettin Bey. I don't know what.'

'Were those Christian articles?' Kerim asked.

'I've no idea.'

'So the client was probably Christian?'

'I imagine so, yes. Foreign, I think.'

'You said that you stored artefacts for Muharrem Bey,' Kerim said. 'Did you witness those items leaving your apartment, or did Canan or her father do that?'

'They did it,' he said. 'I only saw two men, once. They were both Turks. They told me they had come to collect some things for Muharrem Bey.'

'What about the ricin?' As Kerim said the word, a shiver ran down his spine.

Osman Aslan took a deep breath. 'When Fahrettin Bey died, things became very dark,' he said.

'What do you mean?' Eylul asked.

'He was the artist. Without him, there was nothing. Canan spoke to Atyom Bey to see whether he could take over. He used to obtain the supplies Fahrettin Bey needed. The right type of gold . . . whatever. But Atyom Bey said he couldn't. He didn't have the skill and he also said he had no more money, although that I didn't understand. His atelier does well, and what did he need money for? The client paid for the materials.' He ran a hand through his hair. 'Anyway, the ricin . . .'

He was becoming excessively nervous. Kerim said, 'There's no rush. Take your time.'

Osman Aslan breathed in deeply a couple of times and then said, 'I knew that there were people within the police who were involved. Canan was with me the night Müftüoğlu killed himself. An officer telephoned her. She told him to get rid of her husband's phone, and then the next day she went to police headquarters. Her husband's apartment was full of artefacts for our client. She had to find a way to get them out, but the place was crawling with police. She tried to get one of your officers to . . . to turn a blind eye.'

'Who?'

'He wouldn't take the bait,' Osman Aslan said.

'Being what?' Kerim asked.

'She tried to seduce him.'

Süleyman's phone was on silent, but when he saw it light up on the table in front of him, he looked at it. The caller was Arto Sarkissian.

He picked it up and said, 'Doctor?'

'Inspector,' the doctor said, 'I have some news for you. From forensics.'

'Ah. Let me just go somewhere else so I can talk to you in private.'

'Very well.'

Süleyman stood up. 'Ömer Bey, would you please wait here with Muharrem Bey. I need to take this call outside.'

'Yes, Inspector.'

'And keep the tape rolling.'

'Yes, sir.'

He left the interview room and went out into the corridor. Once the door had closed behind him, he said, 'Yes, Doctor?'

'Now I don't want you to raise your hopes too much,' Sarkissian said, 'but it appears our forensic scientists are fairly confident they can extract DNA from those intestines we found in that apartment in Vefa.'

'Oh, that would be so good . . .'

'The mummified head is a long shot, as you know.'

'So we hope, and if it is our custom, we pray.'

'Indeed,' the doctor agreed. 'But it's going to take time.'

'How much?'

'You will have been a married man for at least three days. We're looking at next week, if we're lucky.'

'He's called Sergeant Mungun,' Osman Aslan said. 'I saw him today in my apartment.'

'I know who he is,' Kerim said. 'Tell me about it.'

'Nothing happened,' he said. 'She called me to let me know she was going to bring him to the apartment. She intended to compromise him, I was to film them. But he didn't come in.'

'She wanted you to take footage of herself and Sergeant Mungun having sex?'

'Yes.'

'And how did you feel about that?' Kerim asked.

He shook his head. 'Horrible. But as I said, things were falling apart. Without Fahrettin Bey, we had nothing. The only thing we could do was get hold of the items he had already made.'

'Did you know Fahrettin Bey killed himself?'

'Not for certain. I think it was probably because he didn't want to be part of it any more.'

'I can understand that,' Kerim said. 'Anyone who will use ricin . . .'

'Oh, that was before . . .' Osman swallowed hard. 'Canan got that.'

'Where from?'

'I don't know. She gave some to the jeweller.'

'Mafyan?'

'Yes. It was planted in an item of jewellery in his atelier. The intention was for both that and the Vefa apartment to be sealed off while scientists went in. One of our police officers was on duty and would let Canan in and then help her remove any remaining items. He said he'd take care of the partner who was on duty with him. I didn't think he'd kill him, even if Canan did.'

'This police officer killed his partner?' Kerim asked.

'Yes.'

'Do you know the officer's name?'

'No,' Osman said. 'But I do know he was provided with an alibi by some woman he was seeing. The other man was stabbed, wasn't he?'

'Yes. Do you know anything about any bekçi officers who might have been involved?'

'I know there are some. Ask Muharrem Bey.'

'Does he know?'

'Canan was very protective of her father. But she talked to him all the time and he was in and out of my apartment often. Is he cooperating?'

Kerim said nothing. He knew that Süleyman was interviewing the old man, but he had no idea how he was getting on. He sent him a text asking if and when they could break to discuss their findings.

Eylul Yavaş said, 'To go back to the subject of ricin, the poison you possessed in your apartment was in liquid form, while the example found in jewellery at GülGül atelier was in powdered form. Did these substances come from different sources?' She was still concerned about the possibility of more poison somewhere in the city.

'I don't know,' he said. 'Canan—'

'Canan appears to be taking a lot of the blame, in my opinion,' Eylul said. 'And she's dead.'

Moisture appeared at the corners of Osman Aslan's eyes. He said, 'I wish she wasn't.'

'Any idea who may have killed her, and why?'

'No.'

'I do,' Kerim said, and watched as Osman Aslan turned white.

On the table in front of him, Kerim saw his phone vibrate and light up. Mehmet Süleyman had sent a message saying, *How about now?*

Nothing was happening. He was alone in a cell, with no idea even what time it was. He was sure that he was meant to be home now with Merve and the kids. But they'd taken his phone away and so he couldn't even call her. Yıldırım Yaman stopped pacing and sat down.

What had Pervin told them? he wondered. Had she performed her poor little divorced mother act? Normally he'd have confidence that male police officers would take a male point of view, but he wasn't sure about Kerim Gürsel. There were rumours about him, that he wasn't quite right in some way, not a real man. But would he have been cut any more slack by Süleyman? Probably less, knowing him. He was a hard man, and given how things had run out of control in the city since Müftüoğlu's death, who could blame him?

What if he told them that Pervin had lured him in? That wasn't a lie. She was an attractive woman, she'd seen the way he'd looked at her and fulfilled some of his long-held sexual fantasies. Then she'd told him about the jeweller and how she made a bit of extra cash ensuring that no one found out who came and went from his apartment. It wasn't hard. All he had to do was take her place occasionally when she was sick or on leave. Except that on the night Müftüoğlu died, neither of them had been available. That was why it had all gone wrong. And still he didn't know what 'it' was, even if Pervin did. But did she? And had she seen what he had the night that young policeman had died? He thought she had . . .

He began hammering on the door of his cell and shouting. 'I want to speak to Inspector Gürsel!'

Chapter 25

'I believe we should prosecute all five of them,' Süleyman said.

The three men, Kerim Gürsel, Haluk Keleş and Mehmet Süleyman, had gathered in the latter's office to review their evidence so far.

'We've so much material outstanding with forensics, we'll have to bail some of them at the very least,' he continued. 'The old man is putting any blame he feels might come his way firmly on his dead daughter and Osman Aslan.'

'Aslan's more circumspect, I feel,' Kerim said. 'Although he does paint Canan Müftüoğlu as a . . . what do you call it . . .'

'A tart,' Haluk Keleş put in.

'Yes, frankly,' Kerim said. 'He even claimed she made a play for Sergeant Mungun. Said she was trying to set him up, get him on board.'

'Yes,' Süleyman said, 'I know.'

'Really?'

'Nothing happened.'

The room became silent as they all absorbed what this might have meant. And why Ömer? Was there something about him, maybe a neediness that women particularly could detect?

Keleş broke the silence. 'People I leave to you, but for me this is all about art. Now whether it's art for the sake of its value, for its provenance, or because it's "holy" in some way, I don't know . . .'

Kerim said, 'Provenance?'

'Is it genuine?' Keleş said. 'Can that be proven? Harder than you might think.'

'This is about very rich people purchasing genuine artefacts that should belong in museums and galleries?' Süleyman asked.

'Yeah. Encompassing stealing to order, which we know happens, and possibly, in this case, expert replacement,' Keleş said. 'And don't forget that these are exclusively Christian artefacts, and so there could be a religious element. By this I mean that some of these things, like the statue of St Foy, are supposed to be able to work miracles. Interpol have been put on alert, but so far nothing. And I'm not surprised. In 2004, two Edvard Munch paintings, *The Scream* and *Madonna*, were stolen from the Munch museum in Oslo. Norwegian police eventually made arrests – the men had been armed – and recovered the paintings. But who was the intended recipient is still unknown.'

'Not the armed thieves?'

'No, they were stealing to order,' Keleş said. 'And they didn't talk.'

Süleyman narrowed his eyes. 'Organised crime? Terrorists?'

'If we assume that the copies made by Müftüoğlu were meant to replace the originals, then no on both counts, I think. Money has been invested here, a lot of it. We're talking, I think, about a collector. A fucking rich one, who is fanatical about this sort of thing. Maybe he's ill. Maybe he thinks these things can cure him.'

'Mmm. And my suspect, at least, does refer to whoever this is as "he" . . .'

'Mine too,' Kerim said.

'But if,' Süleyman went on, 'this rich, obsessed individual does exist, then a) he has a considerable number of people working for him, b) he evokes fear, and c) if he was using Müftüoğlu in this country, is he using other craftsmen in other places? And why Müftüoğlu?'

'He was good,' Keleş said. 'And fucking strange. Remember what Atyom Mafyan said about his weird beliefs about putting digitalis in jewellery. People leave the fucking strange alone.'

'But can we trust anything Mafyan told us?' Kerim asked.

'Mafyan was the link, I feel,' Süleyman said. 'He killed himself after your call, Kerim Bey. He must've felt we were getting close.' He sighed. 'And Canan Müftüoğlu, did she kill herself? Doesn't look like it.'

'No,' Keleş said. 'Müftüoğlu's death means the end, I think. With the artist dead, they move out and maybe on. Someone is going to have to contact all the owners of the original artworks he copied to check them out. Just wish I could locate those fucking angels . . .'

'The Ark of the Covenant . . .'

'Yeah, very funny, Mehmet Bey.'

Kerim's phone pinged and he looked at the screen.

'Apparently I'm needed down in the cells,' he said, and rose to his feet. 'Officer Yaman wants to speak to me.'

When he'd gone, Süleyman said, 'I hope I can trust you to keep what happened with Sergeant Mungun to yourself, Inspector Keleş. It has been dealt with by me.'

'The woman was unsuccessful, what's to tell?' Keleş said. 'I'm more anxious about where this billionaire – he's got to be a billionaire to do this – got hold of ricin. It's a very big weapon to use in the art world. Art theft is usually about guns. Ricin is declaring chemical war! I mean, assuming that now Müftüoğlu's dead they're pulling out, why do it this way?'

'Because they can? If we take your maybe sick, maybe dying religious billionaire model to its logical conclusion, then why not? Maybe the thought of being able to, at a whim, take millions of people with him to the next world gave him a kick? Look at these tech magnates. They can do anything – except cheat death. Not even Steve Jobs could do that, so why not gather up every holy relic in the world to at least give yourself hope? Why not use ricin to get what you want? These people are narcissists!'

'You sound like a psych, Mehmet Bey,' Keleş said.

'My ex-wife was a psychiatrist.'

Keleş rose to his feet. 'And I know that you're getting married again tomorrow. So go for five prosecutions. You'll get no objection from me. This thing won't be done before you go on leave, if at all, ever. And don't worry, I'm not letting anything go in your absence.'

Süleyman smiled.

Kerim Gürsel spoke to Eylul Yavaş outside the interview room. 'Do you have any idea what he wants to talk about?'

'None,' she said.

'I hope it's not another round of blaming the dead.'

They opened the door and went into the room, where Yıldırım Yaman was waiting for them sitting behind a table. Kerim and Eylul sat down.

Before either of them said a word, Yaman said, 'I lied to you.'

'About what?' Kerim asked.

'The death of Constable Akar.'

'Are you,' Eylul asked, 'confessing to the murder of Constable Akar?'

'No,' he said. 'But I know who did it, because I saw him.'

'Saw whom?'

'Constable Gölcük,' he said.

'How?'

'I've admitted I was in the house opposite the Kayserili Ahmet Paşa Apartments with Officer Deniz . . .'

'Why?'

'I've already said why!'

'To have sex,' Kerim said.

'You know that! She looked outside while it was happening.

333

She knew. I didn't, but I saw. Gölcük stabbed him in the side and then he ran off.'

Eylul frowned. 'You're admitting, Officer Yaman, to not going to the aid of Constable Akar?'

He lowered his head. 'She told me not to. Said it would mess things up.'

'Officer Deniz?'

'Yeah.'

'And why did you do as she said?' Kerim asked him.

Yaman paused for a moment. 'I'd made a bit of money out of turning a blind eye. I wanted some more.'

They met for dinner at a small köftecisi in Cihangir. Edibe was already seated at a table when her father, Murad Süleyman, and cousin Patrick arrived. They all hugged and kissed and then sat down. 'I hope you like meatballs, Pat?' Edibe said.

'Yes.' He nodded.

'There are other things on the menu if you don't want köfte,' his uncle pointed out. 'And we will have food with our drinks when we meet your father.'

'Food?'

'Yes, we nearly always eat when we go to bars,' Murad said. 'It stops you from getting too drunk.'

'But at the stag you're *supposed* to get drunk,' Patrick said.

'Well, it is a little different in Turkey. We are mostly a Muslim country, so people don't want to do that so much.'

Edibe laughed.

'What?'

'Tell that to Çetin Bey,' she said.

Patrick and Murad ordered köfte while Edibe opted for a vegetarian dish.

'There will be a lot of food at Gonca Hanım's kına gecesi,' she said.

'Aren't you coming out with us?' Patrick asked.

'No. I have to deliver the henna for the party from our family to Gonca Hanım's. The groom's family always buy and prepare the henna. The bride invites all her women friends to her kına gecesi to celebrate that she will soon be leaving her mother's house and going to the house of her husband.'

'But Gonca Hanım has her own house.'

'It is kind of symbolic,' Edibe said. 'There's not usually much food at a kına gecesi, but the Roma do things their own way, and there will be lots of sweets, which I like very much. But you will see for yourself later.'

Patrick looked at his uncle. 'I thought we were going to the pub?' he said.

'We are. But then later the men join the ladies. There is a special dance called halay, which is done by both bride and groom, and then the men go.'

'My dad'll dance?'

'Yes.'

Patrick laughed.

'And,' Edibe said, 'an old woman from Gonca's family will put henna on her hands to make them soft and beautiful and stain them red. In the old days, it showed that the bride was sacrificing herself to her new family. A wedding is both happy and sad, as the bride is leaving her mother. You will see.'

'And then we'll go back to the pub?' Patrick asked.

'We will see,' Murad said.

It didn't feel right to just go. Süleyman emailed his evidence against the five suspects to the prosecutor's office and began to get ready to leave headquarters. Ömer Mungun joined him in his office.

'I've spoken to the prosecutor and submitted my evidence,' Süleyman told the younger man. 'From tomorrow, this will be in the hands of Kerim Bey and Inspector Keleş. You will take your instructions from them.'

'Yes, sir.'

Ömer knew that since both he and Kerim were attending the wedding the next afternoon, they would be absent, if on call, for the duration of the ceremony and hopefully the party afterwards.

'Are we still meeting at the James Joyce at eight?' he asked.

'Yes, and then on to Balat for Gonca Hanım's kına gecesi,' Süleyman said. 'Because the weather is dry, she's having her party in the garden, so wear warm clothes.'

'Sir,' Ömer said, 'this business about Canan Müftüoğlu trying to seduce me . . .'

'It didn't happen, so it's irrelevant,' Süleyman said.

'Yes, but I went out when she called me, when she died . . .'

'You attended in a professional capacity responding to a call from the wife of a suicide – to whom you had given your business card,' Süleyman said.

Ömer sat down. 'Thank you, sir.'

'Don't do it again,' Süleyman said.

Ömer hung his head. 'No. I'm taking two weeks' leave in December. My parents want me to go home to get married.'

'Do you want to be married?' Süleyman asked. 'Do you know the girl they've chosen for you?'

'I know her a little. She's eighteen. But she's . . . well, she's like us, our family. We're few now.'

Süleyman put a hand on his shoulder. Although they never spoke of it, he knew that Ömer came from a family who belonged to a minority ethnic religious group in the east.

'She doesn't speak much Turkish, and so Peri and I will have to help her when she comes to live here,' Ömer said. 'She's pretty.'

'You must do what is best for you,' Süleyman said.

'Yes, but I owe my parents . . .'

336

'We all owe our parents, Ömer Bey,' Süleyman said. 'But in my opinion, we should not sacrifice our own happiness if what they want and what we want do not concur.'

Ömer had picked up that Süleyman's mother probably wasn't coming to his wedding because she disapproved of his fiancée. But then the boss was a lot older than Ömer, a middle-aged man who made his own life.

In response to noise outside, Süleyman looked out of the window. Kerim Gürsel and Haluk Keleş were standing beside a van full of uniformed officers, talking. Keleş was wearing a stab vest.

'I wonder what's going on,' Süleyman said.

'You need to go home, boss,' Ömer told him. 'Leave all this. You've only got two days. And, well, think of Gonca Hanım . . .'

Süleyman turned away from the window and smiled.

She didn't miss a beat.

'He's lying,' Pervin Deniz said. 'I know nothing about the death of Constable Akar.'

Kerim leaned back in his chair. All he really wanted to do was go to sleep. 'Why would he lie? It casts him in a bad light. If proven, he will be prosecuted.'

'He's putting the blame on me. My only mistake was being seduced by him.'

'I don't know who seduced or encouraged whom,' Kerim said. 'All I care about is who killed Constable Akar, and why. Officer Yaman has told me that he witnessed Constable Gölcük killing Constable Akar.'

'Gölcük was with his mistress.'

'So he says.'

'What do you mean?' Deniz asked.

'I mean, although having spoken to the lady in question already, we are interviewing her again,' Kerim said.

She looked away.

'The more you tell us now, the easier it will go for you later,' he said. 'You know that!'

She turned to him, her eyes filled with fury. 'You don't know what this is!'

'So tell me!'

'Let me speak to my parents!' she said.

Gonca Şekeroğlu hustled her sisters out of her bedroom, retaining only her daughter Asana to help her dress. She stepped into the traditional red velvet bindallı – an ornate kaftan-like gown – and her daughter tied a belt loosely around her waist.

'Can't you pull it tighter?' Gonca said.

'I can, but you'll be uncomfortable,' Asana said.

Gonca looked at her and Asana pulled it tighter. It was ridiculous to think she could argue with her mother and win. She changed the subject.

'You know the henna hasn't arrived yet.'

'Mehmet Bey's niece is bringing it,' Gonca replied. 'She'll be here soon.'

'Well, at least we have a lot of candles,' Asana said.

Her mother looked at herself in her dressing-table mirror. 'Is Auntie Sibel ready?'

One of her old aunts had travelled from Edirne in Thrace to come to the kına gecesi and the wedding. For both occasions it was Auntie Sibel's job to arrange Gonca's hair in elaborate curls and waves around the various tiaras she would wear.

'I'll go and wake her up,' Asana said.

Gonca, alone, peered deeply at her image in the mirror. Without make-up, her hair loose, she fixated on the lines around her eyes and the way her neck, though smooth, was no longer firm. She knew that people said she had bewitched her groom into marrying her, and there was some truth in that. She had magic, and he

338

knew that even if he didn't understand it. But she also knew that he adored her just as much as she adored him. Yet those who were jealous of her or wished her ill still whispered in corners. How long could Gonca Hanım retain her hold over Mehmet Süleyman? they asked each other. How many pretty faces would he turn down to be faithful to her?

'We're talking US dollars, not lira,' Haluk Keleş said. 'We believe this fraud involves billions of dollars. Which means that whatever your boyfriend was being paid – and we will find that out – was in comparison nothing.'

Fındık Elvan sat opposite him, her face drawn down in a glower. It made her look a lot older than her forty-three years.

'And if that, coupled with the murder of Constable Akar, doesn't bother you, then maybe think about who these fraudsters are,' he continued. 'They're the type of people who use chemical weapons to cover their tracks.'

'I heard there were poisonings in Beyoğlu and in the Grand Bazaar,' she said. 'But that was terrorists, wasn't it?'

People listened and read selectively, especially since the coming of the Internet. Fındık Elvan, fixated on her mythical future with her lover, clearly had a very loose grasp of current events.

'No,' Keleş said. 'What happened in Beyoğlu and the bazaar is linked to this. I don't know what Mustafa Gölcük told you . . .'

'Nothing!' she said. 'He was making some money for us. On the side, so we could go away. I didn't know what it was about! I never asked and he never told me!'

'Did he tell you what to say if anyone asked you about his activities?'

She looked down. 'He said I wasn't to talk about it. That Inspector Süleyman came to see me, and I told him what I'm telling you.'

'Well, since Inspector Süleyman visited you, things have

changed. We have a witness to the murder of Constable Akar, and that person named Gölcük as the perpetrator.'

'He was with me that night!' she said. 'I told you!'

'You told Inspector Süleyman he was with you for an hour,' Keleş said. 'Is that true? And listen to me closely now, Fındık Hanım, I will only ask you this once, so if you're lying to me . . .'

She began to cry. Haluk Keleş muttered under his breath, 'Fuck!'

But he waited for her to stop crying, then he just looked at her while she hiccuped and gasped and regained something of her composure.

She said, 'He came to tell me that if anyone asked, I was to say I was with him for an hour.'

'Didn't you ask why?'

'No.'

'Why not?'

She began to cry again. 'He brought me my favourite perfume.'

The Süleyman brothers, plus Patrick, made their way to the James Joyce pub in Taksim, the boy full of excitement about attending his first stag. As they approached Balo Sokak, they saw that a group of Mehmet's friends had already assembled outside the pink and green nineteenth-century building.

'Mehmet Bey!'

Çetin İkmen's son Bülent was already drunk, by the look of him. Holding a glass of something aloft, he was leaning on his brother Kemal for support. Their father, who looked so strange without his moustache, said, 'Mehmet, dear boy, what are you having to drink? Jameson's or Bushmills?'

Mehmet Süleyman didn't know much about Irish whiskey, but he did know that the best one from Patrick's point of view was Jameson's, because it was distilled in the Republic as opposed to Northern Ireland.

'Jameson's. Thank you, Çetin.'

'What about for the boy?'

'Coca-Cola.'

Once he had asked the other men what they wanted, İkmen disappeared into the bar. Patrick, whilst not understanding much of what had been said, knew that he was probably getting Coca-Cola. 'Can't I just have a beer?' he said.

'No,' Süleyman replied. 'Your mother would lose her mind if she found out.'

'So don't tell her.'

But his father was adamant.

They were a small group, the Süleyman bachelor party, comprising the groom, his brother and his son, joined by three İkmen men, Arto Sarkissian and Ömer Mungun. Kerim Gürsel had sent Süleyman a text to say that he would be along later.

Once everyone had a drink and Patrick had taught them all to say 'sláinte' – Irish for 'good health', the men broke up into twos and threes to make conversation. Because so many of them smoked, they had to drink outside even though it was cold. Not that anyone complained. This was Mehmet's bachelor party, and so they would all do what he wanted.

When he'd met up with Murad and Patrick at his apartment, Mehmet had talked to his brother while the boy had taken a shower. Murad had told him about his argument with their mother, and Mehmet had wanted to phone her and tell her that she was no longer invited to his wedding. But Murad had stopped him. Even if the old woman did rail against Gonca and all she stood for, she had sent her that very valuable emerald necklace, which probably meant she was conflicted about her. Mehmet himself had been entirely cynical about the gift which he felt his mother had sent only to increase any sense of guilt he may have had regarding his marriage. Sadly for Nur Hanım, he possessed no such feeling.

341

However, now was not the time to think about his mother, and so when Süleyman found himself standing next to Arto Sarkissian, their conversation turned to work.

'I am told,' the doctor said, 'that you still have officers sifting through the contents of the Müftüoğlu apartment in Vefa.'

Süleyman shook his head. 'I don't know whether that will yield anything significant or not. But given that this investigation has become as serious as it has, what else can we do? Maybe there's something from there, yet to be found, that may help us identify who was using Müftüoğlu and Atyom Bey's services.'

'I didn't know Atyom well,' Arto said. 'But of course if anyone in any given community has an interesting addiction, one does get to hear whispers.'

'Poker, wasn't it?' Süleyman asked.

Arto nodded.

'I've requested his bank records and those of his business,' Süleyman said. 'I imagine that Atyom Bey wasn't the sort of person to become involved in criminal activity unless he was desperate.'

The doctor put a hand on his shoulder. 'Let us talk of other things,' he said. 'I should not have raised the subject of work. Tomorrow you are going to be married, and that is such a wonderful, happy thing.'

Chapter 26

'I've charged Gölcük.'

Kerim Gürsel was smoking in headquarters car park with Haluk Keleş. It was dark and cold, but neither of them could bear to spend any more time inside the building. Keleş, though less haunted-looking than Kerim, was nevertheless extremely pale. It had been a long day.

'We're still waiting on forensic evidence,' Kerim continued, 'but I'm convinced he's guilty. There are, I'm told, unaccounted-for amounts of money in his bank account. Not large amounts, which is why his involvement is so fucking stupid.'

Keleş said, 'It's always fucking stupid at that level. Little lookouts, turn-a-blind-eye men, making a few lira to take the girlfriend out for a meal or buy a new phone . . . It's nothing and yet it's just enough to tempt those who have fuck-all.'

'Have you ever seen anything like this before?' Kerim asked.

'I've had artefacts from Syria and Iraq through my hands, allegedly on their way to Switzerland or some other tax haven. I've seen stuff advertised online by IS. But nothing on this scale.'

'You honestly think someone would go to all that trouble to get their hands on original artworks?'

'People are greedy,' Keleş said. 'The rich are too rich, they get bored. But then maybe it means more because all the stuff is religious. If you believe a statue can cure you of terminal cancer, you'll do everything you can to get hold of it.'

'These are multiple artefacts,' Kerim said.

Keleş shrugged. 'As I say, greed. Even if the money man behind this is dying, why does he need so many of these fucking things? Should be in museums anyway. It's just fucking theft. What about Officer Deniz of the bekçi? What's her story?'

'She's blaming her lover,' Kerim said. 'I let her call her parents, which was . . . unexpected.'

'In what way?'

'I get that she didn't want me to listen in,' Kerim said. 'But I couldn't have made anything out even if I had.'

'Why?'

'She spoke Italian,' he said. 'Not what you expect to hear from a working-class woman supposedly on the phone to her parents. But then I am stereotyping. Maybe her mother's Italian? I don't know. She was calmer afterwards, so . . .'

Keleş said, 'Aren't you meant to be with Mehmet Bey in Beyoğlu?'

Kerim sighed. 'Yes. I'll just have to drive straight there now. I had hoped to go home and get changed, but . . .'

Keleş put his cigarette out and began to walk back towards the building.

'What are you doing now?' Kerim asked.

'Going to see if anything's been found amongst all that shit from Müftüoğlu's apartment. Even at this stage, you never know, maybe something'll turn up . . .'

There was always a moment in the midst of customs like kına gecesi when the true meaning of the practice came through. Generally it was a thinly disguised act of sorcery, which in this case was when Gonca's Aunt Sibel placed a gold coin in her hand and then smothered her palm with henna. This happened in Gonca's bedroom. Surrounded by her female friends and relatives, each one holding a candle to light the darkened room, she lay on her bed wearing her richly embroidered bindallı, a crown of crystals and sequins on her head.

The old woman, muttering ancient spells and incantations under her breath, wrapped the bride's hennaed hands in lambswool and then bound them tightly with white cotton. Traditionally the groom's female relatives were supposed to grab the bride and pull her off the bed, in order to deliver her to the groom, who had just arrived with his friends. But the only Süleyman female at the kına gecesi was Mehmet's niece, Edibe. Besides, that part of the ceremony was specific to virgin brides, which Gonca most certainly was not.

But for all the departures from the usual etiquette, it was still, Edibe felt, a powerful ceremony. When Gonca's old aunt anointed her feet with henna, her voice rising and falling, saying words that Edibe would never understand, she felt a shiver run through her body. Gonca Hanım, clad in red, her hair thick and deep red with henna, her feet and hands bound in white, looked both beautiful and powerful, and Edibe found herself unable to look into her fierce black eyes. Her dear Uncle Mehmet was marrying this witch woman from an unknowable culture – a woman whose love for him was intense and primal. She remembered when she had first seen them together, and how shocked she had been. Her uncle had always been, in Edibe's experience, very much in charge of the women he married or dated. But Gonca Hanım had wrapped herself around him like a snake, touching him and licking his face. Edibe knew that Gonca would rather die than lose Mehmet. She'd rather kill him than lose him to another woman.

When the bride got down from her great bed, now covered by a second, unsullied, intricate bedcover, she was supported by two of her daughters. Edibe didn't know their names, but one was a very sleek and tailored woman whom she had been told was a lawyer, the other a very beautiful, more traditionally attired

Roma girl. Tiny girls, their hair covered in glitter, their hands sticky with small balls of henna, weaved in and out of the women's legs, laughing. Gonca's many granddaughters.

Edibe moved the bedroom curtains aside a little and looked down into the garden of the old Greek house. There was a small Byzantine cistern in one corner, at the entrance to which a fire blazed, tended by a hugely fat woman in şalvar trousers. A large open-fronted tent covered half the garden, draped with multi-coloured fairy lights, beneath which tables groaned under the weight of food and drink, much of the latter alcoholic. Underneath the ancient lone olive tree, three men played mournful, haunting music. One played a cümbüş, a metal mandolin, another a wood-wind instrument called a zurna, while the third measured out the beat on a davul, a bass drum. A woman who possessed the same arrogance and time-trammelled beauty as Gonca Hanım sang a song that, while Edibe didn't understand the words, made her want to cry. The kına gecesi was about loss as well as joy. And now that the groom and his men had arrived, there was no way back.

The two men spoke quickly and intensely. Kerim had only just arrived in Balat, and his pale face looked exhausted in the fire-light.

He told Süleyman, 'Haluk Bey is far more invested in this case than the rest of us. I'll be honest, Mehmet, I've charged Gölcük because I truly believe in his guilt, but the art side of things is beyond me.'

Süleyman put a hand on his arm. 'Don't worry,' he said. 'Keleş is more qualified to move forward with a case like this than we are. I get the feeling his mind is forever sifting through the various scenarios that might be played out. He will make connections we can't.'

Kerim nodded.

'Now join me in some rakı,' Süleyman said. 'My fiancée and the other ladies will come and join us soon, and I would very much like you to dance the halay with me.'

Officer Deniz of the bekçi was a looker. Keleş peered at her through the hatch in her cell door, but she didn't look up. He hadn't wanted her to. She, of all the people they had in custody, puzzled him. An attractive young woman, an Italian speaker, apparently besotted with some knuckle-dragger . . . He'd got hold of her service record and intended to look over it to see if he could find anything in there that might give him more information.

In the meantime, the room assigned to sorting through what remained of Fahrettin Müftüoğlu's possessions was now unattended, and so he could, theoretically, look at them at his leisure. Entry to the subterranean store was via code, which he punched into the keypad next to the entrance.

Inside was a large suite of rooms, which encompassed the vault used to store valuable items. There were two gold angels in there now. For some reason, this made Keleş shudder. Had Müftüoğlu, who was clearly an artist, really made those? In comparison with the rest of his work, they were crude and poorly executed. They also appeared to be original.

When he arrived at the large room given over to Müftüoğlu's hoard, he was surprised to see that so much remained to be searched through. It was a big job; some of the jeweller's floors had been collapsing under the weight. Scanning the artefacts ranged across four tables, he saw yet more clothes and fabrics, several sewing machines, and piles of books stacked way above his head.

The davul player beat the drum with mallets as the men assembled for the dance. Now that the women had joined them in the

347

garden, it was time for the age-old halay to be performed by the groom and his male friends and family. While the women placed Gonca, her head and face veiled with red lace, on a raised chair opposite the men, Süleyman and his supporters formed a line. Holding the little fingers of their neighbours, the men arranged themselves on either side of the groom: his brother Murad on his right, followed by Bülent İkmen, Arto Sarkissian and Ömer Mungun. To his left, first his son Patrick, then Çetin İkmen, Kemal İkmen and finally Kerim Gürsel, who was the dance leader, or halaybaşı.

When the music began, Kerim called out instructions as the men performed a series of steps, sidesteps and hops. Patrick, who had no real idea about what was going on, just followed the others. The men at either end of the line, Kerim and Ömer, made great play of flourishing the handkerchiefs they were holding, while as the beat increased, both Çetin İkmen and Arto Sarkissian began to sweat. The women clapped, some of the gypsies ululated, and as the dancing became faster and wilder, the firelight combined with the fairy lights made the men's faces change colour in rapid succession. As the line moved forward, and İkmen and the doctor began to feel that they might die in the not-too-distant future, the groom suddenly broke away from his supporters and danced towards his bride.

As he approached her, Gonca Hanım stood, still with the red veil over her face, her supporters gathered at her back. The other men, with the exception of İkmen and Dr Sarkissian, who had gone to sit down, continued to dance as Süleyman stopped in front of his bride. Grasping the bottom of the red veil, he pulled it up to reveal her face.

Dressed in thick red velvet, a shining tiara on her elaborately coiffured head, she wore the emerald necklace his mother had given her, which partly disappeared into her deep décolletage. He kissed her right hand, which he then held up to his forehead,

348

honouring her. Some of the women in her party began to cry, which was traditional. But not Edibe Süleyman, who was far too cynical about men, even if the groom was her uncle; or Asana Şekeroğlu, who had spotted a man in the groom's party she thought she recognised.

As Mehmet Süleyman stepped up onto the platform to join Gonca, he put his arms around her and they kissed. Her women howled in anguish around them.

Investigation of Fahrettin Müftüoğlu's computer, which he had only ever used at work, had revealed details about the items he had produced in his apartment. St Foy, various boxes, the monstrance were all described in detail, photographed from different angles. But all gleaned from open public websites and social media outlets. So far the Dark Web had not reared its head, although Haluk Keleş knew that the technical officers had far from completed their investigations. The fucking angels, however, featured nowhere.

Keleş looked at the book table. There were a lot of books. What did someone like Fahrettin Müftüoğlu read? Predictably, many were about ancient Egypt – some in Arabic, some in French. They were all old. There were also things stuck inside them, bits of paper mostly. Was there any sort of order?

He couldn't see one. Also scene-of-crime had probably just dumped them in no particular configuration. As he began to pull things out, his phone rang. He looked at the screen. It was Commissioner Ozer.

He picked up. 'Yes.'

'Inspector Keleş, would you come to my office?' his superior said.

His first thought was that he'd done something wrong. Told someone he shouldn't to fuck off. But he said, 'Yeah.' Then he ended the call.

349

Some of the things he had pulled out of books were photographs. One he noticed was of Canan Müftüoğlu. He grabbed a handful and left.

The men were supposed to leave the kına gecesi quickly after the dancing. In the old days, they would have kidnapped the bride and Süleyman would have taken her to his parents' house on a horse. But this was the twenty-first century, and Gonca was a woman who had grandchildren.

However, everyone began to eat and drink, and some more dancing happened, though the men and women tended to stay in their own groups, with the exception of the bride and groom. Although it was cold, it was a fine night, and the two of them sat side by side near the fire, drinking rakı.

'You had no sleep last night, my darling,' she said as she stroked his face.

'Does it show?'

She laughed. 'Not at all, I just know that is how it was. İkmen told me.'

'Oh.'

'İkmen also told me that he has fixed our bedcover problem. A poor little girl . . . Oh, it's a long story, but no malice or witchcraft was involved. Just an accident.'

'I told you,' he said.

'Yes, but angel, I needed proof.'

They kissed again, and he put his arm around her. They watched their friends and family dancing and eating in the firelight for a few moments, then suddenly Gonca's whole body tensed.

'What's the matter?' he asked her.

Gonca shook her head. 'Asana,' she said.

'What about her?'

She pointed. 'Flirting with your colleague. Dirty little bitch!' Then she laughed.

But she wasn't flirting with just anyone. Asana had Kerim Gürsel all to herself in a corner of the food tent.

Süleyman said, 'I'd better go and rescue him. He's a married man.'

He kissed her hand and left. As he approached his colleague, he saw Asana's arm snake up to Kerim's collar. Süleyman tapped her on the shoulder, and she turned.

'Mehmet Bey . . .'

'I expect,' he said, 'that Inspector Gürsel has been too polite to tell you that he's married . . .'

'Oh no,' Asana said, 'he's told me that. Sinem, she's called, and his little baby is Melda.'

'I see.' Süleyman looked at Kerim.

'Asana Hanım and I have friends in common, Mehmet Bey.'

And of course, they did. Asana, though a high-powered property lawyer, had lived in Tarlabaşı, where Kerim had an apartment, when she was young. She too had a taste for drag clubs and gay bars.

'And so . . .' Süleyman began.

'Oh, Kerim Bey's secret is safe with me,' Asana said. 'Of course his being . . .' she left what he was blank, 'is an awful shame for me.'

Kerim laughed.

'But at least,' she said, 'I can talk to someone about how awful men can be, and also how absolutely infuriating it is that we need them for sex.'

He didn't know much about cars, but he knew a top-end Mercedes Maybach when he saw one. And this one was top-end. Probably bulletproof too. In fact, almost certainly.

Haluk Keleş watched Officer Pervin Deniz get into the car, assisted by some mirror-shaded flunkey, who then drove her away. His own vehicle, though almost new, couldn't compete.

351

He looked around its very basic interior. Who gave a shit about a Peugeot even if it was new? Who gave a shit about anything apart from money?

Commissioner Ozer had called him to his office to tell him that Officer Deniz was going to be released into the care of her family. Medical reports had been received from a private clinic that suggested she was a very sick woman. Officer Deniz, it seemed, had no child; she did not originate from working-class Gaziosmanpaşa – she didn't even live there. Rather, she lived in a massive and magnificent yalı with her parents in Yeniköy. Her father was a foreign businessman, Ozer had told him, but he didn't specify what type of foreigner.

Kerim Bey had heard her speaking Italian. But Keleş hadn't alluded to that with Ozer. All he'd said was 'How did she get to join the bekçi if she's a fantasist?'

But all Ozer had said was that he didn't know, and to take it up with her bekçi commander. Then he'd gone on to tell Keleş how nothing the young woman had told them could be relied upon. Her statement was to be struck from the record as unsafe. Apparently she had in the past run away from her parents and this clinic many times, and had always assumed other identities, created other lives, loved different men.

But so what? Keleş thought. She'd been involved! The poor little rich girl had left her latest piece of cock to rot in a cell. What was happening stank. And yet if Deniz was deemed unfit to give evidence, Keleş could appreciate there was little Ozer could have done.

So who was Officer Deniz's father, with his Maybach and his flunkeys in mirror shades? Was it too fanciful to imagine he was Mafia? The good old-fashioned Cosa Nostra had been sniffing around Turkey for years – even before former Italian prime minister Silvio Berlusconi had introduced Turks to his stripping housewives on his ubiquitous TV channels. Haluk Keleş loved

Italy and hated to see that country's enormous contribution to the art world cheapened.

Too wound up to drive home, he sat in his car and began to look through the pile of photographs he'd taken from the Müftüoğlu evidence room. He shouldn't strictly have taken anything out of that room, and he knew that he'd be pulled up on it when the camera footage of those areas were reviewed, but it was proving difficult for him to give a shit. All the great art he had grown up worshipping, all the values of integrity and the absolute right of people to see and experience works of genuine genius he had absorbed from his novelist father were just crumbling away.

As he shuffled his way through the photographs, he was struck by how many of them were black and white. Tiny prints of old-fashioned cars in a desert. Probably Egypt, given that Müftüoğlu's mother had been Egyptian. However, when he turned one of them over, he saw that he was wrong. But he kept on looking until he saw something that he stared at with his mouth open.

Chapter 27

'I'll drive you home,' Kerim Gürsel said to Süleyman. 'I've only had a few sips of rakı and that was an hour ago.'

'Patrick and I can get a taxi,' Süleyman said. 'You go straight to Tarlabaşı.'

'No.' Kerim took his arm. 'You're tired and it's your wedding day tomorrow. It will be my pleasure.'

They were standing in the street outside Gonca's house. Çetin İkmen and his sons, the doctor, Murad and Edibe and Ömer Mungun had already left in taxis. Dr Sarkissian, unaccustomed to Roma moonshine rakı, had required someone else to tell his driver where to take him.

The two men and the boy walked to where Kerim had parked his car and got in. In spite of dire warnings from his father, Patrick had tried the moonshine rakı too and was half asleep. As they drove away from Balat, down towards the Golden Horn, Süleyman said, 'I'm sorry you got cornered by Asana Hanım.'

Kerim smiled. 'I enjoyed seeing her. She's a great fan of drag. She knows Madam Edith. She won't tell anyone.'

Süleyman sighed. Everyone had secrets, some more potentially damaging than others.

Outside, although the sky was still clear enough to see the stars, the temperature had dropped considerably, and he hoped they didn't get an early flurry of snow in the morning. The stars reminded him of the wedding rings he'd had made, and he smiled. Gonca was not an easy woman to be around sometimes, but he

354

was glad he had asked her to marry him. Even after all these years, she still fascinated him, and he was still bewitched by her. Just before they had left and against all wedding etiquette, she'd asked him to stay the night with her, but he had refused. Apart from being just plain wrong, he had also known he was too tired to submit to another night of little sleep.

By the time they arrived at Süleyman's apartment building, Patrick was asleep. Also, and annoyingly, another car, bounced up onto the pavement, was parked across the building's entrance. While Süleyman opened the back door and hauled Patrick out and up into his arms, Kerim went to see if the driver of the other vehicle was inside so he could ask him to move.

He was, but Kerim didn't ask him to move. Instead he said to Haluk Keleş, 'What are you doing here?'

'What are you doing looking at that thing?'

İkmen turned towards the voice, which had come from a very pale and, without her signature make-up, very old-looking Samsun, wearing a tattered candlewick dressing gown.

'What are *you* doing?' he countered as he put one cigarette out and then lit another.

'I've just taken two aspirin,' she said. 'Headache. I was going to sit down in here for a bit before I went back to bed.'

'I'm not stopping you.'

'No, but that thing . . .' she pointed to the laptop he was peering at, 'flashing away . . .'

İkmen, realising he was defeated, shut the lid and turned around in his chair.

'So, do you want to talk or what?' he said.

'No. I'd like to know what you were doing with that thing. Çiçek said you came in drunk.'

'Çiçek exaggerates,' he said. 'And as for "that thing", I was seeing what I could find out about Atyom Mafyan the jeweller.'

355

'Garbis Aznavourian's cousin? Why?'

'Because it seemed he killed himself last night,' İkmen said.

'I heard.'

'Trying to work out why.'

'Probably money,' Samsun said. 'He gambled.'

'He did. But some of the things he was involved with went beyond that, I believe.'

'Like what?'

'If he needed money to cover his debts, he could have gone to his bank.'

'What, for gambling debts?'

'He wouldn't tell them it was gambling debts; he'd make something up!' İkmen said. 'Then there's his apartment in Tarabya. Worth a good couple of million euros. If he was in that deep, he could have sold it. But instead he committed fraud.'

'Did he?'

'Yes, but don't tell anyone. He acted for someone unknown, producing fake artworks.'

'I knew a girl in Üsküdar did that,' Samsun said. 'Photocopies of ancient masters. Used to sell them door to door.'

'I'm not talking about things like that!' İkmen said. 'I'm talking about things made to look exactly like famous, extremely valuable works of art.' Then his face fell. 'Sacred things, things people will die for.'

Haluk Keleş put the small photograph he'd found in the evidence room on Süleyman's dining table, while the exhausted groom made them all cups of coffee.

Peering at the tiny image, Kerim Gürsel said, 'What is it?'

'From what's written on the back, it was taken in Abyssinia, now Ethiopia, in 1936,' Keleş said.

'I didn't ask when it was made, I asked what it was.' Kerim

356

was tetchy. He had wanted to go straight home after dropping off Süleyman and his son. But Keleş had insisted he stay.

Süleyman picked up the small image. 'Looks like Müftüoğlu's angels. Who is that in the background?'

'I don't know,' Keleş said. 'But he isn't local.'

Kerim Gursel, still annoyed, began to sort through some of the other photos and pieces of paper that had been tucked behind the image.

'And we can't see the angels' faces,' Süleyman added. 'So these may or may not be the models for the jeweller's angels. Have you got any more of these photographs?'

'No,' Keleş said. 'There may be more amongst all that shit still at headquarters, I don't know. But if this was taken in Ethiopia in 1936, then that was the time when fascist Italy ruled over it. See that white man standing between the angels? He's Italian. I'd lay money on it.'

'And so?'

'And so if Müftüoğlu just had this picture to copy from, it could mean he made up the faces.'

'Why?'

'Why?'

'Yes, why?' Süleyman said. 'If your thesis is that Müftüoğlu made things to order, to act as replacements for original works, then that wouldn't work in this case. Any copies made would have to be exact.'

There was a pause. He was right. But then Keleş said, 'Not if no one knows what those things look like.'

Another silence. It was Süleyman who ended it. He said, 'You're suggesting, I think, that these angels are in fact the angels that sit on top of the actual Ark of the Covenant?'

'Yes. Some experts think the real Ark has been in Ethiopia for centuries held in one of their ancient churches, guarded by a single priest.'

357

Kerim Gürsel, though not agreeing with Keleş, was intrigued, and took a photograph of the small snap on his phone.

'And if I were to say to you that I think you are putting fact together with myth and creating a reality of your own making, what would you say? You want me to phone the authorities in Addis Ababa and tell them that someone, we don't know who, may have been in the process of having a copy made of a national treasure they may or may not own? They'd call Ozer and have me locked up.' Süleyman picked up his phone and called a number he had on speed-dial. 'However,' he continued, 'don't just take my word for it.'

He waited for an answer, which, when it came, sounded like a bark.

'Asana? Are you awake?'

Gonca hadn't wanted to be alone the night before her wedding, and so her daughter had agreed to share her bed for the night.

Asana turned over to look at her mother. 'Well I am now.'

Gonca put her arms around her eldest girl and kissed the side of her face.

'I'm sorry, Asana, but I just can't sleep,' she said. 'I know I'm an old woman now who really should be sitting by my fire smoking a pipe, watching my grandchildren play . . .'

'That's not you, Mum.'

'I know!' she said. 'But am I deluding myself, Asana? I will be that crone in a few years' time, whether I like it or not!'

'You won't.'

Asana just wanted to go back to sleep. In the morning, she had to help her mother prepare for her wedding amid, no doubt, the hysteria engendered by her younger sisters and her aunts.

'But what if I am?' Gonca said. 'I will admit to you, Asana, and no other living soul that when people say I bewitched Mehmet Bey, they are right.'

'I never thought you didn't,' Asana said. 'Not that you needed to. He loves you.'

'Ah, but I did my work just before Çiçek İkmen gave him up!' Gonca said darkly. 'It's buried in these walls.'

'Up here, in the bedroom?'

'Yes!'

Asana sat up and put on the bedside lamp. 'Mum,' she said, 'it's what you do, and now it's done. Leave it. Or not. If you carry on like this, you're going to be tired out tomorrow, and then you'll just go on about how you looked like shit at your wedding.'

She lit a cigarette and then gave one to her mother.

Relentless, Gonca continued, 'And now Çetin Bey tells me that I shouldn't allow Şehzade Mehmet to buy that house on Büyükada. He says it will cost too much money, that he will have to get loans, which will make him vulnerable to corruption, and only I can change this . . .'

'So tell him you don't need him to buy the house!' Asana said.

'He wants to make me happy.'

'So tell him that you'll only be happy if he doesn't buy the house!'

'Oh, but Asana, our family have all been looking forward to going to Büyükada in the summer. And his son, Patrick . . .'

'Well then, we'll all have to just get over it, won't we?' Asana said.

She'd rarely seen her mother anything other than supremely confident, and so Gonca's current state of anxiety shocked her. Unlike her mother, Asana was unsure about the role of magic in her life, and tended to believe only what she could see with her own eyes. She had no doubt that Mehmet Süleyman loved her mother as much as she loved him. But what Gonca seemed to be seeking was assurance that it would always be the same. And no one could give her that.

Eventually, when they'd both finished their cigarettes, Asana put her arms around Gonca and lay back down again. She stroked her hair. 'Go to sleep, Mum. Everything'll be all right.'

If Mehmet Süleyman looked ghastly, Çetin İkmen was horrific. Stinking of stale cigarettes and rakı, red eyed and haggard, he looked as if he'd just recently got up from his own grave.

Süleyman had explained on the phone some of what was keeping him and the other two officers up. Now that İkmen was in his apartment, he finished his story.

İkmen looked at the old photograph. 'How do you know it's not a fake?'

'A fake? They didn't have Photoshop—'

'No! I mean the thing in the photograph!' İkmen snapped. 'God! I can't believe I'm saying this, but Haluk Bey, the whereabouts of the Ark is a story. It may be true, it may not be. I am not qualified to say and neither are you. In addition, what you have found in that photograph proves nothing. I'm assuming that your contention is partly informed by the possibility that this bekçi officer's father might be Italian. But we don't know that. Suspects are removed from the system due to lack of mental capacity all the damn time. The only outstanding facts you need to worry about, in my opinion, are the death of Constable Akar and the appearance of ricin in this city. Other than that, you have two suicides, which may or may not be connected to your investigation, and some fake religious artefacts.'

All the men fell silent. Then Keleş said, 'The ricin incidents are connected. We know this. Osman Aslan, who was part of this conspiracy, has as good as said so.'

'I know,' İkmen said. 'But if the people behind this fraud are as frightening as I've been told they are, it's unlikely that the Aslan man and Canan Müftüoğlu's father will tell you anything more, whatever you do. And they are the only people who really know now, as far as I can tell. Lean on Officer Yaman and Constable Gölcük, who may or may not come out with something you can use. From what Mehmet Bey tells me, it seems that Yaman has implicated Gölcük.'

'And we have another witness, a prostitute,' Keleş said.

'So charge Gölcük with murder,' İkmen said. 'He may offer up more information to try to reduce his sentence.'

'Yes.'

'What really puzzles me,' İkmen continued, 'is how all these people came to meet each other in the first place. I'm sorry, Haluk Bey, but I think your concentration on these artefacts may have cost you dearly in terms of trying to establish what this apparent network of individuals actually means.'

Süleyman cut in. 'To be fair, Çetin, it has been very difficult to disengage one from the other . . .'

'I know it's hard!' İkmen said. 'You're dealing with someone we know is utterly ruthless and lethal. I also know, Mehmet Bey, that it's your opinion that now that Müftüoğlu and Mafyan are dead, these people are moving out. GülGül has always been a unique atelier in this city. Innovative, highly skilled, and possessed of the bonus of having Müftüoğlu amongst its jewellers. He was not only brilliant, but also odd and antisocial. What more could you want? As for Atyom Bey, I think he was in debt. Maybe to these people, maybe to some other. How the cops got involved was to do with money, of course. But . . . Gentlemen, you have to work with what you have. You're still waiting on results from forensics; Müftüoğlu's things are still not properly catalogued. I get that Ozer released the bekçi woman because of either her state of mind, fear of a diplomatic spat with a foreign power, pressure from above or all three. I rarely agree with anything that man does, but in this case he was probably in an impossible position. And if the woman was a fantasist, her testimony would be unsafe...'

361

'But at least we now know that Müftüoğlu definitely killed himself,' Kerim Gursel said as he held up a piece of paper.

'What's that?' Suleyman asked.

Kerim read, '*Canan no longer loves me. I cannot bear it. I will die by my own hand.* And then he signs it, F. Müftüoğlu'

'Is it dated?' Suleyman asked.

'No.'

'So it could be... irrelevant... I mean why hide such a thing with an old photograph...'

'Unless the photograph were relevant,' Keles said.

'What do you mean?'

'I mean,' he said, 'that he'd lost his Canan and maybe he felt that was in part because of this. It must've taken him a long time to make those angels. Perhaps he felt that in a way they'd taken him away from her, allowed Osman Aslan in to take his place.'

They all looked down at the floor, all aware they would probably never know what Müftüoğlu's motivation for anything he had ever done were. In spite of this note he remained unknowable.

Eventually İkmen said, 'Present your Ethiopian evidence to Ozer, Haluk Bey. Take copies of everything, but expect this whole situation, so long as ricin doesn't make a reappearance, to subside. No artefacts have so far been stolen. With the copies in our care, they won't be. I understand that you want to find out who was behind this because people have died. You want justice, it's what you do. But there is always another day on which you can fight, and provided we have this information carefully catalogued, then if this operation starts up elsewhere, at home or abroad, we are in a position to be ready to assist. And because it would appear to target artefacts worldwide, we need to share our intelligence.'

Kerim said, 'Everything you say is true, Çetin Bey . . .'

'And were I in your position, I too would be frustrated and angry,' İkmen said. 'But what you have uncovered here . . . just looking at the amounts of money involved . . . this is organised crime, a terrorist organisation or someone with too much money and too much power. These situations can take years to fully expose, and even then you may never get to the bottom of it. Going back to Italy, look at the Cosa Nostra. The authorities in Rome have been waging war, mainly in the south and in Sicily, for decades. You have something. You've lifted the corner of a blanket covering a murky world. See it as a start. Do what you can, always bear this in mind, and move on.'

Once Keleş and Kerim had gone and İkmen was alone with Süleyman, out came a bottle of brandy and they went into the living room.

'I want you to go to bed soon,' İkmen said as he lit a cigarette. 'Gonca Hanım is not in the business, I believe, of marrying a ghost.'

Süleyman smiled. 'I will. But I insist you stay over. You can't go home now. You can have my bed.'

İkmen shook his head. 'I will not! You're the one who needs to look handsome tomorrow, not me. I'll stay, but the sofa will serve me well enough. Quite honestly, I could probably sleep on a spike at the moment.'

Süleyman was too tired to argue. 'Do you really believe everything you told Haluk Keleş and Kerim Bey?'

İkmen took a drag on his cigarette and then slowly exhaled.

'You know me so well, Mehmet.'

'I do. And so?'

'We both know that some of our colleagues are vulnerable to persuasion, especially if money is involved. And I truly believe you won't get much more out of Aslan or Canan Müftüoğlu's father. Both men are traumatised by the loss of the woman and

363

the power of those they are protecting, made violently manifest by the use of ricin.'

'I think the old man knows far more than he is saying about how it all began,' Süleyman said. 'But he's trying to save his own skin.'

'Of course. I've been reading a lot recently,' İkmen said, 'about Colombian and Mexican drug cartels. Impenetrable. Largely because of the way they treat those who do speak. They set up torture houses where people are literally chopped to pieces, bit by agonising bit. Can you imagine? And they own whole provinces in their countries, which is not surprising. We fight what are effectively private armies these days, Mehmet.'

'And yet, what you said about that photograph . . .'

'Ah.' He smiled. 'As I said before, you know me so well.'

'You think it's genuine?'

'I think it could be.'

'Why?'

'Why shouldn't such a thing exist? It's as probable as the possibility that it doesn't. And if I were going to get my hands on a religious artefact, why not go for the big one? Yes, it will burn your eyes out if you are unrighteous, but the sort of people who in this instance we think want it won't believe they are.' He smiled. 'There's part of me that hopes it does exist, that they get their hands on it and then melt like the Nazis in the Indiana Jones films. Anyway, you must get to bed, Mehmet. I'll be fine here.'

Chapter 28

Rambo Şekeroğlu senior had procured a large wedding car for his sister, a white Lincoln stretch limousine. He'd hired it from another Roma man in exchange for certain favours he wouldn't specify. Wrapped in red ribbon and decorated with red rosettes and flowers, it was a fitting vehicle for one who some called 'the Queen of the Gypsies'.

Traditionally Gonca would be accompanied by her close female and male relatives, who would joyfully fire bullets into the air. But Mehmet had made her promise that no guns would be worn to their wedding. Rambo felt the loss keenly.

'If Dad was still alive, he'd be horrified,' he told Gonca as he helped her into the back of the car. Her wedding dress, which was made from purple velvet encrusted with small patches of golden sea silk, had a two-metre silk train, and she wore a pink veil that was almost as long. On her feet were rhinestone-encrusted purple stilettos. She carried an enormous bunch of orchids.

'Between Mehmet Bey's job and the hotel rules, we must keep things as quiet as we can,' she said.

Rambo pulled a face.

'Oh, don't be such a child!' Gonca snapped. 'Mehmet Bey is paying for all the food, drink and entertainment today; the least you can do is stop yourself firing bullets into the air!'

It was midday, and Gonca and her daughters and granddaughters were not due at the Çırağan Palace Hotel, on the European side of the Bosphorus, until 2 p.m. But the weather, though cold, was sunny, and Gonca, like most brides, wanted as many people to see her going to her wedding as possible. Also, the İstanbul traffic was likely to make their journey much longer than it should be.

Rambo took the driving seat, alongside Erdem, Gonca's eldest son, while other Şekeroğlu men pushed piles of relatives into old VW Beetles, ancient Chevrolets and modern, if battered, Minis, both in Balat and down on their home turf in Tarlabaşı. As far as Gonca knew, two hundred relatives were due to attend, plus ten friends and business associates. Mehmet's contingent hardly made up the forty places remaining. Although his extended family was actually bigger than Gonca's, many of them lived abroad, some he barely knew and many he didn't like. His party consisted mainly of friends.

As Rambo drove out of Balat, Erdem said, 'We're booked into the Sultan Suite, which is where you will spend your wedding night, Mum.' He'd helped Süleyman organise the wedding and was in charge of making sure that the bride and her party were at the right places at the right times.

'Well, that sounds wonderful,' Gonca said.

'You wait until you see it,' he replied. 'And let me tell you, it was Mehmet Bey's idea. I picked something much less grand and not nearly as expensive. But he wouldn't have it. Only the best for you.'

Sinem Gürsel looked at herself in her bedroom mirror. Her husband, who had been in to headquarters that morning, had only just arrived home, and they were now both dressing for the wedding. The ever-reliable Madam Edith was entertaining Melda in the living room and would be looking after the baby so that the couple could enjoy the celebrations on their own.

When Kerim came out of the bathroom, a towel tucked around his waist, Sinem said, 'Do you think this dress is good enough?'

'I think you look sensational in it,' he said.

'Yes, but is it good enough? You know how all the gypsy women dress up for weddings. Is this a bit plain?'

Sinem was curvy but slim, and could wear almost anything she wanted – or she could have done if not for the fact that her limbs were twisted by arthritis. Block colours, like this blue fishtail dress, suited her well, even if they were plain.

'It doesn't matter,' Kerim said. 'Dress it up with some of your scarves and jewellery if you feel like it. And anyway, you won't be the only lady not dressed like the Roma. Çetin Bey's daughters are coming, and Mehmet Bey's niece.'

Sinem sat down on their bed and watched Kerim get dressed. He had a new dark blue suit for the occasion.

'Do you feel better about things today?' she asked as she looked through her jewellery box.

'What do you mean? I charged a man with murder this morning,' he said. 'Something I must put to the back of my mind for a few hours now.'

'No, I mean about . . .' their eyes locked, 'us.'

Kerim sat down next to her and put an arm around her shoulders. He kissed her nose. 'It's work in progress.'

'What does that mean?' she said. 'When you told me you went to Pembe's grave and cried, I was so sorry for you . . .'

He put a finger on her lips to silence her.

'I will always love Pembe,' he said. 'I know you know that. But I will limit my visits as much as I can.' He kissed her lips. 'You know I love you, Sinem. Even when we're not having sex, I . . . Some things are easier than others . . .'

'I don't suppose Mehmet Bey and Gonca Hanım only have sex when it's "easy",' she said bitterly. 'But then they're properly in love . . .'

'And so are we!' Kerim said. 'Sinem, I have known you for thirty years and I have loved you all that time!'

'Not like a man should,' she said, and then regretted it. 'Oh Kerim, I'm . . .'

He shook his head sadly, but then he hugged her.

'You're right to want the romance you deserve,' he said. 'I owe you everything, Sinem. Without you and Melda, I am nothing.'

He was a cop who was a cop killer. Mustafa Gölcük had been certain that Fındık Hanım would stick to their story, but she hadn't. And then those bekçiler had seen him do it and so that had been the end of it. If only the jeweller's wife hadn't died, he could have shared some of the blame with her. But they'd poisoned her and so he was alone with his murder. Those who'd employed Canan Müftüoğlu were unknown to him except by their actions. They were horrific. Using ricin was unforgivable. But then so had been the killing of Constable Akar.

He'd only done it because the jeweller's wife had told him to. Another distraction. He'd told her he thought the Armenian's idea of halting the police operation using ricin at his atelier was enough. But she'd insisted. She'd been an evil bitch! He wished he'd never met her. He blamed that female bekçi for that. Vefa was her beat and so they met up from time to time. Nothing sexual happened, she wasn't his type. But she'd been nice to him, and when she'd asked him if he wanted to make some easy money, he'd said yes.

It had started out with turning a blind eye to stuff turning up for the jeweller late at night. He'd arrange to be in the area so he could take care of it. It was easy – then. But then with Akar on board, it became harder to do. The young man cramped his extracurricular work, which affected his earnings, especially when the bekçi woman got herself a boyfriend she could use instead.

Gölcük had pleaded with her to let some work go his way,

but she didn't. His relationship with Fındık began to suffer. But then the jeweller's wife told him she had to get as much finished work as possible out of her dead husband's apartment the night after the scientists left. She'd told him to kill Akar, and he'd obliged – for a price.

But now that he'd been charged with murder, would anyone, Gürsel particularly, believe his story about how he had been manipulated by a woman who was now dead? He couldn't give them any information about who had been behind her and the jeweller Mafyan, because he just didn't know. And now that Mafyan was dead too, it was hopeless. Canan, the jeweller's wife, had always said that her husband's death had been unexpected. She'd said he probably killed himself because he was tired of doing so much work, day and night, for people he knew could end him at any moment. But then the bekçi woman had told him that Müftüoğlu had killed himself because Canan had been unfaithful to him. Who knew?

What he did know was that he was going to prison, and as an ex-cop, he was not going to do his time easily. Before that, however, he also knew that he would be questioned again by Süleyman, and *he* was a bastard.

Patrick Süleyman walked out of his bedroom and stood in the hall in front of his father. Dressed in a black suit, white shirt and bright green tie, he was very smart, except for one small detail.

'I am so proud of you,' Mehmet said as he rearranged Patrick's messy tie into a neat Windsor knot. 'Just this . . .' He finished and patted the boy's chest. 'There.'

'Thanks, Dad.'

'I'm surprised they don't teach you how to put on a tie properly at your school.'

'We all hate wearing ties,' the boy said.

369

Süleyman smiled. 'So, are we ready to go now?'

'Yeah.'

'Do you have everything you need? Remember you will be going home with Çetin Bey tonight.'

Patrick picked up his suitcase.

'Good.' His father picked up his own bags. He was about to open the front door when . . .

'Dad . . .'

The boy looked troubled. Süleyman said, 'Yes?'

Patrick put his hand in his jacket pocket and took out his father's wallet. 'Beware of pickpockets and magicians.'

Süleyman laughed as he took the wallet back. 'You're improving,' he said.

He couldn't help himself, but he didn't care. Inspector Haluk Keleş had been told to leave the subject of bekçi Pervin Deniz alone, but he couldn't. When he should have been doing his job, obtaining estimates of the value of Müftüoğlu's creations from art dealers and gold merchants, he was concentrating on tracking her down.

Of course, the home address she had given the bekçiler was not where she really lived, which was in Yeniköy with her parents. He didn't know where, and so he began to look at strange and slightly silly articles and websites cataloguing the lives of the super rich who lived in Bosphorus yalıs. No Italian names came up, but there was one Deniz and he vaguely recognised the name, Nilüfer Deniz.

A quick search revealed that former film star Nilüfer Deniz lived in Yeniköy. Back in the seventies, when the local studio, Yeşilçam, had dominated cinemas all over the country, Nilüfer Deniz had specialised in ingénue parts – ruined village girls, jilted brides, virgins in danger. Haluk Keleş didn't remember any of these films, although they occasionally turned up on TV. But he knew of Nilüfer Deniz because his mother had always liked her.

She had, of course, retired many years ago and had gone to live in Yeniköy with her first husband, Fırat Sasmaz. However, that marriage had broken down in the early eighties, after which she became involved with an Italian aristocrat, whom she married in Rome in 1985. He was called Cavaliere Gianluca Sforzo, and he had a daughter with Nilüfer Hanım, born in 1987, called Mihrimah. Making sure that he still had the small photograph from Müftüoğlu's apartment in his wallet, Haluk Keleş set off for Yeniköy.

They were married on a raised platform under an archway constructed from fresh flowers on the vast Çırağan Palace Hotel terrace, overlooking the Bosphorus. And although the civil ceremony took only a few minutes, when Gonca Şekeroğlu and Mehmet Süleyman exchanged their unique night-sky rings, tears began to form in their eyes. Then they kissed.

Gonca's sister Didim, while approving of the outdoor ceremony – which Gonca had insisted upon provided there was no rain or snow – was outraged by the kiss. Standing at the front of a huge crowd of relatives, she registered her disgust with her sister loudly, in Romani, and then busied herself keeping her grandchildren under control. Cameras and phones flashed as both official and unofficial photographers attempted to capture images of the couple before the light faded. It was a beautiful afternoon, but it was autumn now and everyone wanted to get inside the huge heated marquee the hotel had set up for the champagne reception, during which the bride and groom would greet their guests and accept their wedding gifts. These would consist mainly of money and gold, and both bride and groom would wear red sashes around their necks to which these items would be pinned.

Erdem Şekeroğlu, as designated wedding organiser, took the

newly-weds into the marquee and attempted in vain to arrange the guests into an organised queue. The couple were mobbed, people kissed, shook hands and waved champagne flutes. Children ran around and frequently fell over, laughing. Gonca was delighted. Holding tight to her husband's arm, she was soon lost in a flurry of banknotes and gold, and by the time Mehmet's family and friends came to greet them, she was crying. Everyone had been so generous.

Finally, bringing up the rear, Kerim and Sinem Gürsel embraced them both and pinned two gold coins on Mehmet's chest. He, in turn, kissed Sinem's hand.

'Thank you for coming, Sinem Hanım,' he said. 'You look most beautiful.'

Sinem saw the fierce glance Gonca Hanım aimed at her husband, and thought that now they were married, she was going to question all and any interactions he had with other women. She felt a tiny devil inside prod her to continue their contact.

'It must be so lovely for you to get married in one of your family's palaces,' she said, aware that her husband was anxious to now move along.

Süleyman laughed. 'It is simply a wonderful venue, Sinem Hanım,' he said. 'Thank you.'

And then to Gonca's horror, his phone rang.

'It's every fucking woman for herself,' Samsun Bajraktar said to her cousin, Çetin İkmen, as they watched people arrange themselves around numerous round dining tables.

İkmen, brandy in one hand, cigarette in the other, said, 'That is because Erdem Şekeroğlu is a realist.'

'What do you mean?'

'I mean,' he said, 'one of the reasons I have always admired the Roma is for their independence of spirit. Also, and this isn't so good, a lot of Gonca's more distant relatives can't read.'

372

'I didn't think of that,' Samsun said. 'Anyway, look, I'm going to go and grab us a table.' She began to leave.

İkmen said, 'Take Kemal and Bülent to help you in case you need backup.'

At that moment, he saw Süleyman wander out from the other end of the marquee looking at his phone. İkmen went to join him. 'Anything wrong?'

Mehmet embraced him. 'No, not really.'

'Which means yes,' İkmen said.

Mehmet laughed. 'Haluk Bey thinks he has discovered the identity of Officer Pervin Deniz's parents,' he said. 'Her mother, he thinks, is an old Yeşilçam film star.'

'Who?'

'Nilüfer Deniz.'

'Really!' İkmen said.

'You remember her?'

'I do. Pretty little thing.'

'Well, according to Haluk Bey, she married an Italian called Cavaliere Gianluca Sforzo back in the eighties. They settled in Yeniköy and had a daughter . . .'

'Did they indeed?' İkmen said.

'I think Cavaliere is some sort of aristocratic title,' Süleyman said.

'I think it is too. I also recall that name.'

'Why?'

'I think,' İkmen said, 'that Gianluca Sforzo was once a person of interest.'

The yalı was enormous. But then if Nilüfer Deniz had bought it back in the seventies, she'd probably paid almost nothing for it. A brilliant white four-storey baroque building, it was the sort of place Haluk Keleş sometimes had fantasies about owning. In his hands, he promised himself, such a place would be furnished

373

with original nineteenth-century furniture and fittings. He'd rip out any ugly radiators and heat the place using a wood-burning soba – even if it did mean he almost died in the winter. Walking up to the front door, he noticed that the Maybach he'd seen Pervin Deniz get into the previous night was parked in the drive. He rang the doorbell and waited.

A man answered the door; not the same man who had driven Pervin Deniz away from headquarters, but one very similar. Young, mirror shaded, hair gelled.

'Yes?' he asked Keleş, who showed him his badge. 'What do you want?'

But then a small elderly woman pushed the man out of the way. 'Police? Again? I thought we'd sorted all that out.'

She looked him up and down in a way he did not find comfortable or approving. He could see that she had once been pretty, even though she was now skeletally gaunt.

Keleş, who had managed to put together a reasonable cover story on his way to Yeniköy, said, 'Just following up from last night, hanım.'

'Oh,' she said. Then, dismissing the young man with a wave of her hand, she added, 'You'd better come in, I suppose.'

The wedding banquet was substantial. Aware that her reputation within the Roma community was at stake, Gonca knew she had to feed her relatives and friends well. If some tiny little piece of meat with a few leaves on the side was served, they would wonder whether she had lost her mind. And so the meal had started with plain, reliable lentil soup and then moved on to a dish called hünkar beğendi, which was basically an Ottoman-style lamb stew with aubergine and rice.

Patrick, sitting on his father's left at the top table, didn't much like the boiled rice everyone else seemed to be enjoying, and was mortified to learn that the dessert, a dish called zerde, was also rice based. But then with his father texting on his phone most of the time and Gonca Hanım looking on furiously, that was the least of his concerns.

Eventually, unable to contain his curiosity any longer, he said, 'Dad, what are you doing?'

'Doing?' His father looked up.

'On your phone,' Patrick said. 'Your wife's looking at you like she'd kill you given half a chance.'

Süleyman turned to Gonca and whispered something in her ear, but she didn't look amused. Then he said to Patrick, 'It is just work.'

'Work!'

'Yes . . . A colleague is . . . It doesn't matter.'

'I think it does to Gonca Hanım,' Patrick said. 'You know, Dad, this is your third marriage. You can't fuck it up.'

Not only had the boy scolded him, he'd also sworn at him! But Süleyman decided that he would let that go for the time being. There was no way he could argue with his son in public, and besides, what he had been doing had been wrong. He switched his phone off. There was nothing he could add to what he'd already texted to Haluk Keleş, or his mother, who had not come to his wedding, had not called and probably never would. Why she had given that emerald necklace to Gonca was anyone's guess. The woman had always been utterly unreadable.

'Mihrimah is in Italy with her father,' Nilüfer Deniz told Haluk Keleş. 'We thought it best she return to the clinic she always stays in when her condition breaks down.'

She sat across from him in a large brocade armchair.

'Which is where?' Keleş asked.

'Rome,' she said. 'I think in light of this recent event, she may be there for some time.'

375

'Why doesn't she go to a clinic here?' He had assumed the psychiatric report on Pervin Deniz had come from a Turkish hospital. If it had come from Italy, clearly it had been translated very quickly.

The one-time film star laughed. 'Seriously?' she said.

'Some of our clinics are world class these days,' he countered.

'I don't care. I remember how they used to be, and I will not put my daughter through that. Anyway, although I am sure you don't know who I am—'

'You were in Yeşilçam films in the seventies,' Keleş said.

'Yes, but you had to look it up, didn't you? Oh, don't answer that!' she said. 'All her life Mihrimah has had problems. Over the years we've been told she is a sociopath, bipolar, she has a schizotype disorder and latterly she is personality disordered. What can one make of it all?'

'Your daughter was a bekçi for over a year,' Keleş said. 'Didn't you report her missing?'

Nilüfer Deniz frowned. 'Inspector,' she said, 'my daughter has been disappearing, playing at being other people, all her life. This is not the first time she has left us. Anyway, what could you have done? Looked for her for a little while and then given up? My husband is very well connected. He can obtain help in this matter whenever he wants.'

'You husband is Italian,' Keleş said.

'Yes. Our daughter has dual nationality, which is why it is easy for her to go to Italy.'

'Seems to me,' Keleş said, 'that it might be more convenient for you all to live in Italy.'

She looked uncomfortable for a moment, and then she said, 'My husband prefers to live here.'

Süleyman had allowed Keleş to speak to Çetin İkmen on his phone about Cavaliere Gianluca Sforzo. A person of interest in the dim, distant past, but why? İkmen couldn't remember. And was that connected in any way to why he didn't want to live in his own country? Although he was there now . . .

'Hanım, you are aware of the reasons your daughter was under arrest, aren't you?' Keleş asked.

'An art conspiracy,' she said. 'I know of no details.'

'Artefacts being produced to replace original artworks.'

'That's appalling,' she said. 'I'm afraid my daughter does get such fancies. She craves excitement, you see. We are told, her father and myself, that that is one of the symptoms of personality disorder.'

And then he remembered that Ozer had specifically told him that the clinic was in İstanbul. He hadn't assumed that, Ozer had said it. But from what this woman had said, that wasn't true. Haluk Keleş felt both elated, that something could indeed be very wrong about this family, and also afraid. His heart began to hammer.

'I see,' he said, and then, more quickly than he usually did, he rose to his feet. 'I just thought I would make contact to check that everything with your daughter is in hand.'

'It is,' she said. 'As I told you.'

Noticing that one of his shoelaces was untied, he bent down to fasten it. As he did so, everything in his right-hand jacket pocket fell out on the floor. His phone, his car keys and the small black and white photograph taken in 1936 somewhere in Ethiopia. The old woman went over to him and helped him retrieve his belongings.

The dancing began as soon as the hotel staff had moved the dining tables out of the marquee and the DJ had set up his sound system.

Patrick said to Kemal İkmen, 'It won't all be Turkish music, will it?'

'No. Although you might like some of our modern stuff,' Kemal said. 'You know we have Turkish rap now?'

'Yeah, but my dad won't have that, will he. Not at his age.'

Mehmet Süleyman and Gonca's first dance together as husband and wife was achingly romantic and also not. It was romantic because the music, 'Careless Whisper' by George Michael, was both heartfelt and sexy, and not romantic because all the kids kept running through the marquee shouting and laughing.

But those who could blank the children out and concentrate on the couple could see that they were unaware of what was going on around them. Gonca, her feet bare now, held the train of her long purple gown over one arm, her hands entwined around her husband's neck. Both of them had their eyes closed as they gently swayed, their lips locked together in a long, long kiss.

Hülya İkmen, who had come with her husband, the jeweller Berekiah Cohen, said, 'Don't they look beautiful together!'

'I'm very pleased with the fit of the rings,' her husband replied. 'It can sometimes be difficult with older ladies like Gonca Hanım, because by sixty many have developed a measure of arthritis.'

Hülya raised her eyes up to heaven. 'Thank you for that observation, Romance Bey.'

Berekiah said, 'I can only say things the way I see them, Hülya.'

'Really?' She propped her sleeping father up in his chair. 'I suppose I have to be grateful you were a bit more poetic when we met.'

Arto Sarkissian, who had been sitting next to his friend Çetin İkmen, rose to his feet and said, 'I must go outside or I'll go mad. What with the music and the children . . .'

Although a lot of guests remained in the marquee, plenty of people were outside too – children eating sweets from the little bags Gonca had made for them, crammed with lokum and chocolate; elderly Roma women sitting on the ground knitting and smoking; incredibly beautiful young girls making doe eyes at the hotel staff; and Kerim and Sinem Gürsel sitting on a wall next to Ömer and Peri Mungun.

Although she hadn't said anything about it, Ömer knew that his sister was sad because she hadn't been able to bring her new boyfriend to the wedding. To be fair, neither she nor Ömer had asked. But now that she was talking to Sinem Gürsel, who was showing her the latest photographs of baby Melda, she seemed much happier.

Left alone with Kerim, Ömer didn't know what else to talk about except work, and so he stayed silent until they were joined by Eylul Yavaş, who looked absolutely stunning in a long silk evening gown and elegantly tied green hijab. Sitting down beside her colleagues, she said to Kerim, 'I hear you charged Mustafa Gölcük, sir.'

'My evidence may well mostly be based upon hearsay, but I feel it's sound,' he said.

Eylul looked up into the star-filled sky. 'So much death, and for what?' she said.

'Money,' Ömer replied. 'And fear.'

She frowned.

'The suicides,' he said.

'Maybe Müftüoğlu really did kill himself because his wife was unfaithful to him,' Eylul said. 'I've never been married and so I don't know what I'd do if my husband were unfaithful to me. I think I'd be devastated.'

Ömer and Kerim shared a look. Ömer knew that Kerim was gay and that he had loved and been loved by a trans woman. But neither said anything. And then suddenly they all realised that the music in the marquee had stopped.

'What's happening now?' Ömer asked.

'Don't know.'

But then a group of waiters emerged from the marquee carrying the wedding cake. Pure white, with a single stripe of pink roses

379

down one side, it was seven tiers high and, given the number of men who carried it, weighty. Somehow, heroically, they got it up onto the platform where the bride and groom had stood to be married, and then they moved away as Gonca and Mehmet approached the giant structure. Someone dimmed the lights on the terrace and a very smart maître d' stepped forward to give Süleyman a large cake knife.

After first kissing his wife, Süleyman asked her to place her hands over his while they cut the cake together. Their guests clapped, cheered and took multiple photographs on their cameras and phones.

Meanwhile, in Taksim Square in the centre of the new city, police and fire services were being called to a horrific accident that had taken place inside one of the road tunnels underneath the square. Apparently the driver of a Peugeot had lost control of his vehicle and smashed at speed into a concrete pillar. It was being said that he had died on impact.

Chapter 29

Because he was what his wife described as a 'news junkie', Mehmet Süleyman knew about the death of Haluk Keleş the following day. A selection of newspapers had been delivered to the Sultan Suite when the hotel staff brought them their breakfast, all of which reported the terrible accident. Keleş, it was reported, had been on his way to headquarters.

The news made Mehmet Süleyman sad, but he kept it to himself. Gonca didn't need to know, but she did. A large part of her reputation as a witch came from her ability to observe behaviour. She'd seen him look at the papers with more attention than he'd given his morning coffee, and so while he went out on their balcony for a cigarette, she read the story herself and then followed him. As she got out of bed, she smiled at the sight of her beautiful unsullied white and silver bedcover. Her marriage was blessed.

It was another bright, cold day, and when she sat down next to him, she snuggled into his thick hotel dressing gown. When he'd finished smoking, she said, 'Come back to bed, baby.'

He smiled. 'I will,' he said. 'Why don't you go and warm it up for me?'

She stood, kissed him on the lips and then went inside. Alone on the balcony, Mehmet let his gaze wander into the middle of the Bosphorus and tried not to think about what, if anything, Keleş' death might mean. But then Gonca called him inside and so he went to her.

He had just this one day with her before he went back to work, back to the darkness that he loved almost as much as he loved his wife.

Later on, Süleyman and Gonca returned to her house in Balat, where they spent the day eating the food her daughters had prepared for them, listening to music and making love. The following day, however, was business as usual. Gonca's son Rambo came home and Süleyman went to headquarters full of trepidation.

The shock everyone felt at Haluk Keleş' death lay like a thick coating of dust over everything, and because the weather had closed in again, it was cold, grey and damp. Süleyman interviewed Mustafa Gölcük once again regarding the death of Constable Akar – he was still protesting his innocence. But forensic evidence was coming to light that was not going in his favour, and so unless he started giving them something that supported his story soon, his was a lost cause.

Muharrem Aktepe had been bailed pending further investigations, while the old man's daughter's body remained in a sealed container in the mortuary. Osman Aslan was on remand awaiting trial for possession of a toxic substance injurious to public health, and threatening police officers. However, in spite of the fact that Kerim Gürsel had now personally sorted through all Fahrettin Müftüoğlu's remaining paperwork, nothing of any further interest had been discovered. He'd died by his own hand.

It was only at Haluk Keleş' funeral on the Sunday that anyone remembered the Ethiopian photograph. The dead man's personal effects had been sent to his parents, but his father recalled no photograph amongst them. Only towards the end of that week did Kerim Gürsel remember that he'd taken a photograph of the thing in Süleyman's apartment.

The two men were looking at it, together with İkmen, while

they had coffee at a table outside a small büfe on İstiklal Caddesi. İkmen had just taken Patrick Süleyman to the airport to catch his flight back to Dublin, and had been telling the boy's father how much he was looking forward to coming back.

But Süleyman, strangely, looked sad about that.

When İkmen asked him why, he said, 'Because of the house on Büyükada. I know he has been really looking forward to going there, but Gonca now doesn't want me to buy it.'

İkmen asked, 'Why not?' Knowing full well why not.

'She's worried about money,' he said. 'With prices going up so much, she's concerned, and quite rightly. But I still feel bad, even though it now appears my Uncle Beyazıt has decided to give his share to Murad and myself.'

İkmen, who also knew that Mehmet's childless uncle had been planning to do this for some time, said nothing. Then Süleyman's phone rang.

'Oh,' he said, as he looked at the screen. 'It's Dr Sarkissian.'

He stood up to take the call and wandered aimlessly in front of the church of St Antoine as he listened to the doctor. Alone with Kerim Gürsel, İkmen asked after his family, and then they chatted about the wedding until they were joined by an unexpected guest.

'Inspector Gürsel, Inspector İkmen,' Bishop Juan-Maria Montoya said. 'I have been thinking about you and your worrying artefacts.'

They invited him to join them, and İkmen called into the büfe to bring another coffee.

'I have hardly been able to get what you showed me out of my head since,' the bishop said. 'That people are debasing that which genuine believers hold so priceless . . .'

'We think we've managed to stop it, at least here in the city,' Kerim said.

'Greed is everywhere,' İkmen said. 'You stamp on one greedy

383

bastard, another one just falls in line to take his place. Sorry, Bishop.'

'Oh, think nothing of it,' the Mexican said. 'The world as it is at the present time is enough to make a saint curse.'

Süleyman returned to the table and greeted the bishop. 'Well, that was interesting,' he said as he sat down.

'The doctor?'

'Oh, would you rather I went if you are to talk business?' the Bishop said.

'No, no,' Süleyman replied. 'Provided it goes no further – and knowing as I do that you are a man who can keep a secret . . .'

The bishop smiled.

'It seems that our jeweller, Fahrettin Müftüoğlu, mummified his own mother,' Süleyman said.

'You mean those intestines in that jar,' Kerim said, 'the ones Ömer Bey thought might be tripe . . .'

'Isis Müftüoğlu.' Süleyman nodded. 'Not enough information for us to be able to discover whether he killed her or not. But if some of the books found in his hoard are anything to go by, he embalmed her. Or rather, he embalmed her head. Who knows where the rest of her might be.'

'But why?' Kerim asked.

'Why not? He was of Egyptian origin, maybe he was curious,' İkmen said.

'No, why would he kill his mother?' Kerim said. 'When he met his wife, he wouldn't live with her because he didn't want to upset his mother!'

'Maybe he changed his mind,' Süleyman said. 'After all, if we are to believe his suicide note, he killed himself because she was unfaithful to him with Osman Aslan."

'This is the man who made the statue of St Foy?' the bishop said.

'Yes, although why and for whom, we still don't know.'

'We may never know,' Kerim added. 'Our poor colleague Inspector Keleş had some theories that even now may be viable.' He frowned. 'Mehmet Bey, that photograph he showed us . . .'

'Of the Ark of the Covenant,' İkmen said.

'Yes, well . . .'

The bishop's mouth dropped open. 'You know where the Ark of the Covenant is?' he asked. 'Is it here?'

'No,' Süleyman said. 'Our colleague found a small photograph amongst Müftüoğlu the jeweller's possessions that had the word Abyssinia and the date 1936 written on the back. Abyssinia is now what we call Ethiopia, and at that time it was ruled by the Italians. One of our suspects at the time we discovered had an Italian father. Haluk Bey put these facts together and . . .'

'And when he died, the photograph was not amongst his effects,' Kerim said. 'He had just been to see the suspect's family . . .' He paused for a moment, then took his phone out of his pocket. 'But I took a photograph of it. Here!'

He laid the phone on the table in front of the other three men.

The bishop looked at the screen and shuddered.

İkmen put a hand on his arm. 'Bishop?' he said. 'Are you all right?'

The cleric took a deep breath. 'I don't know, to be honest. You know, when I was a young priest, I worked in a city called Juarez on the border with the USA. A lot of gangs, guns and drugs in that city. Many of the cartel members, violent, ruthless men, would pay homage to a deity called Santa Muerte, St Death. Like a statue of the Holy Virgin, but a skeleton.'

'Gruesome,' İkmen said.

'In the extreme,' the bishop agreed. 'But powerful. Ask Santa Muerte to curse your enemies and they will die. I have seen grown men do just that.'

'The power of suggestion,' Süleyman said.

'Maybe. But still they die. And they die because evil exists.'

385

The bishop pointed towards the photograph. 'The Ark, as we know, is both good and evil, and that someone intended to replace it makes my heart race. That, whatever it is, should not be out in the world.' He turned to Kerim Gürsel. 'Inspector, you once asked me whether I could tell a genuine relic from a fake . . .'

'Which I think you did with St Foy.'

'Maybe.' He picked up Kerim's phone and stared at it. 'But that was not like this . . .'

Çetin İkmen watched the bishop closely until Kerim took his phone back, then he said, 'I'd like a copy of that picture if I may, Kerim Bey.'

Without a word, Kerim sent a copy to İkmen's phone. Nobody asked why he wanted it. They didn't have to.

Whatever had started in Vefa was still not over, and they all knew it.